The Hidden Treasure Files

by Martin Herman

194 Rodney Press

The Hidden Treasure Files

...A WILL JAMES MYSTERY

Copyright ©2016 Martin Herman
ISBN: 978-1-945211-01-0 PRINT
Library of Congress Number: 2016905027

First printing: May, 2016
Second printing: August, 2016
Third printing: January, 2017
Fourth printing: September, 2017
Fifth printing: October, 2018

Printed in the United States of America
ALSO BY MARTIN HERMAN
The Jefferson Files
The Jefferson Files -- the expanded edition

521 Simsbury Road, Bloomfield, CT 06002

Acknowledgements

When you spend much of your life writing fiction for your own amusement – as I have – it is a true eye-opener when one day you find that others are interested in reading what you have written. My first published novel resulted in such an interesting series of events for me. First, the lovely Lora Chan, single-handedly sold about 100 copies of my first novel, *The Jefferson Files* to virtually every person she came across. Her conversation starter went from, *"Do you read mysteries?"* to *"Would you like me to ask him to autograph it for you?"* before most of those nice people even knew it, they had actually purchased a book.

Then there was the book launch party that my daughter, Aimee, threw for me in Brooklyn. Family and friends – many of the friends who attended that evening were my daughter's – and all who attended were supportive. These wonderful people not only came and listened to what I had to say, but also purchased copies of my novel. Some may even have read it!

Then came the exposure on Amazon.com... it was like being the subject of a worldwide party line.

I am so appreciative of professionals like Carol Lennig, Librarian, Adult Services, Prosser Public Library, Bloomfield, Connecticut, who was the first public librarian to purchase my novel for her library; she placed *The Jefferson Files* into both Bloomfield, Connecticut Library branches. This is my home town library which made this particular placement so special for me.

Subsequently I was permitted to speak and sign copies of my book as part of a new author's night at the North Haven, Barnes & Noble store. Thank you, Bianca Bancroft, Community Business Development Manager...

Closely followed by a radio interview on WESU – Middletown, Connecticut – thank you, Donovan Longmore and Yvonne Davis...

And that warm and supportive reception during the Bloomfield Book Fair, where I was permitted to read passages from my novel and sign copies; thank you Marie Robinson...

At the Bloomfield Book Fair I met the hard working and very effective June Hyjek. June was the President of the Connecticut chapter of APSS, a writer's group, at the time. As an APSS member I had numerous opportunities to present my novel to many new audiences. It was June Hyjek who tenaciously fought the politicians in Hartford and didn't stop until the Governor declared September 1st, 2015 as Connecticut Author's Day, proving once again that the right man for a job is more often than not, *a woman!*

All of that happened just around the time I turned 75. Imagine starting a new chapter in life at 75?

What a treat this all has been.

Fortunately, my first novel, almost 10 years in the making, enjoyed surprisingly steady sales; leading to the writing of this second novel – this time in only 5 months; I have so enjoyed this newest chapter in my life and now that I am hooked, I hope to continue writing for as many more days as I may still have on this earth.

Hopefully, there will be readers who will continue to want to read what I write.

To Allan Pepper...

Allan was one of the principal continuity editors for this book – not because he decided to be a book editor in his latest incarnation but because he is an avid reader and is and has been a very special friend of mine. His thorough and precise notes and follow up questions along with his intelligent suggestions helped make this a far better "read" than the 13th re-write I first shared with him.

Allan is known throughout the music world and a fair share of New York's general population as one of the two founders of New York's legendary *The Bottom Line*, in the Greenwich Village neighborhood of New York City. For almost 30 years The Bottom Line was "the" go to venue for new and established performers – the place many first discovered Bruce Springsteen and K D Lang... where Prince appeared as did Dolly Parton and Billie Joel as well as Aaron Copeland. Where Richard Price read from the galleys of his book, *Clockers*... where Lou Reed recorded the album *Live: Take No Prisoners*, and where Harry Chapin held his 2000th concert.

It was where I learned to appreciate Handel's Messiah through the Bottom Line's creative version, the *Downtown Messiah*. Where I watched, with more than a few mixed emotions, one of Soupy Sales's last performances... saw Ringo Starr light up the stage during a rare late night surprise appearance; where I first discovered how great a guitarist Janis Ian was; and where I rediscovered the Jefferson Airplane and David Johansen, (aka Buster Poindexter).

If you enjoy this mystery– as I hope you will – you can thank Allan.

The Hidden Treasure Files
by Martin Herman

This is the second in the current series of Will James mystery novels, this time, the anti- establishment private investigator and his crew are asked to help unravel a mystery that begins in a Brooklyn antique store and ends in the most unlikely of locations.

Every Sunday morning, precisely at 10:30 sharp, there is an auction held in a sparsely furnished back room of Better Times Remembered, a small neighborhood antique store in the Williamsburg section of Brooklyn. Albert Froog, the owner of the store and self declared auctioneer, personally chooses the items for each week's auction. Generally these items are fairly ordinary but become more interesting because of the back story he is able to weave around them. At times there is even a speck of truth in the story he tells.

At this particular Sunday morning auction, one of the items he offers up is a prohibition era permit in a battered old wooden frame authorizing the manufacture of alcohol. It was one of many items he acquired in an estate purchase. On his inventory sheet he has assigned a value of 50 cents to one dollar for this item because so many similar permits were issued during prohibition and the frame is of little or no value.

Hoping he will wind up with something between 50 cents and a dollar he starts the bidding at $2.00.

To his surprise and amazement two separate people quickly bid the price up to $100,000.

"Who would pay $100,000 for this piece of junk?" Froog asks himself. "What do they know that I don't?"

When the head of the New York Mafia family also shows interest in the item Froog becomes doubly convinced that he really has a hidden treasure on his hands.

If you think you know how this will all end you are so very, very wrong.

As with all Will James Mysteries, the numerous twists and turns will keep you reading and guessing until the very last page.

Part 1

Chapter 1

Better Times Remembered, a neighborhood antique store in the Williamsburg section of Brooklyn, was opened in the summer of 1940 by Evelyn Zaleson, who lovingly built the business into a major financial success.

She was an avid reader and for her ninth birthday asked for and received a complete set of Compton's Encyclopedia. Earlier that year, Evelyn had been diagnosed with scarlet fever and not given much of a chance for a complete recovery. The family saved and sacrificed for many months before and after the purchase in order to make her birthday wish come true; her mother, four brothers and three sisters did whatever they could to make her comfortable and when the doctors all but gave up, her family set out to prove the doctors wrong. Their love and attention helped move her almost completely back to better health. Meanwhile, Evelyn read each and every volume of her very own copy of the Compton Encyclopedia, page by page – some sections over and over again. Through its pages she learned about the world and much of what it had to offer. Her Compton education served her well for the rest of her life. The many facts she retained helped her to establish her store's reputation for more interesting antiques. She used her knowledge of history and geography and developed a lifelong interest in various kinds of memorabilia and popular types of collectibles. Eventually, she developed an ability to buy and sell truly unique items.

Evelyn also had a natural talent for creating interesting window and in-store displays that seemed to spark an *I must have that* reaction from area shoppers. But the real secret of the store's success was how universally pleasant the experience was for buyers and browsers – as well as those who just came in out of the rain.

Each and everyone who entered the store was treated with the same level of courtesy and personalized attention. From the fresh pot of coffee, to plates of freshly baked cookies, and the information – freely shared. If Evelyn didn't know the answer to a question she said so, and then did the research and quickly reported back.

When Evelyn's daughter, Mary Froog, took over the day to day operations, she built upon her mother's love for the business and the shopping experience offered to all. The store continued to prosper until Mary was diagnosed with a terminal illness. She tried to keep the store going but by the time she died and her son, Albert, inherited it, the business was a financial mess and little more than a tax loss against the rest of the family estate.

Albert Froog refused to have anything to do with the business while his mother was still alive but after she passed away and he learned that his entire inheritance would be given to charity if he abandoned the store, he channeled his energies to make it profitable or at the very least, bring it to a break-even point.

Unlike his mother and grandmother, Albert was not what could be described as a people person. He seemed to be cold and uninterested in anyone but himself; gave off signs of being above those with whom he had to deal; but at the heart of his anti-social behavior was the basic fact that he was painfully shy. The few who knew him best understood that his seemingly out of control temper, rudeness and generally unpleasant outer layer was just a well-rehearsed act.

He moved the basic business model from welcoming browsers towards a less personal internet and mail order business. He was one of the first antique dealers to make the most of the enormous reach of the internet and began buying and selling entire collections throughout the globe – often without seeing or directly speaking with either the people he bought from or sold to.

Froog's anti-social behavior knew few limitations – he treated customers and suppliers as well as employees with equal disdain. As a result, he quickly went through a series of clerk/assistants, each of whom quit because of the verbally abusive way he treated them. It wasn't always what he said, more about how he said it, especially when customers were around. One employee walked outside to take a cigarette break less than half an hour after he began work on his first day and never returned – leaving his coat and hat behind.

Finally the fates smiled down and Froog found Elizabeth Hillsonrat, an undocumented Russian refugee – or more accurately, Elizabeth Hillsonrat found Froog. Elizabeth had been in and out of tight situations for most of her forty years. The past few years, in particular, had been all too challenging and personally draining – but somehow she survived. Elizabeth always survived. All she wanted now was little or no pressure – personally... professionally... period! She felt drained and decided that for her own sanity; at this point in time she needed to drastically simplify her life.

Now, as always, she had to earn enough to pay her bills but since she lived modestly, the need for money did not have to dictate what she did or where she did it. The deciding factor at this time in her life was to work at something that was simple, uncomplicated, and undemanding. She was on such a job, cleaning apartments for a slum landlord when she read the small space ad that Froog had placed in the Village Voice newspaper. She read the ad through several times and thought, this could be just what she needed.

**WANTED: ONE WITH STRONG WORK ETHIC
AND
WILLINGNESS TO WORK HARD
ABLE TO TAKE ORDERS
AND
LEAVE ALL PERSONAL BUSINESS AT HOME
OWNER IS SMART AND CAPABLE
OF MAKING ALL DECISIONS
AND IS NOT LOOKING FOR AN ADVISOR
– WE NEED SOMEONE TO DO THE WORK
COMPLAINERS NEED NOT APPLY
REPLY TO BOX 194, C/O THE VOICE**

According to the rate card printed at the bottom of the page, '*56 words for 56 days for $56.00*' *–300 characters with spaces, maximum - additional characters - letters, numbers, spaces, or punctuation marks, will be charged at 25 cents each*', was the paper's special, no frills *bargain* rate. She looked through the ad again - it was exactly 56 words and 300 characters. *We either have a really precise person here or one of the cheapest S.O.B.'s in town*, she thought.

After her brief interview with Froog she was convinced that this was precisely what she needed at this time in her life. He asked her only one question – "Did you come here today to work or to play?" She told him, in broken English, that she needed the job and came here to work. "Good," he said, pointing to a pile of assorted objects behind the counter, "throw your coat over there, and get to work."

He walked away from the conversation feeling good that she never asked him how much the job pays; she walked away from the same conversation feeling even better that he never asked for her social security card or to see her documentation as a legal alien.

For years, Elizabeth had successfully outsmarted the Russian Komitet Gosudarstvennoy Bezopasnosti, or as it was better known, the KGB, and so she knew she would have no problem dealing with the likes of an Albert Froog. And, she thought, if she was wrong and he became a problem, she could always cut his arms or anything else off – after all, that *had* worked for her before.

Elizabeth quickly figured out that Froog had little patience for, and even less interest in, the day to day minutia of running a neighborhood store and volunteered to meet, greet, and service the customers; keep the store clean and neat, keep track of the inventory, use the tools Froog provided to research and help value whatever he chose to purchase; and keep the books – both sets of books - the one for the tax people and the real one that he kept in his safe in the back of the store. Elizabeth agreed to be paid off the books... *both sets of books.*

She was paid less than minimum wage which she knew could not support even *her* modest living expenses but that didn't matter because she was confident that she could quickly find ways to augment the cash in her weekly pay envelope. It didn't take long for her to figure out how to stuff small items such as ceramic figurines or vintage toys or collectibles from the store's vast inventory into a pocket she had sown into an inside panel of her dress and sell them on Saturdays at a flea market near her small apartment in Freehold, New Jersey.

Chapter 2
About four months later...

Every Sunday morning, rain or shine, promptly at 10:30 A.M., Albert Froog held an auction in a back room behind the store. It was the only time he actively invited customers into the store. These auctions were held to show the lawyer in charge of his mother's estate that he was trying new ways to grow the customer base. He aggressively touted the event as an opportunity to purchase a *selected hidden treasure* at a bargain price, although he privately referred to it as an easy way to palm off meaningless crap.

Usually the event attracted one or two local residents, a stray passerby, and a homeless person just seeking a warm, dry place to sit for an hour or so. The only constant, almost every Sunday was Howard Hill. Howard had played guitar in some of the biggest bands during the late 1940s, '50s, and '60s. Later in his career he owned a small club and recording studio in Hartford, Connecticut, and was always on the lookout for old 78 rpm records and just about any examples of *Big Band* memorabilia that he could use to decorate his club.

Another constant was a huge pot of coffee and on very rare occasions, a box of stale donuts; a half-hearted attempt to pay tribute to what his grandmother once told him was the very least they could do to properly welcome, "friends, new and old, and neighbors who were gracious enough to enter the little store so as to spend a bit of *their* very limited time on this earth with her and her priceless reminders of times past."

For some reason, this week's auction was attracting a full house. By 10:15 A.M. every seat was taken – all five of them, Elizabeth quickly set up a sixth chair and three people were leaning against the back wall. For an Albert Froog auction – *this* was considered a mob scene.

Elizabeth burst into Froog's office at 10:22 declaring excitedly in her heavy accent, "It's like New Year's eves in Times Square out there, Buss. There must be hundreds of pipples waiting for the auction so it should to begin."

Froog put down a competitor's catalogue, slowly removed his reading glasses and stared angrily up at Elizabeth. "How many times do I have to tell you to knock and wait to be invited in *before* you burst into my office, Elizabeth?"

"But Buss –"

"Don't 'but boss' me, Elizabeth."

"But Buss, the room it is packed with pipples. I never seen so many pipples in there at the same time, and there are more pipples outside on the sidewalks waiting for to come in."

Clearly annoyed, Froog stood up, still glaring at her; he slowly walked past her into the area set aside for the weekly auction. He took a quick look around, nodded good morning to Howard, and returned to his office. "As usual," he sneered, "you have grossly exaggerated the situation. There are about ten people in there, nowhere near the *'hundreds of pipples,'*" he said, mockingly.

"So when was last times we had ten pipples in there?" she quickly responded. "You wants I should make another pot of hotted coffee?"

"I already put almost a full pot left over from Friday out there. When it is gone, it is gone. Who do you think I am, Starbucks?" Froog screamed, "Now, get back in there and make sure no one steals anything."

At precisely 10:30, Froog entered the small stuffy room holding a cup of freshly brewed coffee. By now there were 12 people in the small space, waiting for the auction to begin. He recognized one or two from previous auctions. He did not think any of the others had ever been there before – many of the new people looked like grotesquely bloated football players – tall, wide shouldered, muscular, and noticeably disinterested in the goings on. He squeezed past two of them, walked to the rear of the room, and carefully set his coffee cup down on the floor next to him. One quick look around, then he noisily cleared his voice, bringing a hush to the room. "Welcome one and all to my weekly auction," he began. "Once again, I have carefully selected a series of precious collectibles, hidden treasures, objet d'art and one of a kind reminders of times past for you to snap up at bargain prices."

He held up the first item, a bugle he said dated back to the 1920s and began his pitch. "It is believed that Old Satchmo himself played this rare instrument on the very first record he ever made." Even though there were three or four times more people attending the auction this Sunday morning than any Sunday morning in recent memory, he could not get anyone interested in this or any of the first few items he presented. His best chance for a buyer for the bugle would have been Howard Hill, but Howard knew Satchmo and could clearly see that this was *not* a 1920's bugle. Finally, Froog reached out to Elizabeth and was handed the next item, a 1928 government issued permit to legally produce alcohol during Prohibition. The document, originally given to a Michigan manufacturer of vanilla, was encased in a thick and crudely constructed wooden frame. The glass over the document was dirty and had a hairline crack running along the left side.

"I know that you are going to love this next item," he said with a broad grin. "It is a very rare and highly prized document from the prohibition era – 1920s America. This," he said proudly, "is one of the few surviving official *Registry of Stills* certificates. Look at this little beauty," he said, holding the piece high above his head and slowly moving it from side to side, "in near mint condition, I should look this good when I am as old as this precious document." He waited for laughs. When none came he just moved on, "It has all of the necessary *official* signatures and government seals and has been certified to be 100% authentic by yours truly."

He stopped speaking to try to gauge the item's reception, and then said, "This was issued to a Michigan company, on November 5, 1928, giving them legal permission to process alcohol for their primary business – the manufacture of food grade vanilla flavoring. In 1919 the United States federal government declared the manufacturing of alcohol to be illegal with very few exceptions. *This* was one of those rare exceptions; what am I bid for this unique hidden treasure and prized memento of early twentieth century America?"

There was some shuffling among the attendees but no verbal response.

"Oh, come on", he chided, "this would look great on any wall in your home or as a conversation starter for gatherings of friends and family or anywhere you can think of. Who will start the bidding off?" He gave it the widest grin he could and said, "Do I hear $2.00?"

Nothing; no movement; the sign of death for any auctioneer – there was not a raised hand in the room.

He looked around, clearly disappointed, "Come on, $2.00. Do I hear $2.00?"

Howard Hill raised his hand, "I'll bid $2.00," he said meekly.

Up until the moment Froog decided to include it in today's auction, the permit was just something he had been using to prop open his small office window and had the dents and deep scratches on the frame to prove it. Froog was about to bang the gavel down to insure a two dollar windfall, but, before he could make the sale final an older lady, with a dark shawl covering most of her face yelled out, "I will bid $5.00."

Howard Hill stared at the older woman. He fished through his pockets and scooped up a handful of small change. He quietly added up the total and defiantly yelled out, $5.37."

The old woman countered with, "$5.75".

Howard dug deeper into his pocket and screamed out, "$5.77."

"I'll bid $5.87," the older woman said defiantly.

Froog looked around and said, "Do I hear $6.00?"

A middle aged man leaning against the wall slowly removed his dark glasses, wiped his forehead with a checkered hanky, rolled his eyes upward, and said with contempt, "$500."

A hush fell over the room as everyone turned to look at the new bidder.

Froog couldn't believe his ears. "I beg your pardon," he finally said in disbelief.

The man stepped forward and, emphasizing each word, said, "I. Will. Give. You. Five. Hundred. Dollars. Cash. For that item."

Without missing a beat, Froog looked around the room. Do I hear six hundred dollars?"

Howard Hill jumped up, waved his hand, wildly, "Albert, Albert, you know me, I have been coming here for a very long time – can I place a bid on credit? You know I am good for any amount I commit to pay."

Albert looked at Hill and gave him a friendly smile, "I'm really sorry, Howard, but there are rules and unfortunately, even though I do know you and yes, you are definitely good for any commitment you make, bids have to be paid, in full, at the time of the sale."

Hill sat down, clearly upset.

The older woman who had started the bidding war had a portable phone against her ear and cleared her throat as she said, "$1,000."

"So," the previous high bidder said, "Someone has come to life. Okay, I will bid $5,000."

With the phone held closely to her ear, the woman raised her hand and said, "$30,000."

The man glared at the old woman, and said, "$50,000."

The older woman, listened intently to the voice on the other end of the phone, then put the portable phone into her handbag and shouted, "$75,000."

The room went silent. The man cleared his throat and then said, "I bid $100,000." Then, looking straight at the older woman he yelled, "Beat that, you old bag."

Froog was speechless; he stood with his mouth open, unable to make a sound. Elizabeth walked over to him and whispered, "Say something, Buss."

Froog pushed her away, bent down, grabbed his cup and took a large gulp.

"Well, it looks like I just bought the item," the man said, arrogantly.

"Not so fast," the elderly woman yelled back, taking the phone out of her purse as she said, "I need to make a phone call."

"Forget it," the man growled. "I made the high bid, you want to bid higher, bid higher, but if you don't or can't then this item is now mine." He waited for a response and when none came, he smiled and said, "Then it is a done deal!"

"The woman quickly stood and in clear and measured tones said, "It isn't a 'done' anything until he bangs down the gavel and he hasn't banged down the gavel – yet!" Then, looking at Froog she said, "I insist that you permit me to make a phone call."

Froog looked bewildered, almost shell-shocked. He stared at the woman then the man then back again to the woman. "Okay," he said, "one call, but make it a quick one."

"Hey," the man yelled, "what kind of place are you running here?" He held up a huge roll of bills, "I have $100,000 in cash here. I bid fair and square, no one bid higher, so it is mine."

"Who says so?" the woman yelled.

"This says so!" he responded, waving the roll of money at her.

"Hey," Froog said defiantly, trying to recapture control of the runaway train that today's auction was quickly becoming; "This is *my* store and *my* item and *my* auction. *I* make the rules here and *I* say that she gets to make a phone call. Got it?"

The man gave the old woman an icy glare, stuffed the roll

of money back into his pocket, then pointing his finger at Froog he said, "Okay, *I got it!* She gets to call because *you* say so but now I get to walk, because *I* say so." With that he stormed out of the room.

Elizabeth ran after him.

The woman sat down and with a broad smile said, "If you do not mind, I would like to see this item up close. Please pass it down to me for a moment."

Froog handed the piece to one of the people in the front row who passed it on to the old woman.

The woman pushed her glasses up onto her forehead and brought the item close to her eyes, examined both the front and the back, and then seemed to be sniffing around the outer edges of the frame. She handed the piece back towards Froog and said, "Since that rude man walked out I guess the previous highest bid stands – that was mine in the amount of $5.87, but given the electricity now in this room I will raise that to an even $10.00 – five times your initial opening bid request."

"But your last bid was $75,000," Froog stammered.

"We are all adults here," she countered. "I think he was just a plant to push the bidding up. I am willing to go much higher than the $5.87 bid which was the one to beat before that man... or I should say, *your plant*, first spoke up. Perhaps just because I have class and a sense of right and wrong I will generously bid $10.00 - take it... or leave it."

Froog reached down again for his coffee cup and drank it all down in a single gulp. He wiped away the sweat forming on his forehead with a handful of tissues he grabbed from under the podium and said, "I don't think so. I am taking this valuable treasure off of the auction block for one week. I will accept sealed bids and next week, at 10:30

A.M. sharp, I will open all of the sealed bids received by that time and declare the highest bidder *above $100,000* to be the new owner of this rare hidden treasure."

He slammed the gavel down and added, "This week's auction is now over; everyone out!"

When the last person left the store, Froog locked the door and put up the "closed for lunch" sign. He grabbed the newly declared rare hidden treasure, and went looking for Elizabeth.

He found her standing by his desk. "Did you catch up with the high bidder?" he asked excitedly.

"No, by the times I was on the outsides of the streets," she said, excitedly, "he was not anywheres that I could see."

She moved closer to him, "Why you dint just take his money; a hundreds thousands of dollars; why?"

He stared at the frame in his hands, and then looking at her, whispered,

"Can you believe that someone would offer to pay $100,000 for this, this, piece of junk?"

Ignoring his comment she said, "So a hundreds thousands of dollars was not enough for you; you expecting more?"

He brushed past her and sat down at his desk, "Okay," he yelled, "I want you to get me anything and everything there is to know about this valuable document. And I want you to do that immediately. Do you hear me?"

They should be able to hear you in the jungles of Africa the way you are yelling, you fat cow, she thought, but the actual words that came out of her mouth were, "Yes, Buss."

Chapter 3
A little more than a year earlier -

Albert Froog was definitely not happy to be an antique dealer. For him, the store was a means to an end; nothing more... nothing less.

When his grandmother died, her estate included several million dollars' worth of AT&T stock along with her prized possession, *'Better Times Remembered'*, the small antique store at 70 Lee Avenue, near Rodney Street in Brooklyn, New York. Her entire estate went to her only child, Albert's mother, Mary Froog. Unlike her son, Mary shared her mother's love for the antique business in general and this antique store, in particular. She loved everything about the store; both women considered themselves to be lucky caretakers of priceless reminders of simpler, more glorious days. Their feelings towards the business helped them to make it one of the most successful shops of its kind in the tri-state area.

Froog knew that one day it would be handed down to him, as the only child and last remaining member of the family, so he spent many hours thinking of ways to dump the business when that day finally came. "No one is going to trap me in that hell hole," he would tell anyone who would listen, "I can't imagine a worse fate than that."

As a small boy, growing up in the neighborhood, Froog constantly complained about having to be stuck in that 'suffocating little space'; with its *sickly sweet* clientele of little *old biddies* and pretentious yuppies; and 'all of those dirty, rusty and tattered old things that were crammed within its four walls' and seemingly endless basement that stretched out below the next two buildings on the block. And yet, from the time he turned eight and was given the *privilege* to cross the street on his own, he went to the store almost every day after school and almost every Sunday.

At the time of his mother's death the family "estate" had grown to six point nine million dollars between the antique business inventory, assorted stocks, bonds, and pieces of local real estate, which included the building that housed the antique store and all but the last building on the block. Both his grandmother and his mother considered the store to be 'the crown jewel' of their holdings and hoped that Albert would eventually learn to care for the business and keep it alive and well for as long as possible after they were dead and gone. However, knowing her son as well as she did and convinced that he would rush to get rid of the store as soon as it was in his control; his mother gave strict instructions to her lawyer to write her will in the strongest way in order to make it difficult for Albert to walk away from the business. "Fill this will with the kitchen sink of escape proof language," she requested, "I want Albert locked into preserving that jewel if at all possible. Don't give him an inch of wiggle room."

"Now Mary," he assured her, "our firm often handles such matters for our clients, many in your situation. I assure you that the final document will be executed according to your specific wishes and the laws of the state."

"I doubt that many of your clients have a son like Albert to contend with." Mrs. Froog said. "He is a genuinely good man and I love him but he can be pigheaded and he has made it quite clear that he does not want anything to do with the store."

"Then, is it really worth the struggle if he has to be brought to it kicking and screaming," her lawyer asked.

"That's just it," Mrs. Froog said, "While he was still in grade school he walked to that store almost every day. No one asked him to or made him go there. I think if he gave it half a chance he would see the value in it as I have and as my mother did before me."

"Then you have nothing to be concerned about," the lawyer said.

"He is such a contradiction. Worst of all, I think he may just be using the store as a stand-in for his anger towards both me and his grandmother. He seems to think we loved the store more than we loved him, which is silly and couldn't be further from the truth. I believe in my heart that if he gave it half a chance he would learn to enjoy what it has to offer and might even build on what we have established."

"So you want to *force* him to *give it a try?*" the lawyer asked.

"I don't like the sound of that... but, if I am to be honest with you and myself, yes. He likes the lifestyle that our family's money can and has supported, so I am just hoping to make it just a bit harder for him to quickly walk away from what I believe to be the real soul of the family estate."

"I will do my best," the lawyer responded.

Almost as a second thought, she asked, "He is my only heir; if you write in strong language *making* him retain the store can he fight the conditions of the will?"

The lawyer tried to reassure her. "Yes, wills can be challenged, but only for specific reasons and each one must be supported by sufficient evidence to the satisfaction of a judge. Albert *could* claim that someone exerted undue influence on you but he would have to identify a specific coercive element; he can claim that you were not mentally or physically competent when you signed the will, but you are clearly competent, you do not have a history of treatment for mental or physical problems that I know of. In fact you seem to be enjoying very good health, mentally and physically; to prove the opposite he would have to present medical evidence to the contrary. I can also arrange for more than the required two witnesses of your signature to confirm that you were of sound mind and body at the time you signed the final document."

"You know how persistent Albert can be," she sighed.

Continuing to reassure his client, the lawyer said, "Mary, it would be different if you made no mention at all of him in your will, disinheriting him entirely, even accidentally, then he *might* have grounds for legal action. However, you *are* mentioning him, and detailing a willingness to bequeath everything to him with a single proviso – that he maintain what would be a third generation family business; a business that means more to you than anything else in your estate. I believe that works in your favor. He can't claim forgery or fraud. I think we are on high ground here. I can and I will provide you with a legal document that should hold up in any court should he choose to fight it. In addition, challenging a will in court can be very costly and *he* would be entirely responsible for his own legal costs while he would be forced to watch his potential inheritance shrink to the extent that the executor or trustee's legal fees and court costs mount as the estate defends itself from him. Any court in the land would have to acknowledge that the estate was doing its job as legally defined; no, I don't believe he would be able to contest this will under usual reasons. At the end of the day any judge would clearly see that the estate was defending your wishes."

The lawyer continued to assure her that he could write an easy to defend document that would at the very least, ensure that the store would stay open and continually operated after her death. "If Albert decided that he can't or won't continue the family operation then *he* would be required to walk away from *all* of the estate, and inherit nothing. In that case your favorite charity – the Salvation Army – would be given the entire estate on the condition that they would maintain the antique store for an extended time into the future. I think I could get such assurances from the Salvation Army in exchange for such a huge transfer of assets."

Mary Froog and her lawyer spent many hours discussing this and finally Mrs. Froog said, "I know that now I am going to sound like I am giving you completely different marching orders, but... I really wouldn't want him to be penniless. Maybe we could leave him with something, not a lot, but something. Yes, if he opts out then give the rest to the Salvation Army; they do wonderful things and will spend my money wisely, of that I am certain."

Several weeks later the lawyer met with Mary Froog and presented her with the document he had prepared. She read it through quickly and when she came to this section she read and reread it over several times:

> *The estate is a collection of cash, precious metals, jewels, patents, trademarks, land, rental properties, stocks, bonds, receivables, and a family operated antique store, Better Times Remembered, along with its entire inventory and store furnishings, located at 70 Lee Avenue at the cross road of Rodney Street, in the Williamsburg section of Brooklyn, New York.*

> *Better Times Remembered has been designated as the central most valuable portion of the estate by Mary Froog and so it is with her wishes in mind that Better Times Remembered never be reduced in importance, divested, or dissolved.*

> *To ensure the continuation of Better Times Remembered for the foreseeable future, after the death of Mary Froog a series of individual bank accounts are to be opened, no single account may ever contain more than 90% of what is designated as the*

minimum amount that could be federally insured against loss. The combined total value of these accounts may never be less than two million dollars, U.S. ($2,000,000). These accounts may never be liquidated; any and all interest earned from these specially assigned accounts must remain with these specially designated accounts. All of these accounts must be established before any other distribution of Mary Froog's estate can be made.

Others may be hired, from time to time, to assist with the day to day operations of the antique store but no one other than a family member may ever own a controlling interest in it.

A family member must be physically present on the selling floor; during <u>every</u> <u>minute</u> it is open for business, to ensure proper care of the loyal customers and protection for each and every item in the inventory.

Under <u>no</u> circumstances is Better Times Remembered ever to be sold or closed for an extended period or downsized in any way. In the event of a fire or act of God or legal condemnation of the property, another location MUST be secured within walking distance of the existing space and the business reopened within 30 calendar days from the time operations are halted in the original location.

Furthermore, should relocation be required, EVERY effort, regardless of cost, must be made to inform the current customer base as well as the neighborhood as a whole of the change of location.

The store must be kept open for business every day but Saturday and federally recognized holidays, from 10:00 A.M. sharp until at least 5:00 P.M. – during rain or shine, blizzard or act of war. The store may close for lunch - sometime during the day - at any time of the managing family member's choosing.

Once the previously described series of Federally insured bank accounts have been created, the remaining contents of the estate, other than the antique store, Better Times Remembered, may be retained or divested, as the inheritor of the estate chooses.

These are to be binding conditions. Should any clause in the will be legally contested or if the store is not personally operated by a family member, then the balance of the estate's holdings – less $1.00, (one dollar), is to be turned over to the Salvation Army. The inheritor and any future family members are to share the remaining $1.00 (one dollar), and not a penny more."

Mrs. Froog told her lawyer how much she appreciated his understanding, and quickly signed it. As one additional level of insurance against the possibility that Froog could fight the will, her signature was witnessed by no less than six licensed lawyers – two from Mary Froog's lawyer's office and four from another law firm located in an adjoining building.

The lawyer then said, "Because of your earlier concerns let me assure you that I am prepared to work *Pro Bono Publico* – at absolutely no cost to the estate - to fight any efforts if he tries to reverse your wishes; I give you my word in front of these six witnesses."

Albert almost exploded when the family lawyer read the terms of the will. "Why would my mother saddle me with that disgusting rat hole? She knew I hated that dirty rotten business. There must be a way to break those clauses."

The lawyer, who had never liked Albert anyway, smiled as he said, "If you fight it you will lose everything but $1.00. The terms are quite clear and binding. This will is ironclad; I wrote it and will gladly defend it up to the highest court in the nation, if necessary."

"Well she may be able to hang that pathetic little dump

around my neck," Froog yelled, "but she can't make me like it." He then stormed out of the lawyer's office, slamming the door behind him.

Albert read and re-read the will until one of the lines stopped him; it was the line about lunches. *"The store may close for lunch - sometime during the day - at any time of the managing family member's choosing."* It didn't take too long for the devious Albert Froog to work this to his advantage. He had a huge sign made for the front window:

UNDER NEW MANAGEMENT
OPEN EVERY DAY
FROM SUNDAY THROUGH FRIDAY
STORE HOURS:
OPEN: 10:00 A.M. to 5:00 P.M.
CLOSED FOR LUNCH
10:01 A.M. – 4:59 P.M.
CLOSED SATURDAY
&
ALL FEDERAL AND RELIGIOUS HOLIDAYS

He showed the sign to the family lawyer who delayed his response as long as he could and then told Albert, "It definitely does not meet the spirit of your mother's will, but legally, I have to admit that it meets all of the conditions."

Froog gave a hearty laugh.

"Hey," he said, "don't worry. Of course I will keep it open for more than 2 minutes a day. I just want to be the one who makes that decision. I realize that you will hide in the shadows to make certain that it stays open. I don't really care what you do. I know what that pathetic little dump meant to my mother and grandmother and even though I would prefer to burn it down, I will just hold my nose and make certain that it stays open as long as I live. Not because of you or anything you might or might not do; the real reason is because I loved my mother and will do it in her memory. Frankly, I don't care if you believe it or not

– the money really doesn't mean that much to me. I am capable enough to earn my own money and will if need be. You can trust me on that."

"Trust, but verify, I can!" the lawyer said. "Trust but verify, I will. You can count on *that*, too! Just remember, the will clearly requires you to be *on the selling floor*, during *every minute* it is open for business... even all of those additional minutes you now say you will take from the lunch hour described on this sign."

Albert built a wall enclosing the rear third of the already small space to form a private office for himself. He had a one way glass built into the connecting wall and brought in a sign maker to stencil *this way to the selling floor* in gold leaf letters on the new office door.

The day it was completed he invited the lawyer to the store and showed him the new office; "Any questions?" he asked the lawyer.

The lawyer just shook his head from side to side, gave a huge sigh, turned around, and left the store.

Chapter 4
Sunday, May 5, 1996 –
Williamsburg, Brooklyn, New York – 11:41 A.M.

Elizabeth told Froog that she was unable to catch up with the high bidder after he stormed out of the store, which was true. But she failed to tell him that she believed she could get in touch with him any time she chose because she had his contact information; he had filled out the initial questionnaire she automatically passed on to each auction visitor as they walked in and made certain it was completed and returned to her before the 10:30 start of the auction. She did this even if they had been there before and filled out an identical card during a previous visit.

Later in the day Elizabeth picked up the phone in the back storage room in hopes of reaching everyone that had attended this particular auction. Some had answering machines, so she left messages along with her home telephone number. Others answered the phone and let her know that they would not be making a bid for the framed document. She really only cared about the two high bidders. When she called the highest bidder she got his answering machine. She left a long message, emphasizing her willingness to help him be the successful bidder and own this "treasure" for himself. The second highest bidder, the older woman, did not answer the phone and did not have an answering machine. Elizabeth set the woman's sign-in card aside so that she could try again later; silently hoping that one or both of these bidders would get in touch with her before the next week's auction.

She started her research on the framed document. None of her tried and true research tools, the store's extensive microfiche files, bundles and bundles of old magazines and newspaper back issues, copies of census and other government and industry source reports - some going back as far as the last half of the nineteenth century - plus the almost endless data easily retrieved from the world wide web, proved helpful in this search.

Elizabeth researched the United States Prohibition Service of the Treasury Department, the governmental agency that had issued the original document in the frame; she researched all active vanilla flavoring manufacturers across the country during the years before 1928 and years after 1928; she typed in the actual name and address of the company as shown on the document without a single response.

She continued her efforts through the rest of the day and well into the night. It was now more than twelve hours since the auction ended and she still did not have a clue as to what made this specific piece valuable enough to go from the two dollar forced opening bid to a hundred thousand dollars within minutes.

She was not surprised that the company was no longer in business – after all, many businesses went under during the Great Depression. What did surprise her was that she couldn't find anything to document that the company had *ever* existed. How could that be?

Tired and sleepy, she rested her head on her desk and soon fell asleep.

Chapter 5
Sunday, May 5, 1996 –
Crown Heights, Brooklyn, New York – 11:09 P.M.

Albert Froog had difficulty getting to sleep. He tossed and turned, unable to get the events of the day out of his mind.

After what seemed like an eternity of staring at the ceiling, he got out of bed, dressed and drove to the store. He could see a light coming from the area where Elizabeth kept her desk.

He stood watching her, and then tapped her on the shoulder. She jumped up, still half asleep.

"Did you sleep here all night?" he asked.

She yawned loudly, stretching both arms up and out. "I think I may have done that. What time it is now?"

He looked at his watch. "It is just past three in the morning."

"So it is now Monday? I will be going to home now," she said.

"Wait; first tell me what you have found out so far?" he asked.

She shuffled through the piles of notes on her desk. "It is of utmost surprising to me. So far I have finded that the United States' government did given out a lot many of this permits. It says in one of the books that theses permits was sometimes hanged up on a wall in the maybe times that a policemens comes to investigate. But, it really did not makes such much difference because there was such many of this permits was given out and very little amounts of policemens to ever come in to check anyway. You know what

I am talking about?"

"So why did those two people bid so much to own it?" he asked. "This entire event makes less sense than any ten of your sentences all rolled up in a pile." He pulled up a chair and sat down. "And the man who made the best offer makes the least sense of all. He was just a few minutes away from getting what he seemed to want so badly, but he just lost his temper and walked away? *Empty handed!* None of this makes any sense to me."

"I cannot make understanding of such things either," she said, yawning again. "But I thinks you should had taken his monies when he tried to gives it to you. That is my opinions. I also thinks I need it better to go home now."

"Will you be all right driving?" he asked.

"You worried for me?" she asked, smiling.

He grunted. "You're a big girl, Elizabeth, I can't worry about everyone. Just make sure you're back here by 10:00 this morning, bright and ready to continue this research. I have to figure this thing out. I certainly don't want to leave a spare penny on the table."

"Of courses not, buss," she said, "no pennies for the table... not anythings for the table."

*****

After she left, he sat down at the computer and typed in, *"prohibition, legal exceptions."*

The screen came to life. There were pages and pages listing legal exceptions to the prohibition law. It seemed that all anyone had to do was declare that they needed an exception for religious or medical reasons or that they were in the business of making any one of a variety of products which traditionally required alcohol in the manufacturing process, such as the manufacture of vanilla, as in the case of this particular permit, and they would get a full government pass from the provisions and penalties in the Prohibition Act. *This permit is just a meaningless piece of paper*, he thought to himself; *a $100,000 meaningless piece of paper in an ugly and heavily damaged wooden frame. So what makes it worth $100,000 plus... to two different people, no less? I'm really stumped by this*, he thought.

"It was a grand old time to be a pretender priest or a medical quack," he said to the screen, "looks like the only ones who couldn't get a legal drink were those poor shmucks who were too dumb to get out of their own way. And I guess every one of the exceptions got one of these worthless permits. So with all of this paper floating around why would anyone want to give me $100,000 for one in a cheap wooden frame?" He got up and pulled out a cigar from his jacket pocket, lit it, and returned to the computer. "She was right, I should have grabbed that bankroll when I had the chance. I hope that boat hasn't sailed away forever."

Chapter 6
Monday, May 6, 1996 –
Williamsburg, Brooklyn, New York – 10:01 A.M.

The high bidder walked into the store as soon as the "open for business" sign was placed on the door. Elizabeth saw him first but Froog pushed her out of the way and quickly ran over to him.

"So you came back?" Froog said with a toothy grin.

"Where can we speak, privately?" the man said solemnly.

"And your name is?" Froog demanded.

"My name is of little importance. Where can we speak privately?" the man repeated.

"Well, *Mr. Of Little Importance,* first I would like to know your name, your real name, and then we can talk," Froog said, in a mocking and confrontational tone.

"Okay, you can call me Simon."

"And what would I call you after I looked at your proof of identification?" Froog asked.

"Just call me Simon; now, either we talk or I walk right out that door and this time I walk for good!" Simon said defiantly.

Froog led him into his office and closed the door. Elizabeth tried to look through the keyhole then put her ear to the door.

Froog offered the man a cigar. The man waved his hand, dismissively, and said, "I don't smoke and even if I did, you're not the kind of guy I see myself sharing a cheap cigar with. Now, let's cut to the chase, okay?"

"Suit yourself," Froog said as he leaned back in his chair, put his feet up on his desk, lit his own cigar; then, after filling his lungs to capacity he slowly blew a stream of smoke rings towards the ceiling.

"I came here to pick up the permit," the man said.

"Sorry, but I don't think so. Had you not run off in such a huff on Sunday you would know that I decided to turn this into a sealed bid," Froog said.

"Don't be a fool," the man said. "I made a very generous offer. No, let me say that my bid was more than very generous. You know it, I know it, and I know that you know it. No one was ever going to bid anything close to what I bid for that worthless piece of paper in a stupid beat up frame."

"I don't know about that. There was at least one other bidder who was quickly raising you, bid for bid. Who knows, maybe she will come in above a hundred thousand dollars by the time I open the sealed bids on Sunday."

"And maybe she was just a shill you planted there in order to get the bidding to a higher level," the man responded.

Froog looked as if he had just been insulted and said, "Funny, that was exactly what she said about you after you stormed off. Well, as I told her, I do not do such things."

"Whatever," the man said in desperation. "Look, I showed you my bankroll all she showed you was her phone, *if I remember correctly.*"

"So you want to place a sealed bid?"

"You are being short sighted," the man said, "so let's just do this the easy way; a quick transfer of money for that piece of junk; and I'll be on my way a hundred grand lighter."

"First a worthless piece of paper in a beat up stupid frame... now a piece of junk?" Froog asked sarcastically. "If it is of no value why did you offer me $100,000 for it on Sunday? And why did you return and why are you *still* offering me so much for it now?"

"Hey," the man argued, "I am already sorry that I returned. All I know is that I was asked to go to your sleazy skeasy store on Sunday and buy that item. I was given a roll of money and told to make sure I left with the framed permit."

"But you didn't leave with it, you could have but instead you stormed out of here. And who are you calling sleazy skeasy?" Froog screamed with as much false pride as he could muster.

"Whatever," the man mumbled. "You want the money I want the worthless piece of crap. We quickly exchange one for the other and both get what we want. So, let's just get it done and I'll be on my way."

Froog blew another series of smoke rings, this time towards the man, and then said, "From whom?"

"What?" the man responded, obviously annoyed.

"Who asked you to come to my – er, ah – place of business?" Albert asked almost indifferently.

"I don't know who."

Froog stood up, waving his hands in the air. "How can you not know who? You expect me to believe that a complete stranger gave you a hundred thousand dollars – in cash yet - and directed you to come here? And you didn't even ask who they were or why they wanted you to do it or why they didn't just do it themselves?"

"I don't care what you believe, it is the truth and that's that. And one more thing, even if I did know I wouldn't tell you. It is none of your business. You got something to sell; I got someone willing to pay for it. That is the beginning and the end of it."

"But if you really thought that no one would bid even close to what you bid, why didn't you hang around, hold onto your ground when the other bidder clearly didn't have enough money to continue bidding, and walk away with that little historic gem, instead of skipping off like a distraught little school girl only to limp back today and whimper about it like a homesick puppy dog? Froog chided.

"Hey, I didn't come here to dance with you. You gonna sell it now or not?"

"One more question - you will probably not answer," Froog said. "If you think that it is not worth what you bid for it... why didn't you bid just a few dollars above the previous highest bid, like most human beings with half a brain would have done and tell your *mystery shopper* you used up all of the hundred grand and just pocket the difference?" Froog asked.

"Look, when those two amateurs were nickel and diming their bids it was all I could do to keep from heaving up my breakfast and then strangling the two of them. I couldn't believe my ears – first $5.00 then $5.00 and 30 something then $5.00 and 90 something..."

"It was 95 cents", Froog corrected, "Not five ninety something... $5.95 was her bid."

"Yeah, yeah, Okay, when she upped the offer a few pennies or an entire couple of nickels or dimes I almost puked. Who has time for this? Second of all, I am not like you. I would never steal someone's money *and* pocket their fee."

"Not like me?" Froog yelled, "Not like me? You don't know me!"

"Oh! I know you all right. I have been dealing with disreputable, unethical, and unscrupulous people like you most of my adult life." The man said, "Hey, you don't think I checked you out and looked into this seedy little operation of yours before I showed up on Sunday? I'm not like the usual *dewy eyed* fools you probably see most days; the ones who eat up the phony baloney stories... the totally bogus lies and misrepresentations; the fools to whom you palm off your *hidden treasures from the past*," he said, "and I am not interested in your snide comments. You don't run a classy operation. Even you must know that! What you are is a class A carnival barker; I could tell the minute you opened your mouth on Sunday. And this 'document' of yours - if it is real, and only you know if it is or isn't real – it is just a simple permit like the tens of thousands of similar permits they issued that year alone much less during the entire time prohibition was the law of the land. Prohibition was a joke, even back then. Only the stupid and naive took it seriously. Prohibition never affected the priests and rabbis who claimed to need liquor for ceremonial purposes or the makers of dozens if not hundreds of things like cough syrups or after shave lotions or foodstuffs like vanilla which all needed alcohol in their manufacturing process before prohibition, during prohibition, and after prohibition. If anything, more people got into those businesses *because of prohibition!*"

Froog started to applaud, "Very good!" Froog said, "Very, very good! Possibly Oscar nomination good! Soooooooooooo," Froog mused, "it is a worthless piece of paper; no better or worse than the thousands..."

"Tens of thousands," the man interrupted, "Maybe hundreds of thousands."

Froog bowed down. "I stand corrected, hundreds of thousands of similar pieces of paper. Is that what you told the person who gave you that wad of money to buy it with?"

"Please, if someone is stupid enough to think that it could be worth $100,000, who am I to set them straight? All I want to do is deliver the goods and grab my fee. Case closed."

"So you're just like me."

"Okay, similar church," the man said with disgust, "way different pew... I probably draw the line well before you might and don't pretend to be anything that I am not. I do things for people that they can't or don't want to do for themselves. But at the end of the day, I break no laws – that I know of, and deceive no one – especially myself."

Froog grinned at the man, and finally said, "So, I suggest that you put in a sealed bid, hope it is the winning bid, and if it is, pick up your mystery person's purchase on Sunday."

I can't," the man said. "Why don't you just let me take it now, I'll give you the wad of dough and no one will be the wiser."

"*I* can't," Froog said.

"I thought it was *your* store and *your* item and *your* auction and so *you* make the rules," the man said contemptuously.

"Tell me, then, *Mr. More Honest Person than Me*, what makes this particular item worth $100,000?"

"I don't know and I don't care," the man said.

"I'm just trying to understand what happened in here on Sunday," Froog said.

"Hey, it is pretty clear, my guy and that old lady – assuming she wasn't just *your* plant - wanted that useless thing about as much as the other and seemed to have enough money to pay tens of thousands of times its real value to own it. The big difference between my guy and that old lady is that my guy put his money where his mouth was and the old lady just had a phone; for all I know, the phone may not even have been connected to anything or anyone."

"It is that simple?" Froog countered.

"That simple," the man responded, "play it smart before either or both realize what fools they are making of themselves. I think you should just give me the item, take the money, and call it a day; the beginning and end of story."

"Well you had your chance to make it the beginning and end of *your* story on Sunday, unfortunately, now you will have to submit a sealed bid, *above $100,000*, and wait until *next* Sunday, like everyone else."

"Or, I can go looking for another one of these. There must be others around. One is probably just as good as any other. My client probably wouldn't know one from another – I know I don't."

"Froog sat down, leaned back in his chair and began puffing on his cigar. He blew a smoke ring towards the man and said, "Okay, maybe you should just go and do that."

"Have it your way," the man said as he stood up and walked towards the door.

Froog quickly jumped up and wedged himself between the man and the door.

"Just put a sealed bid in," he said nervously. "How about this, make it worth my while and I will let you know if any bid is higher than yours so that you can beat it by a few dollars or so," Froog said.

"I need to have the permit in my hands for my client's representative to pick up before the end of the week – those were the instructions when I let my client know that you and that old broad were playing footsie with each other," the man said.

Froog thought for a moment, and then said, "Okay, okay, here's what I'll do; give me an extra $2,500 above the hundred thousand and it's yours."

"How do you know anyone else will even submit a bid?" the man asked.

"Now you're negotiating?" Froog asked.

"I only got $100,000. Take it or leave it. It is all the same to me."

"And why should I do that?" Froog asked.

"A bird in the hand is better than two in the bush – if you know what I mean? I'll bet my bottom dollar that you have been beating yourself up every minute since I walked out on Sunday that you didn't grab the money while you could."

Froog stared at the man and finally put his hand out, "Done!" Froog said. "Let me see your money."

"Let me see the piece."

"You don't trust me?"

The man stared at Froog and laughed. "You're kidding, right?"

Froog said, "Show me the money and I'll get the permit."

Slowly, the man pulled out a thick roll from his pocket; he

undid the roll and then straightened the bills, swept the clutter away from the corner of Froog's desk with his outstretched arm, and proceeded to make ten piles of ten one hundred dollar bills each. When he counted down the last bill Froog reached across the desk towards the money. The man quickly grabbed Froog's wrist and pushed it away. "First I see the piece. I already let you see the money – so now I get to see the piece. That's the only way this thing is moving forward. Got it?"

Froog slowly nodded yes.

"Now, I don't want to be here a minute more than I have to, the money is sitting right here, give me the permit and I'll be on my way," the man said.

Froog walked across the room to his safe. He blocked the man's view as he dialed in the combination, heard the lock click, pushed the handle down and opened the heavy door. There were numerous bundles of currency, trays of loose jewels, stacks of documents and a ledger book, all in clear view. Excitedly, he thrust his hands into the safe and pushed the contents around. "It's gone!" he yelled. Elizabeth, get in here, NOW!"

Elizabeth rushed in. "You want me, Buss?"

Froog pushed her into a side chair and yelled, "What have you done with that valuable document?"

She stared back at him with obvious fear in her eyes. "I dunn nothin' with nuthin,' Buss."

"Don't give me that, I put it in this safe last night, you were here all alone last night, and it is gone now. You better turn it over or I'll make sure you are on a fast boat back to borschtville before you can say 'boo,' do you understand me?"

The older man got between them and pushed Froog away. "Hey, I don't know what the two of you are trying to pull here, and I don't care to know. If you have the piece, I am happy to buy it and leave, if you do not have it, I'm out of here *now*."

Froog looked at the man. "You can bet I will find out what she did with it. Call me tomorrow."

The man gathered up the ten piles of hundred dollar bills, shoved them into his pocket, and quickly walked out, slamming the door behind him.

Chapter 7
Monday, May 6, 1996 –
Williamsburg, Brooklyn, New York – 10:27 A.M.

Elizabeth sat frozen in the chair.

Froog relit his cigar and sat on the edge of his desk, inches away from her.

"I swear to you, Buss", Elizabeth said, breaking the long silence, "I did not took this thing or anythings elses from that safe. I did not took it from you. I swear on my mudder's eyes."

Froog smiled. "I know you didn't take it," he said calmly, puffing on his cigar. "You couldn't have taken it. It was never in there in the first place. I would never leave a hundred thousand dollar item in a two bit cheese box like that safe."

Her face quickly turned from fear to rage. "Then why you say that I taked it from you?" she asked.

"Look, Elizabeth, if a buyer is out there willing to give some loser like him a hundred thousand dollars in cash and agree to pay a fee on top of it for something *I* own, then *I* need to find out who that person is and get them to pay me what it is really worth."

Elizabeth stood up, spit in his direction, and ran out of the store.

Froog dropped his cigar in the oversized ashtray on his desk and ran after her.

When he caught up with her he threw his arms around her waist. She slapped him.

He started to laugh.

She slapped him again.

He grabbed her hands and put them behind her back. "Stop," he said, "listen to me".

"I should keel you, you animal!" she screamed.

"Don't be stupid," he said. "If you help me find this mystery buyer I'll give you a big bonus."

"I don't want your stinkin' lousy bonus!" she screamed.

Passersby were beginning to look their way. A huge man walked over to them and said, "You all right lady?"

Froog stepped away, "Nothing to see here," Froog said over his shoulder. "Just a little misunderstanding among friends, that's all."

"Would you like me to call the cops?" the passerby said to her, ignoring Froog.

Elizabeth ran her hands through her hair and smiled, embarrassed, at the man. "No," she said, "I weel be all good. Thanks you."

"You're sure," the man persisted.

"I am very much sure. You are good and kindly man; not like that animal," she said, tipping her head towards Froog. "I thanks you".

The man gave Froog a dirty look. "Hey, I don't know who is right and who is wrong here but I do know that if you don't leave her alone or grab her again I'll give you a lesson you won't soon forget," the man threatened.

Elizabeth started to walk back towards the store; Froog followed a short distance behind her. The Good Samaritan stood and watched them until they were at the next corner.

When they got back to the store Froog made a fresh pot of coffee, something he rarely did for anyone but himself. He poured her a cup and one for himself and sat down next to her.

"I'm really sorry," he said. "I had no idea it would hurt you so much. All I wanted to do was buy us some time so that we could try to find *his* buyer for ourselves."

"We? Us?" she asked. "For ourselves?"

"Yeh, *we, us* for *ourselves*," he repeated. "We are a team, you and me. I was serious out there. If you help me find this buyer and we can get more money for that useless piece of crap I will gladly share the overage with you."

"You are not only animal... but a cheap and a rotten stinkin' animal."

"Okay, even if we don't get more than the hundred thousand I will give you a share."

"That *useless pieces of junk,* she said mockingly, "was used to keep your weendow open just a few hours before you tried to sell it as a *'treasure.'"* she sneered. "I know you like the cheap rotten animal you are, Albert Froog. You would have screamed for joy if you gotten some dope to pay you $2.00 for it. If you was not so... so... so..." She seemed to be looking for the right word.

"Foolish?" he suggested.

"No!" she said

"Unwise?" he tried again.

"No!" she said.

"Greedy?" he tried again.

She stared at him. "No! Don't not put wordses into my mouth. What I trying to say is if you was not such a cheap sheet you would have grabbed the two dollars and that would have been that!"

"Okay, okay, okay," he said, "But there can be a really happy ending here for both of us. This could be a real win/win if we play our cards right." He smiled, and then added, "Together."

"Tell me what you are saying", she yelled, "and tell me straight truth or I swear to you I weel find a way to cut your leetle thing off and feed it back to you wrapped up in sewer sludge. You understanding *me*, Albert Froog?"

"He squirmed in his chair, "I understand," he said slowly. "Now listen to me....."

Chapter 8
Monday, May 6, 1996 –
Williamsburg, Brooklyn, New York – 3:22 P.M.

Elizabeth tried calling the old woman many times from her home phone, on Sunday and again today from the store. Each time it rang and rang without being picked up.

She sat down at her computer to send the older woman a message, carefully copying the address from the sign-in card. Almost instantly the message on her screen told her that it could not go through. *What is going on here,* she thought. *Maybe I copied the wrong address?* She retyped the address that appeared on the sign-in card in clear, block letters. Once again, she received the same response. She got up and went into Froog's office.

He was looking through some papers. Without raising his head, Froog barked, "I am not going to tell you again, you are to knock and wait to be invited in *before* you parade into my office, Elizabeth. What about that sentence do you not understand?"

So much for friendly and together, she thought. "I have it here a problem, Buss."

"Then go and solve it."

"I think it is your problem also."

He looked up. "What are you babbling about?"

"I been trying for to get in touch weeth the old lady woman from Sunday."

He put down the paper he was studying and leaned back in his chair. "You know how to reach her?" he asked.

"Elizabeth showed him the sign-in card. "I ask it each of the pipples at the auction to sign in," she said.

"Why didn't you tell me this before?"

"You never asked it me before," she said.

"Don't play games with me, Elizabeth," he screamed. "Why didn't you ever tell me that you had this information?"

"I dint because I dint," she said. "You wants to keep asking me such silly stuff or you wants to help solve it the problem?"

"Let me see that card," he said, grabbing it out of her hand.

"This is great information, Elizabeth," he said, excitedly. "This was very good thinking on your part. If we work this right we now have leverage over that holier-than-thou pompous ass with the wad of bills."

"But I thinks this is not good information, Buss."

"Why?"

"I call to the telephone number and no answer. I send messages from computer and it come back, bad address."

"You probably entered the wrong information," he said. "Here, give it to me, I'll do it." He picked up the phone and dialed the number. Half a dozen rings later, he hung up. "Strange," he said.

He walked out of his office, card in hand, went to her computer and typed in the e-mail address shown on the card. Within seconds he got the same 'unable to deliver' message. He stared at the screen and then turned to Elizabeth.

"I'm going to check out the physical address on this card for myself. She was an old lady, maybe she mixed up the phone and e-mail numbers."

"And the streets address she wouldn't mixed up also?" Elizabeth asked facetiously.

"Hey, I got to at least try," he said as he went back into his office for his car keys.

"I think it is you going to be on a wilded geeses chase," she yelled after him.

"It is the only lead we have. I have to make the effort."

"I think you wrong," she persisted.

"You don't get to make that judgment, Elizabeth, I do." As he ran for the front door he yelled back, "If my mother's lawyer calls for me, tell him I'm in the bathroom."

*****

Monday, May 6, 1996 – Staten Island, New York – 6:03 P.M.

The address on the card was 875 Jewett Avenue in Staten Island. Froog circled the block several times, not wanting to believe that 875 was actually the address of a city fire station. Finally, Froog pulled over to the side, turned off the ignition and slammed his hands on the dashboard. "Son of a bitch!" he screamed. "It is a goddamned fire house!"

Froog shifted between anger and disbelief. Clearly, the old woman had given Elizabeth a phony address and probably a phony phone number and email address. "But why?" he screamed, "Why?" This thing keeps getting *curioser* and *curioser*, he thought to himself. Staring at the fire house he said, "She could have just left the damn card blank – she didn't have to write in anything. It was just a damn card from a Russian illiterate, not a subpoena from the feds."

Froog got out of the car and entered a nearby pay phone

booth and dialed Sol Weiner. He had been updating Sol about the strange events since Sunday's auction but felt the need to go over it again with Sol, every strange detail by strange detail.

"I am parked across the street from a Fire Station in Staten Island," he shouted into the phone.

"Great!" Sol responded, "Now if you or your car spontaneously combusts you are covered... you'll just have to yell over to the other side of the street for a couple buckets of water."

"Don't fool around, Sol, this is serious."

"Tell me why you felt the need to run out to Staten Island on such a frivolous lead," Sol responded.

"It was all I had. Why in God's name would that old lady feel the need to give us a fake address at all? She could have left the damn card empty, but no, she gave an address and a phone number and an email address. None of which seems to be legit. And this address of a Staten Island fire station. Why? I feel like Alice in Wonderland and I don't like the feeling."

Sol knew Albert well enough to just patiently listen, after allowing Albert to vent he calmly said, "First of all, Alice only existed in the dark imagination of Rev. Charles Lutwidge Dodgson, and that is definitely *not* the real world."

"Who the hell is *he*?" Froog yelled into the phone.

"Albert Froog," Sol chided, "if I could get you to read something other than your competitor's literature you would know who Rev. Charles Lutwidge Dodgson is, or I should say, was."

Froog took a deep breath, slowly counted to ten and in a

much calmer voice said, "Okay, Sol, you win, as usual. I am calmer now, so maybe you can just tell me who he was and why I should care?"

"Well, dear Albert, Rev. Charles Lutwidge Dodgson," Sol said, stretching out each word, "dear, dear Albert, my very young and easily excitable friend, Rev. Charles Lutwidge Dodson, was also known as Lewis Carroll. And so, Lewis Carroll *never* really existed, *nor* did Alice, *nor* did 'Wonderland'. They were all figments of Dodgson's imagination. And in his wildest imagination, even Dodgson could never have conjured up an Albert Froog."

"Come on Sol," Albert said. "You are as baffled by all of this as much as I am. Even you have to admit that the events of the past few days make absolutely no sense whatsoever."

"Albert," Sol said, calmly, "let me remind you that I am a trained photo journalist. The primary thing you learn as a journalist of any kind is that even the most senseless act made sense to someone or it could never have occurred at all. It may be a very troubled someone; it may be a very disturbed someone; but to *that* someone, it made all the sense in the world. And so, the first thing a seasoned journalist would do is to try and work out what *probable* sense the *seemingly* senseless act could have made to the person or persons responsible for the act. That usually narrows the field and more often than not helps you to zero in on *the* one or ones who *were* involved and their motivation. In order to do that you have to dismiss what makes sense to *you* entirely; and I don't know any better way to do that than to carefully study whatever photo documentation you can gather up. Unlike humans, who are subject to what their eyes *think* they see and their brains *believe* to be real, photos *never analyze, only document.* Now, have you calmed down enough to listen to me?"

Froog took in a deep breath and exhaled noisily. "Yes, Sol,

I am calmer."

"Okay," Sol said calmly, "now please tell me if you still have the video taping system in place that you told me about in the auction room?"

"Yes", Albert answered, still agitated, "so what?"

"I'll tell you, 'so *what*', but first just tell me why you put that surveillance camera in that room?"

"Please don't patronize me, Sol."

"Answer my question; why did you put that surveillance camera in that room?"

"It was to have a record in case something went missing while the people were in there," Froog said, clearly annoyed.

"No," Sol said, calmly, "I suggest that you put that camera there so that you could have an independent record of what happens in that area."

"It's the same thing," Froog said, now screaming into the phone.

"I suggest that it is *not* the same thing at all. Now, please tell me if you saved the tape from this past Sunday?" Sol asked.

"Come on Sol, you know that we tape over each week to save tape costs." Albert said.

"Of course you do, after all, you *are* Albert Froog. So, now tell me, when do you tape over the Sunday auction tape?"

"Every Sunday we tape over the previous Sunday's tape," Albert said, clearly annoyed.

"So you still have this past Sunday's tape?" Sol said, calmly.

"Yes," Froog responded with an exaggerated sigh.

"At last! Now, that didn't hurt, did it?"

"Please Sol, I'm really not in the mood."

"Hey, you called me, I didn't call you. Now, let me help you... or at least try to help you. I respectfully suggest that you go back to the store and get the tape and bring it to me."

"Why?"

Sol counted slowly from one to ten and then said, "I might be able to see something that can help you unravel the *Alice in Wonderland* experience you *think* you are now encountering."

"I am not making this up, Sol. I *am* experiencing it and I don't like the experience; that tape can't help," Froog said.

"Albert Froog," Sol said calmly, "it can't hurt."

Chapter 9

Despite all of his complaining, Albert Froog actually idolized his grandmother. She knew something about everything; and shared whatever she knew openly and graciously. She was like no one else he knew, she never got angry, he never heard her say a bad word about anyone, she befriended everyone and seemed able to find something good in everyone – including him. People just seemed to like her; opened up to her; felt free with her. He wished with all of his might that someday he could have that same effect on people.

The only problem was that she never seemed to leave the store. At an early age, he realized that if he wanted to spend any meaningful time with his grandmother he had to go to her antique store. Evelyn Zaleson spent virtually every waking hour in the store, even at times and days when the store was closed to the public, she found reasons to be there, among what she referred to as her *hidden treasures*.

On Saturdays and holidays the store became her personal sanctuary, a safe haven of sorts. She often referred to her times in the store when she had it all to herself as what it might be like to own a *free from care* time machine. She considered the store to be a mystical place where she could shed all of her troubles and inhibitions. It was not unusual for her to bring a box lunch on a Saturday or holiday and play dress up, trying on some of the early fashions that filled the many racks and storage boxes in the store. She especially enjoyed looking in the mirror as she tried on some of the many feather boas or hats she had acquired over the years.

In the basement of the store she had a special area built to house *her* personal record collection. These were not for sale; they were hers and hers alone. She stored them by artist and then by type of recording, special one sided World War II records then two-sided 78 rpm records... 33 1/3 LP records... small 45's with huge holes in the center, and then there were the heavy and brightly colored record albums. She loved the music but even more, she enjoyed revisiting her many memories... those very precious memories... *her* very special memories. Reminders of times that were not as fast and furious as they were today; when she was young and beautiful and life still offered so many options for her. So many of the items in the store represented very specific memories of long gone experiences; years before, she established theme days for when she was alone in the store; there were ladies' days – the ones she could *spend* with Ella Fitzgerald or Billie Holiday and big band singers like Jo Stafford; many sunny days she would *feature* Jazz or 'Big Bands' – Benny Goodman... Artie Shaw... Glen Gray and his Casa Loma Orchestra... George Auld and His Hollywood All Stars... the Dorsey Brothers, individually and collectively... Eddie Duchin... the George Gee Swing Orchestra, particularly the records he made with the Make-Believe Ballroom Orchestra, and of course, Paul Whiteman, 'the snap happy king of jazz'. She had every record ever made by Eddie Sauter and Bill Finegan and played them all on a wind up RCA Victor portable record player that she moved from area to area while she puttered around the store.

From time to time she would invite Howard Hill to join her there for lunch so that he could share the inside stories about the artists, many of whom he had played with during the early days of his career or the background gossip he picked up during studio recording sessions. As a black man he had to watch his P's and Q's – never stray too far from the areas and facilities earmarked "black only," even in his home town of Philadelphia, but as a first rate musician, he was free as a daisy to come and go as he chose but only while he was on the bandstand.

On rainy days, for some reason, she preferred to smother herself in Broadway original cast recordings and opera, especially Caruso. She had a special thing for Caruso. His recordings always brought back memories of the tiny apartment her parents had above the butcher shop in Boston. Her mother would be by the stove, making supper; her father by the radio, leading the orchestra behind Caruso... she would close her eyes and raise an imaginary glass to the good times.

She spent very special days with former imaginary heart throbs – Rudy Valley, the Connecticut Yankee... Bing Crosby and the Rhythm Boys... and Frank Sinatra; handsome, sexy, skinny as a rail, blue eyed Frank Sinatra; she still had the ticket stub and never tired of looking through her now yellowed scrapbook from the day she cut school and took a train to downtown Brooklyn so that she could wait on the long line at the Brooklyn Paramount to see Frank Sinatra *in person*. She saved everything connected to that day even the Junior's restaurant menu and the two paper straws from the vanilla malted she bought before taking the train back home. She still got shivers up and down her spine when remembering what it felt like to be in the very same building with him. Yes, there were thousands of other, screaming bobby soxers in the same building at the same time; but here, in *her* refuge, while his voice filled the room, it was just him – with his dreamy blue eyes – and her.

There were Saturdays when Albert would come by, sit and watch his grandmother prance around in a dreamy state while Sinatra crooned as only Sinatra could croon. Sometimes Albert felt as if he was the third wheel on a date. He so wanted to be as important to her as Sinatra seemed to be. There were also times when he thought she just used the music to block him out.

After some of the visits he would return home in a deeply depressed and negative mood and complain to his mother, "It is just crazy, the way she cuddles up to those useless and rotting old things. She seems to love them more than human beings."

"So why do you keep going back there?" his mother would ask. "I don't force you to see your grandmother in the store, no one does. You are her only grandchild, Albert, she loves you. Why can't you just accept that?"

"Yeah, yeah," he would respond.

"Well she does love you. Once and for all you have to understand that you are not competing with anything for her love, you are especially not competing with the antiques for her love."

The more his mother tried to talk him out of such thoughts and feelings, the more resentment he seemed to express.

*****

Friday, May 8, 1964 –
Williamsburg, Brooklyn, New York – 11:42 A.M.

There was one particular visit to the store that seemed to make up for many if not all of the depressing ones. It was a rainy Friday morning in May, 1964. His school was closed for some kind of teacher's conference and he spent the day with his grandmother in the store. Albert's grandmother asked him to watch the store while she went to the bank to make a deposit. Just before noon, Sol Weiner, a tall well-dressed man with a noticeable limp, walked into the store. Sol had some time to kill and stepped into the antique store because of a collection of old picture postcards he saw in the window.

The 23-year-old Sol explained to the 14-year-old Albert that upon graduating from high school he became an assistant to a professional photo journalist and had actually worked in some of the very same countries pictured on the cards. Froog removed the cards from the window showcase and placed them on the counter. One by one, Sol shared his experiences in the various places pictured. When he came to the one showing Hyde Park in London, he pointed to his right leg and said, "That was where I got this lovely souvenir."

Albert cautiously asked, "In the war?"

Sol smiled, no, nothing that glamorous; I was involved in an auto accident. They drive on the other side of the street there and I never saw the car coming."

"Oh, I'm so sorry," Albert sputtered.

"Don't be, it taught me a good lesson," Sol said.

"It taught you to watch both sides of the street for oncoming traffic?" Albert asked, innocently.

"No," Sol laughed, "It taught me not to drink martinis before noon."

The conversation continued even after Albert's grandmother returned to the store. She asked Sol if she could help him and Sol said, "Your sales person here is already helping me, thank you."

Sol bought the entire collection of cards that day and returned to the little store fairly often. He and Albert's grandmother never seemed to be at a loss for things to talk about. A warm and pleasant friendship developed between the three of them over the years.

Sol was a huge New York Yankees fan; he and a group of his friends regularly went to games at Yankee Stadium. From time to time they would take Albert along with them.

The generally shy and reclusive Albert enjoyed those days; he was becoming more open and sociable as a result of his exposure to Sol and Sol's friends. Through Sol, Albert also seemed to find more positive things to talk about and *almost* enjoyed being around the store from time to time.

*****

When his grandmother died, Albert called Sol. Sol listened patiently to his friend as Albert shared his anger and confusion. Albert rambled on about how he felt he should feel more sadness but instead just felt relieved. Suddenly, almost in mid-sentence, Albert, with tears streaming down his face, apologized for bending Sol's ear and quickly hung up.

Sol went to the funeral and when the ceremony ended he walked over to Albert, put his arms around him and suggested a way to ease the pain he knew Albert was experiencing. "Write your grandmother a letter." Sol suggested, "Have the conversation that might have made all of the difference if you voiced the words to her while she was still alive. Maybe acknowledge that pride or ego or confusion or just fear of how she might have reacted kept you from saying it to her when she was alive. Share every bit of your anger; spell out how you feel now and how you felt all of those years; why you think it should or could have been better between you if *each* of you had made more of an effort earlier on. Don't leave anything out. Pour it all onto the page. Then tell her you love her – because I know you did love her, I watched the two of you together. She loved you and you loved her. Of that there is no doubt. Tell her you realize that you could have done more, might have tried to see her side of things to build a better relationship. If you think so, tell her that you forgive her and hope she forgives you. When you are done, come back to the cemetery, sit near her grave and read the letter out loud. Then rip it up into small pieces and let the pieces fly away into the wind. I promise you, you *will* feel better."

Albert couldn't get himself to take his friend's advice, at least not then. It just seemed like a silly exercise and the thought of returning to the gravesite sent chills up his spine. He thought that it would be too much like so many of his earlier visits to the store; her body would be near but her spirit would be somewhere else.

One evening, several months after the funeral Albert was having dinner alone in his apartment when thoughts of his grandmother suddenly swept over him, he pushed his plate aside, got up from the table and sat down in front of his desk. He began to write the letter Sol had initially suggested. It was actually just a page and a half but it took him several hours to complete. He folded it neatly in half and gently placed it on his desk and went to bed.

He tossed and turned for the better part of an hour, when he was certain he would not be able to sleep until he *delivered* the letter, he got out of bed, quickly dressed, grabbed the letter and got into his car. He couldn't quite get himself to go to the cemetery so he drove to the antique store on Lee Avenue. He sat on the front step by the entrance to the store, unfolded the letter and began reading it out loud. By the last few sentences he could barely see the words through his tears. He slowly stood up, gently placed the two pages on the front step and brought his cigar lighter to the edge of the bottom page. He watched the flame build as the papers changed form under the heat. When they were no more than a small pile of ashes he gave a huge sigh and returned to his car and slowly drove back home.

It was almost 4 in the morning when he returned to his apartment. He picked up the phone and called Sol. Still half asleep Sol answered on the third ring. Albert told him what he had just done and then, in mid-sentence, started to sob. Both were silent for quite some time until Albert said, "Good night, Sol."

Sol responded, softly, "Good night, my young, and I hope, less troubled friend."

"Good night, and thank you so very much, my very *best* friend." Albert answered.

*****

Years later, when he learned that his mother died, Albert went to Sol's apartment. Sol could see the sadness on his friend's face. After several deep sighs Albert said, "My mother died today."

Sol put his arms around Albert and led him inside. Sol made a fresh pot of coffee for the two of them and sat next to his friend at the kitchen table. "You know what you have to do now, don't you?" Sol asked.

Albert looked up and said, "I am not going to write her a letter!"

They both laughed.

"No," Sol said, "well maybe not right away."

They both sat silently once again, finally, with tears welling up Albert said, "I feel so very lost and alone. Tell me Sol, what *do* I do now?"

Sol put his hand on Albert's arm and said, "I do believe that you need to allow yourself time to grieve – not morbid, *pity party* kind of grief, but the kind of healthy grief which brings back all of the good memories. Don't let the grieving process go on indefinitely; just long enough to resolve your deeply personal loss with a tender smile instead of an angry howl."

"How will I know when the time is right to forget?" Albert asked softly. "You will never forget, Albert. You should never forget. But you will know when you are ready to re-enter the world of the living!" Sol assured him, "You will most definitely know."

Another long silence passed. Albert broke the silence by asking, "Will you stay with me through this process?"

Sol smiled and said, "You can count on that."

Sol held Albert's face in his hands and said, "You are not alone, dear Albert." He sighed and then said, "I love you, Albert."

After a very long silence Albert said, "I think I have always loved you, Sol!"

Chapter 10
Monday, May 6, 1996 –
Crown Heights, Brooklyn, N.Y. – 10:47 P.M.

Sol had a fresh pot of coffee waiting when Albert arrived from his wild goose chase in Staten Island.

"I don't know what you expect to see from a tape recording that I couldn't see in *real time*," Albert said as he walked in, clearly annoyed, "but, here it is."

"Look Albert," Sol said, gently, taking the tape from his friend, "sometimes just a fresh pair of eyes can pick up a little thing here or there that was previously missed, and even if I can't add any sense to this mystery, what harm can it do? The time you took to come home by way of the store has at the very least allowed you to shake off some of that intense anger you were expressing."

"Oh Sol", Albert groaned, "The damned glass is always half full with you."

Sol took the tape and placed it into their VCR machine.

Albert was in the kitchen making himself a sandwich when Sol called to him, "Hey, come here, I think I have something."

Sol locked onto a frame that showed all of the people who attended the auction. When Albert walked in Sol pointed to each person in the frame and assigned each a number.

"This is the man who made the final high bid of $100,000," Sol said, "let's call him number 1 and for the older woman who *seemed* to be counter bidding with him, let's call her number 2."

"What do you mean, '*seems to be counter bidding*'?" Albert broke in. "She did counter his bid."

"Don't interrupt," Sol said, sternly, "let me continue."

Sol pointed to a large man dragging a chair towards the back row. A few frames later all three huge, body builder types were sitting in the back row. Sol said, "Let's call these men numbers 3, 4, and 5."

He then pointed out another body builder type along the left side of the room and said, "Let's make him number 6; two more huge men are here on the right side of the room, one on either side of the small table with the coffee pot and donuts. Let's call them numbers 7 and 8; the well-dressed man who started the bidding when it was at two dollars, will be number 9..."

"That's Howard Hill", Albert said.

"I asked you not to interrupt." Sol said, impatiently, "Now, where was I? Oh, yes, the bald headed man in the ruffled overcoat, who also never bid, is in the center seat on the first row. He'll be number 10; the young woman at the end of the front row is here, let's call her number 11 and finally, that big grumpy looking guy is number 12. So now we have the full room – big bruiser types well placed throughout the room; on both sides, filling the rear, and all but one seat in the second or back row. Did you notice that all of the husky guys seemed to be wearing really stylish suits? He pointed at the ones visible in that frame. Those are almost certainly Brioni suits, from Italy. The cheapest Brioni is thousands of dollars."

"I never heard of that brand," Albert said.

"You aren't alone, few people know the brand, much less own one. Some of the Brioni's suits stitching is made of white gold and sells for tens of thousands of dollars," Sol said longingly.

"How can you possibly know that?" Albert sneered.

"I know that because I spent enough time in Italy dreaming of owning one someday," Sol said.

"So what does it matter how they dress?" Albert asked.

"Just seems strange that so many Brioni suits would wind up in your store on the same day, that's all."

Sol then put the tape in reverse motion and stopped on a frame with the time/date stamp on the bottom right of the screen reading 10:04 A.M. May 5-camera 3.

"Okay, number 11, the young woman, is already seated in the front row; next to her is number 10 neatly folding his overcoat and next to him, completing the first row is your Howard Hill, my number 9. There at the end of the center row is number 2, the '*old woman*", Sol put his fingers up in the air to suggest quotation marks, "with what looks like a partially knitted scarf on her lap."

"Why the stupid air quotes?" Albert asked.

Sol smiled, "You'll see, you'll see!"

Sol let the tape run until the time/date stamp read 10:09 A.M. May 5-camera 3. Sol tapped the stop button. "Numbers 3, 4, 5, just entered together..." Sol started the tape again. "Now, look here," he pointed at another part of the screen. "Number 2 seems to be motioning to number 4 and number 4 then turns to numbers 3 and 5, says something to them behind his hand. 4 and 5 fill the rest of the seats in the back or second row while number 3 is pulling up a chair and placing it in the second or back row next to number 4."

The tape continues and at 10:21 A.M. May 5-camera 3 Elizabeth is seen leaving the room as numbers 7 and 8 walk into the room; each nods discreetly towards number 2; they separate and take a position along the right side of the room, one on each side of the small table with the coffee maker and box of donuts. "Now, look there, number 1 is walking into the room, looks around, and slowly positions himself against the back wall."

Sol pointed to the time stamp, 10:23 A.M. May 5-camera 3. "This is where you stick your head into the room and almost as quickly, turn and leave."

At 10:26 A.M. May 5-camera 3 Number 6 walks into the room, nods towards number 2 and stands against the wall on the left side. At 10:28 A.M. May 5-camera 3 number 12 enters the room, looks around, and moves to the back wall a few feet away from number 1.

"Albert slowly sat down in front of the VCR machine, "You think they all knew each other?" he asked.

"Maybe not all of them but it definitely looks to me like a fair number of these people were not in the same room with each other for the very first time." Sol said.

Sol fast forwarded to 10:51 A.M. May 5-camera 3, "Now, look at this," Sol said, watch number 2, she has the phone to her ear and... there, *she* put it into her purse without turning it off." Once again, Sol put his fingers up in the air to suggest quotation marks as he said, '*she*'.

"Hey", Albert yelled, "you did it again. What is with you and your air quotes for the old lady?"

"Things aren't always as they seem, Albert," Sol said.

"What does that mean?" Albert asked.

"Maybe nothing, maybe something; just keep watching. I want you to see it the same way I saw it."

They ran through the tape two more times and then Albert said, "So it was all an act? They were actually just putting on a show? But for whom?"

"Looks like they were putting on a show *just* for you!" Sol said. "Look at this"; again he fast forwarded the tape to 11:07 A.M. May 5-camera 3 "This is where the '*old lady*' asked to see the document. Watch her right hand... there," Sol said excitedly, as he stopped the tape, "she seems to be attaching something to the frame. Where is the frame now?"

"It's in the bedroom." Albert said.

"Quickly," Sol said, "bring it here."

Albert went to the bedroom and a few minutes later returned with the framed document. He handed it to Sol who took it to the kitchen table. Examining it carefully he pointed to a small, thin disk on the bottom outer edge of the frame. He carefully peeled it off of the frame, took it to the sink, and dropped it into a glass as he slowly filled the glass with water. They saw a series of sparks in the glass.

"What was that?" Albert asked.

"That, little Alice, was an electronic bug."

Albert picked up the glass and stared at the small disk resting in the base of the glass. He gently put the glass on the table and sat down in front of it. "So the minute I moved the document from the store and brought it here they knew where it was?"

"She knew where it was." Sol said.

"Well if they were all in this together, then *they* knew where it was."

"We don't know that they are all in it together – all we

know is it looks like a bunch of them may know each other. Anyway, I don't know who, *'they'* are – but the only reason to put an electronic bug on something is to be able to keep track of its location."

"But the guy who came to the store on Monday didn't act at all like he knew it wasn't going to be in my safe."

"Who knows?" Sol shrugged.

"Well why would he have come to the store for it if he knew from the electronic bug that it was not in the store or anywhere near the store? He could have trailed it here and just taken it?" Albert said.

"So maybe they are working together but *not* necessarily sharing whatever they know with each other." Sol said. "Hey, why guess? What we do know is that the bug is no longer working so that alone may push one or all of them to become a lot more aggressive and soon."

Albert stared at Sol and said, "This is just plain crazy, I'm somehow involved with a real bunch of spooks."

"Maybe, maybe not; all that we can be certain of is that now that they can no longer track its location, someone or some ones are going to have to get moving. Neither you nor I are really capable of forming a meaningful defense. Maybe it is time to call in a protector of our own." Sol said

"Know anybody like that?" Albert asked.

Sol thought for a while then said, "I may know someone who knows someone."

Sol went into his study and came out with a huge Rolodex file. He looked through it then pulled out a card.

"Is that the one who can help us?" Albert asked.

"No, but it is someone who can connect us to one who might." Sol answered. "I was on an assignment for the Washington Post a few years back. We were investigating a congressman from Ohio. We kept running into brick walls; every secret seemed to be wrapped in other secrets, until the assignment editor brought in a guy who seemed to thrive on unraveling mysteries. He had this unique ability to dig into anything and anyone on our radar. I don't know how he did it but I do know that each and every time we asked him to check something out he was able to get us what we needed, and quickly. Tomorrow I will pay my guy at the *Washington Post* a visit. This looks like just the kind of challenge our maybe investigator seemed to thrive on."

"You're going to drive all the way to Washington, D.C. just to talk to your friend at the *Post*?" Albert asked.

"Some things are better done in person. I'll start out early in the morning. It won't take all that long and it will be good to get a way for the day."

"Why can't we contact this guy directly?" Albert asked.

"He never gave me a business card – and I *did* ask." Sol said. "For all I know he doesn't even have business cards. He's a really non-conformist type of guy; but he did say that he would be happy to work with me again, given the right assignment, and could always be contacted through the assignment editor at the *Washington Post.*"

"This guy is a real spook?" Albert asked.

"A whole lot spookier than any *spook* I ever met before or since," Sol said.

"Do you remember this guy's name?"

Sol turned the card over and in block letters it said, *Will James.*"

Chapter 11
Tuesday, May 7, 1996 –
Editorial offices, the *Washington Post* – 11:02 A.M.

Sol woke early, grabbed some fruit and a few bottles of Perrier, stuffed it all into a small cooler and began the long drive to Washington, D.C. When he reached his contact at the newspaper he was told, "James isn't the easiest person to reach. Not like he works out of an actual address."

"What do you mean he doesn't have an actual address?" Sol asked, "Doesn't he run an ongoing business?"

"Not so that you would notice," the editor laughed. "I really don't know how he pays his bills. He works where and when he wants. In fact, *just* the business that I know he has turned away could support another couple shops. At times he is quite visible and at others, it is like he has fallen off the edge of the world. I seem to be one of the few people he responds to in a fairly timely manner."

"I know that a call from the Washington Post is almost certainly going to get answered – on the first try, but, why you? I can vouch for the fact that you are not the easiest guy to work with." Sol said.

"He thinks I helped him when he was in a pinch about thirty or so years ago."

"What did you do for him?" Sol asked.

"Truth be known, all I did was my job, it looked to me like he was being railroaded by the Feds and I kept street reporters on the story to stop the bullies from being bullies; but as I see it, why look a gift horse in the mouth? If he thinks he owes me, let him think he owes me. James can be the best and easiest person to deal with that you could ever want, or the most persistent pain in the rear," the assignment editor said.

"So how do *you* reach him?" Sol asked, "do you send a beam of light into the sky, like in the Batman comics?" Sol laughed.

The editor smiled, "Actually, from what little I know about Batman, it can be easier connecting with him than with James." The editor picked up one of his own business cards and held it out to Sol, "There is a public bulletin board at the courthouse. I pin a card like this on the board and most of the time he gets in touch with me the same day." The editor said. "But there have been times when it takes longer. What do you want him for?"

After a long silence Sol said, "A really good friend of mine needs someone with James' unique talents."

"That may not prove to be enough to get his interest, and he *only* works on things that get his interest."

"What *does* get his interest?"

"In broad strokes, he seems to have a real *thing* against those who wield power, seemingly without conscience or empathy for the underdog."

"Narrow the strokes a bit for me."

"He really likes to work on problems that others have given up on... that supposedly, 'experts' have labeled 'unsolvable'; he seeks out, seems to thrive on right vs. might struggles; especially when those with a lot of power have been using it to silence those with less or none. I have worked with him on quite a few assignments over the years and if there is a more specific model that interests him most, I have yet to find it."

"Well," Sol said, "this situation is all of that, and more."

"Then I would say that James will probably be interested."

"I should tell you," Sol said, hesitantly, "My friend can be a handful. How does James react to clients with little or no social graces and a *trust factor* of minus ten, to the hundredth power?"

The editor laughed, "Look, there is no *preferred type* of client where James is concerned, but one thing I am certain about – your friend can be the worst human being on earth to everyone else, but as long as he is straight with James and treats anyone James brings into the mix with respect and dignity... *and* is one thousand percent honest *and* truthful in his or her dealings with James, there won't be anyone better to work with. There is no guarantee that he will even take your friend's problem on, but if he does, I suggest you make certain that your friend understands that James *will* take over. *He* will decide what to do, when to do it, who to get involved – and I have known him to get help from people who are at the top of their game, generally unreachable to the rest of us."

"Sounds expensive. What is this likely to cost?"

"It will cost a dollar more than your friend is willing to pay and probably a lot of dollars less than James is worth. I think James would work for free if it allowed him to resolve a problem others might consider beyond any possible solution."

"How does he survive? Is he independently wealthy?"

"I have no idea about his finances, but he's a survivor, all right – that is for certain. Don't worry about him."

"Why do you keep giving him assignments if he is so unpredictable?" Sol asked.

"Because he is great at what he does; he's smart, very smart, usually doesn't wear his intelligence on his sleeve but very little gets past him and his results always check out; that's the *how* and the *why* of it." The editor said. "I would bet the ranch that he could think his way out of a sealed cube with no windows... no doors... or any *apparent* way out. He is *that* good."

Slowly at first, then after being assured that all confidences would be honored, Sol shared the events since last Sunday's auction.

"Sounds more like a story for me than an assignment for James," the editor finally said.

"I really don't know what we have here." Sol said. "But my instincts tell me that my friend is already well over his head; and the journalist in me believes that he may only be dealing with the very tip of the iceberg so far."

"And your role in all of this is?"

"He is my friend and I would like to save him from being hurt."

"And your role in all of this *is*?" The editor repeated.

Sol smiled. "You haven't changed a bit, have you?"

"And *your* role in all of this *is*?" The editor persisted.

"I'd like to get a better look at the full iceberg before my friend crashes into it."

"Well", the editor said, "if and when the big mass of this iceberg comes into sight and it looks like the kind of a story my readers would want to know about, I hope you will bring it to me, *first*."

Sol reached out to shake his contact's hand, "You can count on it!"

Once outside the newspaper building, Sol called Albert.

"Will he help us?"

"I don't know," Sol said.

"You got up in the middle of the night to drive a thousand miles and you don't know?" Albert said, sarcastically.

"Oh, Albert, it wasn't a thousand miles and it wasn't the middle of the night. I'm trying to help here, let the process unfold. If he agrees to work with us we should know fairly soon. If not, we'll jump off of *that* bridge after we crash into it."

Chapter 12
Twenty nine years earlier...
Saturday, May 4, 1967 –
Bailey's Crossroads, VA – 7:13 P.M.

In 1946, Murray Leinster first published a science fiction short story, "A Logic Named Joe" in the March 1946 issue of *Astounding Science Fiction* Magazine. The story predicted massively networked personal computers and their drawbacks, and appeared at a time when computing was in its infancy.

By 1960, when the vacuum tube technology moved to transistors and finally integrated circuits; computer main memory slowly moved away from magnetic core memory devices to solid-state static and dynamic semiconductor memory, which greatly reduced the cost, size and power consumption of computer devices. The mass increase in the use of computers accelerated with 'Third Generation' computers. These generally relied on the invention of the integrated circuit or microchip. The first integrated circuit was produced in September 1958 but computers using them didn't begin to appear until 1963. Some of their early uses were in embedded systems, notably used by NASA for the Apollo Guidance Computer, by the military in the LGM-30 Minuteman intercontinental ballistic missile, the Honeywell ALERT airborne computer, and in the Central Air Data Computer used for flight control in the US Navy's F-14A Tomcat fighter jet.

In early 1967, Will James's High School science teacher, Jack Lazarus, was given permission to head an after school science club dedicated to the new challenges in science. Although nineteen students signed up for the club, only Will James remained by the third time the club got together. The club then moved to the James's garage where teacher and sole student regularly met every Saturday morning. Will and his teacher built an early version of a computer. From then on, Will James was hooked.

It didn't take very long after that for fifteen-year-old Will James to be able to hack his way into just about anyone's computer system, anytime he chose. Although some systems took a little longer than others, eventually he found a way into and out of each one he had targeted, apparently without leaving any sign that he had even been there. The Department of Defense system proved the most challenging but eventually, it too was no match for him.

He had mixed emotions about accessing the Department of Defense servers. His first reaction was that he had outfoxed the best, but that quickly turned to concern. He was bright enough to realize that if he could do it then so could real enemies of the country. He anonymously sent a letter to the Secretary of Defense in the Pentagon, in which he detailed the vulnerabilities of their systems. He suggested changes they could make to improve their system's security. Several weeks after sending the letter he went back into their system only to find that nothing had changed. They had clearly chosen to ignore his suggestions, which was no problem for him but what did concern him was that they did not see the potential risks as sharply as he had and as a result had not made any changes to secure their data. It was as easy to hack into their system now as it had been the previous time. *Could it be that they just didn't care*, he wondered?

He sent another letter, this time much stronger and more detailed. He waited another few weeks and still was able to move in and out of their system as freely as before. Well, he thought to himself, maybe they just need a louder wake up call. He infected their programs, changed some of their commands and created "back doors" to access sensitive employee passwords and usernames. He read and copied a series of files that had been marked confidential and sent them all, anonymously, to the *Washington Post*.

His involvement might never have been traced back to him had he not been so brazen as to send the Secretary of State's personal security code to one of the underground newspapers. This brought his activities to the personal attention of the United States Attorney General who created a special task force led by no less than the Director of the FBI. They swooped down on the underground newspaper with a vengeance. It didn't take too long before the editor of the newspaper gave them James' name and address.

*****

**Thursday, November 14, 1968 –
Bailey's Crossroads, VA – 4:19 A.M.**

Just before dawn, two weeks before Thanksgiving, the James family home was surrounded by armed agents of the Department of Defense, the FBI, and the City of Falls Church Police department. With the FBI in the lead, they broke through the front door and quickly moved from room to room until all family members were accounted for. Two armed agents stood at the foot of Will James' bed, a third stood along the right side and a fourth agent shook him out of a sound asleep while standing on the left side of the sleeping boy. The fourth agent told him to get out of the bed and put his hands behind his back. He was handcuffed, read his rights and with his father by his side, led out of the house, then not too gently shoved into the back seat of the middle car of a three car motorcade. Two Falls Church Policemen on motorcycles took positions on either side of the middle car, and with sirens blasting and lights flashing they sped away from the house. The remaining members of the household were individually threatened with possible prosecution for charges of violation of federal anti-treason, sedition, and subversive activities acts against the government of the United States of America.

James' parents were advised that they *might* face additional charges as accessories before the fact for crimes against the United States government.

The house was thoroughly searched; all computers, electronic devices, and most of the contents of Will James' bedroom and the family's garage were catalogued, packed into boxes and evidence bags, and moved into an FBI van.

Within weeks the government officially brought federal charges against Will James and 'to be named' co-conspirators. He was finally sentenced just shy of his 16th birthday; making him the youngest person ever convicted of computer hacking. Because of his age, he received a six-month sentence to be served under house arrest followed by public service until the age of eighteen. He was also required to write a letter of apology to the Department of Defense and was banned from using computers for recreational purposes until his eighteenth birthday. He wound up serving the six months in prison for violating the terms of his parole.

He was taken into custody by the United States Marshals Service and flown to an Alabama federal correctional facility where he ultimately served the six months. Local radio and television stations interviewed various legal experts who suggested that, given the extent of his actions, he would have been sentenced to at least ten years for his crimes if he had been an adult at the time they were committed.

While at the correctional facility, James was befriended by Robert Schless, two years older than James, a repeat offender with a long history of petty crimes from New York's lower east side. Computer wizard James taught street tough Schless how to use a computer to find out whatever he could possibly want to know - whether for *good* or *evil* - regardless of how well the information was being protected and no matter who was protecting it. For his part of the deal, street wise Schless taught James how to protect himself from the guards and various youth gangs within the facility.

The government never stopped watching James. He, every member of his immediate family and it seemed like anyone he ever knew, were regularly followed and frequently brought in for questioning. According to the authorities he was still considered to be a threat to the nation's security. Meanwhile, he became a living legend to the underground hacking community.

On the morning following his eighteenth birthday James went missing. When he next surfaced he and Robert Schless were operating a small security service just outside of Washington, D.C.

Chapter 13
Friday, May 10, 1996 –
Crown Heights, Brooklyn, N.Y. – 3:14 A.M.

Sol and Albert woke up to a series of heavy thumps against their apartment door. Still half asleep, each jumped out of bed, reached for their robes, and went to see who could be at the door in the middle of the night.

Sol looked through the small lens in the door and saw two tall thin men in front of the door. One seemed to be leaning on a walking stick. "Who is there?" Sol asked.

"It's Will James and crew," one of the men said softly.

Sol looked at Albert with a quizzical smile and opened the door. "Do you always show up in the middle of the night?" he asked the two men.

"We show up when we show up," the man with the walking stick said.

"You actually were able to sleep at least three hours longer than we did," the other man said.

The two men walked inside. Looking around, one said, "I am Will James. That guy leaning on a whittled down tree trunk is Robert Schless. He is the '*and crew*' of Will James *and crew*. You can call him Schless, everyone else does; I don't care what you call me, I don't tend to answer to any name."

"Nice walking stick," Sol said to Schless.

"Damn fool fell off his roof shoveling snow last winter," James said. "I'm not sure what you want us to do but Henry at the Washington Post asked me to talk to you and whenever Henry asks me to talk to someone I usually find it to be really interesting. Hope this doesn't turn out to be the glaring exception."

"Want coffee?" Sol asked.

Schless stepped past Sol and Albert and began walking from room to room until he had been through the entire apartment. When he returned to the main hall he nodded to James and said, "Coffee sounds good to me."

"Okay, I'll put up a fresh pot," Sol said as he led them into the kitchen. "How do you like your coffee?"

"We tend to like our coffee the way we like our women," Schless said, "strong and hot."

James rolled his eyes at Schless and moved the conversation to the auction. "Henry at the Post gave me a quick update on the events since last Sunday but it would really be useful to hear it all again in your own words."

"We might be able to do even better than that," Sol said as he turned back from the kitchen and led them into the living room, "we can show you a VCR tape of the actual auction."

The four men moved into the living room and watched as Sol turned on the VCR and pushed the play button. After a few minutes James moved closer to the screen and said, "Can you start it from the beginning again?"

Sol did as requested.

When it played through, James took out a small pad, made several notes, and then said, "Do it again, please." He knelt down closer to the screen. When the tape played through the third time he made another few notes on the pad then said, "Once more."

"Wow," Schless said, moving towards James, "did I just see what I thought I saw?"

Sol and Albert looked at each other in utter confusion. "What are we missing?" Albert asked.

"May I have the VCR control?" James asked. He took the control unit from Sol and hit the reverse button; he stopped motion, and then hit play, gradually slowing the tape to a single frame at a time. A few minutes later he hit stop and locked onto a single frame. "Right... there," he said, pointing to the screen.

"Right where?" Albert asked.

"Right.... *there*," James said pointing to the old woman's head. "Your little old lady seems to be having a bad hair day, or I should say, a *no hair* day. It is entirely possible that this *little old lady* isn't so old and may not even be *a lady!*"

As he replayed the next series of frames they could see that at one point, the *lady's* shawl slipped off of *her* head, exposing an extensive bald area of scalp. *She* quickly repositioned the shawl; no one in the auction room seemed to notice.

"Not only can that possibly be a man, it could be a *young* man." James said. "Look at how quickly she/he reset the shawl. A seemingly old '*woman*' hobbled into the room looking like she was at death's door. But a few minutes later *she/he* is able to move like a blur to reset the shawl. I am not surprised that no one inside the room seemed to notice the bald head; it was exposed for barely a split second. I am, however, surprised that no one seemed to notice how quickly the shawl was reset."

Albert stared at Sol, "So that was what you meant by those strange air quotes?"

They watched the rest of the tape without further comment. When it was done James asked Albert to tell him about the events since the auction. "Please, don't leave anything out," James said, "No matter how trivial you may think it is".

Albert brought the two men up to date and then Sol told them how he realized that there was a tracking device attached to the frame.

"May I see the device?" James asked.

Albert went into the kitchen and returned with the glass of water that still held the device.

James took a pen from his pocket and carefully raised the device up above the water line so that he could get a better look at it. "Okay," James said, now tell me the entire story again."

"But we just told you," Albert complained.

"Soooooo? That only means you may have to tell us three or fifteen more times," Schless said.

Albert started to complain but Sol cut him short. "I saw this man in action, Albert. He really knows what he is doing. If he wants to hear it fifteen more times just tell him fifteen more times."

Albert cleared his throat and began retelling them about the events of the past few days. When he finished James said, "This time you mentioned the actual address of the fire house in Staten Island. You left that out last time."

"So it was a fire house on Jewell Avenue in Staten Island, a stupid fire house; there has to be dozens, I don't know, maybe thousands of neighborhood fire houses in New York and I would guess that some of them are in Staten Island," Albert, yelled, "what possible use to you can that be?"

"Hey," Schless yelled back, "he clearly told you not to leave anything out. We're trying to help you here. If you think you can decide what is important and what is not important then maybe you should just handle this *mystery* of yours all by yourself."

"Then answer me," Albert yelled. "What possible difference does that particular piece of information make?"

Sol broke in, "Look Albert, you asked me to get someone to help you. Now cut the crap and let them help you."

"Wait a minute," Albert argued, "two men come into our home in the middle of the night; one walks through the rooms without a 'how do you do, the other barks orders. I realize that you may have a warm and fuzzy feeling about them but I haven't had *that* pleasure, yet! I still don't understand why I was dragged out of bed in the middle of the night."

James held up his hands. "You're right. Let me tell you why that little piece of information may be important. That particular fire house is just two blocks away from where the current head of the Gambino crime family lives. That very same fire house is also where the same head of the Gambino family chooses to meet people; especially *new* people that he doesn't know very well and, as a result, may not yet totally trust. The house is actually in an old building that is relatively easy for his bodyguards to protect; it is also hard to bug conversations there because of natural dead sound zones, which drives the Racquet Squad and FBI guys crazy. That device in the glass is the style of electronic bugs the Gambino family has begun to use because it is designed to avoid normal discovery. Notice how thin and flexible it is. It has a very limited frequency range and for some reason the Feds have not yet been able to counter it. They will, of course, it is only a matter of time until they do, but as of this moment in time, they can't. That is why my ears perked up when you mentioned the actual street address."

"Okay, Okay," Albert said.

James sat back with his eyes closed and his hands behind his head while Albert ran through the events again. After a few minutes James opened his eyes and asked, "You still have the framed document here?"

Albert went to his bedroom and returned with it in his hands. James took it from Albert, being careful not to add any additional fingerprints of his own. James then asked him if he noticed anything missing or rearranged when he got home; especially in or near the place where this item had been stored.

"No," Albert said, "Sol was home most of the day and he would have told me if someone had been here. Do you think they sent me on a wild goose chase to Staten Island just to be able to get in here and snatch the framed document?"

"I really do not think so; especially since you yourself made the decision to go to Staten Island without any prompting. They had a *bug* attached to it so they knew where it was." James said, "All they needed was a little time to get in, track the piece to its exact location within the apartment and leave, no one would have been the wiser."

"No one could break in here," Albert said confidently.

"Really," Schless said, "You think your locks are strong enough to keep anyone and everyone out?"

"Yes, I *really* do!" Albert responded, somewhat sarcastically. "I do think these locks can keep *all* strangers out."

"Do you have a hairpin?" Schless asked.

"Do you see any need on his bald head for hair pins," Albert said, pointing to Sol, "or any women, with hair or without, around here?"

"Never mind," Schless said, taking out his wallet and removing two hairpins. "I never leave home without them."

Schless walked to the front door, let himself out and closed the door. From outside the apartment he whispered, "Are each of the door locks engaged?"

"Albert moved closer to the door and said, "Yes, they are."

"Are you sure?" Schless asked.

"I am sure," Albert said, obviously getting annoyed.

"Are you really, really certain?" Schless asked.

Before Albert could answer, the door opened and Schless walked in.

"It would have taken me less time but I stopped to make a three minute egg," Schless said, sarcastically.

"Don't show off!" James said.

"Forget what they say in the sales brochures, there is no such thing as an intruder proof lock," Schless said, "At least I have yet to see the lock that I cannot neutralize in a matter of minutes. And if that makes you nervous I need to quickly add that I am *not* the best lock picker *I* know."

Sol quickly reached for a loose paper and pen and scribbled a quick note, then showed it to the others. It said, "Should we check to see if they have listening devices in here as well?"

Schless smiled. "I did check; it was when I walked through the apartment without a *how do you do*."

Albert blushed. "Okay, so how would they know when I would decide to go to the address on the card?" Albert asked. "It has been days since they seem to have planted the bug on the wooden frame and I didn't even know we had an address, phony or not phony, until way past then."

"Well," Schless said, "for one thing, there are a couple of people camping out in a white Chevy with Michigan license plates up the street. The car has not moved in at least the last 30 hours although the individuals in the car did change every 6 hours or so. They seem to be watching this building. I would guess they have just been waiting for both of you to leave so that they could break in. I don't know for certain, but I would also guess that you and your assistant and possibly even you, Sol, have been under their surveillance since the auction on Sunday – and maybe even before Sunday."

James broke in, "Unless your assistant is also in on the plot."

"That makes no sense at all," Albert said. "If she wanted she could have walked away with that frame at any time. Up until a couple days before the auction I was using it to prop open a window. It had zero value as far as I was concerned. If they waited long enough they could have fished it out of a garbage can."

"How can you possibly know that there are people in a car watching us?" Sol asked.

"We've been parked several cars behind them for almost two days," James said. "That's how! Okay, now tell me again."

Albert looked at Sol and slowly repeated his story.

When he was finished, James asked, "Tell me how and when you got the piece you offered up at the auction?"

"It was part of an estate that I bought. It only just arrived here from Michigan a short while ago," Albert said.

"How did you first hear about the estate sale?" James asked.

"I regularly subscribe to a group of major city newspapers so that I can stay on top of public notices. I read in one of those papers that an independent evaluation was about to be made on a small estate in suburban Detroit. In the past I have done quite well by rushing in before an estate is packaged for auction. I usually make a lump sum offer and after they consider the time and expense of a full blown process, the executors often decide to take my offer and my money and run. This particular lot was being offered for sale by a bank that held a small mortgage on the property. All they really wanted was to get the loan paid off plus a little extra to help them market the house to a new potential buyer. That is the best situation of all. Banks have no personal attachments to personal property – especially other people's personal property. For banks, time is money and the quicker the sale the better. Add to that the economic hell the entire Detroit area has been buried in and you get a lot of really valuable pieces beginning to surface, most selling at rock bottom prices. So every time I hear about a sale anywhere near Motor City I drop everything and race out there. This particular piece of junk," Albert said, pointing to the framed document, "came with a lot of other pieces – some a little valuable, some, such as this framed document, not at all valuable, but I paid so little for the entire lot that I will probably make plenty of money on most of it." "I told you, I have been using this little beauty," he said, pointing again to the framed permit, "to prop open a window in the store. There really wasn't anything about this piece that made me think it was worth more than a couple of dollars, and even a couple of dollars would have been a stretch."

"Where do you advertise so that potential bidders could learn about the auction and what might be offered for sale?" Schless asked.

Sol started to laugh. "Advertise? Albert doesn't believe in advertising."

Schless looked at Albert, "So how could anyone have known about this piece before the actual auction? You told us that the turnout was many times that of an average Sunday morning. There had to be some way for these *new* people to know about it."

"Yes, Albert," Sol asked, "How would anyone have known what would be included in this week's auction?"

"I don't really know the answer to that," Albert said. "I don't advertise which items are to be auctioned off. In fact, *I* didn't even know that I was going to include this piece in Sunday's auction until the Tuesday or Wednesday before."

"Had anybody looked at this piece in the store, recently?" James asked.

"I don't usually encourage browsers," Albert said. "And it was never on display, I told you, I was using it to wedge open a window."

"You told us that the total attendees for this particular Sunday morning were two or three times any previous Sunday," James said, "So there had to be some way for these people to know that this was going to be a more interesting auction than any of the earlier ones."

James took a jeweler's loop out of his pocket and carefully examined the piece. He then turned it upside down on the kitchen table and took a ring of keys out of his pocket and detached a short, squat tubular object from the rest of the items on the key ring. He slowly rolled the object along the surface of the frame. At one point it lit up and began to beep.

He took a Swiss army knife from his pocket and gently used the thinnest blade to remove the back panel. Each of the men moved closer to the table.

Albert was the first to speak, "Well, I'll be a monkey's uncle – there is a key wedged between the mitered edges of the frame. How did you know to look for it there?"

Ignoring his question, James said, "Now tell me everything there is to know about the estate this came from. Don't leave anything out – no matter how meaningless a detail it may seem to be."

Chapter 14
Friday, May 10, 1996 –
Williamsburg, Brooklyn, N.Y. – 8:27 A.M.

Albert got to the store much earlier than usual. Elizabeth was already there and was dusting a shelf when he walked in. "Just the person I wanted to see," he said. "Do you have any idea how so many people knew we had an auction last Sunday, or to be more specific, that I was going to auction off that little item that has thrown our lives into such a spin?"

"I told the pipples," she said, with a bit of pride.

"What do you mean, 'you told them'?" he asked.

"Every Wednesday there is in newspaypis lots and lots pahges full of coopins and advertisisments for things to buy. I made deal with one newses pipper to advertising the auction and in return they gots to put a box with their newses pippers in front of this store for free."

"You did what?" he screamed.

She moved closer to him and poked him in his stomach with her index finger. "No more screaming, Okay?" she yelled back. "I dint screaming at you so you don't not screaming at me – not today, not tomorrow, not to any udder day; you understanding me, Albert Froog?"

Albert stared at her, "What has gotten into you?" he asked.

"I not longer taking all of that badness treating from you ever again. You want it for me to be working here then you be nicer to me. Take it or go."

He smiled, "The term happens to be 'take it or leave it,'" he laughed, adding, "But since this is *my* store, if anyone would have to go I assure you it isn't going to be *me*."

"Just start to be treated me with more decentness," she said.

"So, the worm has turned," he said.

"First I a stealer crook and today I a worm. I want you should know, Albert Froog, I not animal or bug and you not treat me like either one no more. No more! You understanding of me Albert Froog? *No more!*"

She was still poking her finger into his chest. "Okay," he said. "Okay." He gently moved her index finger away and then pointed his finger at her, "You want to be treated better? That's okay with me. But, treating people better goes both ways. I don't think you are treating me with very much respect when you take it upon yourself to barter the valuable space in front of *my store* without asking *me* first."

"You are with seriousness telling to me that it was *not* good idea to make more pipples knowing about our auction?" She asked, indignantly.

"Now you ask me for my opinion?" he said, raising his voice. "The time to ask my opinion, Ms. I Want To Be Treated Nicer is before, not after; *before*, not *after* you do something of this magnitude. Now, who gave *you* the right to rent out space for newspaper boxes and to place ads without my approval? Or am I not allowed to even ask for an explanation anymore?"

"First," Elizabeth said, defiantly, "you lowering your voice to me, then answer me this, Albert Froog, you thinked it was *not* good idea what I dunned."

"What you *dunned*," he mocked, "was to expose us to all sorts of trouble."

"It was good idea," she insisted. "If you did have thinked of doing this you be saying it was great idea – but you dint thinking of it – I thinking of it – so you yelling on me that I do terrible thing?" she screamed back.

"Good idea or not, you exposed us to all sorts of bad," he yelled. "Maybe I would have applauded the idea before, maybe not. You know, it isn't like I have ever encouraged people to rush through our doors. I have done all right, so far, thank you very much, converting our business into a virtual store with buyers using the mail or internet. I like it that way. If given a choice I am not so sure I would have given you a 'go ahead' on this. But we will never know, *will we*? You made the decision for me and I don't like anyone making decisions *for me*. Is that nice enough for you?"

"It was good idea." She repeated, as she began to walk away.

"It exposed us to who knows what." He insisted, "The jury is still out on it being a good or a not so good idea."

She turned around and stared at him, "It was good idea." She said. "You should be thanking of me for this, not yelling on me."

"Do you have a copy of the ad for last week's auction?" He asked. "Please and thank you!" He added with a flourish.

She went to her desk and returned with a copy of the previous Wednesday's *New York Daily News*. She opened it and pointed to a small announcement, "Here is it." She said, shoving the paper at him.

He took the paper from her and sat down...he smoothed it out with both hands and began reading it to himself. He turned to the front page, scanned the headlines, and then turned back to the advertisement. He sat back, put his hands behind his head and closed his eyes. Outwardly he was trying to look angry and disappointed but inside he knew that she had accomplished something that was both positive and meaningful. The notice was very nicely positioned within the paper, the price was right – no cash, well written, and in a mass readership paper, that is a pretty large deal. It was just the kind of thing that his mother and grandmother would have looked at and said, *"Good job Albert. Nice work. You are a good boy and we love you."*

Then reality set in, he opened his eyes, sat forward and glared at her. "This idea of yours brought danger and trouble into my life. You are *never* to do something like this again without first checking with me. Do you understand?"

"And hows about the chances for to make $100,000," she snapped back. "I should be gotting a raise and plenty happy words not a meanness like you are always giving out to me."

"This created horror for me. Don't you understand what you did? he screamed.

She gently took the paper off of his desk and began to slowly but clearly read out loud:

Don't miss out...
Come to this week's auction at:
'Better Times Remembered'
...the best little antique store on the planet
70 Lee Avenue, near Rodney Street,
Williamsburg section of Brooklyn.
Rare, previously hidden treasures
from the personal estate
of Mark Regan,
a former Michigan Teacher of the Year,
among other stunning artifacts up for sale -
will be a prohibition era permit
issued to the holder
to make booze – legally –
at a time when the government
said NO
to everyone else!

Sunday, May 5 - Starts 10:30 A.M., sharp
Be there or be square!
(Free refreshments!)

"Tell to me, Albert Froog", Elizabeth said proudly after reading him the copy, "You still theenks that I made it such bad mistake here? You don't not believe inside that, that, that little black heart of yours that I did it a good theengs for this business?"

"You wrote that?" he asked in amazement.

"No, I dint writed it. The newspaper pipples writed it, just like they writed it every weeks before," she said.

"Why did they feature that worthless permit?"

"Each week they asked to me for a list of what you be auctioned off and I tell to them. This week when I tell to them this permit for to making alcohol when alcohol making not legal their eyes opened big like dinner plates. The writer pipple said many would be wanting to buy this items for to be showing their friends such a hidden treasure."

"But it is no treasure, it is a worthless little nothing. They issued thousands, no hundreds of thousands of these worthless permits during prohibition." He said.

"It not matters if it is worthless to you it only matters if it is interesting to them and it was interesting to them." She said. "When I see the look on the writing pipple's face I knew it was good way to interest more pipples come to the auction. Each week I look for one items to make more excitement. This week it be this permit and it worked good, we never seen so many pipples come to auction as this week."

"I can't believe you did this and had the nerve to have done it before? What absolute gall! Get out of my office," he barked. "I need to think in peace and quiet." He remained sitting upright at his desk, staring straight ahead.

A dispirited Elizabeth walked out of the office with her head down. Under her breath, she mumbled, "It was good idea!"

He yelled after her, "How about closing the door, or am I being too mean to ask?"

She walked back, glared at him, and then slowly closed the door.

He looked at the advertisement again then reached for the phone and dialed Sol.

"You can tell the James gang that last week's auction was advertised in the Wednesday *New York Daily News* food section. That was how word got out."

"Well, at least that clears up one mystery. But, why didn't you just tell him that when he first brought it up?" Sol asked.

"I didn't know it then. I just learned that little piece of information from my new CDMO."

"Your what?"

"My new Chief Decision Making Officer, Elizabeth." He snorted.

"Elizabeth placed an advertisement without your knowledge?" Sol asked.

"So it seems."

"And she paid for the ad, how?"

"She *bartered* for it."

"She what?"

"Hey, don't get me started."

"So what happens now?" Sol asked.

"I begin cataloging everything I got from the Regan estate sale for the James gang," Albert responded.

"If I were you I would stop referring to them as the 'James gang,'" Sol said. "They don't seem to have a sense of humor and right now you need all the serious minded help you can get. What about this week's auction. What are you going to do?"

"I called my mother's shyster lawyer and told him what had happened and given the circumstances I asked for a few days relief from the 'show up or lose everything' clause in the will. Oddly enough, it didn't take a lot of convincing. He said that as long as I keep him fully informed and get the store opened again without too much of a delay, he will temporarily waive that condition of my mother's will."

"Does he have that kind of authority? Wouldn't he be handing you a valuable precedent to use against him later? Sol asked.

"Let's not look a gift horse in the mouth."

"So Elizabeth got you free exposure in the great *New York Daily News*; on Wednesday, Food Day, yet, with the very popular and well-read food store ads and manufacturer's coupons," Sol said. "Did you tell her what a great thing she accomplished?"

"Hell, no; I told her never to do something like that without my approval again," Albert responded.

"Of course you did. After all, you *are* Albert Froog." Sol said, facetiously. "My, my, will wonders never cease?"

"Will wonders never cease, indeed," Albert repeated.

"She has a real good head on her shoulders. Maybe if you showed a little appreciation she could help you build that little business of yours." Sol said.

"I like my *little* business just the way it is." Albert said. I'm not looking for partners right now, thank you very much." Albert said.

"We all need help of some kind Albert." Sol said.

"Right now all I need is a good night's sleep. I haven't had one since that damn fool auction."

"I don't know, Albert. Something tells me that a few sleepless nights might not be the worst thing facing you right now." Sol said.

Chapter 15
Forty-three years earlier –
Friday, October 2, 1953 –
Grosse Pointe, Michigan – 8:03 P.M.

Mark Regan was a barely satisfactory substitute teacher for several years before he was asked to become a full time teacher. He kept to himself... rarely sought out any of the other teachers... didn't seem to be engaged while in the school building... it was a job and he needed a job – nothing more, nothing less.

The principal called him at home, late in the evening of October 2nd, 1953 to take over for a Gross Point High School teacher who suffered a fatal heart attack earlier that day. It paid a bit more and would guarantee a paycheck for at least the rest of the current school year, so he agreed.

His first days as a high school teacher were rather shaky. In fact he spent the better part of the first two weeks on the job drafting his letter of resignation. To put it mildly, he hated the work. Fortunately, he was convinced to remain at least through that term. His principal put it as well as he could – "We just don't have anyone else available right now and having you there is marginally better than having nobody at all."

Without the pressure of thinking that this would be his job for the rest of his life, Mark felt freer to experiment and a number of his new ideas proved to be very effective. Before the term was over he and his students formed a strong bond and ultimately he blossomed as an extremely effective teacher for more than the next forty years. For three of those years he was named Michigan Teacher of the Year, a title that embarrassed him more than anything else.

Mark eventually wore two hats – he was an advanced chemistry teacher and the head of the growing science department at Grosse Point High. Late in his career he also volunteered one night a week to be the only German language teacher at the Beacon School in Downtown Detroit. The first and third Monday nights of every month he taught Basic English to native German speaking war wives as they prepared for their citizenship tests and new lives in America. The second and fourth Monday nights of each month he taught conversational German to World War II veterans, their parents and siblings who were seeking to better communicate with the wives that the soldiers in their family brought home from the Great War in Europe. On the occasional fifth Monday night he organized a neighborhood job fair where local businesses could interview and, hopefully, hire both out of work veterans as well as their new American spouses.

Even though he maintained a wide professional space between himself and his students; when his students talked among themselves about their teachers, many rated him to be the best teacher they had; possibly ever had, and maybe ever would have. His fellow teachers envied the way his students prepared for his classes, especially when many of the same students just drifted robotically through theirs. What his fellow teachers never seemed to grasp was that he defined teaching as a two sided intellectual adventure. He learned from his students – his students learned from him. Or, as he liked to say, "There are no *innocent bystanders* in my classes; we each have an important role to play."

His students believed that he seemed to be teaching to *their* specific abilities. Those who quickly grasped the subject matter rarely felt bored even when he retraced his steps to help the others catch up. He did this by adding nuggets of interesting information when returning to a part of the lesson plan already discussed. For example, while teaching the chemical interactions that are harnessed to make an atomic bomb he could see that only a few students had really absorbed the data, the rest of the class looked lost. He repeated the basics again but this time also talked about the conflict at the time within the scientists involved. More than anyone else, these men understood the devastation such a weapon could generate in the wrong hands.

His students also appreciated that he wasn't afraid to openly admit when he did not know the answer to a question. Instead, he gave himself the assignment to find out and report back to them at their next class; and he always did.

He instructed... supported... encouraged... anticipated; plastering his class room with copies of what he called, *"A short list of your rights and mine."*

> *You have the right to learn –*
> *I have the honor to teach.*
> *You have the responsibility to question, respectfully –*
> *I have the obligation to respond, respectfully.*
>
> *You have the right to be here in this class –*
> *I have the honor of your presence.*
> *I have the right to demand your full attention –*
> *You have the right to expect no less from me.*
>
> *We must treat each other with respect!*
> *I have the right to be treated with respect –*
> *You have the right to be treated with respect.*
>
> *I commit to share my knowledge with you to the best of my ability.*
> *You are entitled to the best I have to give –*
> *I will settle for no less*
> *than the best you have to give."*

He was no pushover but he never stopped reaching out to the few students who repeatedly failed to turn in assignments on time, or any whose mind seemed to be elsewhere during one of his classes. The other students were not always as understanding. They usually made it quite clear to their few disruptive classmates that any distraction – no matter how small – was robbing the rest of them of the opportunity to learn – and that they did *not* consider such antics to be the least bit cool.

For students who put in the time and effort to learn, Mark was always available for after class tutoring; he was 'the source' for little known scholarship program information; the writer of glowing reference letters; as well as a dependable soft touch whenever a student was in need, financially or otherwise.

For all who knew him, especially during the past decade or so, it seemed as if his life began and ended within the four walls of a classroom. It would have come as a complete shock and surprise to all who knew Mark Regan the 'teacher', that after dinner most week days and practically round the clock on weekends and holidays, Mark had a completely different mission in life.

His early days as a substitute teacher could not predict how well he would turn out as an educator; his early childhood could not predict how calm and peaceful his later years would be.

*****

Mark Regan was born Markus Obereder in *Braunau am Inn*, a small Austrian town on the south bank of the Inn river, which separated Austria from Germany. His family lived on *Salzburger Vorstadt*, diagonally across the street from number 15 Salzburger Vorstadt, which almost four decades earlier housed a small craft brewery and several housing flats, one of which was rented by Alois Hitler and his third wife Klara for themselves as well as Alois' children from a previous marriage, Alois Jr. and Angela, and their new baby, Adolf. Although Adolf Hitler and his family no longer lived at number 15 Salzburger Vorstadt by the time the Obereders moved onto the street, the building was already a place of interest for Germans and non-Germans alike because of its status as the Nazi leader's birthplace.

Marcus's father, Karl, ran a very successful family business that manufactured custom embroidered priestly garments used by the Greek Orthodox Church as well as prayer shawls used by those in many of the Orthodox Jewish communities throughout Eastern Europe. It was his great grandfather who revolutionized the hand embroidering process first used in Russia and Poland by developing a proprietary method which allowed him to more easily introduce larger quantities of pure 24 karat gold threads into the finely woven garments he made. The family company quickly became the most sought after supplier of such items in all of Europe. As word spread the small shop grew until it had a constant backlog of orders. Many customers gladly paid in advance and then waited 24 to 30 months for delivery.

Never very politically engaged, Karl ignored the growing influence of the Nazi Brown Shirt movement in virtually every aspect of his small community's life. However, by the early to mid-1920s even he could no longer ignore the existence of the formidable nationalistic movement that was bleeding into Austria from neighboring Germany.

On November 8, 1923, Hitler held a rally at a Munich beer hall and proclaimed a revolution. The following day, he led 2,000 armed 'brown-shirts' in an attempt to take over the Bavarian government. It took a while for word to get to the little town on the south bank of the Inn river, but when it did, it sparked a local group of Nazi sympathizers, spurred

on by their proximity to the birthplace of 'home town boy',
Adolph Hitler, and thrown even further out of control by a
local brewer's offer of *free beer for everyone'*, to *show his
support* for *the Führer'*. Small bands of young toughs paraded throughout the neighborhood. By the next morning
broken glass and rubble was everywhere... entire streets
were in shambles and local authorities declared a state
of emergency. A curfew was put in place; quickly printed
posters were tacked on to light poles and outside of public buildings warning that anyone on the streets after 6:00
P.M. would be arrested.

It took almost three months, during which time the town
started its return to normal; the rubble was eventually
cleaned up and carted away; effected buildings were re-
paired or superficially patched up, and soon, what the town
officials publicly referred to as the insignificant though
disruptive outburst was little more than a bad memory.
However, for Karl Obereder, and everyone in the Obereder household, it was a wakeup call, and left an indelible
impression on each of them.

Hitler's rants against what he called the West's unusually harsh demands for reparations after World War I rang
clear to many in the lower middle class and the peasantry
alike. He used nationalism as a basis for all things good
and the Marxists, Internationalists, and Jews as the source
for all things bad. Hitler promised the re-establishment of
Aryan pride and more prosperous times. *Let's make Germany great again,* became the broader message. Verbal
and financial support began to pour in from professional organizations of physicians, teachers, lawyers, and civil
servants as well as individual bankers and industrialists
from around the world – *including* America. Inside Eastern Europe Hitler tapped the strongly nationalistic political views of his home audience; for the rest of the world he
fed fears that the depression would deprive them of their

standard of living; and with every day came new charges blaming the Jews for inflation, political instability, unemployment, and Germany's humiliation after the end of World War I. The Nazi party began drawing thousands of new members, many of whom were victims of hyper-inflation and found comfort in blaming the Jews for their troubles. Hitler's solution was the annihilation of the Jews and the strengthening of the Nordic 'Master' race, which, 'would rule for a thousand years over its inferiors'.

When Markus turned 6 years old and was considered to be old enough to walk to school un-chaperoned, his mother, Ilsa, returned to the work she did many years before as an infectious disease researcher for a small independent laboratory, walking distance from their modest apartment.

Although generally outgoing and talkative, Ilsa Obereder preferred not to speak to anyone about her work at the lab. When friends or family asked what she was working on, all she would say was that she enjoyed being around the people she worked with, but the work itself was rather boring and probably wouldn't be interesting to anyone. Her pet phrase was that it was just a way to fill an otherwise empty day. If anyone persisted she became quite good at redirecting the conversation around some local gossip or cute little thing one of the children had recently done or said; few ever seemed to notice that she had changed the subject.

She did, however, share everything, including the smallest details of her work with her husband. They would lie in bed at night. He holding her close as she sadly shared the details of the many failures and disappointments she and her team were experiencing.

On some of those nights when the day's results were particularly disappointing, she talked about giving up and leaving the lab to "those more capable than me." "My heart and soul just cannot take any more of these disappointments," she would say between heavy sobs and tears. On these nights her husband insisted that she would never forgive herself if she just walked away from such important work. He'd try to reassure her by saying, "...the work was too important to trust to anyone else."... "*You* will find the answer."... "...Ultimately, *you* will not fail"... "It is meant to be..." "*You were born to do this...*"... "I believe in you." And when no other words seemed to connect, the most powerful of all messages was that she just had to continue her work: "*You must do whatever is necessary so that no other human being suffers the way your mother suffered.*"

On a precious few of these nights, when she was able to report a breakthrough – even a very small breakthrough – and these occasions were few and far between – her spirits were high and she was filled with hope. On these evenings she would smother him with kisses and they would make love well into the night.

More turmoil followed, along with stepped up attacks on local Jews and *perceived* 'Jewish sympathizers'; then came the formation of a local para-military community watch organization. Karl was warned against continuing to manufacture garments used in Jewish religious ceremonies.

Fearing the growing antagonism from her neighbors, Ilsa began taking Marcus and his sister to school each morning and scheduled her lunch times for when the children's school let out for the day. She often brought them back to her lab until she was done for the day. Both children did their homework in one of the empty offices. After homework was done, Marcus would wonder into his mother's lab to watch her work. His sister had no interest in the goings on of the busy lab and usually rested on a couch in the reception area, paging through various fashion magazines.

During the family's dinner one night, Karl told his wife and children that the Nazis would eventually bring more bad than good to their world and that he was thinking of moving the family away. "But where would we go," his wife asked. "This is our home," she reasoned. "Can we really be any safer anywhere else in the world?"

For years Karl had been writing to a second cousin, whose parents immigrated to America after World War I. Karl couldn't understand how famous Americans like automobile maker, Henry Ford and aviation hero, Charles Lindbergh could be saying such supportive things about Hitler. Did they not see the evil in this man?

The daily newspapers often showed pictures of Hitler with wealthy and influential American businessmen such as William Randolph Hearst, Joseph Kennedy, John Rockefeller, Andrew Mellon, and Prescott Bush. Karl clipped out the photos and enclosed them with his letters to his cousin. He also questioned the news that big American companies – Ford and General Motors and Chrysler Motors were building Hitler's trucks and troop transporters while investing their money in German companies; Standard Oil was supplying necessary fuel for Hitler's war machine... United States Steel and Alcoa Aluminum supplied critical metals... DuPont and I.B.M. and International Telephone and Telegraph and General Electric... plus many other American based businesses and banks seemed to be propping up that monster with the silly mustache.

The follow up letters from his cousin tried to assure him that these men and companies did not speak for the average American, and *definitely NOT* for the two most important Americans of all, Franklin and Eleanor Roosevelt; the letters continued to repeat his cousin's firm belief that these two Americans knew Hitler for what he was. He begged Karl to flee Austria while he still could. He said that Karl and his family could stay with him until they settled in – no matter how long it would take.

Meanwhile, Karl became more vocal, repeating his concerns as the Nazis' influence increased only to be shunned by many of his neighbors and former friends and even threatened by members of his wife's family that they would report him if he continued making such treasonous comments. Everything around him seemed to be moving him closer to the breaking point. The possibility of getting caught within a worldwide war against Hitler's Germany was becoming more likely with each new day. But where could they possibly go to be safe?

Every letter from his cousin was now ending with the same plea – "Come to America, don't wait until it is too late."

He appreciated the offer... but this country had been home to so many generations of Obereders – they all stayed during good times and bad - how could he be the one to leave?

When the few like-minded neighbors began disappearing in the middle of the night he was finally ready to make a move. "Maybe just for a year or so," he told his wife. "Surely Hitler couldn't last longer than a year or so. Could he?"

Karl discreetly sold off most of the family's holdings and used the funds to buy bulk uncut diamonds and other precious jewels and to make a series of pure 24 karat gold purchases. He converted the gold into spools of metallic thread which he then carefully embroidered onto pieces of clothing for him, his wife and young son and daughter. He then sewed the rest of his gold thread along with the diamonds and other jewels into the linings of their under wear.

On Sunday morning April 1, 1934, the Obereder family, all dressed and ready for Easter services, walked out of their home with little more than the clothes on their backs. The father held onto his son's hand, the mother carried her family bible, their daughter carried her well-loved doll, and their son clutched a small toy car. Karl waived to a neighbor looking at them from her kitchen window, as the family slowly walked to the railway station and calmly boarded a train for Berlin. From there they went on to Zurich, Switzerland and finally, early Friday morning, October 26th they safely sailed into the Port of Montreal, Quebec, Canada.

Finally, finally, Karl's plans to leave Austria were almost complete. He had not told his family exactly where they were going to wind up. They would have to wait until they were literally within walking distance from his cousin's automobile.

After a light lunch and a brief but democratic 'family meeting', they discussed the need for new American sounding names... Karl became 'Carl', 9 year old Markus became 'Mark', 11 year old Helga and her mother, Ilsa, refused to take on American names. When Karl insisted that he and he alone would decide for the family – he announced that the family name would now be Regan, after Charles Regan, the popular English cricket player.

With that now firmly decided, they leisurely walked across the border to the American side; at the end of the day they moved in with his cousin in Grosse Pointe, Michigan.

It would take Carl only a few weeks to convert a small assortment of his hidden gems into enough American currency to buy a place of their own.

The last of the Austrian Obereders... make that the new Regan family... had come to America! *In Henry Ford's back yard.*

Part 2

Chapter 16
Friday, June 16, 1989 –
Grosse Pointe, Michigan – 4:49 P.M.

The day before Mark retired from teaching there were several small gatherings organized by both former and current students and colleagues. He was never very good at small talk and although he believed that the compliments and good wishes were all sincerely meant, he was visibly uncomfortable during the various gatherings throughout the day. There were a variety of little gifts to be opened, memories to be revisited, cookies to be eaten and cups of cider and tea and coffee to be sipped. The final event was a gathering in the teacher's lounge with a variety of wines and finger sandwiches served by the president of the school's Parents and Teachers Association.

Mark's fellow teachers got together and presented him with a new fishing rod and a tackle box filled with bottles of dark German beer as a going away gift. But Mark had no intention of spending his retirement hours fishing or even drinking beer, for that matter. He knew that the end of his teaching career would enable him to spend even more time on what already filled so many evenings and weekends since his mother died.

*****

Fifty-five years earlier...
Early Sunday morning, April 1, 1934 -
Braunau am Inn, Austria

The night before they fled Austria, Mark and his sister listened from their bedroom as their parents argued about a metal box. Seems that their mother took the metal box from the research lab earlier in the day and made it clear to her husband that she was planning to bring it with her; their father insisted that the box would quickly be missed by the laboratory workers and might bring the authorities after them before they could safely get out of the country. He also warned that if they were stopped and searched it would surely be found and would just as surely get them all killed. Their mother kept insisting that she couldn't possibly leave without it.

After they began arguing their mother decided not to add fuel to the fire by telling her husband that the metal box wasn't the only thing she took from the lab that day. She also brought home two very thick six by eight inch spiral pads filled with her team's lab notes.

The arguing continued through most of the night.

When it was time to leave, the next morning, neither Mark nor his sister knew for certain who had come out on top of the argument.

*****

After her husband fell into a deep sleep, Ilsa individually wrapped each spiral pad in heavy gauze and then securely strapped each one onto her body with surgical tape.

With dawn about to break, she picked up the metal box and placed it on top of her family bible. She stood there, staring at the two objects for quite some time. What she was now considering to do went completely against every-thing she had been taught and believed to be sacred, but she was desperate, running out of time, and knew – all too well - that whatever she did might bring harm to the ones she loved the most, her children and her husband.

She slowly carried both objects into the bathroom and locked the door behind her.

She took her husband's straight edge razor off of the sink top and sat on the edge of the bathtub.

She grew up believing with all of her being that the bible *was* the word of her Lord. Then she remembered what her father had often said. He was what her mother referred to as a *still seeker*. He was neither a believer nor a non-believer. He kept asking questions and seemed to consider religion, especially organized religion, in the terms of the scientist he was. His attitude about the bible itself was that the messages inside might have special meaning but the actual ink and paper was just that – ink and paper – and it should not be revered more than any other reference guide.

Now, sitting alone in a room that was the furthest place from a place of worship that she could imagine; she needed to decide if she would go to hell if she actually did what she was now trying to convince herself to do.

She could quote the passages about not worshipping a fake idol and debated within her own mind if holding the physical book up to the same level of reverence as she did her Lord and Savior would be conferring upon the ink and paper equal status to the Lord, himself?

What to do? What to do?

The clock in the hall began to chime and she counted along with it, "one... two... three... four... five." She had to decide, *now*, she thought to herself.

She opened the bible, folded back about an inch of pages and then carefully placed the metal box on the top of the next page. She centered the box so that it was flush with the binding and somewhat equally distanced within the three open sides of the printed page. Carefully, she placed the tip of the razor against the side of the metal box. She couldn't quite get herself to drive the point of the razor into the pages.

Her mother's face came to her. Not the loving, peaceful face of the healthy woman she grew up with and loved more than life itself; the vision that came to her now was of her dying mother, wracked with pain and filled with drugs in order to make her final moments as tolerable as possible.

Finally, decisively, she tightly gripped the handle of the razor and pushed the blade into the pages, carefully tracing the outer edges of the metal box until she had created a cavity just large enough to fit the metal box. She lovingly gathered the cut out portions of the book, brought them to her lips and kissed them several times; gently placing them in the bowl of the sink. After a silent prayer for the travels to begin in just a few hours as well as for the individual safety of her two children and her husband, she asked for guidance and forgiveness from her Lord. She made the sign of the cross over the cut out scraps of paper, and with tears rolling down her cheeks, set a lit match to the pile of papers.

Later that morning, she held onto her precious bible as they left the house. To anyone looking on, it seemed so natural for her to be clutching that book on an Easter Sunday morning. For her, the combination of the metal box and what was left of the bible represented the work she was hoping to do, whenever they arrived at the *safe haven* Karl had selected for them – in this life or the next.

*****

Years later, as his mother lay dying; Mark finally learned who won the argument about the metal box the evening before they fled Austria. She pulled him close to her and – with her last remaining bits of energy - told him what she had been working on before they left Austria and where he could find her notes *and* the metal box. She stared into his eyes and asked him to promise to devote the rest of his life to continue her work.

How could he refuse her dying wish, he thought.

"Tell me you will do what I ask", she pleaded.

Finally, he said that he would.

A smile came across her face; she closed her eyes and died.

Chapter 17
Eighty-five years earlier –
Monday, April 18, 1904 –
Strehlen, Germany – 2:19 A.M

Young Ilsa Ehrlich woke to a series of screams coming from her parent's bedroom. She jumped out of bed and ran to the small room to see her father kneeling by her mother's lifeless body, begging her for forgiveness. Also by the bed was her father's older cousin, Carl Weigert and her mother's doctor, Lazerus Gold.

When Weigert noticed Ilsa standing by the door with a look of horror on her face, he rushed over and took her in his arms and said so softly that she could hardly make out the words, "I am so sorry, dear Ilsa, but she is gone."

Ilsa's mother had been in constant pain from the cancer which had taken over her already frail body. They all knew the end was near and that it would even be a blessing for death to come because it would finally end her pain. But at this moment all Ilsa could feel was deep sorrow for her loss and uncontainable anger towards her father.

Ilsa pushed Weigert away and ran to her father. She was pounding both of her fists against him when Dr. Gold grabbed her and pulled her away.

"How could you let her die?" she screamed to her father. "You could have saved her. You *should* have saved her."

He turned to look at his daughter. "You don't know what you are saying. I loved her more than life itself."

"You loved the awards and the banquets; you loved the admiration and how those stupid little people fawned over you," she yelled back. "If you really loved *her* you would have saved her from this. You *could* have saved her... from *this."* She fell to her knees, sobbing hysterically, *"You should have saved her... from this."*

*****

At the time of his wife's death, Paul Ehrlich was already a celebrated medical researcher. He had published a number of papers documenting many of his landmark discoveries.

When his wife was first diagnosed with cancer he worked even harder to try to forestall the inevitable but the scientist in him knew that she was already too far gone.

Ilsa went on to university and wrote her father a long and emotional letter in which she blamed him for the greatest loss of her life and committed herself to do whatever she could to help find a cure for the dreaded disease that took her mother from her.

She knew how irrational it was to blame her father for her mother's death but her relationship with her father never returned to a loving one after her mother died.

In 1908, Paul Ehrlich shared the Nobel Prize for his work. Ilsa sent a short note to him, congratulating him for winning the prestigious award. She ended the note with, "Always time for another award and more praise, just a little too late to help my mother... your wife. You are and have always been a tremendously good researcher – until the day I die, it will be my greatest disappointment that you were not *as good* a husband, father, family man."

They never wrote or spoke to each other or said the other's name out loud, again.

Chapter 18
Friday, June 16, 1989 –
Grosse Pointe, Michigan – 7:13 P.M.

Mark grabbed a quick supper after he left the last of the retirement party celebrations. He was honored and deeply moved by all of the attention but now he was anxious to put this part of his life in the rear view mirror so that he could concentrate on the enormous task ahead. He could feel his mother's spirit pulling him towards the work he committed himself to do as she lay on her deathbed.

Later that evening and over the next few days he virtually moved into the small lab he had set up in his basement. He had plenty of work to do and a fire in his belly to do it; his only concern was if he had the right stuff to be able to build upon all that was first begun by his Nobel prize winning grandfather and then furthered by his exceptionally gifted mother.

Mark knew that his sister was capable of anything once she made up her mind, and she had clearly made up her mind to cash in on their mother's research. He feared that she would break into his home one day while he was teaching to grab the metal box and lab notes.

His fears about his sister's likelihood to come looking for their mother's research was fed by a series of break-in attempts at his home during days he was either at school or out of town. There had also been a small fire mysteriously started by the side of his house near his guest bathroom window. Fortunately, each time a combination of alert neighbors and his alarm system chased the intruder or intruders away before they could actually gain access to the house. Although she claimed to be totally innocent, after he threatened to report his sister to the police if there was one more such incident, the attempted break-ins stopped.

He knew the contents of the metal box would not be used in his initial lab work and so his bank's vault provided safe and reliable dead storage leaving him with the challenge of where to hide the keys. He picked up a simple wooden block frame from a yard sale and cut a thin wedge along the back of the frame – just long and wide enough to hold the key to the metal box. He attached the safety deposit box key to his own key ring – which never left his body. The wooden frame came with a print of some kind. It was a very modern design which he realized would look out of place among his more traditional decorations so he removed it and in its place put a government permit issued during the prohibition era that caught his eye at a going out of business sale for a local bar. He cut a piece of heavy flex board to fit over the back of the frame – screwed it onto the frame – then hung it in his guest bathroom.

His mother's lab notes were different; they would have to be readily available – at any hour of the day or night, for him to have any hope of continuing her work.

He obtained permission to leave his mother's lab notes in the school safe. His justification was that these were notes for a book he hoped to write one day. As a department head he had keys and alarm codes available to him should he ever need to enter the school on weekends, evenings, or holidays. He understood that he would have to continually go back and forth to where they were being stored but that was a small price to pay for the peace of mind knowing they were just about 100% guaranteed safe.

He rested easier after the metal box and lab notes were safely out of his home and the keys well hidden. He didn't think anyone would ever look in the guest bathroom for the key.

During one of her rare visits to his home, while freshening up in the guest bathroom, his sister noticed the clunky frame. She took it off of the wall and examined it carefully. Thinking it was such an ugly piece to hang in a bathroom she laughed it off as an example of her brother's poor taste in decorating. She sat staring at it and as she lifted it to put it back on the wall she thought she heard a rattle of some kind. She rummaged through a vanity drawer and found a small nail file. She unscrewed the backing and then saw the key. Having seen her mother's key ring many times she instantly knew the key was for her mother's metal box. She refastened the backing and returned the frame to the wall, muttering to herself, "Only Mark would hide a key in such an obvious hiding place. Book smart but street dumb – always was... always will be."

Now that he would be able to devote entire days to his research and needed constant access to it all, he had no choice but to bring all elements back into the house.

Earlier that day he went to his bank and accessed his safety deposit box. Then he retrieved his mother's lab notes from the care of the school safe. He walked around all day with these items in his briefcase, nervously conscious of the substantial risk he was taking by keeping them out in public. The briefcase never left his sight or his mind during the entire day.

Over the past few weeks, as he counted down to his last day of teaching, he spent time thinking about possible safe hiding places within his home. The research papers could be out in the open while he was working on them but he needed to come up with dependable hiding places while he slept or had to be out of the house.

Now, in the privacy of his home he placed the contents of his briefcase on the lab table in front of him.

Other than his sister, no one knew that he had his mother's lab notes and the precious metal box; he regretted telling her almost as soon as the words left his mouth. She wanted him to sell it all to the highest bidder. He closed his eyes tightly in an effort to block out the memory of the last time she and he were together; the obvious contempt she had for him as she tried to push him... pull him... manipulate him... "You fool; don't you realize that we could both be rich beyond our wildest dreams?"

"But this is mother's life's work – it was her dying wish for the work to continue," he pleaded.

"You are still no more than a pathetic little boy. The *'work'*", she mocked, "can still continue, but instead of through your feeble efforts some huge corporation can take it over, and pay us for the right to do so."

"How can you even think of doing that?" he argued, "Mother specifically did not want some big company in charge of it, she knew how they priced the drugs her father created so that only the rich could afford them. She wanted to save *all* people from that horrid disease, not just the pampered few."

"'She wanted'... 'She knew'... 'She desired," his sister said, scornfully. "What about our wants and desires? *She is dead... we* are still alive*! We* are very much alive, and *we* deserve to prosper from the fruits of her labor."

*****

From now on, these precious items would have to be with him all of the time in order for him to make progress on his mother's research. The lab notes were relatively easy to hide inside the house – he separated them from the spiral pads and scattered them, seemingly in random order, among the piles and piles of papers that already covered his cluttered desk. The metal box proved to be more of a challenge. He racked his brain for a safe hiding place and then it came to him, almost as if his mother was talking to him from the grave. He grabbed the metal box and went up to the attic. After digging through several rows of huge moving cartons he came to the one marked, MAMA'S THINGS. He carefully moved the carton to an open space on the floor and kneeled in front of it as he gently pulled the flaps open. Towards the bottom of the box, wrapped in her favorite sweater, was his mother's family bible. He lovingly lifted the leather bound book out of the box and placed it on the floor next to him. He carefully re-folded the sweater and returned it to the carton.

He opened the bible and ran his fingers along the sides of the cavity his mother had made the night before they left Austria. He gently placed the metal box into the cavity. A perfect fit, he thought to himself. "Yes!" he screamed, "A perfect fit!" God will not mind, he thought, and Mama would approve. God would understand that he was not defacing the Lord's book but instead was insuring the safety of this valuable connection to his mother's life's work. The cause was a noble and worthy one.

"It fits like a glove," he said softly.

*****

The evening before they escaped from Austria, the two children listened in horror as their parents fought well into the night; their mother arguing that she must take the metal box with her when they leave their home in the morning; their father dead set against it.

Ilsa had a temper, when all else failed – she screamed; and screaming usually won her the argument. Karl was a negotiator. He rarely raised his voice above a whisper. Tonight's argument was particularly confusing to the children because their parents seemed to be reversing roles. Tonight it was Karl who was screaming and Ilsa who was the calm negotiator; and it sounded to the young ears that she was losing this argument.

"The minute they see it is gone," he argued, "they will know what you have done and send the police after you... after us. They will find us and bring us back or kill us on the spot. Is *that* what you want?" he yelled.

"I will not leave without it. Go without me, then," she cried.

"What can be so important that it is worth risking the lives of our children – as well as your life... my life?" He demanded. "For once in your life, put us... our children... me... ahead of *your work.*"

"The box may contain the cure," she pleaded, "At the very least it will allow us to prove our findings, once and for all. I can't leave it... I won't leave it. If you loved me... you would never force me to leave it behind."

Karl slumped down on a side chair. Seemingly drained both physically and emotionally he said, "Dearest Ilsa... where, just tell me where, would you *hide* this box of yours; *in your pocket?*"

Frantically, she looked around the room and picked up her daughter's favorite floppy doll. She knelt in front of him and in a low whisper she said, "Look... I could sew it into the upper body portion of Helga's doll." She pointed to the seam connecting the upper body to the legs, arms, and head. "It would fit!" She exclaimed, excitedly. "Look... look... it could fit."

He reached out and held her close. "I love you... I want to agree because I love you. But you need to understand that the risk is just too much. Ilsa... think of the children's lives... think of my life... for God's sake, Ilsa, think about your own life."

"But the work", she interrupted, "The work *must* continue."

He held her tighter, "The work cannot continue if we are all captured and killed or thrown into some jail cell for the rest of our lives. Please Ilsa... be reasonable."

They went back and forth through most of the evening. She made every argument she could think of – moving back and forth between logic and emotion and threats. Finally, she stood her ground. "If the box must stay than so will I."

"You are opening us up to additional danger," he said.

"We are on the side of the angels, Karl," she quickly responded. "The Lord will protect us."

"So, tell me Ilsa," Karl said facetiously, "when the storm troopers point at you and say, '*Please, if it is not too much of an imposition... and if you do not mind... would you be so kind as to tell me... what have you there, pretty lady,*' what are you going to say? '*It is a little gift from my God?*' Are you going to wrap yourself in the gold edged pages of the bible and read them the words of the Lord?"

All was quiet for a moment.

Then the children heard their mother laugh, almost hysterically.

"I asked you a question," Karl said, still pretending to sound like a border guard, "what has your Lord given you in that little box lovely lady... if you do not mind my asking?"

"That's it!" Ilsa whispered. She reached over and smothered him with kisses. "That's it... that's it!"

"What's it?" he said, in a harsh whisper.

"That is how we will get the box through the inspectors at the border," she said.

"What's it?" he responded. "Have you completely lost your mind?"

"You have given me the perfect solution, you wonderful man." She pulled him closer and again smothered his face with kisses.

He pushed her away. "Now I am really worried. You have gone over the edge."

"Karl," she murmured, "just wait there for a moment."

She ran to her bureau and brought out her family bible. Excitedly, she placed the metal box on top of the bible. Then she placed it side by side with the metal box. "It is perfect," she sighed.

He stared at her in amazement. "Calm down," he said, "just calm down."

"Here it is," she smiled, "the solution." She was speaking now barely above a whisper, "I will cut a space inside the bible to hide the box. It will easily fit. Look." Again she placed the metal box on top and then alongside the bible. "A perfect fit... a perfect hiding place... they will never question us... it will be Easter morning, Karl. What more natural than to be holding onto a bible on Easter Sunday morning?"

He watched intently as she maneuvered the bible above and around the metal box. He then took the box from her and lined it up with the outer edge of the bible and then placed it gently on top of the bible. "It is still very risky." He said.

"This whole running away plan is risky, Karl. But surely, you can see that this *can* work?"

Although the quarrelling continued for some time after, Ilsa knew that the worst of the arguing was now over when her husband stopped in mid-sentence, and as if he was thinking aloud said in hushed tones, "Using the bible to embrace the 'cure'? Embracing the 'cure' in the words of the Lord... the *'cure'*... safely cradled... *in the words of the Lord... the cure, in the words of the Lord!*"

Finally, they embraced; the metal box would accompany them – even to the firing squad if it came to that. It didn't reverse his fear that those at the lab would sound an alarm to retrieve their valuable property; but, finally he accepted the inevitable. They both fully understood that they would now have less than half of the time his original escape plan might have given them to avoid capture, but in the end, he had to agree that no one would be the slightest bit suspicious when they saw her holding onto a family bible when leaving the house the next morning or during their journey out of the country; after all, it *was* Easter Sunday.

Smiles broke out on both of their faces – for different reasons, but smiles were better than tears or angry words and finally he nodded approval, gave her a kiss and went to bed.

*****

Mark knew that the bible held the metal box during their escape out of Austria because his mother told him all about it as she lay dying. His sister knew about the existence of the metal box but never knew exactly how it was transported during their escape. Mark was about to tell his sister about the role the bible played but after she argued so intensely for them to sell the lab notes he no longer had the stomach to discuss anything else with her. Now he was overjoyed that he kept that bit of information to himself. He returned the carton to its place by the wall and took the bible downstairs to his library. He moved several books around and placed the bible on the second shelf from the ceiling. He stepped back and smiled broadly. *That,* he thought to himself, *is the last place she or anyone else will ever look for the metal box. The very last place!*

Chapter 19
Monday, January 1, 1996 –
Grosse Pointe, Michigan – 3:13 A.M.

Mark always celebrated the first day of the New Year by hosting a small dinner party, usually no more than six or eight lovingly selected guests, rarely the same guests two years in a row, with the exception of Gretchen, his long-time housekeeper. This would be the third time she was to be one of *the cordially invited* for this special meal. The first time he asked her to attend the party as one of his guests was because she had no other place to go and he didn't believe that anyone should be alone on New Year's Day – "that's no way to start a New Year," he told her, "and everyone knows that what you do on New Year's Day you are going to have to do all year long. You don't want to be all alone all year long, now, do you?"

That first year she kept trying to get up after each course to clear the dishes until he finally yelled, "Sit down Gretchen. You are *not* the *serverrrr* today. Today, *I* am the server and *you* are the serveeeeee."

"Am I gonna be the *servee* all year long now because you done been the *server* to me on this New Year's Day!" she countered. But inwardly, she was truly honored by this thoughtful gesture.

He had a unique ability to fill the room during these special get-togethers with complimentary personalities so that the conversations were friendly and stimulating and inter-esting – most of all, interesting. Over the years many new friendships began around those "first dinners," as Mark called them; people who entered the house as strangers went on to become lifelong friends.

He enjoyed cooking and usually worked on the menu for weeks in advance. He always dedicated at least one dish to each guest; ever conscious of their favorite as well as least favorite foods and drinks and, of course, any particular allergies.

This year he invited his newest friends, Fred and Mary Archer, the new territorial commander of the local Salvation Army post and his wife. He asked them to bring five or six people who they knew would not have a caring place to spend the first day of the New Year so that they could get a home-cooked meal along with a few hours of undemanding friendship.

He was going to start today's menu off with his great crab cake recipe because he knew Gretchen loved his crab cakes. But that meant that he would also have to whip up a separate batch of a similar recipe substituting shrimp for the crab because Mary Archer was allergic to crab meat.

As the main courses this year he planned to serve a huge roasted turkey, as well as a glazed ham and his mother's brisket recipe. It just wouldn't be New Year's Day without his mother's brisket and boiled red potatoes. Even the year they immigrated to America and didn't yet have everything in place to cook a proper meal, she convinced a local café owner to permit her to make her brisket and boiled red potatoes in his kitchen for her family, and his. That was a wonderful New Year's Day, he thought, just wonderful.

He fully understood that there would be much too much food for just the few people around his table that day but that would be all right. He would make sure that the Archer's had plenty to take back with them for some of the many mouths they regularly fed.

The table had been set almost a week already; wine was cooling in the refrigerator and he even ordered a center piece of African violets – the lucky flower for 1996 according to the Chinese zodiac.

*****

Something must have awakened him at 3:13 in the morning. He wasn't a very sound sleeper but it would have taken an unusually loud sound to get him up in the middle of the night. The Kramers on the next block were always shooting guns into the sky and setting off fire crackers as part of their New Year's Eve celebrations, it might have been something like that that woke him from a sound sleep. Maybe he was just thirsty and wanted to go downstairs for a glass of water. Maybe he was cold and needed an extra blanket. Maybe he wanted to work in the lab a bit before the day's festivities began. Maybe... maybe... maybe... with Mark, and a mind that never seemed to be fully at rest, anything was possible. Of course, there might have been something he thought he had to do that very minute to prepare for the day's special meal. They could all speculate but no one would ever know for sure.

They fixed the time at 3:13 because that was the time on the face of his Bulova wristwatch. The crystal must have cracked during his fall because the mechanism stopped at that exact time... for him... forever.

It was Gretchen who found him at 10:27 the next morning, when she arrived with the groceries. "I couldn't find that brand of anchovies," she yelled as she let herself in. "I wound up buying the store brand, I think they are all the same anyway." She began putting the perishables away, "Are you still sleeping?" she yelled towards the upstairs. "I'm going outside for the cake, I'll be right back." She waited a few seconds for an answer, and then mumbled to herself, "Today ain't no day to sleep late Mr. Regan, too much to do, too much to do."

She lifted the cake from the rear foot well of her car and moved it onto the bottom shelf of the backup refrigerator in the garage. She took a quick look around, then opened the cake box and ran her finger across one of the sides of the cake. "I sure love real whipped cream frosting," she said softly. Then she did the same along the other three sides of the cake. "Got to make it all even now, don't I?"

She hung her keys on the hook by the oven and started to go upstairs, and then she saw him lying all crumpled up at the foot of the steps. "Oh my God!" She screamed.

Hearing the screams, the continuous blood curdling screams - as she later described them to the policeman who responded to her 911 call – Mark's next door neighbor ran to see what had happened. She found Gretchen on her knees, pounding Mark's chest, hopelessly trying to revive him. "I will never forget those screams," she told the policeman, "not if I live to be a thousand years old."

They believed that he tripped on something which made him lose his balance and fall from the top of the steps just outside of his bedroom. His neck was broken. It could have happened during his fall or when he landed. At least they didn't think he suffered much pain – death must have come fairly quickly according to the coroner.

They closed the school the day of the funeral. The teachers agreed to take it as a no pay day because the town claimed its financial situation could not support paying them if they did not work. Mark would have appreciated the financially responsible position taken by those who made the final decision.

It was a huge funeral. It seemed as if every student he ever taught came back to pay their respects. Almost every member of the faculty asked to be able to say something at the church. Some of the few, who didn't ask, would have liked to speak, but they just thought they would break down emotionally and ruin it for the others; many of the other mourners seemed to have a need to share their own Mark Regan stories with anyone who would listen.

Of everyone who spoke that day, it was Gretchen who made the most lasting impression. She spoke slowly and lovingly about his many acts of kindness and how she would miss him. In the middle of a sentence she began to sob. A few minutes later she tried to continue, but the words would not – could not - break through.

Finally, the minister ran to her side, put his arms around her and gently helped her back to her seat. She held on to his hands and whispered, "He was the kindest and most decent man I have ever known. In all of the years I knew him I never heard him say a single bad word about any-one." The minister nodded.

No one believed that he had any living relatives; at least he never spoke of any.

Gretchen knew that he had a sister, Helga, somewhere in Michigan and that they had been estranged from each oth-er for some time. She made the decision not to reach out to the sister. However, even if she had it wouldn't have made much of a difference. At the same time Mark was being laid to rest his sister was dancing to a Latin rhythm band in Argentina, celebrating her third divorce.

Since he did not have a will on file in the county courthouse and no other document among his papers that named an executor; a public notice was placed in the local newspa-per announcing that creditors had four months to make a claim against his estate. Eventually, when no relatives or creditors – other than the bank that held the mortgage on his modest home, came forth, the bank decided to sell all of the belongings in the house so that they could get the house and property ready for a quick sale, satisfy the mortgage, and close out the estate.

An ad was placed for the contents of the house and an antique dealer from New York came to Grosse Point, made an offer for the entire lot; loaded it onto a tractor trailer and had it driven back to New York.

Eventually, word of Mark's death reached his sister. She went to a lawyer to file court papers to take over his home and its contents as Mark's only living relative. That was when she learned that some antique dealer had already purchased all of the contents of the house and moved everything, as it turned out, including a kitchen garbage can, rotting contents and all.

Try as she did, she was unable to get the name or contact information of the antique dealer. The trail went cold until a friend of hers – living in New York – called her to say that she noticed a small public announcement in a newspaper saying that there was going to be a sale of something from her brother's estate.

Chapter 20
Sunday, May 12, 1996 –
Tom's Diner,
Crown Heights, Brooklyn – 7:23 A.M.

Albert, Sol, Will James and Robert Schless arranged to meet for breakfast at Tom's Diner, walking distance from Albert and Sol's apartment. James asked each to travel to the diner along a different route and advised them that he would be the last to arrive. A little more than an hour earlier than the pre-agreed meeting time, James took up a position in a doorway about half a block away and within clear sight of the popular local restaurant.

James decided to check in with one of his operatives before he joined the rest of them in the diner. He listened intently to the disturbing report, then told his operative to remain in place and to try to learn as much more as possible and said that he would call back inside of an hour. He ripped out a page from his memo book and quickly scribbled a brief note. He folded the paper several times and stuffed it into his breast pocket, then ran from the phone booth to the diner.

James noticed them as soon as he walked in. He went towards the table where the other three were sitting and, without actually acknowledging them, pulled the folded piece of paper out of his breast pocket and dropped it near the table as he continued walking past. Schless reached down for the paper, unfolded it and quickly scanned the message, then stuffed it in his shirt pocket and said to the two other men, "A little complication has surfaced. He wants you to take a train to lower Manhattan and make sure you are not being followed. Meet Jonathan and me at 9 Chatham Square; it is a busy Chinese hangout with the best Dim Sum this side of Hong Kong. He only uses it as a meeting place when he wants loud noises and rude civilians to drown out whatever would be the topic of discussion." He got up to leave, stooped down, and in a low whisper said, "Each go separately and do not let yourself be followed!" Albert and Sol nodded, almost mechanically.

One hour and thirteen minutes later...

When they were all finally together, Albert asked, "Is all of this spook stuff really necessary? Maybe you can give us a clear understanding of what all of this is really about."

James looked at Schless and cleared his throat. "Let me make some things quite clear. That little key we found in the frame in your apartment may be able to unlock a medical breakthrough that some very powerful people would give anything to own. I am beginning to believe that you have each got a clear target on your chests and the only thing saving your lives may be the fact that even you do not know the location of the lock into which that key will fit." He paused, and then added, "Is that a clear enough understanding for you?"

"Where is the rest of the Michigan merchandise this very moment?" Schless asked.

"It's in one of thirty two trailers I keep in an otherwise vacant lot near Coney Island," Albert said.

"Who else knows that piece of information?" James asked.

"Now, counting the two of you, five individuals," Albert said, sarcastically.

"Now that Schless and I know this information, who are the other three?" James persisted, ignoring the sarcasm.

"Me, Sol, and Elizabeth."

"Then you need to quickly move that trailer and just hope it is not too late," James said.

"What are you talking about?" Sol asked.

"I am talking about the fact that Elizabeth seems to have disappeared from her home earlier this morning."

"What makes you say that?" Albert blurted out.

"Because it happens to be a fact; I thought it was about time we get an associate of mine to watch her and as of an hour and a half ago, there were a couple men causing a ruckus in her building. When my operative went into the building to dig into what was happening and she was *not* in her apartment."

"So she got past your so-called professional 'watcher?'" Albert chided.

"You know, Albert," Schless said, "you make it really hard for us to even care what happens to you or anyone connected to you; much less put in any meaningful time trying to help you."

"Maybe she went shopping," Albert said, defensively.

"At six o'clock in the morning?" James quickly responded.

"Well, then, let me just say out loud what I am thinking; I don't believe it," Albert said.

James barked back, "Call her."

Albert reached for his phone and dialed Elizabeth's cell. It went to voice mail.

"She's not picking up," Albert said.

"Is it like her to ignore a ringing phone?" James asked.

"No it isn't. Other than today – whatever time or day I have called her she usually picks up by the second or third ring," Albert said, with a confused look.

"Is the trailer with the Michigan lot marked?" Schless interrupted.

"Not really, all of the trailers look pretty much alike," Albert said.

"So how do you know which one is which?" Schless asked.

"I know which one is which by the trailer number on the back door," Albert responded.

"So they *are* marked," Schless and James said, almost simultaneously.

"Do you keep a record of the contents of each trailer by number?" Schless asked.

"Of course I do!" Albert said.

"This is like pulling teeth," Schless grumbled. "Where do you keep that information?"

"In here," Albert said, pointing to his head.

"Okay", James broke in, "now... will you pleeeeeease write down the trailer number and actual location belonging to the specific trailer - where you are currently storing the contents of the Michigan estate - so that I can make arrangements to move those goods to a safe storage place?"

"How you gonna do that?" Albert asked, looking at his watch. "It isn't even nine o'clock, and it *is* Sunday morning?"

James smiled. "Let us worry about that," James said as he pulled out his cell phone. "Meanwhile we still need to find Elizabeth, don't we?"

"Gee," Albert exclaimed, "I almost forgot about Elizabeth!"

Chapter 21
Earlier that morning...
Sunday, May 12, 1996 –
Tom's River, New Jersey – 5:41 A.M.

Elizabeth, always a light sleeper, was awakened by a noise outside her bedroom window. She lived on the ground floor of a small apartment complex and fearing the ease with which someone could break in, she regularly slept with a can of mace under her pillow.

She grabbed the can and rolled onto the floor from the side of the bed furthest from the window. Someone was definitely trying to pry the window open. She reached up for the phone and then realized that someone had cut the connection. She crawled out of the room on her belly into the adjoining kitchen. Standing by an open refrigerator door with a knife in one hand and a turkey leg in the other was a huge man wearing a ski mask over his head.

"Hey, nice of you to come to me and save me the trouble of having to shake you awake," he said.

"Who are you?" she howled.

"How about you let me ask the questions, honey pie, and you just do whatever you can to stay alive," he responded.

She quickly turned the can of mace towards his face and held the button down until the can was empty. The huge man screamed in pain, dropping both the knife and his snack as he clutched his eyes with both hands. Elizabeth grabbed the knife and shoved it into his leg with all the strength she had. She then stood up, gave him a kick in the groin and another to his face, yelling, "Don't call me honey pie you big tub of lard. She grabbed the outer edge of his back pocket and pulled his wallet out. She removed a twenty dollar bill and his driver's license, threw the wallet down and said, "By the way, that turkey leg was supposed to be my dinner." She grabbed her car keys and handbag and ran out of the apartment.

For a brief moment she considered running to her car and then decided to go in the opposite direction, towards a neighbor's apartment one floor up.

Elizabeth banged on the neighbor's door. A door on the other side of the hallway opened and a short, stout black woman poked her head out. "Help me, please," Elizabeth begged. "Someone is trying to kill me. Please let me in, please, please."

The woman stepped aside as Elizabeth ran into the apartment, then slammed the door shut and double locked it.

The two women huddled together as they heard at least two men exit Elizabeth's apartment. They moved to the living room window and saw two men get into a car and quickly drive away.

"Say," the woman finally mumbled, "you're lucky that I have insomnia."

"Luck has nothing to do with it." Elizabeth said, hugging the woman, "Siberian cemeteries are full up with people who depended on luck to get them through tight situations."

What a strange comment, the woman thought. *What could she possibly mean by that?*

Chapter 22
Sunday, May 12, 1996 –
Tom's River, New Jersey – 6:08 A.M.

Elizabeth turned to the woman and said, rather sheepishly, "I don't even know your name. You saved my life and I don't even know who to thank."

"It's Wilma," the woman said.

"I can't believe we have never met, Wilma. Did you just move in?" Elizabeth said.

"No," Wilma said, "I'm just visiting my sister. You probably know her."

"Hey, Wilma," Elizabeth said, "now that we have met and are on a first name basis, can I borrow your car?"

"Borrow my car, for what?" Wilma asked.

"I need to find my boss."

"I don't really like to loan my car out to just anyone, especially someone I just met." The woman said slowly. "How about I go with you? I can drive."

"You would do that for me?"

"Sure," I don't have very much excitement in my life, the woman said. "This will be like an adventure."

"Okay, let's go," Elizabeth said, reaching for the door.

*****

They left from the rear of the building and sped away in a six-year-old Chevy with Michigan license plates.

*****

Meanwhile, upstairs in the backroom bedroom of the apartment Wilma and Elizabeth just left, sat a frail woman, the *actual* renter of that apartment, gagged and tied to a chair.

I am going to die here, she kept thinking, *I am just going to die here!* She was trying not to lose consciousness but it was getting harder for her to breathe.

Chapter 23
Sunday, May 12, 1996 –
On the way to Brooklyn – 7:25 A.M.

Elizabeth pulled out her phone and dialed Albert's cell. "No answer," Elizabeth said to Wilma.

"Well don't leave a message," Wilma cautioned, "he may have been kidnapped by the same people who sent the two guys. Let's stay out of sight for a while and you can try him again, later. If you still can't connect with him then maybe you will have to consider some way of staying hidden for a while."

"Good idea!" Elizabeth said.

3 hours later –
Staten Island side, Verrazano–Narrows Bridge 10:32 A.M.

Elizabeth tried to reach Albert again, on the second ring he picked up, saw her number and screamed, "Elizabeth, how are you? Where are you?"

James held up his hand, signaling for Albert to hit the mute button. He then took the phone from Albert and double checked that the mute feature was activated and whispered, "We still do not know what if any part she might be playing in this little drama – don't tell her where you are or anything about the moving of the trailer load of goods. If you can, try to get her to meet you at the antique store. Got it?"

"I got it," Albert said, clearly annoyed. "I got it, but, enough about if we can trust Elizabeth and her possible involvement in all of this. She is a simple Russian peasant woman. I told you, give me some credit for being a great judge of people, I know who she is and she isn't capable of being or doing anything like that. And another thing, she could have had that frame and the key anytime she wanted. I had absolutely no knowledge the key was even in that frame until you showed it to me."

James returned the phone to Albert who de-activated the mute feature and said, "So where are you now? How are you? Are you safe?"

"Have not you listened to me," Elizabeth whispered, "I tells you I was oolmust kids napped these morning."

"Were you hurt?" he yelled into the phone.

"No, thanks god."

"Where are you now?"

"On my ways to your store."

"Good, I'll be waiting for you. Be careful."

James whispered, "Tell her to meet you at 5:00 P.M., not before."

Albert gave James a quizzical look.

Sol punched Albert's arm.

"No, 5:00 P.M.," Albert said into the phone, "I can't be there 'till 5:00 P.M."

"Whats it is more importants of you this minute? Can't not you drop what you are doings and come right to the store now?"

James lifted five fingers and whispered, "5:00 P.M. – be firm."

Shaking his head in despair, Albert said, "Don't tell me what to do Elizabeth," and then, more forcibly, "Just find a place to hide until five and then meet me at the store, and *do not* talk to anyone, you got it? Not anyone!"

"Yes, buss."

"I'm serious here, be real careful, don't talk to anyone, these are bad people we are up against."

"Don't not you to worry buss; lets the other pipples be careful. Elizabeth Hillsonrat is fearing no one. Does *you* gots that?"

Wilma stared at Elizabeth. *Why is she talking like that,* she thought.

*****

When Albert closed the phone and put it back in his pocket Schless asked James, "What do you think?"

James thought for a while then pulled out his pad and thumbed down to the notes he previously recorded there. He looked up, gave a sigh and said, "I think, Mr. Schless, that we will just have to trust but verify!"

James stood, walked away from the table, and made a series of phone calls.

Chapter 24
Sunday, May 12, 1996 –
C. B. Forster's Public Warehouse,
Coney Island, NY – 2:53 P.M.

After a series of phone calls, it took just under four and a half hours to actually pick up the oversized shipping container with Mark Regan's belongings, move it about five miles to an old public furniture warehouse, unload it and get the empty trailer back to its original location.

"How did you get so many workers so quickly? Albert asked James and Schless as they walked around the cavernous building.

"There are always a lot of very capable people willing to do some physical work in exchange for a good meal and a safe and dry place to sleep," James said, "Especially in a large, often less than hospitable city like New York."

"And why drop it all into a warehouse so close to the original location?" Albert asked.

"We needed to move quickly and the space was available. Anyway, this space is more than just conveniently located – it will almost certainly keep us off of everyone's radar while we check out the contents. I believe the best hiding places for just about anything is usually in clear sight!" James said. "So where better to hide a house full of belongings then in a giant building full of so many other people's belongings.

Sol walked over to them and asked, "How did you get all of the equipment needed to do this on a Sunday morning?"

"It was just around," Schless said with a smile. "It isn't like it was being used for anything else so early on a Sunday morning."

"What will all of this cost me?" Albert asked.

"Much of it will be covered by IOUs I have been holding... you know, barter arrangements, that might have gone un-used anyway," James said.

"They are *your* IOUs, what will they cost *me*?" Albert per-sisted.

"How about we worry about that at some other time?" James snapped back.

"How about you give me a straight answer for once in our short but *interesting* relationship?" Albert demanded.

"I'm not worried so you don't have to worry. Right now, we have enough to think about. For starters," James said, "where is the lock that goes with the key we found in the wooden frame, and *if* it is somewhere in this trailer load of stuff, will we find it in time to do us any good?"

Albert walked away, angry and embarrassed.

Sol took James aside, "He is just trying to make sure that when the final bill comes – and we all know there will be a final bill at some point - he will be in a position to pay it. That's all."

"Look," James said, "When you are dropping from a trou-bled airplane and someone offers you a parachute, your concern – at that moment – shouldn't be about who is giv-ing you that parachute or what they will want in return. All you *should* be concentrating on is will the chute open in time. Frankly, if it fails to open in time the final cost would be the least of your worries."

"Maybe he has enough blind faith in you to believe that the chute *will* open. Then his only concern has to be what will it cost and can I pay that price?" Sol responded. "I probably know Albert more than anyone else in his life... maybe anyone who has ever been in his life. His brashness and high level of constant disagreeability – if I can coin a new word - is nothing more than a protective shield. He is actually very human deep inside and *I* know that he is deeply grateful for what you are doing for him. The Albert *I know* wants to make sure you are fully reimbursed when this is all over."

James thought for a while then said, "For the moment, let us all concentrate on the *chute*. I have no intention of becoming Albert's *next* problem. My final invoice will be honest and fair and we will both work out an acceptable way to take care of it. Now," James smiled, "do you know if Albert brought the key with him as I had asked?"

Sol went over to Albert, and whispered something in his ear. Albert's face flushed, and then he slowly took out his wallet, removed the key and handed it to James.

James nodded to Sol, mouthing the words, 'thank you,' pulled a string out of his pocket and tied it to the key. He hung the key around Albert's neck and said, "Let's get to work!"

"Maybe *you* should hold onto that key." Albert said.

Sol broke in, "*Albert* would be delighted to leave it in your care." Sol then patted Albert on the back and nodded his approval.

Schless shook his head, mumbled something to himself, and then said, "We still don't know exactly what we are looking for."

"I might be able to help with that," James said. "This Mark Regan was a chemistry teacher. His mother was a fairly accomplished medical researcher and his grandfather, on his mother's side, won a 1908 Nobel Prize for his medical research for disease cures. I think we can make a safe guess that the key is tied to something having to do with their combined medical research. And since there seems to be so much interest in getting that little key of yours, it is a better than even chance that the information is very valuable, and at the very least, worth many times the $100,000 they were willing to pay you for that key."

"Doesn't that assume that they also knew that the key was hidden inside the framed permit?" Sol asked.

"I think that is more than likely, but time will tell," James responded.

"And how do we go about finding that information in a trailer load of goods without even knowing what form it is in?" Albert asked.

"An excellent question, and hopefully, we will have an excellent answer to your excellent question after those very capable people who were willing to do some physical work for a good meal and safe place to sleep get that hot meal they were promised and a few hours of needed rest," James said with a reassuring grin.

James took out his phone as he stepped away from the others. When he returned he said that he would meet them at the store at a little past five and asked Schless to stay with Albert and Sol and make sure they were at the store in plenty of time to meet Elizabeth at five.

"Aren't you coming too?" Albert asked.

"I'll be there; you may have to start without me because I may be a little late, but I will be there," James said as he walked towards the exit.

Chapter 25
Sunday, May 12, 1996 –
Williamsburg, Brooklyn, New York – 4:45 P.M.

James looked down from a rooftop several buildings up the block as Sol, Albert, and Schless walked towards the store, unlocked the front door and went inside.

Several minutes later, Elizabeth and Wilma pulled up in front of the antique store. The two women got out of the car and walked towards the store. James put a pair of binoculars to his eyes and stared at the license plate on the car. He pulled out his notepad, made a quick note and continued watching the street. He saw three large men who seemed to very closely resemble two of the people he first saw in the VCR tape from the auction; the men were now rushing towards the women from behind, grabbed each of the women's arms and pushed them into the store. Ten minutes later a black car pulled up to the store, two men, who also looked like they were at the auction, got out of a car and quickly entered the store.

James looked at the license plate on their car and saw that it was a New York plate. He quickly entered the plate number onto his laptop computer. Almost instantly, a name and address flashed onto the screen. He smiled, broadly, took out his cell phone and dialed *911* and reported a robbery in progress and gave the operator the address of the antique store.

Less than five minutes later, three police cars, flashing lights and sirens blazing, came to a screeching stop in front of the store. Uniformed police men jumped out of each of the cars, two ran to the rear of the store, one stood on either side of the front door as two others quickly entered with their guns drawn.

A few minutes later, the five heavy-set men were marched out of the store in handcuffs, pushed into the back seats of the three police cars and with flashing lights and sirens, all three cars sped away.

James smiled as he walked down from the rooftop and entered the store from the rear. Elizabeth was in the middle of telling Albert about her morning adventure when James approached her and said, pointing to Wilma, "You have just 60 seconds to tell me who that woman is and why she is with you when I clearly heard Albert tell you *not* to talk to anyone."

'I'm Wilma, I live in her building and I may have saved her life. Who are you?"

"First of all, I didn't ask you," he said to the woman, then turning to face Elizabeth he said, "I asked *you!*"

Elizabeth looked at Albert and said, "I don't not like how he is talking to this lady, Wilma – she is right, she did save it my life."

Albert started to speak but stopped as James put his hand up. "Whose car are you driving?" James said to the woman.

"It's my car," Wilma answered.

"So you are 'Fusion Pharmaceuticals, LLP, of Dearborn, Michigan?"

"Who it is this Fooshon Farmacooticals?" Elizabeth asked.

"It's the registered owner of the car you were in," James barked, "that's who. Now," he said as he turned again to the woman, "who are you and why are you here?"

The woman slowly reached into her handbag and with two fingers carefully pulled out a small wallet, slowly opening it to show her identification card which read, Alice Stanley of Detroit, Michigan.

"Thank God for trust and verify," Sol said.

"And all of this 'Wilma' crap?" James asked the woman.

"It is my 'street name' for when I'm on assignment. It was just a convenient ruse I used so that Elizabeth would lead me to you."

Elizabeth walked closer to the woman, glared at her for a moment then pulled her hand back and slapped the woman across the face with all of her force. She then said, calmly, "That's for using me. *No one* uses *me*. Do you understand that now?"

They all stared at Elizabeth. Finally, Sol broke the silence, "Elizabeth, what happened to your accent?"

Elizabeth turned to face Sol, smiled broadly, and then said, "What accent, Mr. Weiner?"

"Your Russian accent, Elizabeth," Albert said.

Elizabeth smiled again, "I have no Russian accent, Albert. Only you, because you live on some *other planet*, would think that the gibberish I have been spouting since I came here was a Russian accent. I happen to speak English quite well – in fact I speak a number of languages, quite well."

"I don't understand," Albert said, clearly confused and surprised. "So all of this has been... has been... some sort of performance? This has all been an *act*?"

"I needed a job, you had a job, Elizabeth said. "When we first met I quickly realized that even you would never offer me such a menial job if you knew how qualified I was, so I presented you with a lame, weak, unsophisticated rube to buy me time until I made longer term plans. Unfortunately, for me, I really grew to like the work and even had moments where I liked being around you... at least some of the time. But by then I was locked into this stupid act of mine."

"This is just too much to take on an empty stomach," Schless said, "One little drama at a time, if you all don't mind. I would just like to know how someone from Fusion Pharmaceuticals..."

"Of Dearborn, Michigan," James added.

"Thank you," Schless said, nodding to James, "of Dearborn, Michigan, just happens to live in an apartment in the same building as Elizabeth."

"I don't live in the same building as Elizabeth," the woman said. "In fact, if you will get someone back to that building you will find the real occupant of that apartment tied up and gagged where I left her. Our management felt the need for a backup plan in case Elizabeth somehow got the better of the two men we sent to pick her up."

"'Okay, okay," Schless said, "That's it. We are all going to sit down as each one of you two women – neither of whom is quite what you initially presented yourselves to be - tells the rest of us who you are, I mean who you *really* are; what you know; and how it affects all that has been going on here since last Sunday."

Chapter 26
Sunday, May 12, 1996 –
Williamsburg, Brooklyn, New York – 8:21 P.M.

Wilma was either unable or unwilling to fill in too many of the blanks. Finally, James just put his hands up and told her to leave.

"You're going to just let her walk out of here?" Albert asked in amazement.

"Look," James said, "we aren't getting anywhere with her. She is clearly stonewalling. It has been almost three and a half hours... she won't talk... we can't make her talk... the police might be able to make her talk, but *we* don't have cause to bring them in. I don't know about you, but I think that hitting your head against a wall is not a lot of fun and after three and a half hours even the wall needs a rest. In addition, unless I am very, very wrong – and I don't think I am – this Fusion Pharmaceuticals will be a lot heavier handed with her than we can be when they learn how easily her cover was blown."

Wilma blushed, picked up her pocketbook and slowly walked out.

"Now," James said, "Elizabeth is quite another matter!"

Elizabeth was uncomfortable talking about her life *before* she came to work for Albert, and said so. But she had no problem talking about the time since she came to the shop, in general, and actually volunteered information for the period since the all-important Sunday auction. She strongly defended herself from the auction forward and repeated over and over again that she knew nothing about the reasons surrounding the sudden interest in the framed permit. "I agreed with Albert, it was a piece of worthless junk and getting $2.00 for it would have been no different than hitting a lottery as far as I could see."

When they seemed to be too tired or just too weary to ask any more questions, Elizabeth stood up to leave. Albert asked her to stay back a few more minutes.

"If you don't mind," he said to James, Schless, and Sol, "I would like to visit privately with our *mystery woman*."

Sol walked closer to Albert and whispered, "Don't be too hard on her."

Albert just smiled and pointed to the door.

When they were finally alone Albert made a fresh pot of coffee and sat down across from Elizabeth. "Look," he began, hesitantly, "I know my weaknesses and I will admit that I can be a handful from time to time, but, I need to know what brought you here and why I should ever trust you again?"

Elizabeth cleared her throat and with a deep sigh stood up. "I simply will not... no, make that, I cannot talk about my past. It really has nothing to do with you or this mystery we all seem to be wrapped up in. It is personal... it is painful... and it is far more confusing than even I can make any sense of."

"You think I am just being nosey?" He asked.

"I think you are trying to enter an area that you couldn't possibly understand. I have lived it and I don't really understand it."

"No one is that mysterious," he said.

"I am!" She said, softly.

"Sit, tell me only what you feel comfortable telling me. I

don't want you to walk out like this. I will try to be less of... what did you call me... oh yes, '*a cheap rotten stinkin animal*'? But you, in turn, will just have to trust me more."

She slowly sat down, then, staring directly into his eyes, she began to speak. She had a practiced, public version of her life story that she used from time to time when someone would try to break through her defensive wall, and that was where she began; then, in the middle of a sentence she stopped, took a very long breath, and began again – this time with the truth.

At one point she looked at her watch – it was 4:37 in the morning. "I would say that is more than enough about me for one night?" She said with a smile. "Now, Albert Froog – if I can bare my soul to you, you are going to have to come clean with me. I now have the right to know what sick and demented baggage you are storing inside of you that has made you the one dimensional, '*cheap rotten stinkin animal*' I have been working so close with these past months."

"Yes, I am complicated beyond all reason," he said, slowly, "but how can I tell you what crazies I am made of? If I could so easily pinpoint what has screwed me up then I would have done something about it years ago. Maybe the one to ask is Sol. He seems to know me better than anyone – I believe that he may actually know me better than I know myself. The mystery I live with every day is why a '*Sol*', would still want to be with me after knowing so much about me. You have my permission to ask Sol anything you want and I will tell him to be open with you."

She put her hand on his and smiled. "Okay, then, let's just agree to begin again," she whispered.

"It's a deal, *but*, this time let's do it in good English and being more trusting and mutually understanding?" He said.

She raised her coffee cup and said, "Agreed, we will begin

again, this time in good English, more trusting, more mutually understanding, *and* with something we each failed to bring to the other before – some level of mutual respect."

Chapter 27
Wednesday, October 2, 1956 –
Donetsk, the Ukraine – 4:17 A.M.

Natasha Abruski, an indentured slave, was about to give birth. At fifteen, she was barely more than a child herself; she had been brutally raped by Dmitri Donskoy, the son of the Admistrator of the Roscosmos facility, hidden deep within a series of abandoned mines in Donetsk, the Ukraine.

When her section leader learned that she was pregnant she was immediately scheduled for an abortion. "You will get rid of that thing in your belly or we will get rid of you," he screamed. "I will not let you ruin that young man's life by waving your little mistake at him."

However, when Boris Donskoy, Dimitri's father and the Administration head of the facility heard about it he quickly arranged for the baby – *'if it was born a girl, healthy and with all of its limbs intact'* – to be raised in his home. "The little slut that carried this baby must be sent off to a labor camp somewhere else but my son's baby will be raised as one of my own."

When the baby was born she was placed in a makeshift nursery half-heartedly set up in a somewhat cleaner section of one of the mines. The baby spent the first 9 days of her life with a small band around her right ankle with #100256-13 written on it. They had to wait for a doctor to arrive from Moscow. When he declared the baby girl to be perfectly healthy, with all of her limbs intact, she was brought to the home of Boris and Svetlana Donskoy who raised her as their own. After giving birth to five sons, Svetlana yearned for a daughter and instantly fell in love with this precious little girl. She gave the baby its name,

небольшой попугай, which loosely translated into English as *Lovebird.*

The verbal and physical abuse from her five brothers began for Lovebird as early as she could remember. When their parents weren't around they would call her *'Mine trash'.*

All five boys contributed to the abuse but the eldest son, Dmitri, was by far the most aggressive. When Lovebird turned fifteen her adopted mother planned a huge party. After everyone went to bed that night Dmitri snuck into his sister's bedroom, something he was now doing fairly regularly, and ripped off the bed cover. He was surprised to see several pillows where he expected to find the young girl. Lovebird, having endured other such surprise visits from Dmitri knew that it would just be a matter of time before he came after her again and made up her mind to be more than ready for him if and when he returned. She snuck up behind him and swatted him across the head with a heavy cast iron frying pan. He slumped onto the bed, unconscious, blood spurting from the open wound. She turned him over onto his back, ripped open the fly on his pants and with heavy garden shears, cut off his penis.

She threw whatever belongings she could quickly fit into a huge cloth sack and scurried out of the second story window. She never saw her adopted mother or father alive again.

She created an entirely new identity for herself. She would now be known as Elizabeth Hillsonrat. She chose *Elizabeth*, after the poet, Elizabeth Barrett Browning. Her mother, a true romantic, cherished her Russian translated copy of *Sonnets from the Portuguese,* and often read passages from it to her adopted baby girl. As a tribute to her escape from them, she crafted her new last name from the name she had secretly given to her five brothers – *'extra tiny rat of the hill'... 'tiny rat of the hill'... 'fat rat of the hill'… 'gross rat of the hill'… and for Dmitri, the most vicious of them all, 'puke rat of the hill.'*

Elizabeth Hillsonrat initially supported herself through small robberies, Soon she became quite good at scamming old men out of their savings and eventually drifted onto the radar of Sergei Mikhailov, son of the head of the Solntsevskaya gang, a group of criminals operating out of Vnukovo International Airport, one of three major airports serving Moscow. Opened initially for military operations during the Second World War, the facility was quickly overrun by the Russian mobs and after the war, when it became a civilian airport, the surviving mob members provided security in exchange for a percentage of every shipment that either arrived or left from the busy airport.

Sergei first heard about the attractive young demon when she scammed one of the commercial pilots out of Vnukovo. Instead of being angry, the pilot thought it was funny that the little girl talked him out of his pay envelope with the promise of everlasting love but without giving him so much as a kiss. "She is good," he told Sergei. "Unlike your father's brutes, this girl can talk her way into and out of anything. I have to admit, I was happy to accommodate her." He laughed.

"I never heard of her," Sergei shot back.

"Thank your lucky stars that you haven't", the pilot said, "Believe me, you wouldn't stand a chance. Before you knew it you would be begging her to take whatever you own away from you – and you will want to apologize for not being able to give her more."

"She is that good?" Sergie asked, in amazement.

"She is that good!" The pilot responded.

Sergie spread the word that he wanted her to be found and

brought to him – voluntarily or through force. When she was finally in front of him, he stared at her a long time before he spoke.

"The little kitty cat got your tongue?" She teased, breaking the silence.

"I heard a lot about you," he responded. "I just wanted to see what all the talk was about."

"And?" she shot back.

"I'm not impressed," he said.

"Likewise, I'm sure," she said.

"What gives you the right to work in my father's territory without paying us any tribute?" He asked.

"I work alone," she responded.

"No one works here without paying us for the privilege."

"Anyone ever tell you what a bag of wind you are?" She said with contempt.

He smiled, walked over to her and slapped her face.

She spit at him. "Is that the best you can do?" she said, with a devious smile from ear to ear. "Or is it just because you know I can't hit back because your goons tied my hands behind my back?"

"Watch your mouth," he sneered.

"It is more fun watching you try to act like a big man."

"I am a big man."

"Are you trying to convince me or just yourself of that?"

"Turn around and I'll cut the rope tying your hands."

"Brave little man, aren't you?"

"Hey, I never met anyone I had to fear yet."

"You never met me, little man. But now that you have I will give you a little advice. The last man who lifted a hand to me is now peeing through a tube."

He cut the ropes and pushed her into a chair. "Let's get something straight, little Miss Nobody. Your midnight escapades stop right now unless you pay us a tribute on everything you do – and I mean everything."

"I told you, I work alone."

"Not anymore, you don't."

"Says who?"

"Says me."

"You and how many armies?"

"I don't need no army to crush you."

"You needed an army to get me here. Maybe I should be demanding a tribute from you for everything *you* do."

"You got guts for a nobody."

"It's Ms. Nobody, remember?"

He laughed.

She laughed.

She turned to walk away. "If you don't mind, I will be leaving now so that I don't keep the Queen of England waiting. We're having tea and finger sandwiches at the palace."

"I do mind, you don't go anywhere until I say you can go," he said.

She smiled broadly, waved good bye, and walked out of the room.

The next time they met he was leaning against his car's bumper, outside a house she had just burgled. Two of his men grabbed her and brought her to him.

"I came for my cut," he said.

"Give me a knife and I'll cut you." She laughed.

"Do you kiss your mother with that dirty mouth of yours?" He sneered.

"My mother was more of a man than you will ever be," she shot back.

"Real quick with the words, aren't you?" He laughed. "You know, I could take it all from you and leave you with nothing."

"You could take it all from me and create an enemy for life," she responded. "Or, you can drive me out of this place before we all get busted and I then might not kill you in the middle of the night."

He sent his bodyguards home and opened the passenger door for her, with a gallant wave of his hand.

"Now", she said, "that will get you a lot more than a slap on the face – I assure you."

They drove around until dawn, finally stopping at an all-night café just outside of the airport.

"I don't know if you have had enough of me but I have certainly had enough of you for one night," she said, with a big yawn.

"Come stay with me," he half begged.

"I don't think so," she quickly responded, followed by another, even larger yawn.

"Why not?" he persisted.

"Because you might kill *me* in the middle of the night," she teased.

"I think it is more likely that *you* would kill *me* in the middle of the night," he teased back.

"Well than, the reason I can't stay with you is that I might kill you in the middle of the night and then I would be a murderer. I am a lot of things, but I am not yet ready to be a murderer."

It took several weeks, but eventually, she did move in with him.

It took her much longer to feel safe enough to tell him the story of her birth and about the family that raised her. The first and last time he ever saw her cry was when she told him about how her five brothers mistreated her. He didn't quite know what to say or do but something, deep inside him realized that she needed to be held tightly and reassured that she was free of them now... that he would protect her.

Eventually she stopped crying. He gently wiped the tears away and said, "I will get even with them for what they did to you."

She looked up at him and gently put her fingers on his lips. "This is not your fight, this is my fight, don't get involved. The Donskoy family is rich and powerful – you have no idea how powerful."

He stared into her eyes and said, "From now on, your fights are my fights."

"They are KGB., they can and would crush you!"

He laughed, "Is that right? KGB? Well then, I guess I will need to pull the covers over my head and pretend I am already dead as I shiver in fear."

"This is serious," she scolded, "I know them better than you do."

"But you... you can handle it?" He said, gently patting her cheek.

"I know their strengths... but I also know their weaknesses... If I go after them I stand a better than even chance to get away free and clear."

He stared at her, admiringly. "You are one hot little dish. Remind me never to get you angry."

"It is entirely too late for that. In fact, one night, in the deep dark of night, I may..."

He pulled her closer and kissed her.

Chapter 28
Three days before the auction...
**Thursday, May 2, 1996 –
Dearborn, Michigan – 10:03 A.M.**

Helga Regan sat nervously in the Fusion Pharmaceutical corporate lobby. She had practiced all week on how best to present herself. She did not want to look needy or troubled – even though she was both needy *and* troubled. She did, however, want to make it clear that she was nobody's fool and at least appear as if she was in control of her situation. This was more than likely going to be her last chance at the gold ring. Nothing and nobody was going to kill it for her, especially not the damned, holier than thou, brother of hers, may he rest in peace.

Joseph G. Politeri walked into the lobby, seemingly surprised to see Helga there. "Ms. Regan," he said with a hearty handshake, "you're early." He looked at his watch, "Actually, a day plus almost two hours, early."

Helga smiled sheepishly, "Oh, my," she said, "I thought it was today at 10:15, I am so sorry." She stood up. "I'll leave and come back tomorrow."

"Nothing of the sort," he said. "Just allow me a few minutes to complete what I have been working on and we will get together." Turning to the receptionist he said, "Sally, have you offered Ms. Regan coffee?"

Helga broke in, "She has and I am fine, Mr. Politeri. I take pride in being low maintenance."

"In that case," he laughed, "you are quite unique, at least among the people surrounding me of late – most people in my life are extremely high maintenance. I seem to attract high maintenance people."

"I'll be fine," she said.

"Great," he continued, "just give me a few minutes and I will be with you. In the meantime, if you need anything just ask. Take good care of our low maintenance guest, Sally."

Politeri went into his office, closed the door then quickly reached for his phone and dialed his chief of security. "What the hell is that woman doing here?" he screamed.

"Excuse me, sir."

"That damned Regan woman is sitting outside of my office this very minute. What the hell is she doing here?"

"She must be here to pick up the cash and tickets for tomorrow night's trip to New York, sir. Would you like me to come up and handle it with her?"

"No, no. Like everything else in my life I will handle it. I just cannot believe the incompetence surrounding me." He slammed the phone down.

Still holding the receiver to his ear, Maxwell Trella, chief of security for Fusion Pharmaceuticals, said to himself, "Damn it to hell, I'm really in for it now."

Politeri walked back to the door, quickly replaced his anger with a broad smile, and stepped into the waiting area. He took her hand in both of his and ushered Helga Regan into his office. "Good morning, again, Ms. Regan. Please sit there," he said directing her to a soft white upholstered sitting chair. "It is the most comfortable seat in the building."

He walked around to his massive desk and settled into his own chair. "Now, please tell me how I can be of assistance."

Don't screw this up, she thought to herself as she settled into the chair, *please God, don't let me screw this up.* "Mr. Politeri," she began.

"Please, dear lady, call me Joe."

"Joe," she said, sheepishly, "I am having second thoughts about this trip to New York."

"Oh," he said, seeming shocked by her comment. "Why is that?"

"I am not sure that I am doing the right thing."

"Let's talk about it," he said, reassuringly.

Just then his chief of security knocked on the door and began to step inside.

Politeri looked up. "Yes Maxwell?"

"Would you like me to sit in, Mr. Politeri?"

"No, Max, that won't be necessary. Ms. Regan and I are doing quite nicely, thank you."

Trella quickly stepped back into the outer lobby and closed the door. *Oh yes,* he thought to himself, *I'm really in for it now.*

Politeri stood up and walked around the desk. He picked up a side chair and placed it next to Regan's and sat down. He reached for her hand and held it gently between both of his hands and said, "Please, Helga." He paused. "May I call you Helga?"

"Yes," she sputtered, "of course you can call me Helga."

"Good," he said, hesitantly, "very good. Now, tell me your concerns."

"I think I should try the legal approach first; to serve that antique store owner with some sort of lawyer prepared papers to get him to return my dear brother's belongings to its rightful place, here to me. After all, I am poor Mark's only living relative."

Trying to fight his initial instinct to yell at the top of his lungs that if she had not taken so long to file her papers with the local court the antique store dealer would not have been involved in the first place, he said, "But of course, dear lady, you must know that this dealer is now the lawful owner of your brother's belongings. According to the law, and we must respect the law, he did buy it and currently owns it all, fair and square. We have no other alternative than to deal with *him* now."

"But why must I go there to do this?" She asked.

"Because, as you just said, you *are* your brother's only living relative, who better than you to do this?"

"I'm just so confused."

"What are you confused about?" Annoyance was beginning to enter his voice.

"Why do you want to pay $1,000 for that permit? You know, Mark actually hung the stupid thing in his bathroom for God's sake."

"As I told you when we first spoke, I initially offered to buy that permit from the original owner, before his little bar went out of business. It had sentimental value for me and my family. I would have been happy to offer the bar owner $1,000, cash for it. Unfortunately, he died before he could sell it to me and his heirs, knowing nothing about my generous offer, subsequently allowed it to be sold to your brother for just $5.00. Clearly, if the executor of the bar owner's estate had known about my generous offer they would not have let it go for just $5.00. We did not know that your brother purchased it until much later. Then when you contacted us to say that you were looking for a local pharmaceutical company to help you retrieve your sainted mother's research papers, and realized that all of our interests were connected, we were more than happy to help you."

Politeri left out a few little details – the bar owner actually died from complications *after* Politeri's henchmen beat him so mercilessly that he bled to death internally. That was when the bar was liquidated and the item that Politeri wanted so badly surfaced.

"But why would you pay all of my expenses to New York and give me $1,000 cash just to buy the same document Mark was able to buy for just $5.00? It just doesn't make sense."

"Ms. Regan, I am a very wealthy man. It may be hard for you to understand but for me, $1,000 and the few additional dollars in traveling money is just a rounding error. It is worth that and more to me to be reunited with something from my family's past. I explained that my mother's family owned the vanilla making company that was first awarded this permit so many years ago. It has very personal ties to my memory of her."

He moved a bit closer. "When you added the element of possible breakthrough medical research it changed my interest from a purely personal interest to a sound business interest. You *do* believe that we will acquire information that can lead to a medical breakthrough, don't you?"

"Yes, my mother spent most of her life working on it, and her father before her. I did tell you about his having been awarded a Nobel Prize for his work to find a cure for various diseases, didn't I?"

"Yes, you did. Actually, you have mentioned that to me

each time we have met." He said, slightly sarcastically.

"I am just so proud of my family heritage," she responded.

"And you have good reason to be proud. Why not just take this time to retrieve your brother's possession and while you are at it, see some of the sights of New York. It is such a lovely time to visit New York, anyway. We have put you up at a five star hotel in the heart of the city and you will be accompanied by members of our security staff to insure your safety."

"Do you think I will be in any danger?" She asked.

"No, of course not; did I say safety? I meant to say to ensure your comfort; comfort, not safety, yes, comfort!"

He stood up, still holding her hand in both of his, and so she stood up. "I assure you, everything will be fine." He smiled. "Remember now, if you need further instructions or anything else, I will be no further away from you than that telephone. Just call me on my direct line during the auction and, if necessary, I will authorize you to bid even higher."

"Do you really think it will take more than $1,000 to purchase that item?"

"One never knows. That is why I cautioned you to raise your bid very slowly. This auctioneer, like any professional auctioneer, will try to bump up the bidding in big increments. You must hold back in order to keep others from moving the final price higher than it needs to be. Meanwhile, you will be accompanied by others on our team to help you."

They were standing by the door, "Please fear not, Ms. Regan. The best is yet to come. If your sainted mother's research is as good as you think, you are about to become a very wealthy woman."

He opened the door and walked her to the lobby elevator. As the elevator door opened he gave her hand a final shake and eased her into the elevator, stepped halfway in and pressed the button to the lobby.

As he walked back to his office and past the receptionist, he said, "Get that loser Trella up here immediately."

Chapter 29
Thursday, May 2, 1996 –
Dearborn, Michigan – 11:14 A.M.

Within minutes Maxwell Trella knocked on Politeri's office door and without waiting for a response, stepped inside. He reached for one of the side chairs.

"Hold up," Politeri yelled, "don't get too comfortable. All I want to know is why I shouldn't get rid of you this very second for what just happened? I thought you were supposed to make absolutely certain that the Regan woman was all set for the Sunday grab of that prohibition permit."

"But she is, Mr. Politeri," Trella said, clearly frightened by the man behind the desk.

"Then what the hell was she doing here?"

"I will look into it, sir."

"Now listen to me, Max, and listen good. If anything - and I mean anything - goes wrong on Sunday you will be one sorry little man; one *very* sorry little man. Do you get my drift?"

"Yes, yes, I understand."

"Have you arranged for that other loser... the private investigator... to bid against her?"

"Yes sir. We turned over $100,000 in hundred dollar bills to him yesterday."

"And you made sure he knows better than to fly to Brazil with my $100,000 in hundred dollar bills?"

"Oh yes, sir. He will not do that; and as an added precaution, he is under twenty-four-hour watch by our guys. If he even thinks about taking a penny of our money..."

"MY MONEY!" Politeri interrupted. "Not *our* money, not the U.S. Treasury's money, not *God's* money, not anyone else's money, but *my moneeeeeeeeeey!*"

"Of course, sir, Mr. Politeri, your money," Trella said, now sweating profusely. "If he even thinks about taking a penny of *your* money and running anywhere with it, we will know about it instantly and will be all over him like white on snow."

"Just make sure he doesn't. I want to make absolutely certain that one way or another we lock this thing up on Sunday. I want that stupid wooden frame off of the streets and in my hands. Do you understand me?"

"Oh, yes sir, clearly off the streets... off the streets. Yes sir, I understand crystal clearly."

"Good," Politeri said, beginning to calm down.

"You can just consider it done sir," Trella said nervously.

"And you are also all set to make sure our guys grab the money back from whoever is running the auction the minute either that stupid private detective or that even stupider old lady wins the bid? I don't want a penny of it winding up in some night deposit vault, right?"

"Absolutely," Trella said. "But I have been wondering, is that old document really worth all of this time and money and trouble, Mr. Politeri? And if you don't mind my asking, Mr. Politeri, why don't we just get someone to break in to that store and pick up the permit now?"

"I do mind, you damned empty head; but I will tell you anyway. *If* we broke in and took that permit we would be putting a bright spotlight on the permit. There has been more than enough of a spotlight already on that permit. We do not want or need anyone asking any questions about it. So we will let it be sold, hopefully, to someone we can control, and then we steal the money back so *the money* becomes the story, not the permit. A hundred thousand dollars is a lot of money. That is all I want to be the focus, a hundred thousand dollars. I want the permit to be so far back in the story that it never makes it to the front of the line."

"But won't anyone ask about what was worth the hundred thousand dollars in the first place? Max asked hesitantly.

"You are so dumb you make dirt look like the Book of Knowledge. Do me a favor, don't second guess me. You will only show how stupid you are. Just do it my way and the permit will quickly fall off of everyone's radar. *Do you understand?*"

"Yes sir. The minute the money changes hands our men will be in position to take the money. Then, in a separate move, they will grab the permit. There will be two very separate moves. I have warned them to make sure there is no connection to the two events; first the money then, later, the permit. No connection will be made. Got it! Don't worry one little bit."

"With you in control, Max, all I can do is worry. You may be my wife's nephew, but I warn you, one more screw up and you are burnt toast. BURNT TOAST! Got it?"

"I definitely got it, sir." The security chief was developing a nervous tick along the right corner of his mouth. "I got it in spades, sir. Yes indeed, burnt toast."

"Now get out of here and do something to earn your keep!" Politeri screamed.

*****

Joseph G. Politeri the CEO, and according to all public documents, the sole owner of Fusion Pharmaceuticals, took a great deal of pride describing himself as a self-made billionaire. In fact that was the tag line of his 645-page ghostwritten biography, *Only the Best – The Life of a $elf Made Billionaire*. However, the full story of his early beginnings would have made a much more interesting read.

*****

He was born Giuseppe Politeri on July 4, 1934. He was the first son born to Mario and Rosalie Politeri. Mario was the head of the local plumber's union and Rosalie, a housewife. They named their son after Joseph G. Zerilli, the mother's brother. Zerilli was the point person for Detroit's bootlegging activities during prohibition and created dozens of small shell companies, each of which applied for and received government approved permits to produce alcohol for religious or medical or food manufacturing uses. Most of these so-called businesses existed solely for acquiring these permits, turning all of the alcohol they could produce into pre-prohibition quality booze. He later moved up to the top position in the Detroit crime family from the 1930's until his death, *believed to be* of natural causes, in 1977.

With Zerilli's help, influence, *and* protection, young Politeri turned what had been a small, generic drug manufacturing company into a multinational manufacturer and distributor of second tier prescription drugs and hospital supplies. From time to time, the company was also used to market stolen goods and launder money from the mob boss's many other holdings.

After Zerilli died, Carmine DeStefano of the New York Gambino crime family, and a distant cousin of Zerilli became Politeri's new 'sponsor.'

`Politeri's security chief left the office, breathing heavily and he sat down on one of the reception area chairs, gasping for air. The receptionist rushed over to him. "Mr. Trella", she gushed, "are you all right? Would you like some water?"

He shook his head from side to side. "No... thank you... I'll be all right... I'll be all right."

*****

As soon as he was alone, Politeri reached for a cigar, lit it, and sat down behind his desk. He pressed the intercom button and as soon as the receptionist picked up he said, "No calls, no disturbances, no interruptions, you got it?"

"Yes, Mr. Politeri, of course sir."

He sat with his face cradled in his hands; then he threw the lit cigar across the room. "Damn it! I am surrounded by idiots and they are going to get me killed!"

He was getting up from his chair to look for the lit cigar when the intercom buzzed.

He turned back and punched the button with such force that everything on the desk shook. "What the hell don't you understand about no disturbances?" He screamed into the air.

Ignoring his words the receptionist calmly said, "Mr. DeStefano would like a few minutes of your time, sir."

His faced flushed. "Put him through," he said meekly, dropping back into his chair.

"He isn't on the phone, Mr. Politeri, he is standing in front of me and would like to see you."

Politeri stood up so quickly his chair almost fell completely backwards. He stumbled towards the door as it swung open and Carmine DeStefano stormed in, followed by two tall young men close behind.

"What's this crap about having to be announced?" DeStefano yelled, "I changed your diapers, you dumb shit."

"I'm so sorry," Politeri sputtered.

"Close the door and sit over there," DeStefano barked at the two men behind him.

"What brings you here from New York?" Politeri mumbled.

"A plane brought me here you fool. Now, tell me what you are doing to get that wooden framed permit for me."

Politeri grabbed a handful of tissues from the box on his credenza and began mopping his face, leaving bits of tissue paper all over his face.

"It is all taken care of", he said. "By this time next week it will be in your hands. I guarantee it."

"You can't guarantee that Friday follows Thursday, but I *can* guarantee that you won't if you screw this up any more than you already have. Do you understand me?" DeStefano growled. "When you told me about some piece of crap prohibition permit and your hair-brained scheme to get it off the streets I told you it was a complete waste of time. Who cares what happened sixty-seventy years ago, during Prohibition? All the players are long dead and buried anyway. But when you told me that there was also some link between that frame and a possible cure for cancer you got my attention – big time! And I warned you then not to over think this. I hoped you would know better than to try some smoke and mirror scheme of yours... to respond in your usual amateur hour way... to screw this up as you have everything else that you have ever touched in this worthless life of yours. My immediate next instinct was to just take over and get it myself, but *you* begged me... 'let me show you that I can be a leader'", DeStefano mocked, "that was what you said, *wasn't it?*"

"Yes", Politeri responded, meekly, but..."

"But nothing", DeStefano screamed, now inches away from Politeri, poking his finger deeply into Politeri's chest as he spoke, "you have only been able to delay getting it to me. Isn't *that* right?"

"There were complications..." Politeri said, softly.

"You are a complication!" DeStefano said, with disgust, "Now, tell me again how you plan to accomplish this?" DeStefano growled.

"I have a main plan and a backup plan," Politeri said nervously.

"Oh my God", DeStefano yelled, "he has a plan *and* a back-up plan! We talked about this, it isn't brain surgery, I told you *not* to over think this. It is going up for auction in that two by nothing antique store. The guy auctioning it off has to be thinking that it is near worthless – even the glass in the frame is cracked from what I understand, for God's sake. He'll probably put it up for just a few dollars – just pay the opening bid and take it home. What kind of *back-up* plan do you need for that?"

"Well", Politeri began, "I decided to send the science teacher's sister there to bid on it..."

"Why?" DeStefano interrupted.

"Well, she was the teacher's only relative, so she is the rightful owner of ...."

"Just what I feared, you found a way to turn the simplest of a thing into an overly complicated plot for a dime store novel," DeStefano yelled. "Why didn't you just do what I told you to do?" DeStefano walked over to a side chair and plopped down into it, shaking his head in disbelief. "What if she messes it all up?"

"That's the beauty of my backup plan," Politeri said.

DeStefano put his hands up, leaned back and thought for a while. All that could be heard was the ticking of the huge clock by the door. Finally, DeStefano took a series of deep breaths and said, "You have so overcomplicated this... I can't believe how much mush must be stuffed in that so-called head of yours."

"It's a good one/two punch plan," Politeri broke in, trying desperately to calm his guest down. "I hired a private detective to bid against the sister. One way or another, we will walk away with the frame."

"You turned a teeny tiny molehill into an entire mountain range," DeStefano sputtered, "I don't care that you are Zerilli's godson. You are going to regret the day you were born if that frame slips through your fingers."

DeStefano put his hands up again and then motioned for one of the two men to come closer to him. He leaned into the man's ear, cupping his mouth with his hand; in a barely audible whisper he said, "Freddie, I want you to get in touch with Howard Hill the minute we get out of here, ask him, don't demand, ask him nicely, if he can be waiting at the gate in the airport when we land." The man nodded his head and then walked back to his original place and sat down.

"You don't understand", Politeri said softly.

"I don't understand?" DeStefano screamed back, "I don't

understand?" DeStefano turned towards the men who had accompanied him into the room. "He thinks that I don't understand", he screamed. "Can you believe your ears?"

"I have arranged to grab any money back that is used to buy the frame so that we will have our cake and eat it too, so to speak." Politeri said proudly.

"Imbecile," DeStefano shouted. "The obvious piece of crap will sell for a few pennies – a couple bucks at the very most, let them keep the damn dollar or two... or twenty... or who cares how much? I don't want anyone to begin to ask questions about this. Don't you understand?"

"Well, I thought..."

"No, you never think! That is the problem, you *never ever* think! Well, I am telling you straight out – you are to stop this *plan* of yours now. Did you hear me? NOW! I am taking it over and do not want you screwing it up any more than you already have."

"But Carmine..." Politeri began.

"Don't even think about going against my wishes on this. Continue with this *plan* of yours and you're a dead man."

DeStefano stood up, marched towards the door, stopped with his hand tightly clutching the door knob. He turned back to glare at Politeri, "Final warning, you are now out of this, *period*. Got it?"

"But, Carmine..." Politeri sputtered.

"This is not just business for me, Joseph", DeStefano yelled, "this is very, very personal for me. Go against my wishes on this and you better pray that I die in my sleep because if I don't die first, I will use my last breath to make your life a living hell, do you understand me, a living hell!"

DeStefano then swung the door open, mumbling under his breath, "Damn gutless wonder." He then marched out, followed quickly by the two tall men.

*****

Politeri was visibly shaken. He reached into his bottom right desk drawer and pulled out a bottle of Johnnie Walker and a tall water glass. He emptied the bottle into the glass, then reached into the drawer again for a sealed bottle. He broke the seal and filled the rest of the glass, drinking it down in a series of large gulps. A small amount of scotch was dripping from the side of his mouth so he wiped it away on his sleeve and then filled the glass again. "If my Godfather was alive today you would never have talked to me like that." He took a long swallow from the glass, followed by another, then another. He filled the glass again. "Sure it's personal for you... a cancer cure would be worth billions..." He tossed his head back and drank half a glass full, "maybe trillions.' He finished the rest of the scotch in the glass and then refilled the glass, "Who do *you* think you are talking to?" he said towards the door. "No 'Mustachio Pete' is gonna come in here, to my space, and tell me what to do and what not to do." One more swallow. "Well, old man... I'll - show - you who is a gutless wonder. You will eat your words when I hand you that frame next week."

*****

`When they were all in the elevator DeStefano moved closer to Freddie and whispered, "Do it nicely, with respect, just make sure that Howard Hill is standing at the gate when we land, got it?"

"Yes, Mr. DeStefano, he will be there," the tall man responded with a broad smile.

*****

Their plane landed a few minutes ahead of schedule. DeStefano and his two guards were the only ones in the first class section of the plane and so they were the first ones to walk into the arrival gate area. Howard Hill was leaning against his cane just outside of the gate. DeStefano walked over to Hill and gently shook Hill's hand.

"Do you know who I am?" DeStefano asked.

"Yes sir," Hill answered respectfully.

Freddie led the two men to the airport club. As soon as they were inside Freddie asked to speak with the manager. They seemed to be having a heated conversation when Freddie leaned closer and whispered something into the club manager's ear. The club manager flushed, then walked over to the reception desk and said something to the receptionist. She seemed startled, but nodded affirmatively to her manager and then circulated throughout the club, informing the patrons and club workers that they had to close the room for about an hour, asking them all to leave the club as quickly and orderly as possible. There were a few outraged responses but within minutes the only ones in the club were DeStefano and Hill. Freddie leaned against the door on the airport side to ensure that no one would interrupt the two men inside.

They sat stiffly at a small table. DeStefano touched Hill's arm gently. "I need a personal favor, Howard."

Hill gently pulled his arm away, cleared his throat, and then said, "Mr. DeStefano, you must know that I refused to partner with your guys when Archie first asked. I am not judging what you do or how you do it... I just prefer..."

DeStefano interrupted him, "What I am going to ask you to do has nothing to do with business – not my business... not your business. It is a purely personal request."

Hill looked deeply into DeStefano's eyes. "Personal?"

"I understand that you regularly visit an antique store at Rodney and Lee, in Williamsburg, Brooklyn."

"I do," Hill said, seeming to be confused by the direction of the conversation so far. "Is that one of your businesses, Mr. DeStefano?"

"No", DeStefano laughed. "It isn't one of my businesses."

"Maybe I should just let you tell me what you want to tell me." Hill said.

"They have an auction every Sunday and I understand you attend most Sundays. At this Sunday's auction they will be putting this up for sale." He showed Hill a photo of the framed document. "I want you to buy it for me."

"Now, Mr. DeStefano, I ain't never worked for you before, it is a little late to begin…"

DeStefano held up his hand, "I give you my word of honor, Howard; there is nothing illegal about the item in this picture or about my request. I have my reasons for wanting to own this item and I am merely asking you to make the purchase for me. It will probably cost just a few dollars and I will gladly reimburse you for anything you pay for it. Will you do this simple request for me?"

"It is legal and totally above board?" Hill asked.

"I give you my word of honor, Howard."

"Your word is good enough for me, Mr. DeStefano. Yes, I will do this for you."

"In exchange…" DeStefano started to say, but this time, Hill put up his hand, "No, 'in exchange' needed." Hill said, "I will do this without any need for you to respond in kind, Mr. DeStefano."

DeStefano stood up, took Hill's hand in both of his and smiled. "Thank you, Howard. I will not forget this act of kindness you have agreed to do for me today."

Chapter 30
Sunday, May 12, 1996 –
C. B. Forster's Public Warehouse,
Coney Island, New York – 6:32 P.M.

Now rested and very well fed, James' small army of temporary workers began the task of digging through the massive contents of Mark Regan's estate.

A primary inspection group was formed to look at each piece of furniture. Sol was put in charge of this group. They set up a simple assembly line. Drawers were removed and individually inspected; two separate groups of inspectors rechecked each other's work; portable x-ray machines were used to insure that nothing was hidden or secretly imbedded into any of the pieces.

Albert went to Elizabeth and said that although he agreed that their major focus needed to be matching the key with a lock, he thought he could accomplish at least one other goal at the same time. He asked her to head up a very small team, maybe with just 2 or 3 of the workers, to separate out a few items that could be turned quickly into cash. She said that he should at least pass that by James and he quickly agreed. James quietly considered the request and then nodded approval.

Elizabeth began by pointing out smaller items with possible value; furnishings, lamps, collectibles, etc.; each item was carefully inspected, x-rayed to make certain that they could not add anything to the primary search for a lock mated to the key, then they were placed in a separate staging area. Elizabeth gave each piece an initial recommended rating of save, sell, or dump.

Albert moved between both groups, periodically tagging

specific pieces with colored bands; yellow for items to be donated to charity for a simple tax deduction; red for questionable items needing further research; green for those items ready for immediate resale or wholesale as is, to other dealers for quick revenue.

It was understood that nothing would leave the building until they actually found whatever they were looking for – and frustrating as it was, they still did not know exactly what that was.

James called in several medical researchers that he knew and had worked with before. They were asked to move from group to group, concentrating on and personally inspecting each item from the cartons marked as having come from the lab Regan set up in his basement. Their first task was to skim through each book and document – and there were literally hundreds of books and thousands of loose documents – for anything that remotely resembled meaningful scientific findings. They were told that somewhere in the collection could be important research – they just did not know what form it would be in or what kind of research it documented.

Everyone was shown the key and asked to keep it in mind because *somewhere* in this lot there *could* be something with a lock that would be the mate for the key currently hanging around James's neck.

They worked into the night. By 2:00 A.M., James suggested that a rolling third of the workforce try to sleep for at least an hour or two at a time; then work for an hour or two; then rest for an hour or two. They were instructed to take breaks whenever they felt the need so that fatigue would not result in missing whatever they were hoping to find.

"Take the time necessary to do it right – the first time. I don't want us having to go over the same ground a second time," James said.

Chapter 31
Monday, May 13, 1996 –
C. B. Forster's Public Warehouse,
Coney Island, New York – 7:17 A.M.

One of the medical researchers gave out a loud hoot and ran over to James.

"Will, look here," he yelled, "take a look at this." He handed James a leather bound bible. James had a puzzled look on his face.

"Open it up", the researcher said.

James flipped the cover open, "Yeh?" He said with a puzzled look on his face.

The researcher gently moved a batch of pages to the side and in the center was a small metal box wedged inside with a flat latch across the upper right hand corner.

James gently put the book - in which the metal box was imbedded - on a flat surface. He removed the key from around his neck and placed it into the lock on the latch, gently twisted the key, first from right to left then left to right. It was clear that the key fit the lock even though the latch did not swing open. He was afraid to force it so he called Schless and Albert over.

"What do you think?" He asked. "The key goes in and may well be the right key for this lock but the last thing I want to do is either break the key or jam the lock."

"Do you think we could force the box open," Albert asked.

Several of the researchers came over. One asked to be able to take a closer look at the box.

"Have you ever seen anything like it?" James asked.

"Actually," one of the older researchers said, "it is something they used in European hospital labs a century or so ago. If I remember correctly, it was made to hold a vacuum and was used for highly perishable and uniquely valuable specimens before refrigeration came into more general use."

"I don't know about forcing it." Schless cautioned. "Without knowing for sure what might be inside, I think we must take every precaution."

Gradually, people were beginning to circle around. "Hey," one said, "why not use the x-ray machine on it."

"I think these were made of lead," the older researcher said pointing to the box.

"Well, the only way to find out would be to get the x-ray machine over here and set it up by the box." Albert said.

When the machine was set up, the operator started to scan the box. "Well, it isn't lead. I get a clear image. In fact, I am getting six distinctly clear images."

"What does it look like?" One of the other researchers asked.

"It looks like there are six oblong masses inside," the machine operator said.

"Can you identify the masses?" James asked.

"If I didn't know better I would say they are either alive or floating in something."

By now all work in the area had come to a halt and most of the workers were looking on.

"We can take an actual photo of the x-ray image?" One of the researchers said.

"Okay, do it," James said.

Another researcher walked over from the other end of the building holding a batch of yellowed papers. "I think I have something here but I am not sure."

"What is it?" James asked.

"These look like standard lab notes but they are in some foreign language. I can't make it out."

"Elizabeth," Albert called out, "you said you speak other languages, can you make any sense of this?"

Elizabeth walked over, took a quick glance at the top page and smiled, "That's old German," she said with a broad smile.

"Can you read it?" Albert asked.

Elizabeth gently picked up the papers and began sounding out some of the words. "They seem to be documenting the gradual shrinking of a... *cancer cell*?" She studied it a bit more then said, "Yes, that's it, cancer cell... the shrinking of a cancer cell."

"Are you sure?" One of the researchers asked, excitedly.

Another of the researchers asked to be able to inspect the pages. "These diagrams look like basic cell formations." He turned to Elizabeth and asked, almost in a hush, "Are you sure it says '*gradual shrinking*?' Those exact words?"

Elizabeth pointed to a sentence as she read it aloud, "It says, '*Die betroffenen Zellen fingen am 4. Tage an, sich zusammenzuschrumpfen.*' It means, the cells began to shrink by the fourth day." She read from a section several paragraphs down on the same page, "*Es gelang uns, heute morgen Zusatzversuche zu bringen, das Ergebnis zu wiederholen: die Zellen schrumpften sich wieder zusammen, und zwar fast vor den Augen* which means, 'we were able to duplicate the results of this morning's trials and again, the cells began to shrink, almost in front of our eyes.'"

"Specifically, where were these papers found?" Schless asked.

"No two were in the same specific location. It is almost as if they were placed, a page at a time at random," the researcher said.

"How will we be able to put them in any meaningful order?" Albert asked.

"Well, they are each date and time stamped so putting them in order should be kind of easy. The difficult part will be determining if we have all of the pages. The challenge is to try to find a way to know if anything is missing," one of the medical researchers said. "In my lab, we never continue a paragraph from page to page; each page begins with a new thought. If this lab worked within that system then we would not have the benefit of continuing sentences for us to link page to page. But even then, unless we find a reference to how many pages were created we will have no way of knowing for certain if one or more of the pages are still out there or a clear understanding as to the specific importance to apply to what might be missing."

"Is there at least a way to know if we have all that might be in this trailer load?" Schless asked.

"Let's put more people on the document checking team now that we know what the paper stock looks like," James said.

"Just be careful," the researcher warned, "these are very old documents – some dated almost sixty years ago – I brought some plastic document sleeves with me, let's at least put the ones we have found in a protective sleeve to avoid further wear and tear."

"What do you want to do about this box?" James asked Albert, pointing to the metal box.

"Put the x-ray wand up against the lock," Albert said.

The researcher did as Albert requested. "What do you see?" Albert asked the person at the machine's controls.

"There is something blocking the keyhole. I can't be sure, but it may just be rust."

"Anyone got a little oil?" someone yelled.

"Can you use salad oil from the food cart?" A woman yelled back.

The researchers looked at each other and one finally said, "It really can't hurt."

"Is there any chance it is rigged to explode?" one man asked.

"I don't see a detonator," the person at the controls said.

"Can you have a bomb without a detonator?" Another asked.

One of the researchers said, The quick answer is no, you cannot have a bomb without a detonator. But, you can have an explosion without it being a bomb. You need something to ignite... you need a power source... you need an initiator. Short answer is that you could have an explosion merely by mixing the right combination of chemicals."

"You make the decision, James," Albert said.

"Hey, let's go for it," one man said.

"Okay," another worker said. "Nothing ventured, nothing gained."

"Pretty cavalier in a building full of people, don't you think?" One of the workers said.

"Hey," the second worker answered back, "You don't see me running for the door, do you?"

"I can't say there is no risk but I have a fairly good view of the contents and I think the risk is small if any at all." The man at the controls of the x-ray machine said.

All eyes were on the metal box as one of the researchers carefully rubbed the key with salad oil and gently placed it back in the lock. He tenderly twisted it back and forth a few times. Finally, the latch swung open with a loud click. A thunderous hissing sound came from the box. Those closest to the box jumped back.

A stale, musty odor seemed to fill the immediate area.

"Could it be a dangerous gas?" one man asked.

"If so, I would already be dead, I am standing the closest to the box – or at least I and anyone near me would be feeling the effects, and I feel fine – so far," the x-ray machine operator said.

After a few minutes the researcher gently lifted the top of the box and looked inside.

Chapter 32
Monday, May 13, 1996 –
Southfield, Michigan – 7:35 A.M.

Helga Regan sat at her kitchen table nursing her fifth beer of the morning. She found the sound of the rain tapping on her windows to be almost deafening as the events of the past few weeks paraded through her mind. "No luck!" she softly moaned to her near empty glass. "No luck!"

She had fought her way through three loveless marriages and three angry divorces in her seventy-three years of existence. Money flowed in and out of her grasp at various times from numerous sources but on this dingy, rainy Monday morning in May she had less than ten dollars in her checking account and dozens of unpaid bills stacked up on the entry table of her small, studio apartment in the once grand Providence Tower Apartment building, walking distance from the equally once proud Northland Shopping Mall in Southfield, Michigan.

When her father died her share of his generous savings bought her a ritzy condo, a shopping spree that lasted for weeks, and her second husband. "What *was* his name", she now thought aloud. But, when the money was gone so was 'Mr. Number Two'.

Then there was 'Earl". She picked him up – or did he pick her up? She couldn't quite remember which. Well, they met at a Sanders restaurant lunch counter at Twelve and Evergreen. Boy, those hot fudge sundaes were good. Earl was a real charmer. He introduced her to endless parties and drinking and that glorious white powder that allowed her to get happy and forget her troubles... she broke into song – *"come on, get happy... get ready for the judgment day!"* "not as good as Judy Garland, but not so bad, I've definitely heard worse." She said to the glass.

So what now, she wondered. She reached for another beer. "You know," she said, now talking to the bottle, "that fat tub of lard Politeri wouldn't be ignoring my calls if Earl were still around. Earl would rip out Politeri's black Italian heart and feed it back to him fried in just a little bit of virgin olive oil." She started to laugh, then cry, then laugh again. "Earl fried just about everything in virgin olive oil... the big sap."

What now, she thought, *we could have been on easy street but nooooooo, not straight as an arrow Mark. Not goodie two shoes Mark. I damn you to hell Markus Obereder. You are comfortably in a cushy coffin and I am left here, all alone, having to face life. You rotten bastard, come back here and fight like a man.*

She rested her head on her outstretched arms and soon dozed off. The distant sound of a ringing telephone woke her. She quickly got up and staggered to grab the wall phone, before she could say a word the voice on the other end said, "Ms. Regan?"

"Yeh, this is Helga Regan." Try as she did to sound coherent, she was still half asleep and feeling the hurt of a weekend long hangover.

"Ms Regan, this is Sally at Mr. Politeri's office. He wondered if it would be convenient for you to meet with him at four this afternoon."

She stood straight up and stared into the receiver. "Let me check my calendar."

"If that doesn't work," the receptionist quickly broke in, "then possibly tomorrow..."

"No, it will work." Helga said, now thinking, that her reaction was all wrong, it was far too quick and needy a response. It is a mistake like this that can sink this last chance at survival, and she knew it.

"Wonderful," the cheery voice said, "We'll see you at four, I'll let Mr. Politeri know. Have a great day!" The line went dead.

Helga continued to hold on to the receiver until a loud humming noise brought her back to the moment.

So now he wants to see me, she thought, "Meeeeeeeeeeeee", she screamed, as a wide grin formed. "He wants to see meeeeeeeeeee; that wonderful, wonderful man is finally ready to see meeeeeee. Well I will be ready for yoooooooooooooo, this time, Mr. big Italian billionaire. I will definitely be ready for you; you can bet your bottom dollar on that!"

Chapter 33
Monday, May 13, 1996 –
Dearborn, Michigan – 4:54 P.M.

Helga Regan looked out of the giant picture window. *Not much of a view*, she thought, but she really wasn't here for the view, now was she?

The receptionist walked over to her, "I am so sorry, Ms. Regan," she purred, "Mr. Politeri must have been caught up in traffic. We have a call into his club. I am certain he will be here soon."

"No problem," Helga said, with a smile, "I am enjoying the view."

Almost an hour later the elevator opened and Politeri walked into the lobby alongside three other men. He saw her, looked at his watch, and then said, "I am so very sorry for your having to wait, Ms. Regan. Please, come right in." He said a quick goodbye to the men, shook hands, promising to get back to them in a few days, then led Helga into his office. He turned to the receptionist, "Not to be disturbed, Sally. Got it?"

"I got it, Mr. Politeri," she quickly responded, with a broad smile.

He led Helga to a side chair then pulled one up next to her and sat down.

"Would you like some coffee?" he asked.

"No, thank you. I am fine."

"Then, let me get right down to it. I wanted to speak with you because we seem to have run into a slight problem with *our friend* in New York."

"Our *friend?*" she repeated.

"I am referring to the antique dealer who walked away with your brother's belongings... *your rightful* belongings."

"What kind of a problem?" she asked.

"He seems to have disappeared. The store has been locked up tighter than a drum since late Friday and no one seems to know where he is or when he might return."

"Well, I certainly do not know where he is," she said, defensively.

"Of course not," he said, "How could you?"

"So," she asked haltingly, "How does this affect our understanding?"

"Our understanding... what understanding?" he asked.

"Well... I just thought..."

"Ms. Regan. If we cannot use your special connection to your brother and his ownership of the items moved to New York, then... well... there is no relationship between you and us."

"So why did you ask me to come here today?" she said, angrily.

"I hired a New York based private detective to look into this matter and it seems the trailer that contained your brother's belongings was mysteriously moved sometime during the weekend so your brother's belongings... *your* rightful belongings, are all now missing."

"I don't understand," she said.

"I was hoping I could impose upon you, one more time, to get personally involved in this matter..."

"What could I possibly do now, especially given the fact that this dealer seems to be nowhere to be found?"

"That's just it. Because he seems to have absconded with your brother's precious belongings, *your* lasting memories of your dear brother's existence, it can *only* be you," he said, strongly emphasizing each word, "who has the strongest reason to bring criminal charges against this antique dealer."

"You're kidding," she said in amazement.

"I don't *kid* Ms. Regan."

"But you said it yourself," she said, "he purchased Mark's stuff free and clear. It is over, gone; probably all of Mark's belongings have already been sold off or thrown to the four winds by now."

"I don't think so. First of all, a trailer load of anything doesn't just *go poof* overnight."

"It *went poof* overnight to that dealer," she said, mockingly.

"Don't be flippant with me, I don't like it and will not allow it."

"Look," she said, clearly annoyed, "I have no interest in bringing a claim against anyone, especially someone halfway across the country in New York."

"I believe," he began speaking again, dismissing her last comment with a wave of his hand, "that the possibility that there might have been some sort of cancer research or even breakthrough cure hidden in those belongings is sparking all of this mayhem."

"How can you possibly say that?" She asked. "I have only told you... who did you tell?"

"I have not told a living soul but maybe... somehow... that antique dealer found out and now he has grabbed the shipment and has done 'who knows what' with it."

"What about your family's precious permit?" she asked.

"You are being flippant again. Don't! Now, you are going to fly to New York tonight and be available for whatever use you might be to our people there."

"I will do no such thing! I can't just pick up and fly off because you *think* I might be useful."

"Can't?"

"Won't!"

"Don't ever use the word *won't* around me, little lady. You *will* do whatever I ask, whenever I ask, or else."

Or else, what?" she shot back.

He smiled broadly, "You do not want to know, '*or else what*'. Trust me on that! You will be on a plane this evening, I already arranged it."

"You arranged it?" She screamed. "You arranged it?"

"I did."

"How dare you arrange for anything involving me without first asking me? And what will I be doing in New York?" she asked.

"You will be doing whatever I tell you to do."

"Excuse me?"

"Come on, little lady, you heard me the first time."

"And if I refuse?"

"Believe me, that is *not* an option."

She stood up, "I always have options, and if you call me 'little lady' one more time I will exercise one of those options to kick you hard enough to turn you into a soprano for life."

He grabbed her wrist and forced her back into the chair.

"Do not make me turn your life into more of a disaster than it already seems to be."

"Excuse me?" she yelled.

"You need me, *little lady*, your life is circling the drain, as we speak. *I* may be your last chance at a continued existence."

"That's outrageous; I don't need you or anyone else."

"Don't waste my time. You and I both know that there is a negative balance right now in your checking account," he whispered.

"That is just not true!" she said, with certainty. "I have a *plus balance*- maybe not a huge plus balance, but a plus balance nonetheless."

"Maybe that was true before the bank deducted their $15.00 monthly service fee at 9:00 A.M. this morning, but as of 9:00 A.M. this morning, your checking account has been in the negative to the tune of $6.18!"

She squirmed in her seat.

"Then there is the little matter about your car," he continued.

"What about my car," she said – a bit less arrogantly.

"It was repossessed over the weekend because you were four payments in arrears."

"Now, that is total horseshit! It happens to be in the parking lot of this building this very moment."

"That might be true but I can assure you it was towed away from its parking space by your building Friday night. I paid the towing fee along with the last four and the next two auto payments and had it towed back to your building yesterday afternoon."

She sat back, staring at him in disbelief. Her car *was* parked in someone else's space this morning but she dismissed it as probably being one more side effect of her drinking binge.

"Now let us talk about your *way* past due rent... two months of unpaid credit card bills... back balances due for your utilities... not to mention the threatened cut off of your telephone. I would say that you need this deal of ours because there is no other sign of life waiting for you." He glared back at her, "That *is* the truth, now isn't it... *little lady"* He sat back and glared at her.

She finally broke the silence, "And what if there turns out to be nothing I can do in New York?"

"Then you are in deep doo doo, Ms. Regan."

"Then at the very least tell me the truth about why you want that permit so badly."

"You already know everything you need to know."

She asked a bit hesitantly, "And *if I go to New York as you request,* you will advance me enough to pull myself out of the problems you so tenderly rattled off?"

He laughed again. "You are a real piece of work and I have to admit, you are beginning to grow on me – something like a wart!" He stood up and walked around his desk reaching for a cigar. He lingered a while by the window as he slowly cut off the tip, placed the cigar between his lips, and lit it, slowly puffing the smoke towards the ceiling. He looked out the window, towards the traffic below. Finally, he turned to her and said, "Okay, I'll advance you enough to keep the dogs from your door – *for now*. But as of this minute I don't want there to be any more arguments from you. You work for me... you do as *I* say... if I tell you to jump, you ask how high. Do you *fully* understand?"

She glared up at him.

"I am talking to you, *little laydeee*."

Finally, she looked down at the floor and said, "Okay."

"Okay, *what?*" he yelled.

"Okay, I understand. Can I leave now?"

"Of course you can; after all, you do have to pack for your trip to New York, now don't you?" He said, flashing a broad smile and waving his cigar at her."

"Will I be staying at the same hotel as last time?" she purred.

He stared at her, and then yelled, "I need to warn you that you are pushing the envelope here."

"Was that a yes?" she asked.

"I'll think about it. Now get going before I forget that you *are* a lady."

He watched her slowly walk to the door, and when she opened it he yelled out to her, "Just pack quickly and then get your bony ass on that plane to New York."

She slowly walked through the door without looking back

and closed the door behind her.

Minutes later there was a light tapping on his office door.

"What does she want now?" he grumbled under his breath as Maxwell Trella walked in.

"How did it go?" Trella asked.

"How did you expect it to go? It went great, Max, simply great," he said sarcastically. "Now make sure it *stays* great. By the way, you and I are also going to New York early Sunday morning so that we too can attend the auction."

"If the old lady is going why do we need to go?" Trella asked. "And what if there really is nothing that she or the private eye can do – it is a possibility isn't it?"

"That's not an option. Just make certain they are both in position *just in case* I determine that they are needed. One way or another we better come back with that frame. You let it fall through the cracks once, it better not happen again. Do you understand me, Max, it cannot happen again. Now get out of here and earn your keep."

As Maxwell Trella left the office, Politeri tapped his intercom button and said, "Absolutely no interruptions... no exceptions... got it?"

"Yes, Mr. Politeri, understood."

Politeri slowly opened the bottom right hand drawer of his desk and reached for the Johnnie Walker.

"There can be no chance of a slip-up on this," Politeri said to the bottle. He gave a slight shudder as his mind went back to DeStefano's ultimatum. "There can be no chance of a slip-up," he repeated.

Chapter 34
Monday, May 13, 1996 –
C. B. Forster's Public Warehouse,
Coney Island, New York – 8:19 P.M.

Schless left the building just after 7:00 P.M. and returned about a quarter past eight. He went to James and they huddled for several minutes. James then called everyone together.

"I have some good news and I have some bad news," he began. "The good news is that we will be completely finished by 6:00 A.M., tomorrow morning. The owner of this building has agreed to allow all of you to remain here, in perfect safety, at least for the rest of this week. The nice people who donated the food have agreed to continue serving three hot meals to each of you for the same period of time. All I ask is that you leave no later than 5:00 P.M. on Sunday and make certain that when you leave, the area is as clean and neat as when we first got here."

There was a roar of appreciation from the workers.

James smiled as the workers began hugging each other. "Now for the bad news," he added. "We need to make absolutely certain that we have culled out every possible lab note or reference to the research that took place in Austria, during the 1930s as well as the research done in America by Ilsa Obereder Regan and later by Mark Obereder Regan. We need to be 100% confident that we have captured each and every scrap of paper they might have generated that is still among all of this stuff." He pointed to the piles of still unexamined items. "Any of their notes in English or German or Swahili, for that matter – diagrams, drawings, calculations, formulas... we need it all; we must have that and all of this work completed no later than by 2:00 A.M., this coming morning; shortly after two this morning the trailer will be brought back into this building so that we can reload all of these items back into the trailer, as neatly as before, and then the trailer will be returned to its original footprint in the depot in Coney Island. You all know me. I never issue false fire drills – this timeline is locked and *must* be met. Everyone here has over-delivered so far and I appreciate all that you have done. Now, I need you to work even harder so that we can make this hard deadline."

There was an eerie silence when he finished his remarks. Then, from the rear of the group, someone yelled, "You ain't never let us down Spider, we ain't never gonna let you down."

As the rest of the crew returned to work, Albert and Sol walked over to James. "What was that all about?" Albert asked, talking behind his hand.

"Schless found this stapled to the front door of your store," James said, handing Albert an envelope. The note inside said that a car would be in front of the antique store at 9:00 A.M. sharp to pick him up and bring him to visit with Carmine DeStefano. The note was unsigned. Also in the envelope was a newspaper article in which Carmine DeStefano's mug shot was shown along with a cut out newspaper article with a reporter's claim that DeStefano had been named earlier that day by the Brooklyn District Attorney as the new "Capo de Capo of the Genovese crime family in New York."

"This is getting hairy," Sol said.

"Do they really leave such notes around?" Albert asked in disbelief.

"They do what they want to do," James said.

"How do we know if this is real or just a prank?"

"I would say that you ignore this at your own risk," Schless said.

"Can these people finish in such a short window of time?" Sol asked, pointing to the workers around the building.

"We will see," James responded, "we will see. They are doing the best they can. Hopefully, their best will be enough."

Chapter 35
Tuesday, May 14, 1996 –
Williamsburg, Brooklyn, N Y – 8:42 A.M.

James and Albert stood outside of the antique store, leaning against the still-locked front door.

At precisely 9:00 A.M., a black stretch limousine pulled up to the curb in front of the store. The rear window slid down and a man they recognized from the photo in the article to be Carmine DeStefano, appeared in the window. He pointed to Albert and motioned for him to come closer to the car.

Albert and James walked slowly towards the car.

"Just him," DeStefano said, sternly.

"We are a package," James said softly, "like salt and pepper... both of us or nobody."

The front passenger side door opened and a tall muscular man got out. He removed his sunglasses, slowly folded them, placed them in his breast pocket, and unbuttoned his jacket to show a shoulder holster. He pointed at James and said, "Unless you want to *pepper* the sidewalk with your innards, move away and let Mr. Salt get into the car."

Further down the street, the driver's side door of a bright red Mustang convertible opened. A fashionably dressed short man with a full head of bright red hair got out and started to walk towards them. It was William 'Billy' Aarons, legendary criminal defense attorney.

*****

James pulled no punches late the night before when he contacted Billy at home.

"The client will complain no matter how little you charge plus I can almost guarantee that it will make the mob really angry at you, possibly add a bit of danger to your very existence. They will *not* be happy that you are involving yourself in this and may decide to throw everything, including the kitchen sink at you and us. To make it even *more* interesting, all that you will have to work with is what little I can put together in the next few hours. In short, I need you to make this all go away armed with just some spit, a very little bit of hope and a prayer."

"Whoopee!" Billy responded." "A dream job!"

"No sarcasm, please."

"Hey, you want me to scrap what has already been planned for tomorrow so that I can show up and yell 'surprise' to one of the world's most dangerous men; you have already made it plain that I can't make any money out of this suicide mission; you are arming me with a pea shooter while the other side will have the best and the meanest at its disposal; at least allow the condemned man to serve up some basic sarcasm for his last meal."

*****

Aarons walked directly to the car and smiled at the tall man standing by the passenger door, "Hi Freddie."

"Morning counselor," the man responded.

Carmine stretched his head out of the window and yelled to Aarons, "Hey, shyster, what are you doing on this side of the tracks?"

"Good morning, Carmine. I see you have met my *very good* and *very close* friend, Will James."

"Don't get involved, shyster," Carmine said.

"Excuse us, guys," Aarons said to the rest of the men on the sidewalk as he stepped closer to Carmine's window, leaned down and began speaking, in very hushed tones.

A few minutes later, Carmine moved towards the center of the back seat and invited Aarons into the car. The door closed and as the window was rolled up the driver stepped out of the car.

The two men sat together for several minutes then Aarons opened the door and stepped out. The window rolled down and Carmine extended his hand to the lawyer. "Don't ever show up unannounced again shyster. I don't like surprises."

"Since when don't you like redheads surprising you?" The lawyer teased.

"I don't mind being surprised by cute redheads with long legs, but you don't fit that description and you ain't never gonna be the kind of redhead that I would like to be surprised by. Now go make the world safer for some hippies."

Aarons smiled, threw a kiss at James as he briskly walked back to his car and drove away.

Albert turned to James and began to speak – James put his finger to his lips and under his breath said, "Just walk slowly towards the car and leave the talking to me. Understand?"

Albert nodded nervously.

When the two men were close to the car Carmine pointed to the store – "You gonna invite me in?"

The man still standing by the passenger door leaned down. "But Mr. DeStefano, we aint had a chance to check it out yet."

Carmine smiled. "Now Freddie, do you think these two nice men are going to hurt me?"

DeStefano looked at James, "You ain't going to hurt me, are you Mr. .... what do they call you... *Spider?*"

"You're safe, Mr. DeStefano, I guarantee it," James said, respectfully.

"That's good enough for me. Isn't that good enough for you, Freddie?" Carmine asked, sarcastically.

The tall young man took a long look around – first at the rooftops then the streets below; then nodded and opened the rear door. Carmine DeStefano stepped out of the car and began walking towards the store. He stopped and turned to face James, "Are you coming, Mr. er... ah... *Spider?*" Then he turned to Albert. "You can come too, you little shit."

Chapter 36
Tuesday, May 14, 1996 –
Williamsburg, Brooklyn, NY – 9:21 A.M.

Albert led the two men into the small room set aside for the weekly auctions.

"You wanna go back there and shut off the camera, Mr. Store Owner?" Carmine said to Albert, as he gave James a wink.

Albert began to talk but James stopped him – "It is an automatic system Mr. DeStefano. I don't think he can shut it off without alerting the 911 line it is connected to. I give you my personal word that the tape will be removed and I will personally burn it."

"Your word is good enough for me, Mr. *Spider*."

"Please call me Will."

"Okay, Will, as I said, your word is good enough for me."

Carmine moved three chairs so that they were in a sort of circle; he pulled a handkerchief out of his breast pocket, dusted the seat, and sat down. Carmine looked around. "You run a cheap embarrassment here, Mr. Store Owner. It had class, real class, when your grandmother ran it and even more class – if that was even possible – when your saintly mother ran it. But now... now it is just an embarrassment. First, I want you to clean it up and return it to the place of honor it was before you had it handed to you – along with more money and assets you can ever spend. Do you understand what I am saying?"

Albert nervously shook his head up and down, "Yes sir."

"Next, I understand you have in your possession a little

item that I want."

"An item, sir?" Albert asked, weakly.

"Yes, I think you referred to it in the *Daily News* as 'a prohibition era permit allowing the certificate holder to make booze – legally'".

"Yes sir."

"You are going to give that to me free and clear and quickly, as a sign of your respect and...." He began to cough as if to be choking on his own words, "And your friendship."

"It is valued at more than $100,000," Albert said, timidly.

Carmine smiled, "As I said, you are going to give that to me as a sign of your respect and friendship; at no charge, *of course*."

James said, "It will be his honor to do that, Mr. DeStefano."

Albert began to complain and James stepped on Albert's foot. "As I said," James continued, "Mr. Froog will be honored to give that to you, free and clear." He gave Albert a dirty look and nodded to Carmine. "Unfortunately, the item isn't here in the store, Carmine," James added, "but Albert will be happy to make a call, and have it brought here, won't you Albert?"

Albert stood quickly and went to his office to call Sol.

Sol answered on the second ring. "Don't ask any questions," Albert said, "get the frame with the permit inside it and quickly bring it to me here in the store."

"Are you sure, Albert?" Sol said.

"Just do it, and please, do it right away," Albert urged.

When Albert returned to the room, he assured DeStefano

that the item would be there within the hour.

About thirty-five minutes later Sol rushed in with the item stuffed inside a D'Agostino Supermarket shopping bag. He stared at DeStefano as he handed the bag to Albert who immediately turned it over to DeStefano.

DeStefano slowly opened the bag, quickly looked inside, smiled approvingly, then closed the bag and placed it on the floor by his feet. "Then our work here is done," Carmine said as he slowly got up from the chair. "Maybe you can invest in some chairs that are more comfortable."

Carmine started towards the door, turned and put his hand out to shake Will James' hand. "I would like to spend more time with you Will; it seems as if you and I have some friends in common... as well as some enemies... also in common. I think we can help each other as time goes by." Then he glanced towards Albert, still shaking in his chair, "As far as you are concerned, Albert Froog, you little shit, you should give thanks to your sainted mother's memory that you still are alive and breathing on this lovely day in May."

He reached into his pocket and pulled out a handkerchief. He draped it around the doorknob and as he opened the door he turned back again to face Albert. "There are no copies of this document," he added, nodding towards the bag, "are there?"

"No sir," Albert said.

"Look me in the eye Albert Froog," DeStefano demanded, "I will only ask this one more time; are there *any* copies of this permit?" He had now raised his voice to a shout.

"No sir, I give you my word."

Carmine looked at James.

James nodded and said, "I am aware of no copies, Mr. DeStefano. But I give you my word that I will dig a lot deeper and *if* there are any copies, they will all be destroyed."

"Good," DeStefano said with a broad grin, "very good." He opened the door the rest of the way and then walked towards the car; he stood patiently at the curb as the rear car door was opened for him; he then got into the car. The tall young man carefully closed the door, took another long look around – first at the rooftops then the streets below; returned to the front passenger seat and closed and locked his own door.

The car slowly pulled away from the curb.

Albert and James watched as the car drove down the street.

"You *don't* have any copies of it, do you Albert?" James asked, still staring at the car now getting smaller in the distance.

"No."

"Better not – I think he would be just as happy having you ground up into a meatloaf as he would to whistle a merry tune."

"Don't be so dramatic," Albert responded, the color slowly returning to his face as he began to walk back to his office.

"You have absolutely no clue how close you came to being gone," James yelled after him.

"Gone?" Albert asked as he turned back to face James.

James walked up to Albert and whispered in his ear, "Gone!"

"Gone?" Albert repeated.

James ran his finger vertically across his neck and said, "Gone!"

Albert was now trembling.

"So what are you going to do now?" James asked.

Albert thought for a moment, and then said, "I think I am going to buy some new chairs for the auction room."

Chapter 37
Tuesday, May 14, 1996 –
Menlo Park, New Jersey – 3:18 P.M.

Elizabeth hand delivered the lab notes and bible – containing the metal box - at 3:18 in the afternoon. As promised, Angela and Frank began working on it as soon as she arrived.

Earlier that day they carefully selected a small group of their most senior and experienced researchers; one by one they advised the researchers that they had a very confidential and time demanding assignment. Angela and Frank had regularly handled high security private industry and top secret government assignments in the past and so, this by itself was not unusual. Every member of their staff, from their most senior researcher to the cleanup crew and maintenance personnel had been through numerous security background checks. As an ongoing precaution, every person – including Angela and Frank – had to take an FBI administered lie detector test, without prior notice, twelve to fifteen times a year. It was not unusual for a team of two or three FBI agents to show up at a lab member's home, late at night, for one of these lie detector tests; especially when the lab was working on a government assignment.

The rest of their regular team was told that the lab would be closed for ten days. Each of the furloughed employees was given a check paying their full salary for the next ten days.

Elizabeth's function was to act as a German translator and since she lived in New Jersey anyway, it worked out quite well for all involved.

Over the years Angela and Frank had established a tight control system to efficiently begin all sensitive projects.

There would be two different researchers assigned to work independently to log in each specimen, which in this case would be Ilsa's lab notes from Austria as well as all of her follow up work documents after she immigrated to America, Mark's notes, and the contents of the metal box. Then both *lead* researchers would meet to reconcile any differences between their two checklists.

Finally, each would form a team of their own to write up a series of recommendations for handling the assignment, depending upon what the client requested or what they determined needed to be either confirmed or proven.

Once again, the leaders of both teams would meet to reconcile the two lists. Any differences would be discussed, defended, negated, until both teams were in complete agreement.

That system proved to establish a unique reputation for the lab. Over time, a lab report on this lab's stationery was looked upon as the gold standard, the ultimate findings, respected throughout the scientific community.

From time to time, potential clients would deliver subtle hints as to what findings or results they would *expect* to see. Each time they were told that they could not dictate the results and if they insisted on doing so they would have to find another lab to do their work.

For this project, Angela planned to lead the first team and Frank planned to head up the second team. James made it quite clear that time was not on their side. He would need them to do the work as efficiently as if they had all of the time needed even though they would be expected to turn it around in days and not weeks.

They did as much prep work prior to Elizabeth's arrival as they could.

In order to avoid unnecessary wear and tear on the contents in the metal box they decided to process all of the documents first and leave the metal box for last.

They unpacked the documents and as an added precaution made a 'control copy' of all of the papers. The original set was placed in the labs huge safe. Elizabeth took the copies and began the tedious process of translating each document. When she completed her work, two copies were made of each translated page; her original translated worksheets were placed in the lab safe and she turned one set of the copies over to Angela and the second set of copies over to Frank.

Even though the lab maintained a white glove level of sanitation as their ongoing standard, both teams proceeded to scrub the lab down again while Elizabeth processed the translations. Understanding that they would be processing sixty-year-old specimens, Angela and Frank wanted to avoid the slightest chance of contamination. As an additional precaution they ordered sealed cases of whatever supplies they believed they might need and only supplies from brand new, sealed cartons were to be used for this assignment. They advised all associates that there could be no exceptions to this rule.

By 8:27 P.M. they were ready to begin the first full review of the documents and lab work. Realizing that once they began it would be most efficient to work through the entire process before breaking for meals or sleep, it was agreed that they and all of their associates would have dinner and then begin their work.

As with other time sensitive assignments, everyone working on the assignment understood that they would be required to live, sleep, and eat in the building until final completion of the assignment. A temporary dormitory was set up in the basement. Pre-packaged meals and selected dietary needs for up to two weeks estimated usage was delivered earlier in the day, courtesy of one of James' restaurant contacts. Two food preparers, always on call for such occasions, were brought in to set up a temporary kitchen in a conference room. All of the perishables and other ingredients were stored in an auxiliary refrigerator.

The house rules were simple, all who worked on the project would be paid on a twenty four hour clock... they earned while they ate or slept as well as while they actually worked. Each worker was told, personally by either Frank or Angela that even though every minute was precious, no one would be asked to push themselves to the very limit. "That is when mistakes happen... when accidents happen... when health is compromised," was Frank's message to them all. "We expect your best because you have demonstrated that you are always willing to do your best *but*, we don't want you to ever put the work ahead of your health."

At any time of the day or night, any of the employees were permitted to call a break time – this was pre-approved as long as they did so as a team, with their entire working unit. Barring illness or family emergencies, they began as a unit, they rested as a unit, and they dined as a unit.

At 9:10 P.M. their work began in earnest. The first call went out to James at 9:44 P.M. Frank advised James that all of the mother's notes seemed to be present and accounted for but there was a reference in Mark's notes that said he was storing his research on a micro disc and there was no such disc in the package of documents received by Angela and Frank.

James called one of the lead researchers who had been in charge of the documents during the initial inspection at the public warehouse. The researcher reminded James of the double checking system they had put in place. "Even if one of the inspections missed something it is most unlikely that the second follow up inspection, would have missed the very same thing. Possible sure; probable, not very likely; either of the two tandem inspections would have more than likely picked up any missing piece during the other's inspection. Fortunately, we had a third person who took numerous photos and made detailed work notes as he oversaw both teams and so I will go back and review his notes as well as talk, individually, with all of the other researchers who were there, and I will get back to you."

The researcher called James back an hour and a half later to say that he had gone through the work documents, one by one, and had spoken with each of those involved and was now convinced, beyond a shadow of a doubt that everything they found was included in the package that went to the lab. "Even the most professional humans are still just human, and so I was happy to recheck the work using the many photos and pages of check lists the other researchers generated during the mass inspection. But after this last review, I would stake my reputation that nothing was missed," the researcher said. "We knew how important this was because you made that plain and frankly, none of us had ever known you to get so many people involved unless it was crucial to get quick and accurate findings – the very first time."

James called Frank and Angela back, told them what he had learned and asked them to make certain that such a key element really existed and to get as much information about it to him so that he could dig deeper.

James went to Albert and brought him up to date. "Did anyone have access to that trailer before the night we had it moved, unloaded, and inspected?" James asked.

Albert thought for a while then said, "I sent Elizabeth to the trailer as soon as it arrived from Michigan and asked her to bring back a few things we might be able to sell quickly.

She brought back the framed document and a couple other things – small things – rather useless things. I must admit that the key did get past me. However, I really thought we were being super cautious."

James was clearly annoyed. He put his hand on Albert's arm and said, "Why did you not tell me that Elizabeth had been in the trailer before us? You really need to understand how important it is for you to share everything with me, *every-thing,* no matter how insignificant you think it might be."

"You had to know that we were in the trailer since we had the frame that started this whole nightmare. How else would we have had it for the auction?" Albert asked.

James thought for a moment and then said, "Then it was my error – but you could have advised me that it was Eliz-abeth and not you who went into the trailer."

"It didn't seem to be relevant," Albert said, clearly embarrassed.

"You need to trust me more. What might not seem to be *relevant* to you might be crucial when taken in a wider framework. At any rate, unless you and I do have an open and full understanding I really cannot be of help to you."

"Look," Albert said, "this, *trusting stuff* is really new to me. You have gone so far out of your way to help me that I am angrier at myself right now than you could possibly be of me. I promise to make an all-out effort to be more open and communicative moving forward."

"Okay," James said. "Okay."

"So what do we do now?" Albert asked.

"I think it is time to sit Elizabeth down and get the same commitment to being more communicative from her as I just got from you."

Chapter 38
Wednesday, May 15, 1996 –
Menlo Park, New Jersey – 1:09 A.M.

When James and Albert arrived at the lab Frank came down to let them in. James suggested that he speak with Elizabeth privately before Albert got involved.

Elizabeth was sleeping on a couch in the reception area. James knelt down beside her and gently poked her arm. She woke quickly and sat up, rubbing her eyes and still half asleep, she said, "What time is it?"

James looked at his watch, "a little past one in the morning."

"How are they doing?"

"I don't know yet, I wanted to speak with you first."

She yawned and then sat up straight. "I'm up. Speak."

"I need you to think hard and long before you answer me. You are bright… clearly smarter than your current position requires; you think on your feet like a pro; and if Albert can't make good use of you, moving forward, I am certain that I could place you in a heartbeat with a solid new job. But *not* if I can't trust you and frankly, at this very moment I have more reason *not* to trust than *to* trust."

"Be more specific," she said.

"There is a missing piece and as of this very moment it looks like you either have that piece or had access to that piece," James said, softly.

"You are talking in riddles and I am still half asleep. Just tell me, what you are talking about?" she asked.

"It is a micro disc record containing some or all of Mark Regan's research."

"I can swear on whatever you ask me to swear on that I have not taken and do not have a micro disc of anything by Mark Regan or anyone else."

"That's the rub," James said. "Given Regan's obvious *super* concerns about security, the micro disk probably was hidden in something else."

"Oh," she said.

"Yes, oh; so here is where you either make me a fan or an enemy, so answer truthfully or don't answer at all," James cautioned.

"Ask your question," she said.

"Did you take anything out of that trailer and not tell Albert about it?"

She stared down at her feet.

He stood up. "I guess we are done here," he said, turning to leave.

"Wait," she said, quickly, "let me explain."

He turned back. "I don't want or need an explanation. I need an answer; only 'yes' or 'no' will do."

"The answer is yes but I would like a chance to explain," she said.

"You're wasting your time and mine. I don't need an explanation. Albert sure does, but that is between you and he – you don't owe me any explanation. However, I could use a little truth," he responded.

She swallowed hard, and then said, "Okay, the truth... "

"The whole truth," James interrupted.

"The whole truth," Elizabeth repeated, "I systematically took little things from the store when I first began working for Albert."

"You have been *stealing*," James corrected.

"Yes, you're right – whatever I took wasn't mine, it belonged to Albert, I took it without his knowledge or consent, and so, *yes*, it was stealing. At first, it was just to make ends meet; he paid me so little – not even enough to survive. Then it was out of spite because he treated me like dirt. But, when I realized that he treated everyone like dirt – he even treated himself like that – I eventually stopped taking things..."

"Stealing!" he corrected.

"Yes, stealing – excuse me – I eventually stopped *stealing* from him." She said.

"So if you started to steal in order to survive... and you decided unilaterally to stop stealing... how did you survive without stealing?" James asked, casually.

"There were meals missed and things done without and it was tough but eventually Albert gave me a raise and various bonuses as the business grew and that helped a lot."

"How does that have anything to do with the contents in the Michigan trailer?" James asked.

"I did take one thing from that trailer, but if I thought it could help with anything going on now I would have immediately told everyone about it."

"Begin by telling me what you took from that trailer?"

"It was a package of blank computer disks."

"How do you know they were blank? Did you check each one out?"

"No, I didn't check each one out; it was a pretty full package, each in generic plain packaging; none of the disks were titled or seemed to show 'wear and tear', I just assumed..."

"I used to play this game with my son," James interrupted. "'I called it 'Where is the leaf'?' The purpose was to make him think beyond what might be 'the obvious'; so I gave him a premise, *if* I wanted to hide a handful of leaves, what would be an ironclad safe hiding place for the leaves in my hand so that no one could see them if they had not watched me place them there? Eventually I had to tell him the answer because he couldn't come up with it on his own. Can you think of the answer?"

"Just mix the handful of leaves inside a pile of other, similar looking leaves?" she said.

"Bingo!" he said. "So if Mark Regan was concerned about the safe keeping of a computer disk where would you think would be the best place for him to hide it?"

Elizabeth instantly responded, "I would hide it inside a package of other computer discs."

"Give the little lady a prize." James said. "Do you still have these discs?"

"Yes. We can always use blank discs and so when I saw it among the things in the trailer I thought I would bring it to the store. In fact they are at the store, on my desk, this very minute. I didn't think they had any value beyond what it would cost to buy some new ones and so I actually thought I was saving Albert money by putting them to immediate use instead of running to the office supply store to buy more blanks, which we did regularly because of the many 'lots' he was buying."

"Did you use any of the disks in the package?"

She thought for a while then said, "No, not yet."

"Okay, that makes it a bit easier." James said.

"Does Albert have to know what I did?" she asked.

"I don't see why I would have to tell him but if you want a relationship built on trust with him I think *you* might *want* to tell him."

"He will never trust me again. You know he has really severe trusting issues."

"His *trusting,* or better said, non-trusting issues have developed over the better part of a lifetime, and I think he realizes that his inability to trust is keeping him from getting the most out of life – in general, and making it even more difficult to build positive relationships with people – in particular. I think he wants to trust more. But one thing is certain, eventually everything comes out. It is far better if you tell him than if he learns it on his own. It isn't always the crime that gets you... but, it is *always* the cover up. Just ask Richard Nixon."

She smiled. "When do I have to tell him?"

"That is up to you. However, the longer it takes to *clean* the air the harder it will be to *clear* the air."

"And how is *the air* now between you and me," she asked, hesitantly.

"Do I have all of the truth now?"

She looked directly into his eyes, "I promise you, the answer is yes."

"If you think Albert has trusting issues, you would be

amazed at how much more that statement applies to me." He said, "I haven't given up on you, not entirely and not yet. But I need a lot more in order to say I can and would trust you moving forward."

"Like?"

"For starters, I would need your word that you will be open and honest with me moving forward."

"You would accept my word?"

"I would accept your word."

"You have my word, I will be completely truthful," she said, "At least as truthful as a former KGB agent can ever be truthful. What I will also promise is that there will be no more half-truths between us."

She put out her hand, "I give you my word."

He shook her hand. "Okay, now please get back to the store as quickly as you can and bring those computer disks to the researchers upstairs."

"You'll explain my sudden absence to Albert?"

"I will do that," he said.

She turned and walked out of the lobby.

As soon as he heard her car motor start James took out his phone and called Schless.

Schless answered on the first ring. James said, "Where are you now?"

"I am home, enjoying a dried up and icy cold supper but looking forward to a long, hot shower."

"I would really appreciate it if you would throw that cold

dried up supper into a takeout container and put that shower off for an hour or so; I need you to rush over to the antique store and take up a position in that alleyway a half a block to its right. *If* Elizabeth shows up I need you to let me know exactly what time she opens the front door and goes into the store as well as the exact time she leaves the store and drives away."

"You know," Schless said, mimicking Marlin Brando, 'I could have been a contender'"

"Not with your glass jaw," James responded. "Can I count on you?"

"Is Drew Barrymore America's little darling?"

James closed his phone, looked at his watch. It was 1:27 A.M. He slowly went back upstairs, thinking to himself, in Elizabeth's native language, "*doveryai no proveryai*", (trust, but verify).

Chapter 39
Wednesday, May 15, 1996 –
Menlo Park, New Jersey – 2:38 A.M.

With almost no one else on the road at that hour, Elizabeth was able to make the round trip in record time. As James came down to let her back into the lab, he sneaked a look at his watch and smiled, he greeted Elizabeth and she handed him the package of discs.

Elizabeth went back to the couch to get back to sleep; James went upstairs and handed the package to Angela.

"I believe that at least one of these disks has files on them – Mark Regan's lab files," he told Angela. "However, you may have to open and read each one in order to determine which, if any, are storing the data you are looking for."

"We are almost finished processing the mother's research data. As soon as we do we will begin to log in the son's data," Frank said.

"Elizabeth has been very helpful translating the notes from German," Angela added.

James thought for a moment, then pulled a small pad from his pocket and wrote down a telephone number and a name. He stepped closer to the researchers and in a low whisper, he said, "Choose any 5 of the pages Elizabeth has translated... choose them completely at random, and send them on to this person at the fax number on this paper. Add a quick note saying that I need these pages to be translated into English immediately and faxed back to you. Also send him five other pages chosen at random *along* with Elizabeth's matching translations. Ask this person," he pointed again to the piece of paper, "to review the originals and check them against her translations. Don't tell Elizabeth that you are doing this but have it done as soon as possible. Let me know when you get his response."

"Should we wait until later this morning when they open for business?" Frank asked.

James smiled, and then said, "It isn't a business, it's a guy who never sleeps – please send it now."

"Are you questioning Elizabeth's ability or honesty?" Frank asked.

"You know me, Frank," James said with a wide grin, "*doveryai no proveryai.*"

"What did you say?" Frank asked, with a confused look on his face.

"Nothing," James snapped back, "now, what about the metal box?" James asked.

"We are saving it for last. It may be the catalyst we need to make the best use of the lab notes and we fear that we may only have a couple stabs at it, given how old the specimens are and the unknowns about how well it has been stored all of these years." Angela said.

"I need to know when you think you will have something tangible." James said.

"Give us two or three days. Of course we will call you sooner if there is something to discuss sooner, as we did with that," Angela said, pointing to the pile of discs.

"Time is not on our side." James said.

Both Angela and Frank nodded. "We understand," Angela said.

His phone rang; James turned and walked away as he

flipped it open. "Yeh."

"She got to the store at 2:02 A.M., stayed only 2 minutes, left at 2:04 A.M. carrying a small package."

"Thank you. Now, enjoy your shower," James whispered into the phone.

"You trying to tell me something?"

"Say good night Gracie."

"Good night, Gracie."

Chapter 40
Thursday, May 16, 1996 –
Williamsburg, Brooklyn, NY – 9:55 A.M.

It wasn't until Thursday that Albert felt ready to reopen the store.

At a little after ten the door opened and Helga Regan rushed in. Elizabeth ran to her. "Hello, welcome back."

Helga smiled and said, "May I please speak with the auctioneer?"

"Of course," Elizabeth said, "I will get him for you."

Elizabeth ran into Albert's office.

"Come on, Elizabeth, you agreed to knock..." Albert said.

"She is here!" Elizabeth said excitedly.

"Who is here?" Albert asked, more than a little annoyed.

"The old lady from the auction, *she is here!*"

Albert rushed to the door and peaked through the one way glass window, he smiled broadly, and said, in amazement, "How about that?"

He reached for the telephone and dialed James. "Keep her occupied," Albert said to Elizabeth, "I'll be right there. Please, *do not* let her leave. Understand me? *Do not let her leave!*"

"I understand."

James answered on the first ring, "Yeh."

"You know that *guy* you pointed out in the auction tape –

the one I ignorantly thought was a woman?"

"Yeh."

"Well *he* is back... and he still looks like a woman to me."

"Keep him or her there. I will be there as soon as I can."

Albert hung up and called Sol. "The old lady from the auction just walked into the store!"

"How about that." Sol said, "You need to let James know."

"I did, he was the first one I called."

"Sure, you called him first. Well, at least now I know where I stand."

"Oh shut up. So you were the second one I called. Live with it you big baby."

Chapter 41
Thursday, May 16, 1996 –
Williamsburg, Brooklyn, NY – 10:39 A.M.

Albert called James again.

"Yeh," James answered.

"Just checking on where you are. I would prefer to meet this woman with you but I am afraid if I don't acknowledge her soon she might pick up and walk."

"I'm less than five minutes away. Go to her and stretch out the 'hellos' as much as you can. I will be there soon."

Albert, stood, nervously ran his hands through his hair and slowly walked out to greet the woman.

She seemed to be frailer than when he first saw her during the ill-fated auction. He extended his hand. "Hello, welcome back to my little shop. My name is Albert Froog and I am the owner; and you are?"

She put her hand out and gently shook his hand, "I am Helga Regan; it was my brother's belongings that you purchased in Michigan recently."

He held on to her hand. It was definitely *not* a man's hand. What was James and Sol talking about, he wondered.

He asked her to join him in the auction room. He gave Elizabeth a look, she nodded slightly. He assumed that meant that the auction room recording device was up and running, or at least he hoped that was what she was trying to communicate to him.

They sat in the new chairs that Albert had rushed out to buy as soon as Carmine DeStefano drove away on Tuesday.

"Can I offer you anything to drink? Coffee, tea, water?"

"No thank you," she responded.

"How can I be of service?" he asked.

"I would like to purchase that item you offered up last Sunday. But first I want to be totally honest with you. The money I was planning to buy it with on Sunday was not mine – it belonged to someone else. I could never afford to offer that kind of money for anything, much less something for which my brother only paid $5.00."

Just then James walked in, pulled up a chair and sat down.

Albert pointed to James and said, "I would like to introduce you to one of my associates."

James held out his hand and said, "Nice to meet you, please call me Stan."

Albert stared at James but said nothing.

She put her hand out to shake his outstretched hand. "I am Helga Regan," she said softly.

"How can we help you?" James asked.

"I would like to purchase the document Mr. Froog, here, put up for auction last Sunday."

"Has Mr. Froog not told you that it is no longer in our possession?" James asked.

Instantly her smile became a frown, "Is that true, Mr. Froog?" She asked Albert.

"Yes it is." Albert said.

She burst into tears. Both men reached for the same box of tissues on a shelf. James was a bit faster, picked it up and handed it to her.

"Tell me about that item, Ms. Regan," James asked after she calmed down a bit.

"May I be frank?" She asked.

"Life is complicated enough without frank conversations," James said.

"I don't know a great deal about it – maybe less than you already know," she said.

"Then why are you here to acquire it?" Albert asked.

"I believe it also contains a very important key that my mother would have wanted me to have."

The two men looked at each other and then at Helga.

"Can you be a little *more* 'frank' about it than that?" James said with a gentle smile.

Helga began to tell them about her family's move from Austria and re-settlement in America. She touched on what her mother had been working on as well as what her Grandfather worked on before that. While she was speaking, James reached up and quickly pulled the head covering off of her head. She was completely bald with huge bumps and black and gray scars all over her scalp.

Helga stood up and slapped him, hard. "Why did you do that?" She yelled, as she quickly re-positioned the shawl back onto her head.

Albert jumped up from his seat and said, "I apologize for what just happened. I assure you that I did not know he was going to do that."

James remained sitting. "I'm sorry for that," James said,

totally free of any emotion, "Now can we get back to what we were talking about?"

"No," she screamed, "we cannot get back to what we were talking about. Why did you do that? What gave you the right to do that?"

"Look," James said, sternly, "I am very sorry that I did that, please forgive me. Now, let us get back to the reason for your visit here, today."

She glared at him for a moment, and then moved her seat, a few feet away from James and a bit closer to Albert. As Helga sat down, Elizabeth raced into the room.

"I need you outside, *now!*" She said to Albert.

Both men glared up at her. Finally Albert said, "We are busy right now. Whatever it is, can't you handle it? We are not to be disturbed."

"*If* I could have handled it, I would have handled it." Elizabeth said, annoyed. "I need you outside... now... please."

Albert looked at James, who shrugged and motioned towards the front of the store.

"Please excuse me," Albert said to Helga as he got up from the chair "I will be back post haste, as soon as my assistant's *urgent situation* is handled." Albert followed Elizabeth toward the front of the store.

As Albert walked through his office door he stopped so quickly that Elizabeth crashed into him. "What the hell is *she* doing here?" He said to Elizabeth.

Elizabeth smiled, "I'm sure you will find out *'post haste'*." She mocked.

Standing in the front of the store was Alice Stanley, or

'Wilma' as she was first introduced to them.

Albert quickly walked up to her and asked, "What the hell are you doing here?"

"We need to talk before you make a very big mistake," she said.

"You will just have to take a number. It seems to be old acquaintance day around here. I am with someone right now." He said, flippantly, and then turned and started to walk back towards his office.

"I know," she said, "I followed her here."

Albert stopped and slowly turned to face her, "What did you say?"

"I said, we need to talk," she repeated.

Albert grabbed her wrist and led her out of the store, onto the sidewalk. "What did you say?" He yelled.

"*I said*," she whispered, dragging out the words, "that I followed her here and we need to talk so that you do not do something you will be sorry – very, very, very sorry - for doing."

He looked around and, still holding onto her wrist, led her closer to the curb. "What are you doing following her?" He finally asked.

"My job," she responded, "I am doing my job. I told you I was a field agent for a private detective agency. Well, following people is part of what I do. I am only here speaking with you as a courtesy. I assure you that Helga Regan, or whomever she might have introduced herself as to you, is trouble with a capital 'T.'"

"Tell me and tell me quickly. What do you think she can

possibly do to me?"

"I *know*," she said emphatically, "that she came to the auction, the other day, bought and paid for by one of our clients, a Michigan based drug manufacturing company. I also know that she is more than likely here now on her own personal agenda."

"And that agenda is?" he demanded.

She pulled her wrist out of his grasp and began rubbing the bruised skin.

"I demand that you answer me, and that you answer me *now*!" Albert screamed.

"I believe that her agenda is to separate you from some very personal items that just got swept up with everything else in her brother's home when its contents were sold to you."

"And you are telling me this because..."

"Because my client wants those items; has advanced enough money and time to pay for her travel as well as to pay her debts; so I also believe that my client should have first dibs on the items in question. Is that quickly enough for you, Mr. Froog?"

"Why should I believe you?"

"You should believe me because I have absolutely no reason to lie to you – not about this... not about anything."

"Let me get this straight, you are here on a *good will* mission?"

"Yes."

"And you gain not at all?"

"That isn't entirely true; if you come to your senses here I do get to go home a few days earlier. And that is a major personal gain for me."

He reached out for her wrist but she quickly stepped back.

"What are these items you are referring to?" Albert asked.

She laughed, "Come on, Mr. Froog, either you already know because you found them when the goods were moved out of the Coney Island storage location or you will never know because time has run out and my client will have found a way to just take it all away from you – with or without your approval. One way or another, if I were you, I would cut my best deal now and walk away. And I assure you, Helga Regan doesn't have a pot to... well you know... she certainly can't offer you anything tangible for those items, but my client *can* and for a quick resolution to all of this, my client would probably be delighted to pay some *reasonable* bonus too."

"Well, first of all, you are definitely *not* me. Second of all, I am sick and tired of all of this mystery and phony pulp novel intrigue. Third of all, I don't negotiate with middle men or middle ladies. Get my drift?"

She smiled. "Yes, Mr. Froog, I *get your drift*."

"So here is how this is going to play out, listen carefully because I do not plan to repeat myself." He said. "Go back to your *client* and tell him or her or they that *if* he, she, they want what I have legally purchased and own, he, she, they can come here, *in person*, and ask for it; and tell me, in person, what it is worth and why."

"My client is not used to making field trips," she said. "*He* may be your only bidder and if that turns out to be the case, you really do not want to get *him* angry at you, if you get *my* drift."

"I grew up in this business," Albert said, defiantly, "and if I learned anything it is that things in demand rarely have a single potential buyer. Maybe it is *your client* who should not get *me* angry, not the other way around. Now, if you do not mind, I don't want to be rude to my guest in there."

He turned around and walked back into the store.

*****

Albert walked past Elizabeth on his way back to the office. Elizabeth whispered to him, "What is all of that about?" She said, pointing towards the outside door.

"Your friend Wilma or whatever her real name is, was trying to get me to give her client the frame."

"Didn't you tell her that you don't have it anymore?" she asked.

"Hell no!" Albert said. "I still want to know what was so special about that piece to make her client bid $100,000 for it."

"You don't think it was just the key that they were after?" she asked.

"I really don't know, I'm just hoping to find out."

*****

While Albert was outside responding to Elizabeth's request, Helga wanted James to know how upset she was with him.

"What you did, uncovering my head, was mean by any definition of that word," she said.

"I really am sorry," James responded. "It *was* wrong of me to do that and there is no acceptable excuse. If it helps at all, having seen how it upset you, if I could go back in time I really would not have done it."

"Well... thank you for that," she said, a bit friendlier.

"Chemotherapy?" he asked, softly.

"Yes," she responded, with a sigh.

"You want to talk about it?" he asked.

"It would do no good. The doctor's don't hold out much hope. They have labeled it 'stage 4' and as you probably know, there is no 'stage 5'" She said. "In addition, I am an old lady... I am learning that doctors don't try all that hard to use their magic on sick old people when there are so many younger patients needing their time and attention. I guess they believe that I have already lived my life... if you know what I mean."

James handed her the box of tissues.

There was an uncomfortable silence, and then he asked, "So, why *are* you here?"

She smiled, weakly, "I know that my mother was working on a cure in Austria and continued her work when we im-migrated to America. I also know that Mark was a gifted researcher, even though I never told him that when he was alive. Between them I was hoping that they might have come up with a way to extend my time, here on earth." She began to cry. "Silly, isn't it? I have made such poor use of this life; you would think I would be happy that it is almost over. But I am not. I'm just not ready to go yet. I would like to undo or at the very least apologize personally for some of the horrid things I have done over my lifetime. I would like to make amends before they lay me out and cover me with dirt."

Slowly she composed herself and sat up straighter in her chair.

"You ever hear the old Pennsylvania Dutch saying?" she asked, '*We grow too soon old and too late smart*'?"

James nodded, "Pretty wise, those Pennsylvania Dutch."

She heaved a giant sigh, where were those *wise men* when I was doing all of those stupid, stupid self-destructive things?"

Just then Albert returned, looking a bit disheveled. "Sorry about that," he said. "Now, where were we?"

Chapter 42
Thirty-seven years earlier...
Saturday, April 21, 1962
Tangshan in Hebei, People's Republic of China 4:04 P.M.

Ping Yee Chan and Wai Hing Cheung met at the Easter Dance when Wai Hing was 10 and Ping Yee was 9. If there is such a thing as love at first sight, it definitely did not apply to them, at least not that afternoon. He thought she was kind of pretty, but too full of herself, stuck up and a general pain in the neck – and told her so; she thought he was an okay dancer but a bit wild and an all-around arrogant jerk, but she kept that to herself. What she did not keep to herself was how mad he made her by continually gawking at the other girls. "It is just an insult," Ping Yee argued, "if you want to be with them then go to them... but while you are talking to me and especially while you are dancing with me you need to keep your eyes on me. I'm a lady, *if* you were a gentle-man you would realize that I *am a lady,* and would be treating me like one!"

They met again at a church social 5 years later. They talk-ed about their first meeting – even laughed about it – but each walked away from the other feeling that they might be much better off if they never had to see the other one again. Ping Yee's sister, Ying Yee, was at the same dance and somehow saw a spark between them and said so to her sister. "I think you two were made for each other. I can see you getting married to him one day and having a long and happy life together."

"You are talking crazy!" Ping Yee yelled back.

"You can call me crazy or anything else but I know what I see", Ying Yee responded, "I would bet the treasures of the

Quin Shi Huang's Tomb that you and he will get together one day."

"You are not only crazy but a terrible fortune teller," Ping Yee yelled back. "I would rather marry a dragon than spend my life with that... that... that jerk.

Ping Yee Chan immigrated to America when she was 16. She, her two sisters, and her mother were part of a huge church group that had come on a tour and decided to stay in the country after the rest of the group returned to China. Her mother found work at a Chinese restaurant run by a family friend and gradually, her three daughters were given jobs there as well. Ping Yee took as her adopted American name, Angela. She grew up, attended college and began working for a small research laboratory in Menlo Park, New Jersey.

Wai Hing Cheung, anglicized his name to Frank, and at the age of 17, moved to Montreal with his older brother. He went to university in Canada and moved to New York City upon graduation where he took a series of little jobs before deciding to hitchhike across the country on what little money he had saved.

By the time he was twenty-two years old, as his money was running out, he settled down in the San Francisco Bay area, where he became an apprentice to a group of electricians. He worked hard and soon became a valuable part of their crew.

Chapter 43
Fourteen years later...
Tuesday, July 27, 1976 –
Tangshan in Hebei, People's Republic of China – 3:42 A.M.

At precisely 3:42:53.8 local time, on the morning of July 27, 1976, an earthquake struck, with the epicenter near Tangshan in Hebei, People's Republic of China. The first shock lasted 14 to 16 seconds. The Chinese government official sources reported the magnitude at 7.8 on the Richter scale, although some sources listed it as high as 8.2. It was followed by a 7.1 aftershock some 16 hours later. Tremors from the Tangshan earthquake were felt almost 500 miles away.

Before the earthquake, this old industrial city had been home to slightly more than a million and a half people. The initial death toll from the first shock alone was estimated to be more than 240,000 men, women, and children. Another 400,000 people died in the densely populated areas around Tangshan. An additional 164,000 people were severely injured. It was the second deadliest earthquake in recorded history; second only to the 1556 Shaanxi earthquake which reportedly killed 830,000 people in China.

Given the hour, most inhabitants were fast asleep in their beds, but even if it had been in the middle of the day, the region would still have been totally unprepared for the almost instant devastation. Few could ever imagine such a disastrous event in Tangshan, which had been considered to be a low risk earthquake region.

Eighty-five percent of the buildings in the city itself were now totally flattened or at the very least – uninhabitable. Many who survived the initial earthquake were trapped under the hundreds of thousands of collapsed and destroyed buildings. The Chinese government refused to accept international aid but that did not stop repatriated Chinese from around the world organizing local groups to return home in hopes of assisting their friends, family, and former neighbors.

Angela and her younger sister, Ying Yee, now Lora, drove to Montreal and there they joined 29 other members of their church and flew back as soon as a charter flight could be arranged.

Frank was in Oakland at the time, working on a huge project. He phoned his boss and began the conversation by saying that he needed him to be very understanding – but with or without his permission - he felt that he had to return to China to do whatever he could to help his family and friends. His boss reassured him, he said he did understand, "If anyone can identify with the personal anguish and physical devastation that an earthquake can generate," his boss said, "it is someone like me who was born and raised in earthquake prone San Francisco. Of course you can go, I wouldn't think very much of you if you didn't go. All I ask is that you just hang in at least until I can get to the project in Oakland and take over where you have left off."

Frank's boss quickly threw some clothes and assorted files into a suitcase, grabbed his tool belt and assorted other items he might need on the jobsite and began the relatively short drive to Oakland, arriving at the work location less than two hours later.

Within a few hours, with the help of the Taiwan Visitors Center in San Francisco and the American Red Cross, Frank was able to make arrangements to return home.

Angela, now 23 and Frank, now 24 each went directly to the battered streets of their birthplace. Independent of each other, both Angela and Frank were drawn to the same small group assigned to dig through the rubble of a flattened hospital. This time, when they came in contact with each other, each saw the other in a totally new light.

The enormity of this disaster seemed to bring out the best in each of them. Eventually even they could see that they had fallen in love. During the sorrow and grief filled days and weeks that followed they seemed to find what little comfort available to them was in each other's arms.

The night before they had planned to return to America he asked her father for the right to propose. Angela's father chased him out of their home with a broomstick.

*****

Over the years Angela's cousin, Ivy Chan, was the *go to* person for what Angela described as Ivy's special brew of *judgment free* common sense advice, always offered with love and support. Even as a very young girl, Ivy always seemed to be genuinely wise beyond her years.

When Frank was chased away by Angela's father, Angela suggested they both go to seek Ivy's advice.

Angela introduced her cousin to Frank by Ivy's Chinese name, "敏兒, Man-Yee, it means *intelligent child*, and she has always been that and more for me."

"I do not want to be disrespectful of her father," Frank said to Ivy, "but I know Ping Yee loves me and I love her. What should we do? What, can we do?"

The three of them were sitting on Ivy's porch. Ivy smiled. "Uncle has always had strong opinions about virtually everything. He is accustomed to being in charge of most things, especially that which affects his family. I have always respected that. However, in this case, only the two of you can or should decide. This is the rest of your lives we are talking about."

"I do not want to disobey him," Angela said, tears streaming down her face, "but I do love Frank and the thought of not being with him is more painful than anything I can imagine."

Ivy looked directly into Frank's eyes – but she might as well have been staring into his soul. "I don't know you, Frank. I have nothing by which to measure your depth of character or sense of right or wrong. For all I know, Uncle might have very good reasons to disapprove of one of his daughter's committing herself to spend the rest of her life with you on this earth, much less for eternity after this life has come to an end. But I can clearly see how much each of you cares for the other."

She put her hands on Angela's shoulders and asked, "Do you believe that *not* spending the rest of your life with Frank would be more painful than feeling the wrath of your father's anger?"

Angela clutched Frank's hand in hers and said, "Yes, even more painful than making father angry."

"Then," Ivy said, "you have answered your own question. In time, Uncle will learn to accept Frank... or not. Either way, you must do what you must do. The Lord works in mysterious ways. *He* brought the two of you back to this place, at this time, for a reason. *He* will deal with Uncle."

"My dad is such a proud man," Angela said with a sigh.

"Pride goes before destruction," Ivy said. "Don't allow *his* pride to destroy *your* love for each other."

✱✱✱✱✱

The next day Frank and Angela got married in front of a few old friends and several new friends - volunteers they had been working with since their return to China. They flew on to Montreal so that Frank could introduce his new wife to his brother. A few days later they went to America. He moved into her studio apartment in New Jersey and began looking for a job.

He took whatever work was available, at times juggling three separate part time jobs, but Frank was finding it hard to get meaningful work. They considered moving up to Montreal where his brother might be able to help but instead, Angela introduced him to her boss at the lab. Frank was given a job typing up the daily research notes from the various researchers' recorded tapes. He had no formal research training but began to question some of the assumptions in the notes. "These guys are stepping all over each other," he would tell her at dinner each night – "seems most of them are only working here until something better comes along and don't really seem to care about what they are doing much less the reputation of the lab. To make matters even worse," he complained, "the *results* they are coming up with aren't supported by their support documentation; doesn't anybody read these reports? Better yet, does anybody there really care?"

At first, she laughed at him, "What do you know about our work?" ... "A little knowledge is a dangerous thing." ... "Don't make waves, you need this job."

Then one night he slammed his fist on the table and yelled, "I may not have your degrees, but I know uncaring when I see it. I am telling you that most of them are just sleep-walking... I see them duplicating each other's efforts... none of them seem to want or care to build upon the work already completed. So many of them seem to be disconnected from the supposed goals of the lab... either that or they are just plain lazy... whatever the reason or reasons, it just seems so wrong. That's just inefficient and wasteful, and in the end, worthless." He threw his hands up in the air, "It makes absolutely no sense to me."

She stared at him. He had never so much as raised his voice to her, or anyone else that she knew. She put her hand on his and said, "Tell me exactly what you think is wrong."

They went to the lab several hours earlier the next morning and he pulled out the previous months typed reports.

She re-ran some of the experiments from those reports and then compared her results with those of her co-workers. *Frank is absolutely* right, she thought. She took her results to the senior researcher. He called Frank in and asked him what in particular made him initially question what he was typing. He felt he had nothing to lose since he was certain that they were going to fire him for butting in like this, so he shared his concerns, point by point.

The senior researcher told him to wait in his office, stood up, and walked out.

Frank's first series of thoughts while waiting for the senior researcher to return centered on the disaster before him; he was about to be fired – there was no question about that. His first reaction was shame – how will his wife deal with such an outcome? Her father will gloat – her father would love the chance to tell her, '*I told you so!*' But after a relatively short time devoted to feeling sorry for himself – he began to consider the broader probabilities - Angela introduced him here – maybe they will fire her as well. Then he thought about their bills – how will he survive? How will *they* survive? He and his new wife were about to be destitute – he really needed this job.

"What have I done?" he murmured, "What have I done?"

He stood up and looked through the huge picture window.

He began to calm down as he watched all of the traffic and people down on the street. "Hey," he said softly to himself, "there is a lot of life out there. The people here can fire me but they can't kill me and they definitely can't take Ping Yee's love from me, so now all I have to do is make a plan for moving forward.

He stepped outside of the senior researcher's office and asked the receptionist for a copy of the Menlo Park telephone book, some paper, and a pen. He brought all of that back into the office and quickly skimmed through the listings, finally stopping at the huge 'Automobile dealer – sales: new/used', section. He started to create a list of local auto dealerships. "I bet I could get a job working for an auto dealer." He thought out loud, "I have always had a talent for repairing mechanical things; I like cars; I know a fair amount about cars; how tough can it be? I may even be able to make more money working on cars than I did working here."

Soon the senior researcher returned with the owner of the lab closely behind him. "Tell him what you told me," the senior researcher said sternly to Frank, "don't leave out a single word."

Frank took a deep breath, set his list aside, calmly closed the telephone book and with all of the confidence that comes from knowing he had nothing to lose, he went through his thoughts and, for added measure, finished by rattling off a list of recommended changes he would make if this were his business.

When Frank was finished, the senior researcher said, sternly, "Sit here." Then he led the owner out of the office.

Angela rushed into the room, "What have you done?" she cried.

"Look," he said, trying to reassure her, "they can't kill me.

All they can do is fire me."

"And me!" she said, tears welling up in her eyes. "I recommended you."

He held her close, "Hey, so they fire us. They can't kill us – you or me. All they can do is fire us. That is all."

"That is a lot!" she responded, tears running down her cheeks.

He gently wiped the tears away, "So what if they do. We will still have each other and isn't that all that really matters?"

"We can't live on love," she said.

"Who says we can't? Anything is possible unless we let them drive us apart the world will continue to spin on its axis and we *will* survive." He kissed her forehead, then the tip of her nose, and then both cheeks. "I love you." He said. "*You* are my life, who cares about these stupid geeks. Without you I cannot survive, I would not want to survive. With you I know that I can do anything... I can be anything... it is that simple." He put his arms around her and held her close.

He gently held her face in his hands and smiled, "Let's focus on what really matters. It took a tragedy in Tangshan for us to *find* each other. We knew each other before but we never really took the time or invested enough of ourselves to *find* each other until we were faced with what can and did destroy so many others. Think - but for the grace of God we could have gone our merry way and never found this love we have for each other. Worse yet, we could have been among those that died in that terrible disaster. I am certain that all of those people had hopes and dreams and a fair amount of them had secure, dependable jobs. In a matter of seconds all the hopes and dreams and jobs vanished. Are we really worse off than any one of those people? We are two healthy, young, and I would say good people. All I ask you to do is trust that I can and will find us a way to survive. "

They were still holding on to each other when the two men returned.

"Okay," the owner said. "Do it."

Frank and Angela stared at each other, then at the owner, then back at each other. "Do what?" Angela asked, sounding annoyed and confused.

"Help us to make the changes."

With that the owner walked out of the office and left them standing with the senior researcher.

Over the next dozen or so years the lab paid Frank's way through school and gave him a crash course in their various processes. It was on the job training and he eagerly took it all in.

*****

Eventually, the owner announced that he was putting the lab up for sale so that he could retire. Angela and Frank talked about it well into the night.

Finally, late evening in America, mid-morning in Hong Kong, they placed a call to Angela's sister in the Kowloon section of Hong Kong. After some nervous rambling they asked her for a loan so that they could buy the lab. When they finished asking, each held their breath for what seemed like an eternity but was actually just a few seconds; Angela's sister said she would wire the necessary money before the end of the day. "I wasn't there for you when you fought with Papa to get married," the sister said, "thank you for letting me be here for you now, at this important cross road in your life."

The next morning, with a cashier's check in hand, they walked into the owner's office and closed the deal. He sold it to them for less than he might have gotten from a larger competitor but he told them to look upon it as a thank you for all that they had done to make him a very successful and wealthy man.

*****

Will James first met them when someone asked him if he knew anyone who could help Ping Yee stay in the country. United Sates Immigration had finally caught up with her and wanted to deport her back to China because she remained in the country illegally after her visa expired all of those years before.

James met with the distraught couple, he told them that he did not know anyone who could intercede for her with the government but he did promise to dig deeper and would do whatever he could.

James never talked about the specifics of how he planned to help or what he could do, much less what he actually did do. However, all that really mattered was that less than a month after they met with him a certified letter arrived on the official letterhead of the senior senator of New Jersey. The letter informed them that all charges against Ping Yee were being set aside. The Senator went on to promise to push for her to be allowed to stay in the country, permanently, because of her work and technical abilities.

*****

When James called them to ask for their help to decipher Ilsa and Mark Regan's lab notes they both agreed, instantly.

Chapter 44
Friday, May 17, 1996 –
Williamsburg, Brooklyn, New York – 10:08 A.M.

Billy Aarons reached James early in the morning. He said he had to speak to James but did not want to talk over the phone. James suggested they meet at the antique store after 10:00.

*****

James was deep in thought, going through his note pad, sitting alone in the auction room when Aarons walked in.

"Good morning Mr. James," Aarons said as he sat down. He rubbed the surface of the chair; then squeezed the arms and seat cushion on the chair next to him. "What was Carmine talking about, these are great chairs."

James smiled and said, "So now Carmine DeStefano is an interior decorator?"

They both laughed.

"What is all the mystery about?" James asked.

"Let's go for a walk," Aarons said.

"What's wrong with here?" James said, waving his hand around the room.

"There are indoor conversations and there are outdoor conversations." Aarons said, "*This* needs to be an outdoor conversation."

"I'm really busy, Billy."

"Humor me, let's go for a walk."

With a short grunt, James stood up and began walking towards the door. As soon as they reached the street Aarons said, "How about the diner."

"It's at least a half a mile away," James complained.

"So we get a little exercise," Aarons said, gently tapping James' stomach, "you could use a little exercise too you know."

They began walking, about half a block from the store James turned to Aarons and said, "okay, you said this had to be an 'outside conversation'... we are outside, let's have that conversation."

"You seem to have made a new friend the other day." Aarons looked around and then added, "Mr. DeStefano has developed quite an appreciation for your various talents. For some reason, you have become flavor of the month in his world and he would like the two of you to get together again, soon; emphasis is on *soon*."

"I thought he was happily married."

"Don't be gross." Aarons made a face as though he had just eaten a bug, "He asked very nicely for me to set up a meeting and I would greatly appreciate it if you would just meet with him."

James stopped walking and moved closer to Aarons, "What am I supposed to say to that? What is he really looking for?" James asked in a low voice.

Aarons put his hand on his heart, "He asked me to set up a meeting just between the two of you, which is all that I know."

"I told you before Billy, I'm really busy right now," James said.

Aarons started walking again, "You can tell the Queen of England that you are too busy, you can even tell Bruce Springsteen that you are too busy, but it is definitely unhealthy to tell Carmine DeStefano that you are too busy."

"I don't run in those circles, Billy. You of all people should know that. You should have told him I don't work with gangsters."

"For all you know he is just a businessman."

"Come on, Billy, I was born at night but not last night."

"What can it hurt if you just talk to the man?"

"I am really busy, Billy. I'm being spread too thin as it is and with this antique store thing I am becoming *over busy* and that is never good. *Over busy* almost always leads to mistakes and in my work mistakes can really be harmful to your survival."

"You really need to make time, Will, he could be a terrific friend but he could also be a very scary enemy."

"You know, Billy, I can't imagine any enemy worse than the Department of Defense, and I did survive even after my little misunderstanding with them," James said.

"You must be trying to kid yourself, because you definitely aren't kidding me. The D.O.D. isn't even in the same league with Carmine's family business. The D.O.D. has rules and overseers... they have to answer to higher authorities – he doesn't on either account. Just see him."

"I thought you said he was *just* another businessman?"

The lawyer grunted as they continued walking. Finally, James stopped and moved closer to Billy. "And you have no idea what he wants to talk about?"

"No, he doesn't see the need to clear all of his thoughts with me. But I can guess."

"So what is your guess?"

"He probably sees a future in the kinds of things you do best."

"He wants to get into cooking take out Chinese food at home?"

"Very funny; he stir fries people – not food! Hey, it doesn't take a space scientist to know that brute force no longer has the same level of *success* that it once had. I am only guessing here but I think he sees computer espionage as the *new* wave for bringing people to their knees; and you have turned computer espionage into a real science, if you know what I mean."

"And you think he expects me to work my *computer science* to his advantage?" James asked, in amazement.

"I told you, it is only a guess. For all I know he has an immediate need for something like that or no need at all. Maybe he just likes your spunk."

They walked in silence for another few minutes.

"See him." Aarons said, breaking the silence, "You can tell him no but if that is your final answer I think you need to say it face to face... he would respect that."

"Okay. Set it up." James said.

"That's a quick change of mind," Aarons said, with shock in his voice.

"Let me get this straight," James said, "First you wanted me to agree and then when I agree you start sounding like you want me to disagree? What kind of *schizoid* are you?"

"I just wondered what I said this time that I might have left out all of the other times I asked you to meet with him. Okay, when do you want to meet with him?"

"What's the difference what I say about when or where? He seems to make the rules, doesn't he?" James said.

"Good, now you're just being smart," Billy said.

"I don't appreciate your putting me in a spot like this," James said.

"Hey, you called me to help you with him, now it is the other way around; and anyway, someday you'll thank me," Aarons said.

"And someday pigs will fly, just not today."

Aarons moved over to the curb and put his right hand up in the air. Within minutes a black limousine pulled alongside the curb and the rear door opened.

"Have a nice ride," Aarons said as he started to walk away.

James stared at the limo and then at Aarons and yelled, "Hey, lawyer, you know that you are a son of a bitch, don't you?"

Aarons smiled broadly and without turning back he yelled, "Don't be redundant... using lawyer and son of a bitch in the same sentence is a double positive... even I know that."

Chapter 45
Friday, May 17, 1996 –
Williamsburgh, Brooklyn, NY – 11:51 A.M.

As James stepped into the back seat he felt hands going up and down his arms and legs. "He's clean, Mr. DeStefano."

"That wasn't necessary, Freddie. Mr. James isn't going to hurt me. Now, are you, Mr. James?"

James settled into the rear seat next to Carmine DeStefano. DeStefano asked the driver to pull the car out of traffic and give them a little privacy.

When they were alone in the car, James said, "Do you live in this car?"

"Don't worry so much about my living arrangements." DeStefano responded, followed by a hearty laugh. "I checked you out." DeStefano continued, "You're the real deal."

"How do I respond to that?"

"Why do you have to say anything? What is... is."

"Well, if you checked back far enough you have to know that I am almost always under someone's surveillance. *They* almost certainly saw us together when we met at the antique store and it would be a sure thing that *they* are probably watching us now. I cannot understand why they did not bring me in for questioning after our first meeting unless they are waiting for something bigger in order to reel us both in."

"Let me worry about the surveillance," DeStefano said, good naturedly. "Let's talk about why the key was removed from the frame your little friend turned over to me."

"Oh, that," James said, sheepishly.

"Yes, that," DeStefano said.

"Mr. DeStefano ..."

DeStefano held his hand up. "Call me Carmine."

"Okay, Carmine, you said you were interested in the document – we gave you the document. If you checked me out you also know that I may walk along the thin outer edge of criminal behavior but I am really not a criminal."

"Who said you was a criminal?" DeStefano protested. "Unlike other people I could mention, I don't prejudge. If you are straight with me then I don't give a rap what your relationships are with others... is or was or will be, with others."

"I am aware of your reputation too, Carmine," James said.

"Are you talking about those lies in the newspapers?" DeStefano, said with a warm laugh. "Never believe what you read in those fib sheets. As far as I am concerned the only valuable use for newspapers is to wrap fish in it or cover the kitchen floor after it is mopped."

"Carmine, why am I here?"

"Like I said, I think you are the real deal. *Also,* I want your antique store owning friend to hold his auction again this coming Sunday – and I want him to spread the word that he is going to auction off the permit in the frame."

James stared at DeStefano – "You now have the permit and the frame. I saw Albert hand it to you," James said.

"I know that," DeStefano said, with a wave of his hand, "but only you, I, and the Bobsey twins, Albert and Sol, know that."

"What could possibly be the purpose of such a sham announcement?" James asked.

"Don't question – just do..." DeStefano said coldly, then, almost as an afterthought he added, *"Please and thank you!"*

"And that was why you wanted me to meet with you again?" James asked.

"Not entirely," DeStefano said. "I also believe that you are better than anyone else on my payroll in a number of very important and timely ways; and I like to surround myself with people who are better than me." After a very long pause, DeStefano added, *"And* I would like to know why I did not get the key."

"Carmine, that key had nothing whatsoever to do with the permit... and, as far as joining your organization, you just said that you checked me out so you have to know that I kind of work alone," James said.

"I haven't asked you to join my organization, and as far as you working alone, I'm not so sure about that." DeStefano broke in. "I hear that you are always making good use of other people's talents and abilities. When you need a pro you bring on a pro. Is that any different from the way I operate?"

"If you put it that way, I guess there really isn't much of a difference between us; except of course that the people I disagree with usually continue breathing even if and after they make me angry."

"That's a low blow. Let's not resort to low blows, Will. I have been respectful of you and all I ask is that you be respectful of me. Plus, of course," DeStefano said with a chuckle, "I haven't killed anyone in years." He laughed louder. "Well, at least not for a few months."

"Carmine, we both know that I am not going to go to work for you. Please, tell me, why I am here?"

DeStefano's body stiffened. "I hear that you might have found more in that trailer from Michigan than tables and chairs – *and a key.*"

"Look, I am not going to play word games with you. The general truth is that I honestly do not know. The *specific truth* is that I am in the process of determining if there is anything there along with the tables and chairs."

"And the key?" DeStefano added.

"And the key!" James responded.

"Will, Will, Will," DeStefano groaned. "You brought in a small army of workers... you had the trailer emptied, and I have to assume carefully inspected... you neatly repacked the trailer and returned everything to its original parking space..." DeStefano moved a bit closer to James. "Excuse me, not everything. Seems the trailer weighed 417 pounds less at the end of your all night maneuvers than it did when it first arrived..."

"Carmine, be very specific, what – in addition to the tables and chairs – and the key - are you referring to?"

DeStefano gave a huge sigh and in a short burst said, "A cure for cancer!"

"Whew," James said, with a wide grin, "when you come to the point, you really come to the point."

"Is it true?" DeStefano asked.

"The truth is that I don't know."

"Don't be coy with me, Will; either you do or you don't."

"The truth is that I really don't know. I am doing whatever I can to determine if there is something, along those lines, but as we sit here – at this specific moment - I really do not know."

"Okay," DeStefano said, I'll be more forthcoming with you than you seem to be willing to be with me. I am an old man, Will. I have climbed to the top of my... let's say profession. I want for nothing in this life but the love of my family and good health for my children and grandchildren. I am a very powerful man but my power does not assure me good health for my children or grandchildren. I have a beautiful grandson. He is almost four years old. My greatest wish for him is that he lives to be five years old." DeStefano pulled out a photograph and handed it to James. "I cannot seem to be able to make the wish for good health come true for him."

It was quiet in the car. James stared at the photo in his hand as DeStefano stared at James.

James broke the silence, "And the reason he might not see his fifth birthday is....?"

"He was diagnosed with cancer. He has been to the best doctors money can buy, they pushed and prodded, they tested and retested, and in the end threw up their hands and just gave up." Tears were filling DeStefano's eyes and his lips were trembling as he spoke. "I have lived my life but he has not yet lived his. I would trade places with him in a snap." DeStefano quickly wiped away the tears that were running down his cheeks. "Tell me, Will, was there a chance for my grandson to see a fifth birthday in that trailer of yours?"

James touched the old man's sleeve, and in a barely audible whisper, said, "I give you my word, I do not know."

"This is my grandson's life I am talking about. There is

nothing I would not do to save his life. Do you know of anything that *might* help my grandson survive this terrible disease?" DeStefano had been clutching James' arm, then he suddenly pulled away. Noticing that James seemed to be preoccupied, DeStefano raised his voice. "Hey, am I boring you or something? I am pouring my heart out to you. You need to listen to me..."

James stopped DeStefano and said, "I am really sorry, Carmine, I know how wrong this is but I must take this call and I need you to be understanding of that."

Chapter 46
Friday, May 17, 1996 –
Inside a Limousine, Brooklyn, N.Y. – 12:37 P.M.

James instinctively knew that interrupting his conversation with DeStefano at a time when DeStefano was opening his heart to him would not go well with the older man.

Generally, it was unusual for him to ignore a ringing or vibrating phone. Since he did not have an actual office he also did not have anyone to screen calls so any call at any time could either be about a mundane matter or a life and death crisis. For that reason, he always answered his phone immediately. But that rule along with all of his better instincts were on hold right now; when he felt the phone in his pocket vibrate he forced himself to ignore it, whoever was on the phone at this moment would have to wait; but the caller was not waiting. James could feel the vibrations again, seconds after the call must have gone to voice mail. Quickly followed by a third time, then a fourth time within as many minutes; feeling that he had to at least see who was calling, he excused himself and opened the phone. It was the lab in Menlo Park.

DeStefano was clearly not comfortable waiting on the sideline and showed his irritation. He glared at James and then waived his hand in the air, "Go and answer the damned phone."

James apologized again and then spoke into the phone, "Please be quick."

Both Angela and Frank were on the line. "We have good news and bad news. You started this conversation asking us to come to the point quickly and even though I know you are always more interested in the bad news than the good news I am going to begin with the good news," Angela said.

Avoiding DeStafano's eyes, James spoke into the phone. "I am in the middle of something that cannot be interrupted," James said, impatiently. "I know that you have dropped everything to help me and so I do not want to be rude. *But* please get to the point *quickly*."

Ignoring James' plea, Angela continued. "The good news is that we can assure you that Elizabeth's translations were supported by the double check. The backup translator you sent us to also told us that the quality of her work was far better than average. In fact, the words used were – *'translated like a native born German speaker.'*"

"That *is* good news," James said.

"The bad news is that the mother's lab notes required us to get into the metal box sooner than we first planned," Frank broke in.

"So?" James said, clearly annoyed.

"The contents of the metal box suffered irreparable damage when the seal was broken by your inspection group. Fortunately, they left the box in the bible so we were able to recoup some of the leakage but the specimens are quickly becoming useless."

DeStefano was beginning to mumble to himself.

"I share your pain but what, if anything, do you think I can do to help?" James said, sarcastically.

"We need to get our heads together – and very soon! There are decisions only you can make and the sooner the better. Every minute we wait makes the specimen worth less," Frank said. "Literally, every minute," Elizabeth said.

"What can I possibly add to the conversation," he barked, "I am not a goddamned scientist!" Then he interrupted himself. "Wait, give me a minute." James held the phone to his chest, turned to DeStefano and whispered, "This is so much against my better instincts, but I am going to ask you to quickly take me to Menlo Park, New Jersey so that you can ask your last question directly to the people who can give both of us their best response."

DeStefano stared at James then opened his window and yelled, "Get back in the car, we need to roll, *now*!"

James reminded DeStefano, "Please tell your driver to do whatever he can to shake whatever surveillance has been watching either you or me or both. I have been trying my best to keep the Menlo Park facility and all of the people who work there, off of *their* radar."

"Mr. James will give you the address," DeStefano barked to the driver. "Move it so we get there fast — alive *but* fast — and make sure the tail is shaken so that they don't know where we are going. *Capeesh*?"

"Yes Mr. DeStefano," the driver responded.

James returned the phone to his ear. "Call Albert and tell him he needs to get to the lab double quick. Remind him to avoid anyone who might be watching his movements but he must get there fast. Meanwhile, I'm on my way. But I will be coming with a very special guest."

"Want to tell us who will be accompanying you?" Frank asked.

"No, if I do, you might tell me *not* to bring him, so I won't tell you," James said.

DeStefano stared at James, "What is going on?" he said in a loud whisper.

"We trust you," Frank said.

"Hopefully, you will still trust me when you meet my surprise guest." James hung up and smiled sheepishly at DeStefano.

During the ride to Menlo Park, James shared just enough with DeStefano to emphasize how big a risk James was taking by bringing DeStefano and possibly whoever was tailing him, and although he knew DeStefano could never be expected to just *'do the right thing'*, especially if *the right thing* conflicted with DeStefano's agenda; he made it clear that whatever future relationship DeStefano might want with James would be irreparably damaged if DeStefano broke the trust now being requested.

DeStefano finally put his hands up, "Although I am sure that you are not trying to threaten me, Mr. James, I will tell you that my word has gotten me a long way in this life. You have my word that I will not do anything that you do not want me to do. Is that good enough for you?"

James held out his fist. At first, DeStefano looked confused, and then he smiled and lifted up his fist and gently bumped it against James' fist.

"Whew," DeStefano mocked, I thought I would have to make a small cut in my hand like in the gangster movies."

"Don't be sacrilegious," James said.

Chapter 47
Friday, May 17, 1996 –
Menlo Park, New Jersey – 3:47 P.M.

The driver expertly maneuvered the limousine through narrow back streets and even went up the wrong side of a one way street several times before he took the Verrazano Narrows Bridge towards New Jersey. At various intervals the driver slapped a flashing blue dome light on top of his dashboard. At least one of these times James clearly saw a police car move aside to give the limousine the right of way.

"I'd like to buy one of those invisible rays," James quipped.

"You couldn't afford it," DeStefano said, barely loud enough to be heard.

They entered the lab's parking lot shortly before 4:00 in the afternoon.

*****

When Frank and Angela realized who James had brought with him they gave James a quizzical look. Frank asked to see James in the outer lobby while Angela nervously showed DeStefano around the lab.

As Frank and James reached the outer lobby Frank said, "I learned a very long time ago not to question your actions, but I am having a problem understanding where this is going."

"Look," James began, equally as uncomfortable as Frank seemed to be, "he isn't here as a gangster, he is here as an anguished grandfather."

"How do you separate one from the other?" Frank asked.

"Please, don't fight me on this. I thought it was the right thing to do or you know I would not have brought him here... even though he probably got me here at least half an hour sooner than I could have on my own. Let's play it out. Meanwhile, I am only asking you to share with him what you feel comfortable sharing with him. If there turns out to be anything you feel so strongly about that you would prefer not to discuss while he is present, let me know and I will deal with it."

"You always have."

"And I will again, if I have to; let's just hope that I do not have to today."

They moved to the small conference room upstairs, off the main lobby.

Frank looked at James, then Angela, and finally straight at DeStefano, "Mr. DeStefano," Frank began, there is a rather huge elephant in the room and I would like to address it."

"Let me save you a lot of time dancing around; you are afraid that at any moment - and for no apparent reason - I am going to blow your heads off; stuff what is left of you in a rusty old fifty-five gallon oil drum; fill the drum with wet cement; let the cement harden; then drop it and your dismembered body parts into the middle of the Atlantic Ocean. Is that your elephant in the room?" DeStefano asked with a laugh.

"Something like that," Angela said.

"Exactly like that," Frank said.

DeStefano exploded in laughter. "I am not that monster you read about in the newspapers."

"I think they need more than a wrapped fish and freshly

washed kitchen floor story," James said, rather hesitantly.

"Okay," DeStefano finally said. "Here are the ground rules I would *ask* you to consider. Treat me like any other concerned family member of a four-year-old cancer victim. No more, no less."

"And how do you want us to treat the two obviously well-armed men who walked in with you?" Angela asked.

"Treat them as what they are; two very trusted employees; my personal security team. Would you question the presence of armed men accompanying any politician – local, state, or federal – if one came to visit your facility? Would you think twice if any public person took similar precautions for their personal safety? Would you not expect the leader of almost any sizeable organization to travel with his or her dedicated security personnel in today's violent atmosphere? Those men are *just* that for me. It is how I live or at least remain alive. There are people who would prefer that I not be alive. Should any of them try to harm me while we are all together do you really believe that either of these two men would not defend the threat against your lives at the very same time they enthusiastically protect me?"

"There is also the matter of the *kind* of sizeable organization you lead, Mr. DeStefano," Angela said, meekly.

"What are you talking about? I run a meat packing plant in the Bronx," DeStefano said.

The room was now deathly silent.

James stepped forward, "I will vouch for Mr. DeStefano's presence here today. Is that good enough?"

Again, there was dead silence in the room.

James looked around and finally broke the silence. "Hey, we can discuss this some other time. If Mr. DeStefano wanted to grab the metal box and lab notes along with you and everyone in this lab, I think he would already have done that."

"Wow!" DeStefano said in mock amazement, winking at James, "That's not a bad idea. Why didn't I think of it?"

James looked at DeStefano and shook his head with disappointment. "You're not helping me, here." Then he said to the others, "Let's move on. Okay?"

Frank broke the uncomfortable silence and nodded. "We will move on."

"Now to the real problem facing us," James began, "Is there a connection between the metal box and the lab notes?"

Just then, Albert and Sol rang the night bell and could be seen on the closed circuit television set in the corner of the room. "I'll go get them," Elizabeth said, "please don't start without me."

Elizabeth soon returned with Albert and Sol closely behind. As they entered the room the two men saw DeStefano and his two armed guards. They both looked at James with blood in their eyes.

"What is going on here?" Albert asked.

"Excuse us," James said taking Albert's arm as he began leading him out the door.

"Wait!" DeStefano yelled.

"No secrets. No more secrets! No more *private* meetings, Will! I have given you more space than I would have given anyone else, and I mean *anyone* else. But enough is enough. I am here as an interested party. In addition, I shouldn't have to remind anyone here that I have more than a little influence in some very important circles... I have access to almost unlimited funds and many very devoted employees and friends of employees at my disposal; any or all of that could certainly help you enormously..."

"Or *hurt* us enormously," Frank interrupted.

"Stop it! Stop it this very minute," DeStefano yelled, looking directly at Frank. "Enough is enough! You don't want me here... I get it. But I am here and I am staying here. I gave Will James my word that I will not make him sorry that he has given me his trust. No one, alive or dead, will ever be able to tell you that I have ever broken my word; never... not once... not ever. I will not be treated like something a dog does after a large dinner and a short walk. Now, you two," he said, pointing at Albert and Sol, "sit down and shut up. Everybody shut up, except for you two." He pointed at Angela and Frank. "You can talk but just talk about this science stuff. There will be no more talking about me; period, end of subject."

After a short silence, Angela asked, "So, where were we?"

"Jonathan asked you if you found a connection between some metal box and lab notes," DeStefano growled.

"You've been paying attention," James said, calmly.

"In my business," DeStefano said, beginning to cool down, "if you want to stay alive you pay attention. So, let's *all* pay attention."

Angela, still a bit shaky, cleared her throat and said, "We have chosen to segment all of the data we were given to analyze into four separate groupings. The first and probably most useful group – strictly from a scientific point of view – comes from the materials Ilsa physically removed from the Austrian lab. This group of notes, we believe, will be substantiated by the secrets hidden in the specimens in that metal box. The notes are sharp, exceptionally well documented, carefully detailed, organized in such a way as to help us to better understand the levels they went through in order to come up with their findings; the failures, and why... the successes, and how."

"Did the move from Austria to America help or hurt?" Elizabeth asked.

"That is a very good question," Angela responded. "We believe it actually *didn't* help. Today, America is definitely a leader in this field but back when Ilsa first arrived from Austria, medical research was not quite on the same level here as it was in Europe – especially the area we now refer to as Eastern Europe. Also, it appears as if the Michigan lab into which she moved her research was not as well equipped, lacked the quantity and even quality of really good researchers to back her up, and was missing many of the physical tools and pieces of equipment she had easy access to in Austria."

"I apologize for interrupting again," Elizabeth persisted, "but what tells you that?"

"Mainly the supporting notes in the first batch... they all referred back to respected sources... published independent studies... experiments... findings... with complete and detailed work documents... checked and rechecked and in a few key instances, triple checked; as opposed to the lack of almost any support documentation in the second and third group of notes. It is almost as if after she began her work again in America, she was working alone instead of as part of a cohesive team, which was clearly the case in her Austrian lab. There was also a spread of about fourteen months between the last entry in Austria and the first entry in America," Angela said.

"Wouldn't the time off have allowed her to recharge her batteries and begin again with a clearer head and possibly even more objectivity?" Elizabeth asked.

"Perhaps, if she spent the time off in a peaceful and restful place – both mentally and physically, but we must remember that they were literally running for their lives during most of that fourteen-month period. Her mind could not have been filled with anything but the day-to-day care and safekeeping of her children and concerns about those who might still be searching for them. There was no time to think and contemplate; they had all they could handle just to deal with their life or death existence each and every day. As important as her work was – both to her as well as within the bigger footprint of the medical research community – her struggle for survival took precedence. No, the fourteen months were definitely not conducive to contemplation; and even if it was, there would still be a *re-learning* period after such a long time away from such an intensive project."

"One more factor needs to be considered," Frank added, "*she* was not working on her research during that fourteen month window but others were and so there was quite a steep learning curve facing her when she hit the restart button."

"You said that you have segmented the notes into four groupings?" Sol asked. "What are the other groupings?"

"Yes, so the first group is the Austrian lab notes... the second group covers her early work when settling into the American lab... the third portion of notes covers the period just after being diagnosed with her illness and ends days before she died, and again this is just speculation on our part. Many of her notes in this third group are confusing... repetitious... disorganized... even contradictory at times. This set is of little scientific value and at the risk of oversimplifying it, was merely her attempt to beat the clock – so to speak... she seemed to be working harder but appears to have accomplished little or nothing of substance during this period. There is frustration but little else..."

Sol broke in. "That seems like a contradiction, we are acknowledging her solid credentials as a medical researcher and then saying she was working harder with *less* to show for it?"

Frank took out a folder and spread out some of the pages. "These pages are just a sampling of her 'output' during this phase of her life. There are multiple musings, at one point she asks 'if there is really a God'... here she lists, in the smallest detail, how to cook a pot roast... and here and again here are stick drawings almost as if she was distracted or lost in thought." Frank pulled out several more pages, "Here is an excellent example of what I am describing," he pointed to four sections on two of the pages, "she repeated the same exercise – four times in two days."

"Was it a key experiment?" James asked.

"It looks like she was trying to see at what level heat she might be able to break a glass test tube and if the glass tubes she was using were all from the same lot," Angela said. "This would have no connection to her primary work; practically the same as simple daydreaming."

Frank continued, "She must have been in excruciating pain, especially towards the end. If so, it would have been natural for her to be taking whatever pain remedy was available to her... from an aspirin to heavy narcotics, just to ease the pain and get her through the day, much less to enable her to work."

"As a medical researcher she would have had access to unlimited quantities of the strongest drugs in existence at that time," Angela said. "The incoherent musings and repetitive experiments were the first tip off to us that this data was not going to be as useful as the first two batches. We believe that as the disease progressed and her pain level increased she might have been taking something that created a level of paranoia... fear... mistrust; real or imagined terror. Whatever the cause, her notes in this third batch are scrambled between her new adopted language, English, and her more comfortable language German... and not just *any* form of the German language but more like *slang* or guttural German, a version that we believe was a throwback to her earlier years living in a poor blue collar town on the border of Germany; which brings us to what we are labeling as the fourth grouping of notes, Mark's notes. We have determined that these were only marginally more informative than the second group of his mother's American notes. It is not because Mark lacked ability – to the contrary, he seems to have been quite a gifted researcher – we consider this set to be less valuable because he seems to have begun from where his mother left off – from what *he thought* were her latest, best notes but instead, what we believe were the disoriented notes after she became ill. So his starting point was flawed. In addition, Mark made several key translation errors. We think those errors put him on a totally different track."

"Wait a minute, stop right there," James broke in. "Mark taught German speaking refugees... add to that he wasn't translating some stranger's notes – these were his mother's notes! He knew her phrasing and vocabulary and... and... he grew up hearing her speak. How could he *not* have the necessary language skills to properly translate his mother's notes? What do you base this on?"

Angela looked at Frank and said, "When Elizabeth did her translations she picked up on something that put key factors in a different light for us..."

James held up his hand. After a few seconds he asked Elizabeth to step out of the room for a moment.

All eyes were on Elizabeth.

Without any comment, she stood up and walked out of the room, slowly closing the door behind her.

James whispered to Frank and Angela, "Did you confirm the differences Elizabeth found?"

Angela answered first. "We did."

Frank nodded his agreement.

"Are you absolutely certain that Elizabeth did not confuse the translations – innocently or not so innocently?" James persisted.

Angela and Frank signaled that she did not.

"Hey," Albert yelled, "are you saying that Elizabeth tried to torpedo us?"

"I am not *saying* anything – I am merely asking."

"You are *asking* while Elizabeth is not here to defend herself."

Ignoring Albert's argument, James slowly began again, "So, let me get this straight in my head, Mark, the scientist... Mark the professional German language tutor... Mark, who knew his mother a billion times better than anyone else, especially someone like Elizabeth who had never met her or read her writings before; *the* Mark I have just described, did not pick up any of what Elizabeth, the amateur translator, picked up?" James asked, suspiciously.

"Yes, we are saying precisely that," Angela said.

"You are a woman seeped in science and objectivity, Angela, how in God's name could you believe that?" James asked.

"Will, it is *precisely* because Elizabeth came to the translations without preconceived notions that she was able to *hear* the subtle references that Mark missed. It had less to do with science than with a procedure Ilsa was describing. We sent the original pages covering these passages to the backup translator; we *only* sent the original source data without Elizabeth's translations and the backup translator read it the exact same way Elizabeth did," Frank said.

"You had a *backup* translator check Elizabeth's work?" Albert fumed. "So you never trusted her?"

"Please, Albert," Sol argued, "let him flesh out his point before you roast him."

"Oh! We need to be *patient*... we need to *let him flesh out his point*... but it is quite all right for him to roast Elizabeth, even though she was sent packing without a chance to defend herself?" Albert asked.

"Remember," Angela broke in, "Mark was on a mission... he was walking in his mother's shoes, so to speak. Elizabeth, on the other hand, was quite impartial. There was neither pressure nor emotional involvement for her; she - just like the backup translator – was able to *hear* the subtle differences and translated the notes accordingly."

"So Mark's work was useless?" James asked.

"Not entirely, in fact he opened a possible window that we believe might be particularly valuable for prepubescent cancer victims."

DeStefano perked up. "So this 'Mark...' His work can help children?"

"Please, Carmine," James argued, "let her finish her thought."

Angela looked at Frank and then continued. "We have assigned a couple of researchers to flesh out Mark's work with all new targeted experiments; we just think it is more useful, given the tight schedule you put us on, to separate it from this primary investigation. The important take away for this discussion is that Mark's work just took a turn that put him on an almost entirely different path. It made his work less useful for *this* trail." Angela emphasized. "Mark taught German and so he certainly was fluent in German but in textbook German, not old country, slang German."

"But he was born in a part of the world where German was his *first* language," James persisted.

"All true, however, he left the area at nine years of age... a highly impressionable age, under the best of conditions... Mark was definitely *not* living within the best of conditions at all... nine-year-old Mark was under very stressful life or death conditions. Even if he had used the same phrases as a youth – that would be well buried by his need to block off the memories and fears he experienced while fleeing to America. It is natural to think he would *protect* himself by paving over the old with his new everyday language – English. As far as his mother's notes are concerned; she was a medical researcher, she had to know that she was running out of time and in conjunction with the pain medications, she would have become incoherent at times. It is a fair assumption that she probably found it easier to think and write in the German language she grew up with instead of the more formal German she was exposed to in her adult years or even her newer adopted language, English. So we came full circle and now began to look at the possible contents of the metal box believing that it might have a hint about a cure."

"What is this 'story time'? Can't any of you get to the chase here?" DeStefano asked. "Okay, so how did that result in the need for this *emergency* meeting today?"

"Wait, let's call Elizabeth back in," Albert said. "She has more than proved herself to be reliable and trustworthy. She needs to know we trust her."

James thought for a while and then said, "Albert's right." He got up and slowly went to the door, opened it and called for Elizabeth to come back.

Slowly, almost meekly, Elizabeth re-entered the room and took her seat at the far end of the room.

James broke the uneasy silence, "Elizabeth..."

She held her hand up. "No explanation needed. Please, just continue."

Angela asked, "Where were we?"

"You were saying that you thought whatever was in the box was a cure," DeStefano said.

James smiled, "You'd make a great court reporter."

Angela continued. "If our presumptions are correct, the specimens might be holding onto what Ilsa *might* have believed would be a link to a possible cure. Our inner struggle, the reason for calling this meeting on such short notice is that we need further direction – your further direction – as to when to move forward with our work on the specimens."

"What is the down side for doing that now?" James asked, cautiously.

Frank jumped in, "You only get to properly dissect a specimen once. So that *once* better be the best you can do."

"So?" DeStefano and James said in unison.

"Can't you just work on a little part of whatever you have at a time?" DeStefano asked.

Putting her hand in front of her mouth, to hide her amusement, Angela said, "That isn't exactly possible under these circumstances."

"Remember, these specimens are more than 60 years old and have been shaken up more than a little, through the years," Frank added.

"Anyway, we cannot be certain that we will get it right on the first try," Angela said.

"But you have six specimens, certainly by the second or the third try you would get it right," James said.

"We can't assume that we have six identical specimens. Our initial assessment is that the six specimens were taken over a three to six month period in order to represent six *separate* stages, possibly six different breakthroughs, in her research. *If* that is correct then each specimen is crucial to making the most out of the mother's earliest work."

"I don't understand," DeStefano said, "if you have the laboratory notes why do you also need the stuff or whatever might be in that metal box you are all talking about?"

"We believe that the specimens *must* hold significant value all their own. Think for a moment about the enormous risk she took just to have that metal box on her person while escaping from Nazi occupied borders at a time when the Nazis were drunk with power and convinced about their superiority. Ilsa Regan seemed to be passionately obsessed with the task of bringing the metal box from Austria to the west," Angela said, "Remember this was 1934; the Nazis were already clearly in charge of the region. It would have been difficult to get anything out of the country without plenty of documentation and an easy to confirm story. She couldn't just assume that her word alone would be enough at any, much less all, of the potential check points that they would have had to pass between their home and their ultimate freedom. Any one person – not even a *super sleuth,* just someone doing their job – could have stopped them in their tracks. She had to know that; but it did not stop her."

DeStefano walked closer to the light boxes and asked, "What is in the metal box?"

Angela and Frank looked at James. James thought for a while then said, "Six dead laboratory mice, each one in a glass bottle, floating in some kind of liquid preservative."

"You got a box of sixty-year-old mice here?" DeStefano said in amazement. "All of this is about six dead mice? You gotta be kidding me."

"Yes," Angela responded hesitantly. "It is about six... dead... mice."

"All of this mumbo jumbo is about *mice?*" DeStefano repeated, shaking his head from side to side. "I can get you all the dead mice you want."

"Please Carmine, let them finish." James said.

"As I was saying," Angela began again, "Ilsa must have known that carrying this box would raise questions everywhere they went. Concealing lab notes was no easy task on its own, but concealing lab notes would have been a piece of cake compared to trying to conceal a metal box. So, we asked ourselves, why would she have taken such a huge risk? One scenario could have been that *she* believed the specimens still held answers... maybe a partial answer... maybe a final answer... or they could or would confirm future 'cure' theories. What is almost certain is that she would never have taken such a risk to her children's safety as well as the safety to herself and her husband, if there weren't any larger potential benefit to be expected from the specimens."

"So let us all agree that the specimens are important; *so if* we are running out of time let us not waste the little time we have on what Carmine here has referred to 'long history lessons'; what makes you think that we have even less time to resolve this than we initially thought we had?" James asked.

Elizabeth, still clearly troubled by DeStefano's presence, snapped an x-ray into one of the light boxes on the wall, turned the back light on, and said, "This was taken just before we called you. It is an x–ray of what was in the metal box an hour or so ago."

She then snapped a second x–ray into a matching light box to the right of the first one, "This is the x–ray taken immediately after you broke the vacuum in the public warehouse."

Moving to a third light box she snapped a final x–ray into it and said, "This was taken shortly before the vacuum was broken. The first one in light box 'A' is today; the other two are about two days old."

Frank walked over to the light boxes, "As you can see with the naked eye, there is a noticeable difference between all three images with the most marked reduction between the last image and the first image. We estimate the difference to be about 5.7992%."

"Are you saying that it shrunk about 6% in the couple of days since we removed it from the trailer?" James asked.

"*Not* just from the time you removed it from the trailer – but from the time you broke the vacuum seal," Angela said.

"Yes," Frank added. "The most loss probably happened the instant the vacuum was lost. We have allowed for some natural distortion between the portable x–ray machine you used in the field and our, state of the art x–ray machine, here in the lab. The x-rays tell the tail.'"

"But even after correcting for that, we believe that there is still noticeable shrinkage and that it is *still* occurring," Angela said.

"What do you think is accounting for the shrinkage?" James asked.

"It had been vacuum sealed all of these years. Ilsa Regan's notes made several references to a special *'air sucking unit'* that her lab had been using to keep specimens from deteriorating – her exact notation was, *'we halted the aging processes.'* We believe that as long as the seal was intact the specimens were secure, or at the very least, dormant. In fact, I would go as far as to say that the specimens you first saw when you broke the seal and opened the lid - about two days ago – almost exactly mirrored the specimens Ilsa Regan placed in the metal box, more than sixty years ago," Frank said. "The photos taken in the storage warehouse – immediately after the seal was broken - have easily been the most interesting single element available to us. Our frustration comes from the fact that we can *see* the specimens but we may no longer be able to access their hidden secrets."

"We believe that Mark Regan never opened the box while it was in his possession nor did Ilsa Regan any time after she initially sealed it in her lab in Austria. Either they both knew or assumed that once opened to the air the specimens would almost certainly deteriorate. We both believe that the specimens were to be used as some sort of substantiation once a 'cure' was found. Of course that is just speculation on our part. Angela said.

"They had vacuum technology in the 1930's?" Sol asked.

"Yes, in fact scientists and inventors have been talking about vacuum *type* processes as far back as the 1700s. The general population became familiar with vacuum technology around 1900 when an American coffee roasting company began using a vacuum process to remove air from their coffee cans before they were sealed so that the coffee could stay fresher, longer. First German and then Austrian laboratories such as Ilsa's had already been using vacuum technology for years before Ilsa took the specimens from her lab.

"Ilsa had no way of knowing how long and under what circumstances the specimens she took from her lab would have to endure. We feel certain that the specimens were vacuum sealed just before she removed them from her lab and stayed intact until the episode in the public warehouse a few days ago. As best we can now estimate, the specimens have been losing about seven one hundreds of a percentage point of mass every thirty-two minutes since the vacuum was broken. We do believe that we have been able to slow the rate of loss down but only slightly."

"How can you possibly know that down to such minute measurements?" Sol asked.

Angela looked at Frank and then at James.

"First of all, these people," James said, pointing to Angela and Frank, "have built a team that is about as good as it gets. In addition, they have equipment that other labs only dream about. Finally, the kinds of challenging assignments they get to work on each and every day forces them to think out of the box minute to minute. It is not an exaggeration to say that the next best dozen labs, combined, don't see the challenges in a year that this lab might get in an average month. Just accept as a given that if they say the specimens shrunk 6%..."

"5.7992%", Frank corrected.

"Excuse me," James said, "5.7992%, if they say 5.7992%, their plus or minus is almost certainly in a range that is within ten thousand of a thousandth of a decimal point."

"We can currently calculate up to nine places to the right of a decimal point," Frank said, proudly.

"When were you able to lower the rate of shrinkage?" Sol asked.

"Minutes before we called Will."

"How did you slow the rate?" Sol asked.

"We have been doing a series of tests for NASA," Frank responded. "They keep one of their restricted zero gravity chambers in this building and we commandeered it for this project."

"What is a *zero gravity chamber*?" Sol asked.

Frank laughed, "Of course NASA has a much longer name for it, but for our purposes here we are just labeling it by what it does. We decided to place Ilsa's metal box in a zero gravity atmosphere in expectation that it could reduce the rate of shrinkage. We didn't think it could completely stop it, just slow it down, which it has. We estimate that the specimens will still lose, at a minimum, about one eight hundredth of one percent of its mass every twelve to eighteen hour period. We can't be sure, it is really just an estimate based upon what we have recorded since placing it in the chamber. We are definitely in unchartered waters here. Our best guess is still just that, a guess."

Angela turned to the light boxes and pointed to the three x-rays. "There is more to consider; specific areas of some of the specimens are shrinking faster than other areas. We can also see discolorations forming – just within the past eighteen hours. These discolorations appear to be several shades lighter on the newest x-rays. We suspect that these discolorations are also important, we just don't precisely know to what extent yet."

"And the more mass you lose the less likelihood you can learn whatever Ilsa Regan discovered? James asked.

"Yes, more than likely," Angela said.

"What can be done?" DeStefano asked.

"That's why you were asked to rush over," Angela said, then paused and looking at DeStefano she added, "That is why we asked Will to rush over."

Frank quickly cut in, "We want to have a non-scientific, though definitely interested viewpoint to weigh all options on the table."

"And those options are?" James asked.

"In no special order of preference these are our choices: we can begin dissecting the specimens immediately with the limited knowledge we have from our initial review of the lab notes; we can accept the smaller but still present rate of shrinkage while we take an additional pass at the lab notes, hoping to identify other options; or…" Frank tailed off, "or we can concentrate on the last few entries from Ilsa Regan's first grouping of notes – completely ignoring the second and third and fourth groups, especially anything Mark might have come up with - for the moment."

"If you were to make a purely scientific choice," James asked, "what would it be?"

"That's easy," Angela said, "We would leave the specimens

alone and put all of our time and energy behind digesting the accumulated work documents. That is the safest path but also the slowest path. It could add weeks if not months to the process and even then, there is no possible guarantee that the specimens would have any remaining scientific value when *we are* ready for them, given the slow but steady loss of mass."

"But I think you brought this to us because you wanted more than a 'textbook' answer." Frank said.

"Let's be clear," James said, "I brought this to you because I know and trust you both without reservation. But that trust comes from your having earned it many times over. You earned my trust..." James continued to talk to Angela and Frank then turned his gaze towards Elizabeth. "as Elizabeth has now earned my trust."

Elizabeth gave him a weak smile and mouthed the words, *thank you.*

Albert smiled, and then whispered, "It's about time."

Sol kicked Albert under the table.

James nodded to Elizabeth and then continued, "You run a *'class A'* operation; you have assembled a remarkably capable team; your integrity and commitment borders on super human.

"Is this a mutual admiration society or a serious discussion with a loud ticking clock in the background?" DeStefano growled.

"Look," James said more seriously, "This is not the most difficult problem I have ever asked you to handle for me but I agree, it needs more than just a scientifically purest plan of attack. Give me your best choice from all of the options presented."

"Frank and I have not discussed this yet," Angela said, "but my suggestion would be to begin to work on the various specimens while we allow two or three of our senior staff to bury themselves in the documents; a sort of one, two punch approach."

"That wasn't even one of the choices you gave us," DeStefano said.

Frank broke in, "As Angela said, we have not discussed this among ourselves yet but I would definitely go along with her suggestion because it is a markedly better choice among a list of less than perfect choices."

James turned to Albert. "I asked you to rush over here because this is your property. I would like you to also have a say in what we do next."

"What does he know about such things?" DeStefano argued. "I think we need to listen to the real experts and if those two," he said, pointing to Angela and Frank, "are as good as you say, they should have the last word."

"I have no problem with that," Albert said.

"Then let's do it!" James said, enthusiastically.

Chapter 48
Sunday, May 19, 1996 –
Long Island MacArthur Airport,
Ronkonkoma, New York – 8:12 A.M.

Joseph G. Politeri and Maxwell Trella walked out of the general aviation terminal, each carrying a thin black attaché case. A man in a black suit waved to them from the taxi stand. Trella, waved back and soon a stretch limousine pulled up in the double parked car lane. A short and stocky man wearing an ill-fitting and rumpled black suit jumped out and quickly walked around the car, opened the passenger door, nodding briefly to the two men. As the driver reached for the cases, Politeri growled, "Keep your hands to yourself."

Politeri entered the car first, followed quickly by a very nervous Maxwell Trella. Politeri turned to Trella and whispered, "This better work, Max, or they will be digging up our body parts for years to come."

During the ride into and through Brooklyn each man was wrapped up in his own thoughts – for Politeri, he knew without a doubt that his life, both literally and figuratively could end today if he let the framed document slip through his fingers again. Once considered the heir apparent to the seemingly endless wealth and power still held by the Detroit mob, he was now facing death, if he was lucky – or a life of living hell - humiliation, disgrace, and poverty - if he wasn't.

Trella knew he would be on the losing end of whatever happened today. He had tried with all his might to get out of this trip but that was not to be. His role was clear from the outset – at the slightest sign of defeat, he would be offered up as the sacrificial lamb.

When the limo pulled up to the curb, around the corner from the small antique store, Politeri sat quietly organizing his thoughts while Trella got out of the car and made arrangements with the driver to stay close by until they were ready to return to the airport.

Finally, Politeri willed himself to put on his war face, he got out of the car, stretched his arms out, nodded to Trella and the two men walked slowly towards the corner of Rodney and Lee; then they entered the small antique store and followed the series of arrows towards the auction area. It was about 10:13 A.M. and there were three men already seated. Politeri and Trella took the only seats still open in the front row.

At precisely 10:30, Froog entered the room holding a cup of freshly brewed coffee. He walked to the rear of the room, carefully set his coffee cup down on the floor next to him. One quick look around, then he noisily cleared his throat. "Welcome one and all to my weekly auction," he began. "Once again, I have carefully selected a series of precious collectibles, hidden treasures, objet d'art and one of a kind reminders of times past for you to snap up at bargain prices."

He held up the first item and began his pitch.

Politeri stood up and yelled out, "I would like you to begin with the Prohibition era permit you advertised a couple of weeks ago."

Albert looked at the man and said, "All in good time, sir."

Politeri opened his attaché case and took out a revolver. "My friend here thinks the time should be now."

DeStefano had been carefully watching the closed circuit screen in Albert's office; he stood up and walked to the auction area, then stood quietly just outside of the entrance.

Albert said, "As I was saying..."

"I don't care *what* you were saying", Politeri said, threateningly, "you *will* bring up the permit now, won't you?"

DeStefano walked into the room, "What do we have here?" DeStefano growled.

Politeri pivoted around quickly and at the sight of the old man he shoved the pistol into his pocket and sat down.

"Carmine," Politeri finally said, "how are you?"

"Never better," DeStefano said, motioning to one of the men in the back row. The man stood up, slowly walked over to Politeri and gently took the pistol out of Politeri's pocket. He kicked the two attaché cases out of the way, motioned for Politeri and Trella to stand and told them to spread their legs and put their arms out. He reached over and emptied their pockets, dropping the contents onto the floor. He then proceeded to frisk them both. When he was satisfied that neither still had a weapon, the man nodded to DeStefano, and mumbled, "They're clean now, Mr. DeStefano," and returned to his seat.

Trella thought to himself, *here it comes*. Both men turned around slowly to face DeStefano.

"I told you to shut your stupid plan down, but you insisted on going forward in spite of what I told you would happen if you foolishly defied me," DeStefano said. "Tell me, Joseph, what is happening with that little item I asked you to pick up for me? You remember... the framed permit."

"Soon, I... er a we... no, he," Politeri said pointing to Trella as he moved away from the trembling man. "He assures me that he will have it for you very soon."

DeStefano reached over to one of the men sitting in the

back row who handed him a rumpled D'Agostino super market grocery bag. DeStefano pulled the frame out of the bag and tossed it towards Politeri who instinctively caught it.

"You can't be talkin' about this... can you?" DeStefano said, "I picked it up a week or so ago – didn't I Mr. Antique Store Owner?"

Albert nodded.

"I guess the only way you can get it for me now," DeStefano said, "would be to hand it back to me, but that wouldn't really be how you said you would do it... was it?"

DeStefano walked up to Politeri and in an exaggerated whisper, said, "Was... it?"

Politeri stood motionless in front of the older man.

"I said, WAS IT?" DeStefano repeated.

Politeri was dripping in sweat as he nodded yes.

A slow stream of a yellowish liquid was beginning to surround Trella's shoes.

"Now the big question... the $100,000 question... the foolproof plan *plus* equally foolproof backup plan, question," DeStefano said. "What do I do about it?"

"Let me explain," Politeri started to say.

"What is there to explain?" Destefano said, smiling broadly. "It isn't like I had to send an army of people to get this – actually, all I did was ask for it. I never thought it would cost more than a few dollars but as it turned out, I didn't have to pay anything for it. Not one single penny. Can you believe that? Not one single penny. In fact, the store owner over there was thrilled to give it to me as a sign of his friendship and respect. I guess he has more respect for me than you do... huh, Mr. Self-Made Billionaire?"

This was not going very well at all, Trella thought, a smile forming on his sweaty face, but now at least he wouldn't have to die alone, Politeri would surely accompany him to the grave.

"Hey," DeStefano yelled, breaking Trella out of his trance, "what are you smiling about?"

"Nothing Mr. DeStefano," Trella heard himself say, "nothing at all."

"Well, you can go. Your biggest mistake was going to work for that loser," DeStefano said, pointing towards Politeri; but all Trella could see was the door as he ran towards it.

"That leaves you, Mr. Self-Made Billionaire," DeStefano said as he crept towards Politeri.

"You are going to go back to Michigan... you are going to pack up all of your earthly belongings... you are going find a place that is somewhere I never frequent... you are going to fade away. One more thing to think about as you return home with your tail cut off. Remember that pot-o-gold you kept talking about that you would get when you finally got your hands on the cure for cancer hidden in that teacher's stuff? Well there ain't gonna be no pot-o-gold for you or anyone else."

"There was no cure after all?" Politeri asked.

"Oh, there might still be a cure all right,", DeStefano said, "but if and when that happens, it will be given – not sold – given, free and clear, in my grandson's name, to a group of hospitals that will make certain it is available to everyone. Nice turn of events, wouldn't you say? Now get out of my sight. You disgust me."

Chapter 49
Sunday, May 19, 1996 –
Menlo Park, New Jersey – 7:45 P.M.

James and Schless were at the lab because Angela and Frank told them that a breakthrough might come at any time now.

Angela worked with five researchers trying to pick up where Ilsa and Mark Regan left off. They felt confident – at the very least - that they could soon definitively declare if the mother/son Regan's accumulated findings had come up with anything worth pursuing. In her last conversation with James, Angela said that they still had not learned enough to be able to say – one way or another - if there was any 'there', there, but what she did know was that the mother and son had approached the challenge in ways that were far different from the recognized procedures researchers had used before or even since. "Even if they did not come up with a cure," Angela told James, "they clearly established a series of procedures and protocols which could redefine how this kind of medical research *should* be conducted for years to come."

Meanwhile, Frank and the rest of the researchers were concentrating on the six specimens. They were fighting the clock to be able to get answers they hoped were still hidden within these specimens. Now that the specimens were out in the air the rate of decay was accelerating at an alarmingly quick rate. Frank's last report to James was neither encouraging nor discouraging. "I have not felt this frustrated in years. If our equipment and accumulated experience was not as advanced as it is we would stand no chance at all. But we are still marginally optimistic that we can get some answers before too much longer. He and his team were now working around the clock."

James's phone rang. It was Sol, advising him that three NYPD detectives had come to the apartment and just left. "They wanted to know about our *'clandestine assembly'* with a known underworld figure – Carmine DeStefano. It really shook us up, especially Albert; he was a basket case by the time they left," Sol told James.

"What else did they want to know?" James asked.

"They never got a chance to ask much of anything else. As soon as they flashed their badges I asked if we were under arrest. They said, no. To be honest, I guess I have been watching too many police dramas on television; I began rattling off every cliché that came to mind. I asked if we were being charged with a crime... I asked if they had a court order... finally, I asked why they would be harassing us so late on a Sunday evening... the one who seemed to be in charge said no to everything I asked. So I told them to get the hell out of our apartment. And they did!"

"Is Albert all right?" James asked.

"After they left he told me that it isn't likely they will give up so quickly and he thought they or some of their compatriots would probably be back – and soon." Sol said.

"Unfortunately, Sol, I think he is right. They *will* probably be back, and the next time they will not be so quick to leave empty handed."

"Probably not, but I was outraged and Albert – after the initial shock wore off – said he didn't like their Gestapo approach. I am not kidding here; they came on like storm troopers. Scary in what we like to think of as a democracy."

"I can relate to that," James said. "Would you and Albert be able to meet with me at Tom's Diner in the morning?"

"I guess so."

"Please try as hard as you can to avoid being followed."

"You think they are watching us?" Sol asked.

"It is always a safer bet to assume the worst, Sol," James said. "They can be like a dog with a bone. If they think they might be on to something then they are not going to give up so easily. Put yourself in their place; working you and Albert over can be far more gratifying than sitting in a squad room waiting for the phone to ring."

Chapter 50
Monday, May 20, 1996 –
Tom's Diner, Crown Heights, Brooklyn – 8:14 A.M.

As usual, James arrived earlier than planned and took up a position about a half a block away, leaning against a wall within clear sight of the restaurant.

At 8:30 A.M. he saw Sol arrive in a taxi. Sol paid the driver, scanned the streets, and then walked into Tom's Diner.

About fifteen minutes later, Albert walked up to the restaurant and walked inside.

James could see a blue and white Chevy Caprice slowly moving into sight. The driver pulled up alongside a delivery truck that was parked at the curb across the street from Tom's. James could see the Chevy driver flash a badge at the truck driver. It looked like the drivers of the two vehicles were arguing about something but must have resolved their differences because minutes later, the truck pulled away and the Chevy took its place at the curb. A young woman got out of the Chevy and walked into the restaurant.

James had arranged for Sol to have a non-traceable prepaid cell phone. He thought their regular cell phones would probably be tapped but Sol might be under less scrutiny than Albert; so it was decided that Sol would be the contact person if James ever needed to get word to Albert in a hurry. James dialed the prepaid cell and Sol picked up. James told him that someone was tailing Albert. He described the young woman and Sol said he could see her standing at the front of the restaurant, talking to the cashier. "It looks like she is just placing a takeout order," Sol said. "So should their meeting be called off?"

James was silent for a while and then suggested that Sol and Albert have their breakfast. "Try to act as natural as possible." Then James cautioned him not to talk about anything involving the work at the lab while they were in the restaurant.

"Stretch breakfast out for at least an hour, I will need a little time to set up a few surprises for your minders. By the time you get back to your apartment I will be waiting inside."

"You don't have a key," Sol argued.

"Let me worry about that."

"Okay," Sol responded, "but I do have to say that I don't love the idea of knowing how useless our security system is."

James hung up.

*****

They had been asked not to discuss the specifics of the case so Sol and Albert spent the better part of the next hour talking about *their* relationship and how best to move on after the stress of the past few weeks.

"I have always been strengthened by our relationship," Albert finally mused, "but I now feel like more of an interested party than I ever had before."

"Being face to face with so much conflict – real, life threatening conflicts –tend to help one prioritize what is meaningful and what is just life's foolish crap... it sure has helped me to put things into better focus," Sol responded.

"I am not proud of this but I now see that you have been my rock since the beginning while I flitted from day to day. You have been the *giver* and I have been satisfied to just take." Albert said, reflectively.

"Like a comfortable old shirt?" Sol asked, only half-teasing.

"I want... no, I need you to know that you mean so much more to me than that," Albert said, gently reaching for Sol's hand.

"We can both try harder," Sol said.

"I *will* try harder," Albert said. "*If* we get out of this and can get back to some semblance of a normal life I will never take you for granted again. I so want to be as committed to you as you have always been to me." He smiled, "I guess I have already started down that road, the *old me* would have been more concerned about getting some big monetary windfall from all of this."

"Surviving the challenges while growing stronger together would be windfall enough for me," Sol said, smiling broadly. He lifted his coffee cup, and whispered, "To the rest of our lives!"

Albert raised his coffee cup and clicked it against Sol's cup, "This beats having to write you a letter someday!"

Sol thought for a moment, and then laughed.

Chapter 51
Monday, May 20, 1996 –
Crown Heights, Brooklyn – 9:44 A.M.

Schless drove towards Albert and Sol's apartment house. He circled the block and quickly noticed a black Chevy Caprice parked just three car lengths away from their building. There was a man at the wheel and a woman in the passenger seat. A coffee cup was perched on the dashboard. Schless smiled to himself; the city of New York should really invest in a few less obvious undercover cars, he thought.

He parked several cars behind the Chevy and turned off his motor. In the back seat of Schless's car, chewing a huge rawhide bone was Moish, the forty seven pound basset hound he borrowed from his neighbor on the way to Crown Heights.

He watched a taxi pull up to the building just after 10 A.M.; Albert and Sol got out of the taxi, Sol paid the driver and they both entered the building. Schless watched the two occupants in the Caprice sit up straight.

Schless got out of his car and opened the rear, driver's side door. He reached in and attached an extra-long leash to Moish's collar and then encouraged him to jump out of the car. Schless nodded to a scantily-dressed young woman several doorways down the street and she nodded back. The woman began to walk past the Chevy and seemed to accidentally drop her open purse. Things fell out and she quickly bent down in a valiant effort to retrieve her belongings. The man in the Chevy's driver seat seemed to be watching her every move as her skirt began to slide up.

Man and dog walked slowly across the street and then alongside the curb. As they approached the rear of the

Chevy, Schless bent down, as if to pick up after Moish. He pulled a raw potato from his pocket and pushed it into the Chevy's tailpipe; then continued walking to the corner with the dog by his side.

*****

Albert and Sol stood outside their apartment door.

"You think he is really in there?" Albert asked in a low voice.

"One way to find out is to go inside," Sol said.

"I hate knowing how vulnerable our locks are," Albert said.

"Hey," Sol responded with a deep sigh, "locks only keep honest people out, Albert. You should know that."

"But that Schless guy got in so quickly... so quietly... so effortlessly. It's scary."

"One more reason to be thankful they are on your side."

"Yeh, sure, well time to make the donuts." Albert said.

Sol knocked on the door several times. No one answered. They looked at each other quizzically. Then Sol put his key in the lock. When the door opened they could see James sitting in the kitchen drinking from one of their mugs. There was a half empty bag of Double Stuff Oreo cookies on the table.

"Should we get you a pipe and slippers?" Sol asked, facetiously.

"I'll take the cost of the coffee and five Oreo cookies off of your bill," James said. "You two were able to enjoy a nice hot breakfast this morning – all I am having for breakfast is a very bad cup of coffee and a handful of cookies. Tell me, do you *ever* wash that coffee pot out?"

Albert got right to the point. "I knew that DeStefano meant nothing but trouble, now how are we going to handle this latest development?"

"It is about to be handled," James answered, confidently.

"Do you mind sharing with the rest of the class how you are *handling* this?" Albert asked.

"When we are done here," James began, "you are both going for a short walk. You will walk, as quickly as you can, up the wrong way on this one way street. At the corner a car will be waiting for you and will pick you up and take you to the lab in Menlo Park."

"What if the police or anyone else is waiting downstairs to follow us?" Sol asked.

"They *are* waiting downstairs for you, and they *will* almost certainly try to follow you, but they will have to deal with auto problems first."

"And you know this... how?" Albert asked, clearly annoyed.

"Because I put into motion the major auto problem they are about to have to deal with."

"So what will stop them from just getting out of their auto and running after us?"

"There are two of them sitting in the car this very moment so I am reasonably certain that at least one *will* get out of the car and try to run after you. But he or she will fail."

"And you know *that*... how?" Albert asked, getting even more annoyed.

"He or she will fail because he or she will get tangled up in a long dog leash."

"And you know *that* how?" Albert was now yelling.

"I know that because I set that up too; and by the time he or she frees him or herself from the leash - assuming neither of you dawdle, but instead, move up the street quickly, you will be in a car on your way to the lab in Menlo Park, New Jersey."

"And you don't think all of that will make them so angry that they will come after us with everything they have?" Albert asked, with mounting anger.

"Actually, I am hoping that happens," James responded.

"Have you lost your everlasting mind?" Albert was now standing inches away from James, almost uncontrollably outraged.

James gently put his hand on Albert's shoulder. "Look," he said, calmly, "sometimes you need an elephant to get rid of a mouse infestation. They could be our 'elephant' to help us shake free from DeStefano - our 'mouse problem.'"

"Let me understand this," Albert sputtered. "Your *plan* is to use the big and powerful New York Police Department to save us from one of the most dangerous men in the city... no make that the region, if not the entire country. One of those powers can have us killed with the twitch of a little pinky while the other can put us away, with similar-minded individuals, for the rest of our natural born days. So *if* by some small chance your half-assed plan succeeds, we will only have to deal with one of those horrific threats. *But,* if instead your seemingly off the wall plan fails, *as if that is even a possibility,* then we can spend the rest of our lives in constant fear of both of those behemoths?"

Sol tapped Albert's back and got between the two men.

"And, now that you are being so forthcoming with us, how *do* you plan to *then* get rid of the *elephant*?" Sol calmly asked James.

"Let's just worry about one pest at a time, if you don't mind," James said.

"Pests? Did you say, pests? A flea is a pest, an ant is a pest; either of *our* two new potential enemies are well past any possible definition of *pest*," Albert said, shaking his head. "So you are asking if I mind. Why should I mind? I am about to bring the big and powerful New York Police Department down on my head – on purpose, yet; by plan! And that's what we are *hoping* will happen if this plan of yours succeeds - why should I *mind*?"

"*Our* heads," Sol corrected.

"What did you say?" Albert asked Sol, as if he was now just aware that Sol was standing there.

"I said, '*our heads*,'" Sol said, meekly. "We are about to bring the big and powerful New York Police Department down on *our heads*. You know, Albert, what happens to you will almost certainly happen to me. Each of these forces sees us as one and the same."

"Excuse me," Albert responded, "*Our heads*."

"Calm down, Albert. Let's not make this worse by fighting among ourselves," James said. "I know, full well, that each of these sides is formidable..."

Albert sat down, shaking his head. "Formidable," Albert whispered, "can be impressive... it can be intimidating... I would not categorize either one of these two death machines as just *formidable*, either. I'm thinking terrifying... frightening... why mince words, I would label this plan of yours suicidal!"

"Calm down, Albert," James repeated, "we are not completely at their mercy – at least not unless we just throw up our hands and surrender. I don't know about you, but if that was my way of responding I would have been crushed into dust many years ago. You are just going to have to pull yourself together. That is the *only* way we have a chance to survive."

"Have you given the fact that I have a store to run any consideration?" Albert asked.

"Of course I have thought about the store, Albert." James said, "I asked Elizabeth to open the store at 10:00 A.M. sharp and put the closed for lunch sign up at exactly 10:01 A.M., just like the agreement you finally struck with your mother's lawyer. If you agree with the plan as I will lay it out for you then you can decide to have her reopen at exactly 4:59 P.M. and close at exactly 5:00 P.M. We then will not have to make any decisions about the store at least until tomorrow and by tomorrow a lot can change."

"If only I could be so optimistic," Albert said, shaking his head, but the terms of my mother's lease require me to physically be on the selling floor those two minutes."

"Let's worry about your mother's lawyer after we get through this immediate problem. He has a reputation as an honest guy and I am sure he will understand after we explain all of this to him."

Sol gently added, "Let's hear him out. Unfortunately, we have no other choice. You can't blame any of this on Will; unlike us, he could have walked away days ago but he didn't. He has consciously chosen *not* to wash his hands of us. Instead, by hanging in with us, he faces the same enemies we are facing. He and all of the people he has recruited to help you are now facing whatever we face."

"Okay," Albert said, "I can't possibly win if both of you

tag team me like this." He sat down at the kitchen table and absent-mindedly reached for the mug of coffee James had been drinking from. He drank the contents in a single gulp, popped an Oreo cookie into his mouth, looked across the table from James and with his mouth full of cookie crumbs, said, "Okay, I am ready to listen. What is the *rest of your plan?*"

James pulled his chair closer to Albert; he rubbed his hands together, loudly cleared his throat, and said, "Okay, my co-conspirators... here is the plan..."

Chapter 52
Monday, May 20, 1996 –
Crown Heights, Brooklyn – 10:27 A.M.

Albert and Sol stood in the apartment house lobby, gathering their nerve.

"Ready?" Sol asked.

"As ready as I will ever be," a clearly nervous Albert responded.

"Then here we go!" Sol said as he quickly opened the front door and on the count of three, both ran down the few steps onto the sidewalk and began running up the street.

"As soon as they appeared outside the door, the passenger in the Caprice grabbed the coffee cup off of the dashboard and the driver turned the engine on and gunned the motor. There was a loud popping sound followed by a grinding noise; the car jerked forward a few feet and then stopped. The passenger door swung open; a woman jumped out of the car and began running after Sol and Albert.

Seemingly from out of nowhere, the young lady who had dropped her handbag before was now walking a basset hound across the path of the running woman causing her to trip on the leash. The dog walker kept apologizing. She seemed to be trying to help the woman up but was actually making it harder for her to move past her and the dog.

*****

At the corner, Schless beeped his horn to attract Sol and Albert's attention and slowly pulled forward. The run of less than a city block had winded them both. When they reached the car, Sol quickly got into the front passenger seat and slammed the door behind him. Albert opened the rear passenger door, looked inside and yelled, "There has been a dog in here. When did you get a dog?"

"Please," Schless said, "just get in, quickly."

Albert got into the back seat, closed the door and sat as close to the door as he could; staring at the other half of the back seat. He picked up a wet and partially deformed piece of rawhide that was on the seat with two fingers and tossed it into the foot well on the other side of the car. "I am allergic to dogs, you know," he said, to no one in particular.

Sol just smiled apologetically. Schless rolled his eyes as he put the car into motion. The car sped away from the curb.

*****

By the time the woman reached the corner the two men she was chasing were nowhere to be seen. She stopped several people at the corner, but no one could say if they had seen two middle aged men running up the block or not. She stood at the corner with her hands on her hips in obvious disgust; then she slowly walked back to her partner in the Chevy Caprice.

The two *professional watchdogs* from the Caprice had been played... they had been out smarted, out thought, out maneuvered... and by two middle aged rank amateurs... and they all knew it! A lot would have to be explained to superiors... and they knew *that* too!

Chapter 53
Monday, May 20, 1996 –
Menlo Park, New Jersey – 11:49 A.M.

Frank went downstairs to let Albert, Sol, and Schless into the building. Other than a quick hello, each silently made their way up to the main conference room. Elizabeth, and Angela nodded at the three men as they filed into the room and then continued what seemed to be a deep conversation at the far end of the conference table.

Frank motioned for them to take their usual seats as he went directly to the light boxes, continuing his inspection of the latest group of X-rays of one of the specimens.

Albert and Sol nodded to the others and sat down.

Schless poured himself a cup of coffee. Then, as he carefully set his cup on a coaster, looked from face to face and said, "Hey, it looks like a funeral in here. Is there only gloom and doom to be served up with my coffee today?"

Frank sighed. "You can call it gloom and doom; believe me, I don't give up easily, but we seem to have come to a dead end."

A short while later James rang the bell and they could see him standing outside via the closed circuit screen in the corner of the room. Schless ran down to let him in.

As James and Schless entered the room, James said, "Judging from what Schless here has mumbled on the way up with me... and now after looking at the expressions on your faces, this is going to be a very long and sad meeting.

Angela began slowly, "We had been concentrating on the more recent of the lab notes because of the time pressures we were under; it made sense to us that the latest notes would more than likely represent their best work. Unfortunately, it didn't. We were going in circles and time was getting away from us. Finally, one of our researchers suggested that we reverse the direction we had been following because, as he put it, 'sixty year old failures might be modern day success stories given the reams of new information and interim research at our disposal.' So we revisited the earliest notes and broke down their first experiments, duplicating them in our lab, now with the help of the scientific advances over the years and our lab's state of the art equipment. That was how we learned that they used x-rays to identify where the strongest cancer cells were forming *not* to cut them out or burn them but so as to better predict the direction in which the cancer cells were likely to go *next*. They then systematically applied or *painted* a solution..."

"Did you say, *painted*?" Sol asked.

"Yes I did. They actually painted, or topically applied a layer of a liquid serum directly onto the skin just above the anticipated *new* cancer cell destinations. Their premise was that cancer cells build and then move on... at the moment the cancer cells *first* enter a new area they are as weak as they will ever be. The exhausting battle with healthy cells plus the journey towards the new destination temporarily reduces the cancer cell's best ability to fight too strenuously for its survival and this only occurs at the moment it first settles into a new area."

Sol broke in, "So why not just *paint* the entire body in this solution to cover all possibilities?"

"Because the formula they came up with was quite toxic and possibly – after repeated treatments – could have been as harmful, maybe even more harmful, than the cancer." Frank responded. "They made mention of a miracle reducer, this painted solution, would seep through the skin and into the targeted cells... once in place the combination of ingredients acted together to flood targeted cells with a chemical infused moisture... diluting most of the germs or disease – the actual cancer - within that specific region... a time-released chemical reaction would then be injected with an effect similar to freezing that *moisture* now accumulated within the newly targeted area. By stimulating the skin above the cells at precisely the right moment, the cancer cells were being invaded by the injected mixture, the cancer in that cell and immediate surrounding cells would become cancer free, any remnants of the now inactive cancer would eventually be expressed through the urinary tract."

Angela continued, "So, success depended upon the accuracy of determining the new location in advance *and* a dependable way to control the strength and direction of the serum. We believe the formula they used was too weak in the first three specimens, just right in the fourth, and too much in the fifth and sixth. By trial and error and knowledge of what existed during those years, we think we have identified most of the secondary active ingredients. But with the deterioration of the six mice in that metal box that Ilsa risked her life to transport, we lost our best chance to identify the primary ingredient for the serum. That is why we feel we have hit a dead end and why the long faces."

"I don't know about the rest of you but my head is swimming here," Albert said. "Can you say what you just said in simple everyday English?"

Frank drew a circle on the white board. "This is a cancer cell. It is powerful and dominant and firmly entrenched, here." He filled in the circle with a red colored marker. "The cancer cells became strong by draining all of the power from the healthy cells in its way. Most theories for treating or trying to combat the cancer cell fall into a couple of areas. Without involving ourselves in the pluses and minuses of each of those two methods, the medical profession has argued in favor of either cutting out or burning away – radiating - the diseased section as well as a margin of healthy surrounding cells as an insurance policy to get all of the cancer." He made a wider circle around the first one. He placed a series of dots on and around the circle. "This represents the serum going through the skin onto the targeted cells." He erased the drawing from the board. "Now it is gone! Is that plain enough?"

"Yes," Albert said, amazed.

There were three light boxes, each illuminating a new x-ray. Pointing from one x-ray to the next, Frank said, "These are all x-rays of the specimen we are now calling *'last in line'*. It is what we believe to be the final specimen of the series, but we have no way to verify that. It is important to note," he said, pointing to the x-ray on the extreme left; then to the x-ray in the middle, "the elapsed time between these two slides was only *nine and three tenths seconds* – a blur at best. The image on the extreme right screen is our control slide – it was taken prior to removing the specimen from the security of the NASA tunnel and a fraction of a second before we removed the specimen from its protected place in the metal box." Frank pressed a button on the center screen. "Here is the same specimen, magnified 300 times. As a measure, please note the internal organs in the same general areas as the cancer cells have already shrunk to a point where they are barely recognizable." He then did the same to the extreme right screen. "Again, magnification to 300 times," he pressed another button. "Here is magnification at 600 times." He pointed to a small area. "That is where the heart should be."

"So, exposure to the air shrunk the mass this much?" James asked.

Angela responded, "Yes, there is no doubt that exposure to the air accounts for some of the shrinkage; however, only some of the shrinkage. We believe that a larger percentage of the mass loss and the sole reason for this total melting away of what previously was there..."

"Excuse me, each of you have used the word *melting* several times today. Up until today the references were one version or another of *shrinking*. Has something changed or am I reading too much into this?" Elizabeth asked.

"You are *very* observant Elizabeth – maybe you should work here at the lab with us instead of at the antique store with Albert," Frank responded.

"Wait just a minute," Albert broke in.

They all turned to look at Albert whose face had turned beet red as he stared blankly at Elizabeth.

"Don't worry, Albert," Schless said, "there is no way anyone will be able to match the generous employee package I am certain you will want to put together for Elizabeth after all of this is resolved."

"Yes, Elizabeth," Frank continued, "before we used the term *shrink* exclusively because all we could see was that the specimens were decreasing in size... shriveling in front of our eyes. What we are *now* able to see in far greater detail is a total melting away process." He fanned out what looked like dozens of black and white numbered photos. "Here," he said proudly, "is exactly what happened during that blur. These forty-three separate photos represent what actually took place during that nine and three tenths second blur!"

There were matching looks of amazement around the table.

"How did you capture so much in so short a window of time?" James asked.

Angela said, "We brought in a NASA photo recorder to document our work on this specimen. By studying the charts afterwards we were able to see what was happening in attoseconds."

"Attoseconds? What is an attosecond?" Schless asked.

"An attosecond," Elizabeth responded, "is the time it takes for light to travel the length of two hydrogen atoms. 24 attoseconds is the atomic unit of time."

"How do you even know that?" Frank asked.

Looking a little embarrassed, Elizabeth shrugged. "I guess I read it somewhere."

"I think Frank was only teasing before but I would be serious in asking you to consider working for us instead of Albert," Angela said.

"Enough already!" Albert broke in. "I thought you were all here to help me; I don't see how taking my strongest asset away from me could be anyone's definition of *helping me*. Elizabeth has a job and I plan to make it well worth her while to want to hold on to that job now and in the far distant future."

Angela continued, "We previously reported that some areas were shrinking faster than others – we now believe that it is not entire areas but very specific *cells* – the cancer cells - which were targeted to shrink and yes, melt away, at a quicker rate because the skin just above them had been *painted* with a solution designed to bleed down and attack those very specific cells."

"As with everything else that you see or hear in this building, that information is *not* to be shared with anyone else," Frank said, sternly.

"Why is that so important to be kept secret?" Sol asked.

"It is important because we believe that no other country in the world can break down time in such a microscopic unit of measure. If not for the frustrations we have been experiencing on this assignment, we never would have asked for special permission to use it for a non-government assignment, and the approval only just arrived – it required nine individual sign offs... one going all the way up to the Oval Office. This process gives our spy satellites a distinct edge over all others," Frank said.

Angela moved closer to the light boxes and said, "There is no question about it, this is very good news – we have discovered the process used by the Austrian lab to chart and then shrink specific cancer cells."

"So, then tell me why the long faces?" James asked.

"We have not been able to reverse-engineer the formula used to manufacture the serum. So knowing the process is useless without the serum," Frank said with a heavy sigh.

"So they did find a way to cure this disease... decades ago?" Schless asked.

"They did and they didn't," Frank said. "They *did* in that they developed and may have proved a possibly revolutionary new process. They *didn't* because they were never truly able to pinpoint the specific diseased cells without *bleeding* over to healthy cells, and in the case of this specimen," he pointed to the middle x-ray, "entire organs were dragged in. Furthermore, they did not put the formula for this special serum in their notes – it died with them."

"What does that tell you that you did not know before?" Sol asked.

Frank thought for a few minutes then said, "We learned that there is a short window of time when cancer cells may be more dangerous and when they are less dangerous. Specifically, the instant they attach themselves to a new area. By the time they are ready to move on they are at their strongest. When they first arrive at a new location they have minimal *defensive* strength; that is when we stand the best chance to crush them – not so much before... not so much after... just precisely then!"

"Now that you know this can't you prove the theory with one of the other specimens; by the way, where are the other five specimens now?" Albert asked.

"They are still in the NASA unit." Angela said.

"Have the other specimens also been *melting* away?" Sol asked.

"Not materially; at least not yet." Frank said, "But we anticipate that they will as soon as we take them out of the NASA unit."

"All of this sounds like great progress," Schless said.

"More like an empty victory," Frank said sadly.

"Painted on the surface?" Albert whispered to Sol, clearly impressed.

"How is it that we do not know what they used in that *paint concoction* of theirs? It seems to me that this would have been a proprietary blend that they developed over some series of trials. Can't we track it down through any other source?" Sol asked.

"We have deduced that they tried two different formulations. However, we have no way of knowing the specific ingredients in either one – Ilsa did not identify them in her notes and by the time we cut into the specimen, the mass had already begun to deteriorate. Any remaining traces of the solution had all but evaporated."

"I'm also more than a little lost. Can you boil all of this down again? Please, only use the simplest of terms possible," Schless said.

"Actually, that technique was used by the Russians as early as the 1920's," Elizabeth said.

Frank's head turned quickly to Elizabeth. "How did you know that?" he asked.

"I don't know... I just do," Elizabeth said.

"That was not very widely known, Elizabeth. In fact, I understood that this technique was a deeply held secret for decades and only came out by accident when Russia and America teamed up on space exploration," Frank said, guardedly.

Sol stared at Elizabeth. "Is there anything else you want to tell us, Elizabeth?"

"I don't want to slow down the discussion – it is just something I know about," Elizabeth said, meekly.

"I understand that there was a small but effective elite Russian commando unit that was responsible for burning down an entire research facility – with everything and everyone destroyed within its walls just to keep that process secret," Frank said.

"Come on, Elizabeth, tell us what you know," Albert said.

Elizabeth looked around the table, stopping briefly to meet James's eye, then said, "I just know about this process; it was initially developed during the First World War in Donetsk, the town where I was born... a little industrial and mining town in the Ukraine. The scientists were trying to repair or at least reduce the damage to vital organs from mustard gas. I also read somewhere that it was not a very successful experiment. The Russians returned to the earlier research towards the end of the Second World War in hopes of undoing the damages to their soldier's lungs caused by germ warfare – Germany's final desperate act. From what I read, these experiments failed as well."

Albert broke in, "How do you know all of that, Elizabeth?"

"I told you," Elizabeth said quickly, "I read it somewhere."

James held up his hand, "Talk to us, Elizabeth."

"I thought you said you trusted me," she said, sternly.

"I did and I do. But I can't help but feel that you are somehow holding back something that *might,* just *might,* help us here," James shot back.

She heaved a huge sigh, and then said, "I have already told you that I was born in Donetsk." She stopped for an even deeper sigh, "I was raised by the head of the KGB's Internal Medical Research Ministry and his wife. I saw some things and heard some things and ultimately connected the dots. I am not saying that this is a wild goose chase you are on, but I am saying that it was tried and failed and the KGB really, really tried. The people who ran the facility where I grew up would have gained mightily if they could have found a way to show success but they didn't – they couldn't. They would have been declared national heroes if they could have broken the code. They were pretty smart and had whatever tools they asked for and they still failed – not once but twice. That's all I know."

Angela asked, "How did you know that they used it during

the early 1920's? You weren't even alive back then."

"I read something about it while playing in my father's office, I have this annoying ability to remember anything I read or hear – even casually – virtually word for word. It is how I am able to speak so many languages. All I have ever had to do was read a language lesson or listen to a language tape once, sometimes twice, and then I would be able to speak the language, read it, easily converse with anyone for whom that would be their native language. Usually by the first time around I would have the identical cadence, accent, inflection, of the speaker on the tape. I can't say that I understood everything on the lab papers I translated for you... but I could recite, word for word, including misspelled words, from every page I scanned. I think of it as a nuisance, a parlor trick. For me, it is just annoying."

"You know," Frank said, "We hear a lot about people with a *photographic memory* and tend to think that such people are quite unusual, but I have always believed that most if not all people are capable of retaining far more of what they read or hear if they are able to concentrate. The *secret* is concentration. I watched Elizabeth one day when she was working on the translations. A car in the parking lot backfired and it startled me and everyone around me, but Elizabeth was so involved in her work that she didn't even seem to notice. She was concentrating so hard that she was able to block out the distraction. I mentioned it to Angela at the time."

"Did you ever visit the laboratory in Donetsk?" Frank asked Elizabeth.

"Yes," Elizabeth responded. "I did. My brothers and I had the run of the place and spent many hours in the lab as well as the rest of the facility. But I was very young and did not really know what I was looking at."

Frank looked directly at James as he said, "As we said before, one of the major roadblocks we have encountered is that we have not been able to reverse engineer the liquid formula or even determine the complete list of ingredients Ilsa and her associates used on the six specimens. There was no mention of such a formula in her notes and we wondered how that information could possibly *not* have been included given the high level of detail throughout the rest of her notes from the Austrian lab. The only acceptable reason was that they had merely lifted an existing formula. We knew that the Russians actually began such research and so our internal discussions began to surmise that Ilsa and her group somehow accessed the earlier research and were trying to build upon it."

"Failing to get it from her notes, it is a shame that you couldn't have gotten it from the specimens themselves," Schless said.

"The combination of sixty plus years of mishandling and the deterioration since the vacuum was broken have made it impossible to learn much of anything from the specimens themselves," Angela said. "And of course, the preserving liquid into which each specimen was floated has further hampered our reverse engineering activities."

"Also, as said before, we have come up with a group of possible ingredients that would have been available to them at the time. Perhaps, just perhaps, if Elizabeth goes over our list, she might see one or more key ingredient which she saw either on some document or in a supply cabinet or on a work surface in that lab in Donetsk."

"That's quite a reach," James said.

"Even a spoon can be helpful when facing a brick wall with nothing else around to dig your way through," Frank responded.

"I'm willing to help anyway I can," Elizabeth said.

James put his hands up, and said, "If you think there is even a chance in a thousand, let's do it."

"But if Elizabeth is right and the process was a failure, why invest more valuable time and resources on this?" Sol asked.

"I'm as skeptical as you seem to be", Angela said, "but if we can spark Elizabeth's memory there might be a light at the end of this tunnel."

Albert sighed, "I just hope the light at the end of the tunnel isn't an oncoming train."

Schless yelled out, "Look at the screen, DeStefano and two of his guards are downstairs at the front door."

All eyes turned to the security monitor in the corner of the room.

James quickly stood up and said, "I'll go down and see what new drama is developing."

They all watched the screen as they saw James open the front door. They watched what looked like a very animated conversation between James and DeStefano. Finally, James let DeStefano and his two bodyguards into the building. Within minutes they all entered the conference room.

DeStefano was the first to speak.

"I don't remember being invited to this little party. I thought we all agreed to work together."

He motioned to his bodyguards to sit by the door as he walked over to inspect what was now on the light boxes. "Now that I am here, we can begin," he said, moving his gaze directly towards James.

"We have already begun, Carmine." James said.

"So I see," DeStefano shot back, with a grimace.

From outside the building they heard someone talking into what sounded like a bullhorn.

"This is the FBI. Your building is surrounded. We are requesting everyone in the building to exit immediately. If you fail to heed this warning we will enter the building with whatever force is necessary. If we are forced to enter in that manner then everyone within the building will be taken into federal custody and may be charged with one or more federal crimes. I will need some acknowledgement that this message has been heard and will be honored."

"That is why you were not invited," James said to Carmine with a frown. Then to Frank he barked, "Set the security camera to record and make sure you get both sides of the conversation. If you see anyone barge passed me or if you think it is getting out of control, quickly call your contact at NASA. Tell your contact that their fellow feds are compromising your security procedures and ask them to make whatever calls they can to stop it quickly."

James rushed downstairs as the rest of those in the room looked on through the closed circuit screen.

James opened the door just wide enough to pass through and walked outside. He stood close to the door, well within the range of the security camera, and held up his hands. At the top of his lungs he yelled, "I am not armed. I wish to speak to the agent in charge."

A tall, muscular man, with a short crew cut of deep red hair slowly walked towards him. "I am Agent Allis Murphy. I am the agent in charge. Now tell me what your name is and your specific reason or reasons for being here."

"I am an American citizen," James responded, "and so I have the Constitutional right to be wherever I choose, whenever I choose, with whomever I choose."

"That kind of talk is going to get you into a whole lot of trouble, sir."

"What is *your* reason for being here and threatening the many unarmed, law abiding citizens in this building?" James asked, as he slowly lowered his hands.

"I am asking you to step aside and allow us to enter this building," Allis Murphy said.

"I would like to see your court papers permitting you to forcibly enter this building," James said.

"I will ask you once more, and *only* once more, to step aside and allow us to enter this building," Murphy repeated.

"Just for the record", James said, "and for the television feed that is about to be sent or may already have been sent to every news service in the world," James said, pointing to the camera above the door, "the company operating out of this building regularly works on multiple high security assignments from various branches of the United States government, many who work here have the highest civilian levels of security clearances, with multiple federal departments of the United States of America, so I ask *you* again to show me your court papers permitting you to forcibly enter this building."

"Do those *high security assignments* include the participation of a known member of the Gambino crime family?" Murphy said contemptuously.

Just then, DeStefano was fully visible inside the lobby; he

tapped on the door and motioned for James to move to the side so that he could exit the building.

"What seems to be the trouble?" DeStefano asked with a gentle smile.

"What is your name and reason for being here?" Murphy asked DeStefano.

"You don't know my name?" DeStefano said indignantly. Why, Mr. FBI Agent, I thought both of my pictures," he moved his head from side to side to duplicate a typical mug shot, "was tattooed on the palm of every FBI agent's hand so that they could instantly recognize me wherever I am and whenever I am within their gun sights."

A siren pierced their ears as a jeep, lights flashing and horn blazing, pulled into the lot. Two men, in marine desert fatigues quickly got out of the jeep and walked towards Murphy. "Please state your reason for being here." One of the marines said to Murphy.

Three helicopters appeared from below the horizon and began circling the area.

"You are interfering with an FBI investigation soldier," Murphy said.

"This is now a United States Marine-secured facility, sir. I am officially requesting you and those with you to stand down, holster your weapons, and leave these premises immediately."

"You are interfering with an FBI investigation, soldier," Murphy repeated.

"Show me your papers, sir," the marine persisted, slowly moving his hand to the holstered handle of his service pistol case.

"We followed that man," Murphy said, pointing at DeStefano with renewed confidence, "to this location; he is the known leader of the New York Gambino crime family, and we have reason to believe that others are consorting with him for criminal purposes inside that building."

"And your papers, sir?" the marine said again, unsnapping the cover securing his holstered service pistol while holding out his other hand as if to accept the requested court papers from Murphy.

"I don't have papers," Murphy finally said.

"Then I strongly suggest that you return to your vehicle and promptly leave the premises, sir." The Marine said.

"I will be back", Murphy said to James.

"When you do," the marine said, "you will find a reinforced marine checkpoint at the entrance to this lot and with or without court documents you will not be permitted access to this facility. The citizens in this facility are currently working on special assignments for the Department of Defense and that takes priority over any and all domestic matters."

DeStefano's guards walked closer to him and stood on either side.

DeStefano stepped forward and spoke directly to Murphy. "I merely came here with my friends," he said, nodding towards his guards, "to get a urine test. I was in the process of peeing into their little paper cup when you made this awful spectacle of yourself." He turned to James and said, "I may have left a small puddle when these people's loud noises scared me half to death. Please send my apologies to those in charge and tell them I will pay for the cleanup of any mess that I may have created." He then gave the Marine a gentle smile. "I will be leaving now." He signaled for the limo to pull up, staring directly at Murphy, he said, "I want to thank you for your interest in my health and wish you and all of your associates a warm and personally satisfying good day."

Freddie opened the rear passenger door. DeStefano waved at James and gave him a wink, blew a kiss in Murphy's direction, and got into the car. After securing his passenger, Freddie entered the front passenger seat and the car slowly drove away.

Murphy glared at James. "You haven't seen the end of this 'Spider.'"

"So you knew who I was all along," James said calmly. "Why then did you ask?"

Murphy waved at his men to move out, got into his own car, and sped away.

Frank walked closer to the marine and they talked privately for a few minutes. Finally, the two shook hands, the marine returned to his Jeep and drove away.

"I really like your casually dressed friends," James said to Frank.

"You know of course, that we only get to play that card once," Frank said, as they reentered the building.

"Sure, but if you do it right," James said in a low whisper. "Once is enough and we definitely did it right."

When they returned to the conference room James whispered in Albert's ear, "I guess that will take care of both the mouse *and* the elephant for a while."

"You don't really believe that either one will be giving up so quickly, do you?" Albert asked.

"No," James responded, "neither will be giving up, that *is* for certain, but each side will think long and hard before they try to come after any of us. At the very least it will buy us a bit of time and that may be all we need to resolve this mystery of ours."

Chapter 54
Monday, May 20, 1996 –
Menlo Park, New Jersey – 8:37 P.M.

Elizabeth spent the better part of the rest of the day with Frank and Angela. They pulled out numerous catalogues, some decades old, in hopes that some look or shape or name would ring a familiar note in her mind.

They stopped for dinner around eight o'clock, tired and weary and each feeling defeated. They were picking at their food when one of the senior researchers rushed into the room carrying three yellowed booklets. "I found these in the old archives in the storage room," she said. "Each of these dates back to the early nineteen hundreds. These were very specialized suppliers from the same region in Austria as the lab where Ilsa worked. If this doesn't do the trick I am afraid that we have really hit a brick wall."

Elizabeth reached for the catalogues and leafed through the first book. "No, there is nothing here," she said, sadly. She fanned through the second book and suddenly her eyes lit up. She opened it and turned back, about a dozen or so pages, until she found the image that initially caught her eye. "That's one of the bottles that was *always* under lock and key in my dad's office."

Frank and Angela stared at the picture.

"Are you sure?" they asked in unison.

"Yes, it looked like a perfume bottle and I asked my father if I could have it when it was empty. He laughed and said, 'Not this bottle – even empty, any remaining fumes would shrink your nose down to the size of a snow flake.' He made me promise that I would never come close to that bottle again. He rarely cared about my safety and so it really made an impression on me. That is the bottle I saw in his office, I am certain of it."

Frank jumped up from the table. "We are back in the game!" he said. "Let's get to work!"

Chapter 55
Tuesday, May 21, 1996 –
Williamsburg, Brooklyn, New York– 10:02 A.M.

Elizabeth was removing an item from the front window when Freddie walked into the store. He nodded to Elizabeth and asked if she was alone.

"Albert is in the back." She said.

"And Will James?" He asked.

"Yes, he's also in the back with Albert."

"I would like to speak with them. Can you ask them to come out?"

She started to speak but didn't quite know what to say.

Freddie smiled, held up his hands in a mock surrender sign and said, "Hay, I didn't come here to hurt anyone. Just tell them I'm here."

Will was the first to come forward. He nodded to Freddie, "Hi."

"Hi." Freddie responded, "Mr. DeStefano asked me to come by. "

"After yesterday I thought he would want to keep a low profile." James said.

"Yeh, a low profile, that's probably why he sent me instead of coming himself." Freddie said. "He needs to know, is there anything new from the scientists?"

"It has only been a day, not even a full day, Freddie." Elizabeth said.

"He needs to know if your guys can help his grandson." Freddie said.

James walked closer to him, "They are working on it, Freddie. That's all we know for sure."

"Mr. DeStefano wanted you to know that money was no object – whatever is needed..."

"From what I saw, money isn't the problem." Albert said.

Freddie seemed anxious, "Money... equipment... people..., Mr. DeStefano just wanted you to know that he can and would supply whatever might be needed, no questions asked, no obligation... no problems. Free and clear, he wanted me to make sure you knew it would be *free and clear*."

"These researchers are the very best there is Freddie. No one is giving up but it is slow and tedious work." James said.

"Is there nothing you can do to push it along?" Freddie asked.

"Just tell him to be patient." Albert snapped.

"It is hard for him to be patient while he is watching his grandson get weaker by the day." Freddie said. "Please, give me something to go back with, anything."

"Just tell Carmine that as long as they are working on it there is hope." James said.

*****

That evening, Albert told Sol about Freddie's visit. "They seem to think they can either threaten or own everyone and then snap their fingers and the world just stops for them."

"Hey," Sol growled, "how about a little compassion here. We are talking about a child – not even 5 years old. They are watching him die and he hasn't even lived yet."

Albert gave Sol a quizzical look, "You want me to be concerned about some gangster?"

"No," Sol said, "I expect you to have more compassion for the fate of a small child."

"I can only imagine how many *small children* became orphans thanks to that *grandfather* of his."

"Whatever the *grandfather* did or did not do, the grandson probably never harmed a soul." Sol said.

"I'm sorry Sol; I just can't separate the two." Albert said.

Sol shook his head from side to side, "If you can't see the difference between that or any adult and a child whose life is likely to end before it even begins – then I suggest the problem is somewhere within you and not Carmine DeStefano – regardless of who he is."

"Hey," Albert responded, "whose side are you on anyway?"

Sol pushed himself away from the table and started to walk out of the room. He paused and turned quickly to face Albert, "Who made you judge, jury and executioner? Grow up Albert, just grow up!"

"I'm trying here," Albert finally said.

"Well try harder! Maybe you have spent so much time around those little hidden treasures of yours that you have lost sight of life's *real* treasure, like humans."

"That's really horrible." Albert said.

"What is really horrible is your unwillingness to see beyond the tip of your nose."

When they first got together Albert and Sol set a few house rules for themselves. One of the most important of those rules to Albert was neither would go to sleep angry. This night, Sol broke that rule.

*****

Freddie came to the store every day that week and the next. Each time the news was the same – 'As long as they are working on it there is hope.'

With Sol's argument fresh in his mind, Albert tried to connect emotionally but just further alienated those around him.

Gradually Freddie's visits slowed to once a week, then once every other week, and by the end of the summer they stopped all together.

It was late in August when Albert arrived at the store and found Freddie leaning against the door.

Albert asked him what he wanted.

"A miracle." Freddie answered.

Albert started to repeat the now familiar response, 'They are still working on it and as long as they are there is hope.' But instead he invited the young man in to the store. He made a fresh pot of coffee and motioned for Freddie to sit down. They sat and talked for a while, small talk, polite but without substance.

"You don't like me, do you?" Freddie finally asked.

Albert thought for a while, shrugged, then said, "I don't really know you."

"I don't get the feeling that you give two hoots for Mr. DeStefano's grandson."

"I don't know him, either."

"What's to know?" Freddie shot back. "He's an innocent little kid with a death sentence hanging over his head." Freddie said.

"With a grandfather who would as quickly have someone murdered as decide what color sox to wear." Albert said.

"You're judging the kid by the *possible* actions of his grandfather?" Freddie asked.

"I don't judge anyone." Albert said, defiantly.

Freddie stood up, "You're a real jerk, Albert, a close minded little jerk. Why don't you just pull your head out of your backside? This kid never hurt no one."

"Or what?" Albert shot back.

"Or nothing." Freddie said as he walked towards the door.

"Wait," Albert said, "Let's start again. I really want to understand. Please, let's start over."

Freddie sat down as Albert refilled his coffee cup.

"It's as simple as this," Freddie said, "Mr. DeStefano is watching his grandson die. Like it or not, you guys are his last hope."

Chapter 56
Six months later...
Monday, October 28, 1996 –
Menlo Park, New Jersey – 4:51 P.M.

James called Billie Aarons and said, "Do you have a paper and pen?"

There was no answer.

"I would like to surprise our friend, the limo guy," James said.

"I thought you knew, the limo guy hates surprises," Aaron said hesitantly.

"He'll love this one," James said. "It's a special gift for his grandson."

"Excuse me?" Aarons said. "What do you mean?"

"Just get some paper and a pen," James insisted.

"You know, Will," Aarons said, "if you would like I could come over tomorrow and we could go for a walk."

"Anyone ever tell you that for an expensive mouthpiece you can be awfully thick at times?" James said. "Just get some paper and a pen. You do own paper and a pen in that big house of yours, don't you?"

"Just a minute," Aarons said, clearly annoyed.

James could hear the phone drop and a few minutes later Aarons picked it up and said, "I have a piece of paper and a pen, now what?"

"Just take this down, word for word; tell the limo guy to visit our Chinese friends tomorrow at 2:00 P.M. sharp."

"I don't make his schedule, Will."

"Just write it down," James persisted.

"What if he is *busy* tomorrow at 2:00 P.M., sharp?" Aarons said.

"Billie, you can't possibly be as stupid as you sound right now," James said. "Just tell the limo guy I would like him to visit our Chinese friends at 2:00 P.M. sharp tomorrow. If he is busy then he is busy. I didn't ask you to make his schedule or to guarantee his being there. I am just asking you to deliver a message."

"Okay," Aarons said. "Is there anything else?"

"Yes there is," James continued. "Tell him he should bring his daughter and grandson along for the ride. He should give his friend up front the same instructions he gave him the first time he and I went to see our Chinese friends. Also, tell him it is possible that both mother and son will be going away with our Chinese friends for about three weeks so pack enough clothes and a couple of his grandson's favorite toys. Do you have all of that?"

It was quiet on the other end of the phone.

"Have you gone completely crazy?" Aaron finally said. "What the hell are you talking about?"

"I don't think I am any crazier than I was when you first called me for some assistance some time ago. Do you remember that far back?" James said, "Now that I have answered *your* question please answer mine - have you written down what I said before you blew your top?"

It was quiet for a long time, and then Aarons finally responded, "I don't have the slightest idea what you are talking about. I know you aren't drunk because you don't drink but I am beginning to wonder if you have been into Schless's private stash."

"Okay, let's do this another way. Just tell Freddie that I will be shopping for some antiques later tonight so if he isn't doing anything special, maybe he can come by and help me pick out a few things. Would you just do *that*? *Please*?"

"I don't make his schedule either."

"Billie," James said with a sigh, "just do it!"

"Okay," Aarons said, "but..."

James hung up.

*****

Less than an hour later, Freddie, drove up to Albert's antique store in an un-restored motorcycle from the first decade of Harley-Davidson's existence.

James walked out of the store and greeted him. "I've done a lot of things in my life," James said, "but I have never been on a motorcycle."

"Calling this a *motorcycle* is like calling my momma's fried chicken a between-meals snack," Freddie said, indignantly. "This hog *is* history, man. It was made in 1905; they probably only made a few hundred of these that year. You know what this little beauty is worth?"

James held up his hands in mock surrender, "Okay, guilty as charged. I admit that I know nothing about this. Now, want to take me for a spin?"

"Sure, get on and I'll give you a ride you aint nevva gonna forget."

When James was seated behind Freddie, they quickly took

off. They road for a while, seeming to go around in circles, then pulled into the open bay of a Mobil gas station a few miles from Albert's store.

Freddie took off his helmet and turned to face James. "You wanna tell me what you were trying to get the lawyer to tell Mr. DeStefano?"

"I would like Carmine to bring his grandson and his daughter to the lab in Menlo Park at 2:00 P.M. tomorrow afternoon. Tell him that this is by no means a sure thing but there is a new protocol that might help his grandson. Emphasize *might*. Tell him it must be tomorrow at two because we have arranged for a really knowledgeable team of doctors – the very best of the very best - to be there to examine his grandson. *If* they think he has a chance to be helped, the team will take his grandson and the boy's mother to a place for three weeks of treatments."

"Why don't *you* tell Carmine?" Freddie said.

"I assumed both sides of such a conversation would be bugged. That was why I called Billie."

"Maybe you're *not* so smart. You really think Billie's line is any safer than yours?"

"Whatever, I tried to go through Billie. So you won't pass my message on to Carmine?"

"No, I'll tell him. But I really hope you know what you are doin.' When it comes to his grandson, Mr. DeStefano ain't got no sense of humor."

"Come on, Freddie. Do you think I take his grandson's cancer... no, make that any child's cancer, lightly?" James asked.

Freddie removed his sunglasses and stared into James'

eyes. "I'm here because Mr. DeStefano thinks you are the real deal... he has said he thinks you are smart... he also said he thinks you can be trusted. As far as I am concerned, the jury may still be out on both things, especially after this new piece of business tonight. But I *am* here and just for laughs I want you should know that this is definitely *not* something to screw around with. Okay?"

"Okay." James responded.

Freddie put his sunglasses on and revved the motor. "Okay, get back on the hog and I'll take you back to the store."

"One more thing," James said. "Have him bring a couple of his grandson's favorite toys and enough clothes for three weeks."

Freddie put his helmet on, shaking his head from side to side, then drove James back to the antique store. When they reached the store, James got off of the bike and reached out to shake Freddie's hand.

Freddie extended his hand and quickly pulled it back. "Look at my face," he said to James.

James smiled. "Is this the place where you tell me how you are going to break my bones if this is just a scam?"

"Hell no, if this is a scam, you ain't gonna have no more bones. They gonna quickly dissolve in the acid we gonna put in the steel oil drum after we put your lifeless body inside. But I *will* deliver your message, *Spider*."

"Gee, Freddie," James said, "I didn't know we were on a nickname basis."

Chapter 57
Tuesday, October 29, 1996 –
Menlo Park, New Jersey – 1:55 P.M.

At 1:55 P.M. the black limo pulled into the lab's parking lot and drove up to the front entrance. James was standing outside, leaning up against the front door of the lab.

The front passenger door opened and Freddie stepped out. He surveyed the area, and then opened the rear passenger door. A deeply tanned woman stepped out of the limo. James thought she was in her mid to late thirties. She was dressed in a pair of skin tight leather Capri's, an oversized New York Yankees sweat shirt, high stiletto heels, enough makeup for a carpool of circus performers, and a hairdo that sprang up a good foot and a half above her head.

She was chewing gum as she walked up to James and said, "I'm Mary, Michael's mother, and Carmine DeStefano's daughter."

"Hi," James said, with a broad smile. "I'm Will James."

"I know who you are," she said. "What I don't know and need to know, real fast, is if you can actually help my son?"

"No small talk?" James said. "No, how ya doooin? No nice weather for a drive in the country?"

"I'm not here to dance around with you," she shot back. "Can you really help my son or not?"

James glanced beyond the woman, centering his gaze on the limo.

"Hey," the woman yelled. "I'm right here, why are you gawking at the car? Who you lookin' for?"

James turned back towards the woman and said, "I was looking for Michael's father."

"Michael ain't got no father... well at least not no more. The jerk is dead."

"Oh, I'm sorry." James said apologetically. "I just thought..."

"You thought what," she quickly responded.

"Given the circumstances I thought both parents would have wanted to..."

"Hey, I'm a single mother, all right? Michael's father – if you could call that drunken slob a father - died in a bathtub just after Michael was born."

"I'm so very sorry," James repeated.

"Don't be, the world is a better place without him."

"Was it an accident?" James asked, sorry he asked the question as soon as the words left his mouth.

"Yeh," she said smiling, "you could say it was an accident. He used to like punching me around in places that didn't show marks. He was smart enough to know that marks would lead to questions and the questions could land him in a whole lot of trouble with his father in law. One day he got a little sloppy, he broke two of my ribs. I guess that led to a really bad accident for him when my father found out what he done.

"Freddie and Jimmy 'four eyes' came to the house to *talk* to him about it. He was taking a bath when they showed up. Freddie kicked in the bathroom door and *accidentally* pushed the lousy jerk's head under the water, then Jimmy *'four eyes' accidentally* pumped six bullets into his chest. I gotta say, I aint never seen Freddie or Jimmy move so fast."

"You watched them do this?" James asked.

"I wouldn't have missed it for a million bucks. That lousy drunk raised his hands to me once too often."

James just stood there, speechless.

Mary smiled, took the gum out of her mouth and calmly placed it in a tissue which she folded neatly and then put into her pants pocket. Then she shrugged, "What can I say; my father's friends can be a little overly protective of me."

"I'm not sure why you told me this," James said.

"Well, you asked, and even if you didn't I'd want you to know that my Dad's friends are a little overly protective of me. So... can ya help my son or not?"

"The quick and easy answer, Mary, is that *I* can't personally help your son or anyone else's son. But if anyone can, the medical team in that building right now would be who I would go to if I had a son with Michael's diagnosis."

"You must know that we have already been everywhere and seen everyone and no one gives Michael the slightest chance to survive another year."

"Yes, I do know you have reached out for help and I also know that the *next to the last thing* you need right now is false hope."

She moved a bit closer and poked her finger into his chest. "If that is the next to the last thing I need – what is the last thing I need?" she asked.

"*The* very last thing you need is to have no hope at all!"

She stared at him a long time. Tears were beginning to run down her cheeks, leaving long black lines from her mascara.

James reached for her arm and gently led her to a small bench near the front of the building.

She sat on the edge of the bench and sighed. "What do you think are the chances these people can do what the best in the world said couldn't be done?"

"Look, I don't matter in this discussion. Talk to them, tell them your concerns; you make the final decision. You have nothing to lose."

"And what is in it for you?" she asked.

"Let's just say I am trying to keep a promise I made to the worried grandfather of a four-year-old with a terminal disease."

She took out a small pack of tissues and dabbed at her eyes, slowly got up and walked towards the car and opened the rear passenger door. She extended her hand as a small boy dressed in a Spiderman costume jumped out of the car.

The boy ran towards James and yelled excitedly, "Are you Spiderman?"

James leaned down to greet the little boy, "What makes you think I am Spiderman?" He asked.

"Poppy said you were called Spider," the boy said.

James moved down on one knee and gently put his hands on the boy's shoulders. "Can you keep a secret?" James whispered.

"Sure," the boy said excitedly.

"Well, I'm undercover right now; I don't want anyone else to know that I am Spiderman, so just call me Will." James gave the boy a quick wink and a nod.

"Is that your school day name?" the boy asked.

"My what?" James asked.

"You know, your school day name. Mom says all super-heroes have to go to school but when they are in school they don't want the bad guys to know that they are really superheroes so they have different names, regular people names, you know, for school days."

"Oh," James said. "Yes, I guess Will is my school day name. Please call me by my *school day name*."

"My name is Michael, Spidey... oh, I'm sorry, Will."

James winked at the boy again.

Carmine DeStefano stepped out of the car and walked over to James and the boy. Gently patting his grandson's head, he said to James, "Hello, Will."

James cautiously smiled at DeStefano and said, "Hello Carmine."

"Tell me Will, am I going to like you as much tomorrow as I did yesterday?" DeStefano asked.

James's smile turned to a slight frown as he said, "Let's concentrate on today, Carmine; tomorrow will just have to take care of itself. Let's go inside."

Freddie rushed towards them, leaning closer to DeStefano as he said, "Maybe you and your family should wait in the car, Mr. DeStefano, while I check the place out?"

DeStefano waved him off. "Don't worry, Freddie, I don't think Mr. James would put us at risk or I never would have brought Michael and Mary here in the first place. Let's go in and see what miracles Mr. James has in store for us."

Angela and Frank were waiting in the lobby and they both nodded respectfully towards DeStefano as he entered the building.

Angela walked directly to Mary and introduced herself. "Good afternoon."

"Will it also be a *good afternoon* for my son?" Mary asked.

"I hope so," Angela said. "I sincerely hope so. Please call me Angela, and that is my husband, Frank."

Frank was leaning down with an extended hand to Michael. "Hi!" he said in a loud whisper. "Would you like me to call you Spiderman or Michael?"

"Oh, I'm not really Spiderman," the boy said. "I just dress up like Spiderman. He's Spiderman," he added, pointing to James. "I'm just Michael."

DeStefano pulled James aside. "If I didn't trust you I might still be here," DeStefano said, "because I will try anything if it has even a slight chance to help Michael. But they would *not* be here if I did not trust you. I do not want them to think there is a happy ending only to have their hearts broken again..."

"Look," James broke in, "I asked you to come here because there is a very slim chance that this work we have been involved with might have opened up a different way of looking at how cancer cells develop and thrive, especially when involving pre-pubescent children. Upstairs is a doctor from the Dana-Farber Children's Cancer Center..."

DeStefano's eyes widened. "We went there!" he said, loud enough for everyone in the room to stop and stare. "Did you think that I would not have gone there *first*?"

James maneuvered DeStefano into a far corner. "Carmine,

you may have gone to the hospital and had Michael examined by their doctors, but they only know what they know, or knew at the time you were there. A lot has changed in the last few months."

"If anyone there misled us I will burn that building down with everyone in it!" Carmine fumed.

"Carmine, calm down," James said in a hushed tone. "I am certain that no one misled you. However, they did not know what Angela and Frank and the researchers in this lab learned just a few short months ago. You said that you trusted me, well, Goddamn it, don't just *say* you trust me, *really trust me!*"

Chapter 58

Two days earlier... **Sunday, October 27, 1996** –
Dana-Farber Cancer Institute,
Boston, MA– 11:19 A.M.

Before he was a world famous singer/songwriter, Billie Howl was a struggling street entertainer in Hartford, CT. Howard Hill owned a small nightclub in downtown Hartford at the time and was always on the lookout for bright young talent.

Hill stopped to watch Howl perform one evening on his way to the club and was outraged as he watched a group of toughs pushing Howl around. One reached in to grab a fist full of cash from the open guitar case on the ground. Hill quickly ran over to the case, slammed the lid on the 'would be' thief's hand and then pinned him down until a passing police man took over.

After things calmed down Hill told the young entertainer that he thought he had talent – real talent. He offered to give Howl a chance to perform in his club and said he would be happy to finance his first album when the performer felt ready to make one. The rest, as they say, is history. Howl went on to become the hottest new name in music and a lifelong friendship was formed.

When James learned that Howard Hill was a fairly regular attendee of Albert's Sunday morning auctions he asked Albert to reach out to Hill to help arrange for Howl to accompany him and Frank on a 'special mission'. It was fairly well known that Dr. Ethan London, of Dana Farber in Boston, was a huge fan of Howl. Schless contacted Dr. London's office and asked if Howl could take a private tour of the children's wing and while he was there would like to join Dr. London for lunch. Dr. London quickly cleared a few hours from his busy schedule and arranged to have a small conference room setup for lunch with his favorite musician.

Howl's beat up van pulled into a parking space and they quickly went into the facility with a few minutes to spare. The introductions were made and Howl posed for photos with Dr. London and some members of the doctor's personal staff. Before the tour was to start they were escorted to a private wing of the executive office suite where lunch was served.

As the luncheon plates were being picked up, Howl said, "Dr. London, under *truth in advertising* I want to tell you that I am here because of those men," pointing to James and Frank, "they asked me to make myself available today and when they told me their reasons I enthusiastically agreed. Frankly, if I had to travel from the other side of the planet I would gladly have done whatever I had to do in order to be here today, these are good guys and are working on the side of the angels. I am going to leave you with them now, I hope you will hear what they have to say and help them in any way you can. But, before I leave I would like to give you these two front row seat tickets and a backstage pass for my concert next month at Fenway Park. I understand you played a really cool guitar in a garage band some years ago. I know that you are a busy man but if you are able to attend the concert I'd love to have you sit in with me and my band for the closing number."

"Are you kidding," The doctor said, "I'll be there all right – guitar and all."

Howl shook the doctor's hand, stood up, and walked out of the room, closing the door behind him.

Frank took out a large manila envelope and as he began spreading various documents around the table, said, "You know about some of the work Angela and I have been doing over the years, well here is what we have been working on most recently."

"I'm not complaining, Frank," Dr. London said, "having lunch with Billie Howl will be one of my greatest experiences of all time, but if you wanted to spend some time with me, all you had to do was ask."

"I did ask," Frank said, "and I was told you *might* have fifteen minutes in a few weeks, but there is a little four-year old boy who might *not* have a few weeks left to live."

Dr. London blushed, "Well, Frank, all of a sudden I have no place to go for at least the better part of an hour, so, why don't you just tell me what you want to tell me?"

Frank pointed to a series of lab reports, "Ethan, we believe that we have uncovered a way to actually shrink cancer cells – *in children!*"

"Just in children?" Dr. London asked.

"Yes. In time we may learn how to broaden the age factor. Time will tell."

"What makes children better candidates?" Dr. London asked as he picked up one of the documents.

"We believe that because pre-pubescent skin is softer, more flexible, it is more receptive to this protocol."

*****

Less than an hour later, Dr. London reached for a telephone and called his assistant. He rattled off a list of department heads and senior staffers and asked for them to come up to the room, *immediately!*

*****

Shortly before midnight, the room was buzzing with activity. Dr. London grabbed Frank by his shoulders, "You have our attention, so now tell me what you need."

"I'd like you to come to the lab as soon as you can." Frank said.

"But we have the latest equipment here." Dr. London said.

"It's more than just equipment, it's a process and over the past few months we have perfected the process. Please, come to the lab to see what we have come up with."

Dr. London gathered some of the doctors in the room. They talked quietly among themselves and when London returned he said, "We can all be there this Tuesday, say 2:00 o'clock?"

Frank gave him a bear hug, "2:00 o'clock Tuesday it is!"

Chapter 59
Seven months later, May 24, 1997 – 1:03 P.M.
Montauk, Long Island, New York

It was a long drive from the city, but James appreciated the break from his regular routine. Even though all of the windows were closed tight, the smell of the ocean wafted throughout the car. He was enjoying a lighthearted conversation with his passenger. Concerned that he would bore her to tears during such a long drive he had actually prepared a list of topics in advance. However, the preparation was totally unnecessary. As it turned out, both he and his passenger seemed to find plenty to talk about and the time just flew by.

At about one in the afternoon he turned into the long driveway. About a half mile in, he rolled to a stop. A black Cadillac Seville was parked across the driveway.

A huge bulk of a man struggled to get out of the front seat of the Cadillac. He waddled over to James' side of the car and motioned for him to roll his window down. "Are you lost, mister?"

James smiled. "I don't think so. Are you?"

"Well this here is private property, so why don't you just mosey on back down to the highway?"

"I can't do that," James said.

"Why can't you?" The guard asked.

"Because then I would miss the party," James said.

"What's your name?"

"Will James."

The guard went back to his car and reached inside for a clipboard stacked with papers. He put on a pair of thick horn rimmed glasses. "I don't see yer name here on the sheet, Mr. ..."

"Will James, I was actually invited by the birthday boy himself."

The guard looked through the papers again, "Oh, yeah," he finally said. "I see it now *Mr. Will James*; so what about the lady?"

"What about her?" James asked.

"It don't say *Mr.* Will James *and guest*... it just says *Mr. Will James*," he said with a smirk.

"Well she is one of the birthday presents I am bringing to the party." James said.

"Maybe you don't know, *Mr. Will James,* but the birthday boy is only five years old."

"Oh, but I do know that he is five years old. That is why I also brought that big box in the back seat. The lady, here, is a *backup* gift... you might say."

"She aint on the list... so she aint invited... so she aint goin up the hill wit ya, *Mr. Will James.*" The guard said with an exaggerated grin from ear to ear.

"Is Carmine DeStefano in the house at the end of this driveway?" James asked.

"That is not public information, *Mr. Will James.*"

"Well", James said, slowly and deliberately, "*If* Carmine DeStefano *is* in the house at the end of this driveway, then I have to presume that Freddie is up there too."

"So?"

"Is Freddie in the house at the end of this driveway?"

"Yeh."

"O.K.", James said to his passenger, with a broad smile, "Now we are getting somewhere."

"You aint gettin nowhere, *Mr. Will James,* unless and until that lady in the car exits the car."

"Humor me," James said, "Call Freddie. Tell him that *Mr. Will James* has a guest and would it be all right if he brought his guest to the party?"

The guard smiled. "Why I would be thrilled and delighted to do that for you."

The guard slowly walked back to the car and removed a portable phone, dialed a number into it, and then waited for someone to pick up at the other end.

The guard spoke loudly into the phone. "I got a Will James down here but he ain't alone. There is a lady with him. He is asking if she can go to the house with him and I told him..."

It was clear that whatever the guard had heard from the person at the other end of the phone had made an instant impression on him. He quickly closed the phone, rushed back to James's car and said, "I'm really sorry sir, Freddie says it is absolutely all right for you and any lady you want to go up to the house and enjoy the party. He says to hurry because they are waiting for you to arrive so that they can cut the cake."

The guard was sweating and nervously ran his finger inside the edge of his shirt collar. "I was only doing my job, Mr. James. Honest, it was nothing against..."

James held up his hand. "Don't apologize. I understand, and yes, you were just doing your job. If it comes up I will tell Carmine that you were doing your job. Please don't be concerned. But we really need to get going; we don't want to hold up the cutting of the cake any longer than we already have."

The guard quickly stepped away from the car. "Maybe you can ask them to save me a piece of the cake?" He said, almost as an afterthought.

"You can count on it." James said.

The guard quickly ran to his car and moved it so that James and his passenger could drive by. James gave the intimidated man a friendly wave as he slowly drove past.

The car came to another checkpoint on the way up, this time they were waved on as soon as their car came into view of the guards.

They came to a modest little cottage with a circular driveway. Their car moved halfway around the tree lined circle and stopped by the front door. A burly man opened the passenger door, respectfully watched the woman step out of the car, and then ran around the front of the car to open the driver side door. James had already stepped out of the car and was reaching into the back seat for a package wrapped in brightly colored paper and tied with many different ribbons. He nodded to the car parker and joined his passenger, who had already climbed up the few steps and was waiting for him at the front door. James reached out and rang the doorbell.

The door opened and they were greeted by a short and cheery woman in a brightly colored housedress. "Hi!" she said, as she reached for the package. "Did you bring that for me?" They all laughed as she quickly handed the package to a man who added it to a gigantic pile in the center of the room. "I'm Diana Cerrina, a neighbor," she said to the woman standing next to James. "The little monsters are all screaming and running around in the back. Go find Gary, you know Gary? He'll make sure you're both settled in. Quickly grab a plate and get yourself something to eat. I keep telling them they need to put a small food pantry somewhere along that driveway of theirs. It is such a big distance from the main road to the house that you could just die of thirst or hunger before you get up here."

James gave the woman a kiss on the cheek. It was obvious to James' passenger that he had seen this woman many times before, probably while visiting this house.

Freddie walked towards them with a huge smile. He gave James a fist bump and nodded respectfully to the lady.

DeStefano saw James enter and rushed over. He gave James a bear hug, stepped back and affectionately patted James's face. "Thank you for coming," DeStefano said. Then he saw the lady and whispered in James's ear, "You two going steady, now?"

"No, actually, she is one of the birthday gifts I brought with me today," James said. "I would have gift-wrapped her but I couldn't find a gift box her size."

The lady rolled her eyes, and then asked, "Where is the birthday boy?"

DeStefano led them through the house and into an open grassy area in the back. Children were everywhere. There was a huge tent set up with rows of benches and a buffet line with several carving stations. DeStefano stopped to whisper something into Freddy's ear.

Moments later, Mary rushed towards them. She grabbed James, wrapped her arms around him then planted a wet kiss on his cheek. "Ain't you the man of the hour?" she said.

"Hey everybody, this here is the greatest man on earth." She brushed away tears.

"And who is the lucky lady?" Mary asked, pointing to the woman by his side.

James said, "Actually, she is here for you, Mary."

Mary smiled awkwardly, "For me? I don't understand."

"Well then, let me explain. This lady is Elizabeth Hillson-rat. Although Angela and Frank and everyone in their lab played a major role in Michael's cure; as did Dr. London and the entire hospital staff... if not for Elizabeth, they wouldn't have even looked in the direction that helped Michael live to see this day."

Elizabeth was blushing. "That isn't true, Mary. I merely translated a few papers."

"She did a lot more than *just* translate a few papers," James said, "but the details can wait. Suffice it to say that she put the researchers on a path that led directly to Michael's remission and I wanted you two to meet."

"Hey," Mary said, "if he says you are terrific then you are terrific. And, if you did anything that allowed us to come to a day when my little Michael could sit in front of a cake with five glowing candles on it, then you are more than terrific – you are someone who can have everything I own."

Mary gave Elizabeth a hug and, with tears running down her cheek, whispered, "Thank you from the bottom of my heart."

Diana Cerrina put her arm around Mary and wiped the tears from Mary's face, "Hey," she said, "This is supposed to be a party, a blessed birthday party. Nobody cries at a blessed birthday party. When you gonna cut the cake?"

James turned to DeStefano, "Oh, by the way. I promised the guard at the first checkpoint on the driveway that I would get him a big piece of cake. Can you get someone to keep my promise for me?"

DeStefano stopped one of the roving waiters, "Send *Jimmy 'four eyes'*a tray and throw on a hunk of cake after Michael blows out the candles. Also, make sure someone tells the big galoop not to spill anything in the car.

Minutes later, the guests and family formed a huge circle around Michael as he leaned over the huge cake and one by one blew out each of the five candles.

The little boy was almost crushed by the well-wishers as his mother and grandfather led the singing of "Happy Birthday."

Blessed birthday party or no blessed birthday party, there wasn't a dry eye in the house!

Chapter 60
Saturday, May 24, 1997 –
Along the southern shore of Long Island,
New York –8:05 P.M.

It started to rain as the car made its way out of the driveway. The hypnotic click of the windshield wipers partially drowned out the road sounds as James maneuvered the car over the loose gravel and newly formed puddles. With signs for the main road now in sight, Elizabeth finally broke the silence.

"I can't seem to get one image out of my mind - little Michael with his angelic face all lit up by those five little candles while a mob of people all huddled around him. Are you as surprised as I am that after all that has happened since that hideous Sunday morning auction, it all came down to a gentle breath blowing out five little birthday candles?"

"I have to admit, I don't usually look for happy endings and so I am rarely disappointed when they don't come at the conclusion of a job."

"No one is that cynical," she said.

He smiled. "Okay, you got me. But today was a really nice change of pace for me," James said.

"I would have guessed that you just order up any kind of ending you choose, Mr. James," she teased.

"I learned a long time ago that no one writes the endings in *real life* – I'm usually brought in after all good solutions have been tried and already failed so I *may* have a degree of control as to how or when the journey begins for me. Sometimes I can even pick the moment when the *real* action begins, but once it has begun, the resulting *stuff* almost always takes on a life and direction all its own. That's why they call life, *real* and Hollywood *make believe*. I gave up trying to create *happily ever after* a long time ago. Frankly, I think that if I knew how an assignment was going to end I would be less motivated to get involved in the first place."

"Well, what just happened back there was as *happily ever after* as anything *I* have ever witnessed," Elizabeth said. "And no apple polishing intended, but your fingerprints were all over that happy ending."

"Hey, between false modesty and honest arrogance, I opt for honest arrogance every time! But, you, young lady, are the reason for that young man's birthday cake more than anyone else, including the medical people. Go figure that Mark Regan would totally dismiss *topical application*."

"Well, you remember what Dr. London said about that – if someone would have told him that you could attack a cancer cell without a room full of expensive hardware he would have thought they were '*wack-a-ding-hoy*'."

They both laughed.

"Albert should have been here," she continued. "He needs to know what a *real* hidden treasure is. He throws those words around so much that they lack any real meaning anymore. However, little Michael getting to blow out the candles on his birthday cake is my new definition of a *hidden treasure*."

James stared at her. "I think you put your finger on something. This whole case seems to be a redefinition of those words. It started because Albert thought he had come across a *hidden treasure* worth buckets of cash. Instead he learned that his relationship with Sol was a far more valuable treasure than anything he might have acquired in exchange for that useless framed permit. Maybe in some way everyone involved in this case picked up a new appreciation for the meaning of *hidden treasure*."

"What about me?" She said

"You tell me." He said.

"I'm just a little kid from a mining town in the Ukraine." She said.

He began to laugh.

"No, really, what about me?" She persisted.

"Not a simple question... so there can't be a simple answer," he said. "Hey, we passed a small diner about a mile or so back, what do you say we double back and discuss it over a cup of coffee? We'll need gas soon anyway."

"That sounds fine," she said. "But I'm going to need a lot more than just a cup of coffee. All of a sudden, I'm really hungry!"

*****

They settled into a booth towards the back of the diner. There were only a few other customers scattered around the small restaurant, between a long counter and a few tables with mismatched chairs.

While waiting for the waitress to come for their orders he said, barely above a whisper, "This project involved far more than I had initially bargained for... more time... more assets... the cashing in of many more IOUs than I imagined going in." He opened the paper napkin wrapped around the knife and fork. "And more danger from multiple sources than I really need in my life."

"I had the impression that danger is a *turn on* for you," she said.

"No, contrary to your *impression*, I am usually deep in the background, a place with barely any danger to me or my associates at all. My strong suit has always been to focus a bright searchlight on others while remaining in the shadows for as long as possible. In that scenario, *the bad guys* have to function with a giant target on *their* backs – they are the ones in danger - while I and a handful of really terrific specialists dart in and out." This assignment, starting with Albert and ending with little Michael has been very, very different."

"Different? How?" She asked.

"I allowed it to get personal for me. I traded detachment and remoteness for personal involvement."

"Is that so bad?" She asked.

"It is very bad because the best help I can offer is as an impartial force. Once it becomes personal I am no better or worse than the client. I think that does a disservice to the client."

"At what point did it become personal for you?" she asked.

"When I realized how *they* – the bad guys - were playing with Albert's head, I couldn't just let him try to deal with it himself; even though he started out as the least likable person I had ever met. My normal reaction would have been... perhaps, should have been, to let him circle the drain."

"But you didn't... why?" she persisted.

He thought about it and then said, "Something made me want to help him beat the bastards who were making his life a living, breathing nightmare. You may laugh at this but I tend to quickly catalogue people onto a ledger sheet of winners and losers. From the first time we met, I couldn't quite decide if Albert was a winner or a loser. I think he was trapped somewhere in between and so needed all the help he could get."

"Okay, she said. "So who were the winners and who were the losers on your ledger sheet for this case?"

He smiled, then said, "Let's start with Albert; Albert was a very big winner – although he might not see it just yet."

"His side is that he made and lost a hundred thousand dollars without ever getting to enjoy any of it," she said.

"He might have said that at the beginning... but I think he has grown enough as a result of this trial by fire that he no longer would say it today. And as far as the financial windfall he might think slipped through his fingers, he has to know now that it was never a reality – it was just bait, disguised to look tasty – but never actually there at all. Like a flashy lure, one quick bite and he would have been like an innocent fish in the ocean, caught, gutted, cleaned, and cooked to perfection. No, I believe he was lucky that he got away with his life. But I think he also won because he will never be the same after this. His priorities have changed, I think for the better. Previously he claimed to have no interest in protecting this antique business and yet he seemed to fight to keep it safe, like a tigress protecting her young.

"Sol was also a big winner. Albert and Sol are far more equal in their relationship today than ever before – before Sol was the parent and Albert the misbehaving juvenile. Today they are both adults and I think their future life together will be better for it."

"Then there is poor Helga Regan," he continued, "one of the losers. She died before her mother's work could help her."

"Just like Ilsa - Helga's mother - died without being able to help *her* mother," Elizabeth added.

"That is a very good analysis," he said.

"What about Carmine DeStefano; winner or loser?" she asked.

"Carmine DeStefano," James mused. "Now there is someone who was, is, and probably always will be, on the outer edges of anyone's ledger sheet. I find it to be one of the worlds greatest wonders how someone so bad could do so much good because of the right motivation, his love for his grandson."

"And he didn't have to use any muscle! But you still have not told me where I wound up on that ledger sheet of yours," she said.

"I have been avoiding that, haven't I?" he said, with a broad grin.

"Yes, you have."

"Okay, then let me get right to that."

Just then the waitress returned, "Hello, my name is Belle, I'll be your waitress tonight. Want to hear our specials?"

James motioned to Elizabeth. "You go first."

"I don't know about you," she said, "but I'm famished." Elizabeth quickly looked through the menu and ordered.

"I'll have the same," James told the waitress.

When the waitress left, Elizabeth leaned forward and said, "Saved by the Belle."

He groaned. After a few false starts, he finally said, "Elizabeth, you would be a great asset to me and my group."

"Albert would suffer a coronary if I left him now," she responded.

"I notice that you didn't say no," he said.

"I didn't say yes, either." She said.

"You know, I offered to trade you for whatever Albert currently owes me."

"No, I did not know that! What am I, some property that can be passed around in barter?" She complained.

"The amount due was pretty high and I considered throwing in a corned beef sandwich and a few bags of M&M peanut," he teased.

"And what did *old* Albert say?" she asked.

He laughed. "I didn't ask *old Albert*, I asked *new Albert*. *Old Albert* would have jumped at the offer; I felt I had at least a 50/50 chance with the *new Albert*!"

She howled with laughter.

"Seriously, though, it is only a matter of time, Elizabeth," he continued, "before you leave on your own, anyway. If you didn't outgrow that little corner in Brooklyn before all of these recent events, you certainly have as a result of them."

"What would I do for you in this *group* of yours?"

"You want a job description?"

"That would be a good start, don't you think?"

"Since no two days are ever exactly the same as the days before or the days after for me or anyone else attached to me, it is hard to say exactly what you would be doing. However, there is no question in my mind that you could add value in many ways. You're smart... you can and do think on your feet. You understand the value of loyalty.

How is that for a job description?"

"I don't know, Will."

"There really is no rush – take as long as you need to decide," James said, as his phone began to vibrate. He reached for it and said, "Yeh."

He listened for a while then said, "Hold on a minute." He held the phone against his chest and moved closer towards Elizabeth. "Okay, it seems that your time to decide is up. I have two questions for you, first, how strong is your Farsi, and second, how would you like to help find out why and by whom a Planned Parenthood Center in East Detroit was fire bombed earlier today?

———————///———————

ABOUT THE AUTHOR

Martin Herman was born and raised in Brooklyn, New York. He has lived and worked in various parts of the country and currently lives midway up a small mountain with a breathtaking view of the Connecticut countryside and almost daily reminders of truly natural beauty, which he says is the only way to describe New England sunrises.

He managed businesses for several decades and since 1999 has been an independent business consultant serving *start-ups* and troubled mature businesses – here and abroad.

Since his early teens he has written short stories and full length novels for his own amusement; as his 75th birthday approached he published his first full length historical murder mystery and hasn't stopped since.

Mystery writing is what he does late at night and on long airplane flights.

—————///—————

**Your comments and suggestions are
not only welcomed but invited.
You can contact the author directly at:**

mherman194@prodigy.net

—————///—————

Also by Martin Herman:
The Jefferson Files –the expanded edition
ISBN 978-1-945211-00-3 PRINT

It is 1806, early in Thomas Jefferson's second term. A deeply entrenched secret society arranges for a dissident within their organization to be brutally murdered and left floating in the Potomac River, within clear site of the Jefferson White House.

Clearly, the secret society is challenging Jefferson to either deal with them as equals or suffer the consequences.

Almost two hundred years later, after discovering a hidden diary written by someone living in the white house at the time of the crime, three college students and a world class computer hacker learn about the crime and begin unraveling the modern day version of the secret society.

There are numerous plot twists which will keep you guessing until the very last page.

...some of The Jefferson Files amazon.com reviews:

Marvelous Read   By Shannon Mazurick
This book is wonderful. It is a fascinating and engaging read. The book is a fiction read although it includes historical elements and facts. Sometimes readers need to remind themselves that it's fiction because the author does a fantastic job capturing the reader. He also does great intertwining the 1800's and the 1900's. The storyline is very creative. Personally, I'm not typically known for reading a book connected to historical elements so for me to give The Jefferson Files a positive review means it's a marvelous read.

I loved how the book told of two parallel stories set ...
By Erin Donovan
I loved how the book told of two parallel stories set hundreds of years apart. The present day Max and his love of Jefferson was well developed and included much mystery and suspense as he traveled down a road grappling with the decision to set forth the truth about his beloved Jefferson. The past story was also well developed and worked well with the link to present day that was unfolding before the reader's eyes. At the end, I craved more and found myself wanting to know what was next for Max and the other characters. I also loved the ties to New Jersey, and they made the story that much more realistic. Can't wait to read the next adventure from Martin!

A MUST READ!! Well written.   By Karen Thorne
We really loved the book. It is a real "Page turner," my husband says. Beautifully done.

Gripping page turning thriller with outstanding historical references By jw

This is an amazingly written, fast paced page-turner. There are so many aspects of the history that I didn't realize, and the intrigue is so deeply woven into the story. I picked this book up, as a fan of Jefferson and founding father history, and couldn't put it down until I finished a few days later. I love how the book touched on subjects like patriotism, ethics, family, and others. You can tell how meticulously the author researched this subject. the characters like Bourgess are so compelling and well written. The story line about OOTAP is totally engrossing. I really hope there is a sequel!!

Highly Recommend! By BritChik

It is rare that you read fiction and you are so engaged in the historical elements of it that it inspires you to read more on the topic and feel as engaged in the story as the characters are in the novel! This book takes you to many locations, and many times throughout history, near and far, and yet the author has done a really excellent job making it all make sense. It's a real testament to his writing ability that as a reader the story comes together so clearly, whether you're in the 1800's or 1900's. And how cool that even though this book touches on parts of real American history, it all felt like it was newly discovered nuggets, and the fictional story was so tense and exciting that I didn't know how it could possibly end?! Highly recommend. This could also make sense as a series of "true historical crime" fiction books with some of these characters popping up again.

Well done and interesting.... a good read. By Kristina A. Stevens

Wonderful writing by Martin Herman. I love the pace of the story and his attention to detail. The author had me at chapter one as he juxtaposed past and present and at times left me uncertain where historical non-fiction left off and the fiction began. Nice work, would love to read a sequel.

By Mei

Loving both history and murder mysteries, Mr. Herman's book does a fantastic job of combining the two. Usually a mix like this starts out slow but "The Jefferson Files" draws you in to the setting quickly and skillfully and keeps you there until you finish. Having bought the book on Monday, I sadly completed the book on a Tuesday, loving the tale and wanting more from the writer. I was left with the desire to learn more about our 3rd president. An easy and enjoyable read. I would recommend this wonderfully written book to anyone.

I loved this novel By Lora Y. Chan-Morelli

This story travels along two paths. One, in 1806 when the story begins and the second, almost two hundred years later, when it is finally resolved. Rather than confuse, the two intertwined story lines made the telling of this mystery so much more exciting. I particularly enjoyed the character development - the "bad guys" had so many human qualities and the "good guys" had real faults. I hope there will be a follow up to this novel.. I just didn't want this one to end.

A true page-turner! By A Hon

I found myself immediately struck by the story and loved how Herman sprinkled in historical facts. It is fast-moving; I feel like I truly devoured this story! Herman is an excellent writer with a great attention to detail. This is a great read for young adults looking to learn more about Thomas Jefferson and the politics of secret societies as well as adults interested in murder mysteries! I've recommended this book to many friends!

Also by Martin Herman

The Jefferson Files
ISBN 978-1-945211-00-3 PRINT

... a historical murder mystery

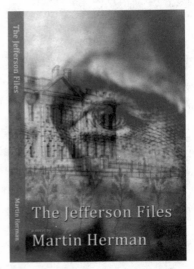

It's 1806 and early in Thomas Jefferson's second term. A secret society arranges for a dissident to be brutally murdered and left floating in the Potomac River. The secret society wants Jefferson to either deal with them or suffer the consequences. A diary — written by someone living in the Jefferson White House — surfaces in the present. Three college students and a world class computer hacker investigate the 200-year old crime and dig into the modern day version of that same secret society. It's still around and now has power over the government, international finance, and the arts.

The Hidden Treasure Files
ISBN 978-1-945211-01-0 PRINT

... a contemporary thriller with international intrigue

The story begins in an antique store auction in Brooklyn. One of the items up for bid is an old government permit housed in a rustic wooden frame. Bidding begins at $2, but within minutes two people drive the price up to $100,000. To a select group of people — including a children's disease specialist, and the head of a New York crime family — the permit is worth far more than $100,000. The reader is taken on a journey to the Ukraine, China, and Germany as the mystery unfolds within these pages.

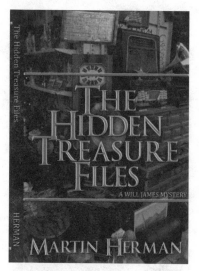

The Hidden Treasure Files describes a unique cancer treatment; unfortunately the treatment is fiction. To turn fiction into reality, 10 percent of this book's sales will benefit The Northeast CT Cancer Fund, which pays for cancer-related screening and treatment for needy patients.

The Sweet Revenge Files
ISBN 978-1-945211-02-7 PRINT

... an old fashioned, whodunit that will keep you guessing until the very last page

A bomb explodes in a crowded movie theater. The authorities quickly find fingerprints and DNA belonging to a convicted murderer ... instantly they realize that he couldn't possibly have had anything to do with this crime because he was executed for being a convicted murderer 80 years ago.

So how did his fingerprints and DNA get all over the crime scene and getaway car?

The Return to Sender Files
ISBN 978-1-945211-08-9 PRINT

"I know who you are and what you've been doing with your deliciously wicked and malicious computer skills ... and I like it."

A computer hacker sees that message on their screen and soon becomes another cog in a scheme far more malevolent than simply stealing someone's bank information. The Return to Sender Files addresses a very modern problem — at a time when everything from power grids to the operation of autos and trains and even planes, as well as the most personal information for almost every person alive is there for the taking by a persistent hacker ... is anyone safe?

With a song and a smile — The Howard Hill Story
ISBN 978-1-945211-09-6 PRINT

This is the story of a professional, black musician who played on the same stage with legendary performers — Billie Holiday, Nat King Cole, Ella Fitzgerald, Oscar Peterson, and others — during the second half of the 20th century.

The Howard Hill Story offers up a backstage glimpse of a time in America when jazz and popular music were at their height.

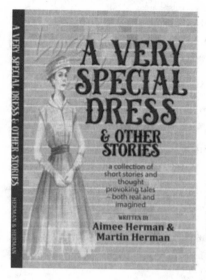

**A Very Special Dress
& other stories**
ISBN 978-1-945211-06-5 PRINT

This collection of short stories is a labor of love from Martin Herman and daughter Aimee Herman. A Very Special Dress & other stories is about budding romances, long term marriages, the search for gender identity, and sexual orientation. You'll meet people who endured bad relationships before they met and fell in love with their soul mates. *Sound familiar?*

To order printed copies or e-books of any Martin Herman book, please go to:
martinhermanauthor.com or write to
mherman194@prodigy.net

Website **martinhermanauthor.com**
Email **mherman194@prodigy.net**
Blog **mhermanwriter.wordpress.com/**
Facebook **Martin Herman-Writer**